THE WARRIOR QUEEN

With all my love,

Aria Moss

THE WARRIOR QUEEN

THE TARRASSIAN SAGA

Aria Mossi

Matador
Unit E2 Airfield Business Park,
Harrison Road, Market Harborough,
Leicestershire. LE16 7UL
Tel: 0116 2792299
Email: books@troubador.co.uk
Web: www.troubador.co.uk/matador
Twitter: @matadorbooks

ISBN 978 1803131 986

British Library Cataloguing in Publication Data.
A catalogue record for this book is available from the British Library.

Printed and bound in Great Britain by 4edge Limited
Typeset in 11pt Sabon by Troubador Publishing Ltd, Leicester, UK

Matador is an imprint of Troubador Publishing Ltd

To my beautiful, brave daughter, Tianna.

"The strongest love is the love that can demonstrate its fragility."

Paulo Coelho

SAN DIEGO COUNTY, CALIFORNIA.

SIX YEARS BEFORE.

I am trying to hold back my tears and it is not because he hates them. Right now, he would welcome them, because he wants me to acknowledge my limitations. I refuse to cry or give him eye contact, for that matter. Another thing he hates. However, it is not defiance that stops me. I know the disappointment on his face might break me, so I don't look.

It took me a long time to understand my father's love was conditional. He is a strange man, my father, one big contradiction. He spoils me rotten, calls me his angel, yet he will let his men hurt me because I needed to learn my lesson. He would have a child, his only child, with a black woman, yet he is a closet racist. Everything is conditional, and everything works until he decides otherwise.

I have my back to him and look out into the garden instead. The sun is about to set over the beautiful Carmel Canyon and soft peach colors kindle the streaky sky. The golden hour. My favorite period of daytime used to fill me with wonder and a thirst for something I could never reach. Now it's just there, basking the world in its gold hue. My father's perfectly manicured garden, surrounding his perfect house, mocks my lack of perfection.

I see my reflection in the large French windows. The failure. The one who refused to comply. I got everything wrong as far as my father is concerned, from the wrong skin color to the wrong hobbies and interests. It makes no difference I am a product of his choices. I didn't choose my mixed heritage. He was the one who put his precious Italian seed in a black woman even though he doesn't even seem to acknowledge the existence of black people. Yet, it is my fault I have the wrong skin color. He was the one who took me to Camp Pendleton ever since I was old enough to walk. Yet, it is my fault I want to become a Marine. Wanted, rather. He found it cute while I was little, following him around the camp like a puppy. It was fine indulging in hobbies like Kendo or my natural affinity for sports. *Male sports,* as he calls them. Of course, he produced a strong specimen, despite its gender. So, he indulged my *sweet boyish behavior.* With him, it is all fine until it is not. If he feels control is about to shift from him to anyone else, nothing is acceptable any more. He shuts it all down with an iron fist. It is how he rules his Marines, how he leads all of us. To him, the best reason for doing anything is because he can.

My imperfect reflection in the glass mocks me more than anything else. My baggy shirt and trousers cover every inch of my skin. I put them on purposely, trying to hide from my own eyes. But there is no hiding from the pain. All of me feels raw. I look at my reflected image, and I don't even understand why I am still standing. Why am I still alive? Can't people just die of pain? My painful skin tingles under my baggy clothes. The bruises have started to turn a strange yellow color, but I still scrape my skin in the shower over and over again. My broken ribs are healing well, according to the doctor. To me, it feels like they will never heal.

The cast came off my arm, but it still hurts. Even in my sleep. Phantom pain caused by PTSD, according to the doctor. But then again, he is my father's friend, and he will say and do what he is told. I pull at the long sleeves of my shirt trying to cover my wrists. The marks of the restraints refuse to heal. Mocking me. Always mocking me.

I look at the girl reflected in the glass. She will be eighteen soon. The beginning of life, some say. Not for me. I am dead. I have nothing. It feels scary inside my head. I am screaming in there; I am kicking, punching, bringing chaos to the whole world, to match my torment. On the outside, there is just this comatose-like girl staring quietly at her image.

"You think I am heartless," he says behind me. "You are my only child. Your bruises hurt me just as much as they hurt you. Your pain... I haven't slept much in weeks. No father should ever have to live knowing his daughter was..." His voice breaks and maybe... just maybe.

"Then let me have my justice! Let me make sure they won't do it to someone else. Please, Dad! I need something, anything, a reason to survive this pain," I say, turning around to look at him. Cold green eyes bore into my empty soul. Stupid hope! I am still not broken. I never learn, do I?

"You don't know what you are saying, little girl," he says, and his hard stare makes me feel small and insignificant. "You will not be able to carry your shame. The press will eat you alive. Everywhere you go, people will whisper behind your back. Every time you hear laughter, you will think it's aimed at you. When you find a man to settle down with, he will always use it against you."

This time I can't help the tears. I can't keep the anger in either.

"Does this look like I had a say?" I scream while pulling my sleeves up. He doesn't look at the bruises left by the restraints. His steely, unblinking eyes are pinned on mine.

"You will not raise your voice at me. You need to learn your place, Gianna. Saying no to men is not enough. Not when you caused the actions you are trying to stop. Saying no might be the prerogative of the Wooks, but girls like you don't have such a luxury. You don't get to flaunt this," he says, pointing at my broken body, "and think it's okay to mingle with men as if you are one of them. You know very well, no one will blame them. Everybody will blame you. And probably me, for allowing it."

"You only allowed it because mother signed my parental permission to join the Marines. You pretended it was your idea all along, just so you wouldn't have to admit defeat to a woman," I tell him, because I want to hurt him, the way he has hurt me.

But once again, I am wrong. People like him cannot be harmed. They have no weaknesses. They are in charge. There is no winning with them, just fighting to the death and there is no fight left in me.

"I allowed it because you needed to learn a fundamental lesson. Your life will be much better once you do." His voice is like a shard. Most people can't tell the fine line between his usual commanding voice and this. There is passion, strength and even emotion in the voice of the Commandant of the Marine Corps. My mother and I only get this coldness that pierces through your gut and tears you apart.

"Let me guess," I say, wiping furiously at my tears, unable to stop them from flowing. "You know best! Is that it? Or did I need to learn that your men, your rank, and your reputation come before me?"

"Yes, all of the above. But most of all, Gianna, you needed to learn the value of a woman will always be less than the value of a man!"

1

—

GIANNA

PRESENT DAY

I may be the center of attention of every high-life event, I may be the tabloids' favorite party girl, and I may fuck my way through every A list. But I don't drink, and I don't take drugs.

No matter how colorful, my choices are my own. Self-enforced sobriety keeps me safe while allowing my wild reputation to thrive. Gianna Romano is the *Man-Eater,* the tabloids' darling and that is fine by me. As long as I get to choose who, when and how, they can call me whatever they want. For the last six years, I worked my ass off for a stupid, useless job I absolutely loathe, but the pay-off is worth the drama.

Being one of the world's two best paid models comes with a lot of benefits. I get to choose my crowd, who I can bully, who I can fuck, but best of all, I get to choose who I don't want to fuck. I am the predator, not the prey.

I cannot do any of the above if I am under the influence, and that is why I am terrified to open my eyes now. This must be a dream. I am quite sure. There is no reality where my tongue fills like cotton inside my mouth, my pupils plump, and my body unresponsive. There is no reality where someone has spiked my drink. I am always sober and only drink from my own water bottle, I never leave out of my sight.

I lie here in whoever's bed I may be, waiting to go back to sleep. I don't ever spend the night, but that's okay. I am not going to turn this into a big deal. I must have been exhausted and partied harder than I thought. London Fashion Week is always full on. Besides, I know the men I choose. They are harmless, and I have them wrapped around my little finger.

My friend Yara calls all my fuck-buddies Ken. After Barbie's Ken. Probably quite suitable considering I drive a pink Ferrari. I find my car just as ridiculous as my job, my wardrobe and the men I fuck. A tiny prick of fear makes my skin tingle. Maybe I am drunk after all. Why else would I admit that to myself?

Forget sleeping; I need to have a cold shower and get the hell out of here. I think everyone around me is wasted, as the noise is rather lively – a fight. People are screaming, a woman or a girl is crying, and the smell of putrid makes me want to gag.

Forget the shower. I need to get the hell out of here! Only... I can't. Restraints. Naked. Pinned to a cold metal table. I know what comes next. I have been here before. Maybe *he* was right, women like me deserve this. I don't fear the pain. I fear losing control. I am, once again, nothing. *No, not this time! No more! Just fight, Gianna!*

I open my heavy eyelids to look them in the eyes. Whoever they are. I will die fighting. I will take as many of them down as I can. I will die, but I will not die alone. Only it doesn't work like that. I have to close my eyelids again, as the light is blinding. I cannot fight anyone because my restraints feel like steel. I have no control because I am naked. I have no value. *He* was right all along. I am nothing.

Someone places a blanket on top of me. It feels like fur. Two large shadows lean over, blocking the harsh light. Their fresh, clean smell covers the stench around me for a minute. The shadows take my bounds off. *Big mistake!* They release my ankles. *Huge mistake!* They pull me up, and the world I can't even see spins around me. Massive hands hold me upright, and I wait for my body to feel steady before I die and take as many as I can with me.

But then... I hear them talk. My job involves a lot of traveling. I know the sound of many languages, but that is... different. The voices are also different. They match the size of the hands, holding me upright. Strangely enough, the touch doesn't hurt my skin. I open my eyes, and I wish I hadn't. Maybe it is a dream, after all. Or perhaps whatever drug I took was created by someone obsessed with sci-fi. Too many details at once burn my brain. Bright lights. Blaring noise. Flashing beacons. Blue smoke. The insides of a ship. *Non-human.* The metal floor shines with a dark gray substance. It stinks. Blood. *Non-human.* There are body parts everywhere. Gray, slimy body parts. The shapes and textures are all wrong. *Non-human.* The hands holding me keep me all wrapped up in a strange large fur. For the first time, I realize they are trying to cover me. Their touch is firm but not restrictive. Is this a rescuing? I look up at the two men holding me steady on my feet. *Non-human.*

I can hear the same feminine voice from before. It could be a little girl. She's crying, calling them monsters. But they are not. They are an alien form of life. The notion throws my plans off. That and their size. I can't fight that. No human could. I grew up surrounded by bulk, muscles, and overgrown men. But this is different. Probably Yara's huge bodyguard would look like a boy next to them. Yara... We were together. Would she be here?

I look around and see the massive aliens carrying some women out. They look asleep or dead. Only the little one is awake. She is talking in Russian now and crying. I can only see a glimpse of bright red curls hanging over the arm of the large creature carrying her out. The alien body parts littering the floor look like a different species than those holding me up and the ones who carried the women out. The dismembered creatures are disgusting. No other word for it. The wrinkly gray skin and the disturbing forehead ridges are not even as horrible as that stench. It reminds me of dead people and hospitals, somehow. I have a feeling they looked a lot more sickening when they were alive.

The aliens by my side are not touching me anymore, and that is the only reassuring thing that has happened to me since I woke up. Maybe the way they smell too. Which is the most stupid thing anyone taken by aliens thought of. What are these creatures? Why am I not laughing hysterically? Asking for the hidden camera to reveal itself. Isn't that what people kidnapped by aliens do? Why am I so calm? They must be aliens, despite the humanoid features. Humans don't get this big. I am tall by any standards and not used to tilting my head up until it hurts, just to have eye contact. They are close to eight feet tall. Their bodies are pure muscle. I don't think I have ever seen anything even close to that. They look like overgrown Vikings. Maybe because of all that wild hair and big bushy beards, my mind makes the connection. They look so human, and yet they don't. Their skin has a strange coppery shade. Something metallic about it and it is covered in a hefty sprinkle of hair. Huge and hairy seems to be the main description. No wonder the Russian girl calls them monsters. But they are not. They are an alien sentient species. Soldiers of some kind. It's in the way they move and act. Soldiers are no different, no matter where they are from.

They all wear the same uniform, a short white leather kilt, which doesn't cover much... Who the hell wears a kilt to war nowadays? Probably the same kind of people who have swords! Massive ones, all dripping with sickly gray blood at the moment. I also notice some type of alien weapon attached to their kilts, but they seem to prefer those huge swords.

Their facial features look incredibly human – a different story with their eyes. No iris, just one solid color. Again, it seems coppery. The one on my right has some red dots in his tense stare. His overgrown muscles shake with unspent energy as he looks over the dismembered bodies. I guess there's no one else left to kill. The one on my left is more in control of himself. Is that a smile? Could that be a kind smile? It makes his beautiful alien face look trustworthy. What is wrong with me? Why do I allow myself to hope again? Hope hurts more than anything else in this world. Maybe because fighting my way out of this is not really an option.

These beings could crush me with a finger. I am all naked under the fur, and not only did their eyes stay on my face, but they kept me covered until they made sure I could do it for myself. Maybe alien men are different. Or perhaps they simply don't fancy human women. I try to control the trembling in my body and look at the alien who's still smiling. I give him a questioning but reasonable look. He needs to understand I am cooperating. I think it works because his smile reaches his eyes. I stay away from big, muscly men who could easily overpower you just because they could. I like my sleek city boys, driving sports cars and flashing new money. But despite these men not being my go-to type, not to mention freaking aliens, my brain does register this is a race of seriously hot men. Could it also be a race of men who don't find me attractive? That would make them just perfect.

The kind one—*do I dare call him that*—speaks to me in that strange language. It's just booming, or maybe it's their force making it sound like that. He is obviously calm and trying to contain it. The one on my left has taken a step back, almost like he's trying to give me space. His eyes scan the room for dangers. Despite his obvious penchant for everything bloody, there is something protective about him. He reminds me of Yara's bodyguard. Is this alien trying to keep me safe? Do I dare hope? The one with the kind smile shows me something trapped in his giant palm. It's a little container made of dark-colored glass. Inside, some sort of an earwig wriggles about. It also flashes red every other second. Is it an alien bug?

I try to control my panic as he gestures to his right ear, then to mine. I get flashbacks from all the scary movies I ever watched. He waits for a reaction I don't give and points at my mouth, his mouth, then at the bug. He wants to put that in my ear, so we can communicate. A translating device. It could also be a hundred other things and none of them good.

But… he asked for permission first. He is giving me a choice before most likely putting it in my ear by force. It may be a fake choice, but I am taking it, nevertheless. I am not in denial, I know all my life choices are artificial. Being able to make those choices, no matter how fake, gives me power – the only type a woman like me can have.

I push my golden curls behind my left ear and offer it to him. He didn't expect that. Respect! There is respect on his face. Despite the alien features and all that beard, there is no mistaking that. Do I dare hope? A sharp pain both in my ear and behind it goes straight into my brain, and my knees turn to Jell-O. I drop the fur, but the two large men are quick to cover me back up and support my body once again.

"The pain will soon fade, Human female," says the strange voice. My head feels like it's about to explode. My ear is tingling, and the visual of that bug in there makes me feel sick.

"I am the Blood Fleet's Healer," says the voice inside my ear but also outside of it…

What is happening? I look at the smiling alien, and as his

beautifully shaped lips move, they start to match the words inside my ear.

"We fitted you with a translating device. You were fearless, Human female. You didn't cry in pain. You are strong, and I am very proud the Blood Fleet has rescued you and your Human companions. You are safe now."

"Safe?" I ask for lack of better words. It's so strange I can understand him all of a sudden.

"Yes," he says as he looks around with a sense of urgency.

Now that I can understand words, I can make sense of the blaring noise. Some form of artificial intelligence coming from the walls is asking us to evacuate. It's now doing some strange form of a countdown.

"We must rush now, female," he says gently. "You and the other Humans have been rescued from the Noorranni slavers. We are the Blood Fleet: Tarrassia's elite force and the most feared Warriors of The Coalition of the Seven Stars. No harm will come to you in our care. You are free. We will now take you onboard our warship. Please allow me to carry you. You have no foot coverings."

The things he says are strange but no stranger than this reality I am in. All I care about is that he keeps asking permission for everything. I am a hundred per cent sure he will make me do all these things if I say no. But he asks for permission first, and to me, that means everything. A stupid sliver of hope makes me feel like crying. Free! That's what he said. Do I dare let that little sliver grow? These two men... aliens, could crush my scalp with two fingers. Yet, they take their time to explain and ask for permission in the middle of a ship about to go down. Maybe I can trust them and...

The noise of heavy footsteps crushing the body parts littering the floor makes me lift my eyes to the vast entrance of the cargo bay we are in. The air seems to shift, and the two large men by my side go all stiff. Hands to their swords, bodies straight, ready to take orders, report, and submit. As the newcomer walks in and our eyes meet, all air leaves my lungs. My body sags involuntarily, and the men by my side hold me up once again. Will I ever learn hope is my biggest enemy? Will I ever understand there is no world where I am anything more than prey?

"High Commander, we are retrieving the last Human. I am sorry for the delay. She is scared, but conscious and I wanted to explain…" starts the smiley one.

"Evacuate now! You follow my orders, Healer, and none of them involved explaining anything to females. Bring her! Move!" says the man watching me with copper eyes, flecked with golden specks. His stare goes through all my protective layers, peeling them off one by one until there is nothing left but raw fear. Then he turns on his booted feet and leaves, crushing the body parts littering the floor.

My brain finds it funny that I would call such a creature a man. He is an alien. A huge, scary alien, covered in the gray blood of his enemies. He looks much bigger than the two males by my side. But then I suddenly remember, for some reason they were all bigger when they were fighting. Perfect killing machines. It really makes no difference what he is, an alien, a monster, or a man. I know his type to the finest detail. They are all the same, regardless of the planet they live on. It doesn't matter what they are; all that matters is what I am to them. I am prey. I have no value.

2

—

GIANNA

It's all a blur after *he* leaves. The Healer grabs me in his arms. The way I feel engulfed by all those huge muscles is just another reminder of how helpless I am against these beings. I can hear the sound of crushing body parts under his boots as he carries me out of the carnage.

We make it to some sort of pod, and only the two of us board it. It's hard to see much around the thick blue smoke. I can feel the heat coming from everywhere, and the mechanical voice doing the countdown hurts my ears, making my head pound. He straps me in a chair fit for his size, while I hold onto the furry covering as if it's my lifeline. My famously long legs can't even touch the floor. I force myself to watch what he is doing. This pod thingy we are in looks… simple, like a minimalist artist created it.

I would have expected an alien spacecraft to look at least twice as complicated as the stuff you would see at a NASA center. Instead, the control panel is something a child could easily learn how to use. Not that he uses it. As he secures himself in the only other chair in the pod, he instructs the ship verbally on what to do. Something he called MI replies to all his commands. My stomach feels like it took a punch as we are propelled away from the larger ship at a dizzying speed. After that, though, it's all very smooth, and it's hard to tell we're even moving at all. There are no windows to look outside, but if this is deep space, it will probably be pitch-dark anyway.

"We will dock to the Blood Fleet's High Command warship, in a few nanoclips. What is your title in Human society, female? What can I call you?" he asks.

"Gianna," I tell him before he makes me.

"What does it mean?"

"Nothing, it's just my name." Probably quite suitable for someone who is nothing. My dad said once it means *God is gracious*. A bad joke, if I ever heard one.

"Humans don't call each other by their title?"

I look at him with dead eyes, and his smile disappears.

He turns his head away but explains that Tarrassians only save their names for close family and friends. I don't reply. I have nothing to say. He seems embarrassed. I also know his type to the detail – the so-called nice guy, who just follows orders with a *heavy heart*. No matter how sorry he feels for you, he will not go against men like his Commander.

"You are afraid, Gianna, but you shouldn't be," he says, almost like an echo to my thoughts. "The High Commander has that effect on even the strongest Warriors. He comes across as harsh, and he likes things done his way, that is all. You and the other Humans have nothing to fear. Tarrassians never hurt the weak."

I wonder if there is a subtle threat somewhere in there. A reminder of my weakness, as if I could ever forget that. I am all but naked under the fur I am holding on to for dear life, I have no idea where I am, and everyone around me is at least twice my size and full of muscles. I don't need a reminder.

"When we get to the High Command ship, I would like to ask permission for taking a blood sample. It has been requested by the Elder of the Healers. It won't hurt; I have a special type of needle we use for cubs and those with fragile skin."

I am so tempted to say no, just to make him cut the crap. But what's the point? I don't feel like playing stupid games. Instead, I don't say anything and stare down at my hands, fisted in the fur covering. At least I can tell my lack of reaction bothers him. Let him grow some balls, then.

The so-called docking to their warship happens without as much as a single jolt. He offers to carry me, but I refuse. The inside of the monstrous warship is strange. What else would it be? The thought of being in space and surrounded by aliens should be a massive shock to my system, but it's not. Nothing could be worse than the way the other alien looked at me. I know that look and I know what's coming next.

The Healer adjusts his large steps to mine as he escorts me along the mirror-like corridors of the alien ship. Every surface is reflective. I try to walk with my legs closer together, as I can see glimpses of my naked body reflected into the floor. Whatever the metal is made of it feels warm and soft like silk under my bare feet. I keep my head down, but I try to take in as many details as I can. Escape route, guards, enemy numbers, and where they tend to show up. I can feel their eyes on me as we pass them by. I don't look at them, trying to avoid eye contact. I am prey, so that should be avoided. I know the rules all too well. However, their eyes are just curious, not invasive. Strange, but maybe it's because the one in charge has already put a claim on me.

Eventually, we make it to an unusual opening, leading to a large room. It's not a door, maybe a slit. Windows. For the first time, I understand the magnitude of this. I thought it would be pitch-black, but that is not exactly accurate. There are traces of light and then random splashes of color, reminding me of Holi, the Indian Festival of Colour. The room has no furniture, except for a metal table jutting out of the wall. There is some sort of a mug there and four cups. Why four? I wonder. I try not to think about the raw meat laid on a metal slab. It has been cut into small chunks, some still dripping blood. It makes my insides feel hollow. Have I misinterpreted the hunger in his eyes? Was that actual hunger? Could this be the meat of someone instead of the meat of something? I surprise myself by finding relief in that. I think I would rather be eaten. Death is freedom.

Many furs lie on the floor and another pile is folded neatly by the far wall. There are no corners, as the room is oval. I just stop in the middle and wait. I can see one of the huge aliens coming into the room through the open slit. There is a glass panel by the entrance. It lights up each time someone goes past it. The alien, all bushy beard, wild hair, and large muscles, hands in something to the Healer. A medical box. I don't even flinch when I see the needle's size or the blood collector container attached to it. *The special needle for cubs*, he called it. It could easily go through the other side of my arm, and probably half my blood can be stored in that container. I don't cower. There is no point. He could just make me. I kind of know that is why the other alien is here. I bring an arm out of my fur and hand it to him without a word or closing my eyes. I can feel firm but gentle fingers holding my arm in place, then... nothing. He thanks me for my collaboration, and that's that. I didn't even feel a scratch.

He offers me a folded white garment, apologizing they don't have anything more suitable on board. More aliens come in carrying women, already wearing the same oversized garments. That is why the four cups. There are four of us. The little girl, who is actually a woman, is the only one awake. She is still crying, and for some reason that irritates the hell out of me. The other two are asleep. The aliens lay them down gently on the furs, and the Healer checks on them. He runs some clear glass device all over their bodies.

The redhead screams, calls him a monster and throws a fur at him. But then again, I already know she is a weird little thing, that one. She gives me a quick look, and to my relief, she decides I am unsuitable to give her any comfort. Strangely enough, she finds safety all huddled into the sleeping form of Sia Bentley. Am I less approachable than the *Ice Queen* herself? Apparently so, and I am grateful for it. Maybe they are friends or something. I don't know, and I couldn't give a peanut.

I quickly change into the massive shirt as soon as the aliens leave the room. At least it covers a lot of skin. I can't even find relief knowing I am not on my own. I am not a bitch, but I don't hang out with people outside my circle. Especially not with women. I get on well with Yara, but that's about it. I know who these women are, but they are not my crowd.

I don't think Sia Bentley has a crowd. She is the industry's other best-paid model. We ran *Victoria's Secret* catwalk for the last few years, and we frequently do photoshoots together. We just exchange banalities when we meet, and that's it. I don't know if the whole *Ice Queen* persona is just some publicity stunt. Probably not, considering her looks. And not because of her long white hair, gray eyes, and pale complexion. The woman looks like she eats icicles for breakfast every single morning. The press nicknamed her the *Ice Queen,* and it couldn't be more appropriate. She keeps to herself, never comes to the after-parties, and probably thinks I am an attention whore, since I go to all the parties. Sia is strange, and I always kept my distance. She does the same, and that's how we roll.

Maybe the redhead feels safer with her since they are both a bit on the weird side. I think her name is Natalia and she is obviously Russian. I didn't even know that until I heard her speak earlier. Unlike Sia and I, she is not a high-fashion model.

She does the hair adverts, and that kind of makes sense. She is not high-fashion material, because she is tiny. The girl only reaches my shoulders, and suddenly I realize how terrifying these aliens might look to someone that small. Her frame is petite, and the huge mane of red curls dwarfs her even more. Her hair reaches her waist, and the volume of it makes her little doll-like face almost disappear in it. Strangely enough, she's got a huge pair of DDs on that tiny frame. This close, she looks even more beautiful than in her adverts. A freckled china doll with big round blue eyes and a turned-up nose. Sadly, I don't think she is right in the head, or… I wonder if she's still a minor or something. That would be bad, considering what's about to happen to all of us.

I only met Natalia a few times briefly while we were having our hair done by the same famous hairstylist. Most of those times, she was either crying or giggling. At times, she was doing both. And there was definitely some talk about monsters. I remember Yara and I were trying to keep a straight face as the hairstylist was nagging Natalia in that colorful British way of hers. I was never a fan of that woman, no matter how good she was with my hair. Which of course, is all too bad since she is the fourth woman in this room.

Jade something, I don't even know her full name, wakes shortly after all the aliens leave the room, and the slit closes behind them. No surprise, her first words are curses.

"What the actual fuck, *Blondie*! Did you drag me to one of your crazy parties, love?" she says using the stupid nickname.

She has no idea how much I hate it or the memories it brings. She has nicknames for everybody, and most are hilarious. Sadly, it's not that funny to me. I know she doesn't do it to hurt me, but it makes me dislike her, nevertheless. Most people do to be fair, except for men. Men go wild for Jade. The wrong type, but she likes them that way. Maybe she'll love it here after all.

"Sadly no, I don't think you would like my kind of parties or get along with my crowd. No offense," I tell her, and I am being mean for no particular reason.

"That's the understatement of the year, love. I don't like rubbish pool parties with skinny bitches, and I don't shag toy boys" she says with a sugary smile and a deep British accent.

Serves me right, I guess. Jade gives as good as she takes, and she is fearless. At least in my book, she is. The type of men she likes scare the shit out of me. Maybe Jade can handle what I cannot. I've seen her with some really rough guys, with terrible reputations. All wrapped up around her fingers to make my self-esteem worse. Jade commands men in a way I haven't seen other women do. Maybe rules don't apply to her. That RULE!

In a room full of hot models and half-naked girls, all men's eyes would always go to Jade. Including the gay ones, crazy enough. It never bothered me; if anything, it made me feel relieved. Fewer eyes on me. The other girls hated it. It was quite common to hear nasty things like *Who would want to fuck the fat girl?*

Apparently, all men. If Jade was to hear, she would reply with equally evil things and sometimes give intimate details of their boyfriends' dicks. No wonder fun-loving Yara adores Jade, and to be fair, Jade is a great laugh. Never heard anyone curse that much, and I grew up amongst soldiers. She is one crazy nut wrapped up in a package all men seem to go mad for.

She is no taller than Natalia, but she is far from petite. Her boobs are oversized; there is no other name for it. So is her jiggly, perfectly round ass. Yet, her waist is smaller than mine.

Jade is very good at advertising Jade. She embraced her hourglass figure in the most brilliant way. She has this unique pin-up-girl style. Wearing corsets, really low-cut tops, and very tight pencil skirts. Her signature red lips and red stilettos add to the bombshell looks. Her hair is a long, wavy bob, shining bright with hundreds of shades of chocolate and mahogany. She is the world's most famous hairstylist, after all. Her beautiful waves frame her heart-shaped face and those gorgeous green eyes, she was probably named after. Yara calls them bedroom eyes. Everything about Jade seemed to have been created for men, yet THE RULE doesn't apply to her. Maybe because she doesn't fight it. She owns her femininity in a way I never could. I might be walking *Victoria's Secret* catwalk, but Jade is the one men picture wearing that lingerie. Even now, the huge shirts we were given look better on her than on me. The other two girls are wearing the same garments. Obviously, they belong to the men. They didn't expect women on board. I pull at the soft fabric molding to my skin as I pace the floor. I hope it's not one of his. I would rather be naked.

"So, since this is not a crazy skunk party, care to explain, *Blondie*?" she says, wrinkling her nose at Natalia's constant wailing.

"We were kidnapped by aliens from the London Fashion Week. To be sold as alien dinner or alien fuck-buddies. Other aliens saved us. Same purpose, no doubt. The end." I wait for a laugh or disbelief. But then again, she can see the deep space outside the windows for herself.

"Are they hot?" she asks instead, and I stop pacing for a while. Is she for real? "What?" she shrugs, pointing at Natalia and Sia. "I was kidnapped with fucking *Elsa* and *Merida*. At least I demand some dick, right?"

I don't know whether to laugh or cry, but Natalia beats me to the crying part. Sia wakes, and as expected, there is no reaction. Nothing. No fear, no tears, just a cold assessment of her new circumstances as she moves her icy grays over us.

"How did they get us in the middle of that crowd?" she asks the one logical question I didn't even ask myself.

"So, it can speak," sighs Jade dramatically, but Sia ignores her.

"It doesn't make any sense," I say without stopping my pacing. I feel strange. Anxious, scared, angry. "I don't remember anything after the first day of the show. I know I was going to attend a party, but I am not sure if I did or not," I say.

Natalia looks at me with those vast baby-blue orbs.

"I remember thinking I had to leave quickly before it got dark, at the end of that first day," she says. "I don't like the dark. Monsters hide in the dark."

"Jesus fucking Christ!" shouts Jade, and Natalia cowers next to Sia, who, surprisingly enough, gives her a hug. "You are fucking nineteen years old, love," says Jade. "I told you before to stop with the monster crap. Especially when I am doing your hair!"

"You are not doing my hair now," says Natalia between sobs.

"I still don't want to hear your bonkers shit. What the fuck?"

"Natalia, you looked at these other aliens, didn't you?" asks Sia, ignoring Jade. "The ones who took us from the other ship. What did they look like? I mean, did they look just as evil as the first ones?" Sia talks to Natalia as one would to a scared child, and the answer doesn't disappoint.

"Yes, huge monsters!" she says.

"Go fucking figure!" comes the expected by now outburst from Jade.

"Were you awake the whole time?" asks Sia. "Actually, how were you awake, Natalia? I am sure I was drugged."

"I think I am cursed," she answers watching us with cute doe eyes. "Monsters always keep me awake."

"Jesus, someone keep fucking *Merida* quiet. She's doing my fucking head in."

"Did they do something behind your ear?" asks Sia, who seems determined to ignore Jade.

Natalia explains how the hairy aliens put something behind her ear in her Russian-accented child-like voice, and she could suddenly understand them.

Their soft chatter, Jade's bickering, Natalia's sobs, the humming of the engines, they all move somewhere at the back of my new reality. With every second that passes, everything takes backstage, and the only thing left to burn my mind is how *he* looked at me. I am about to have a panic attack. They stopped about a year ago, but I can feel one coming now. My mouth pools with saliva, yet I can't swallow; my forehead beads with sweat, my chest hurts. I must concentrate on the girls. On the window, on anything other than how *he* looked at me.

"Hairy?" asks Sia, reacting to something Natalia said. "What do you mean?"

"Oh please," says Jade, rolling her eyes. "Of course, she will say hairy. There's fucking monsters everywhere."

"They are hairy," I say, and resume my pacing.

"You saw them?" asks Jade, a trace of fear in her voice.

"Some sort of explosion woke me up. Naked and strapped to a table." My fists are squeezed so tightly they hurt. Those words are far worse than death. "Then the huge hairy creatures came. They are soldiers. They call themselves Warriors, whatever... I was fighting, trying to escape the binds."

I can feel my own tormented expression as I look at my bruised wrists. The old scars have faded, but I still see them under the new ones. "Two of them got me up from my restraints. And as I was trying to fight them, I felt the pain behind my ear going into my brain. I could understand them straight away, like Natalia said," I tell them because they don't need to know I didn't fight. I let the aliens do that willingly because... it gave me some control – a fake one. My power is always an illusion. Jade is faking it too. I am sure of it. The more I am around her, the more I can feel her fear. Sia is just Sia. Nothing seems to break the ice. Not even a fucking alien abduction. As for Natalia? She has victim written all over her. Her fragility will call to these predators. They will go for her first.

"The two who were holding me up explained the same stupid story to me. Yeah... right!" I say, spitting my words out at the girls, or more likely at myself. The panic attack is coming. If I allow it, I will be like Natalia. Prey. Breathing doesn't work; denial doesn't. Hate. I must focus on my hate for the one who thinks I belong to him.

"You don't believe they were saving us?" asks Sia.

"Of course I don't. There are no heroes in the real world, *Elsa*."

Jade starts laughing and performs an air high-five towards me. Sia ignores me, and I say good on her. I am not like Jade. I hate calling people names. I am not a bully. I just want to be left alone. I can't even find comfort in the thought these women will meet their fate first. All men go for Jade and her EEs, and Natalia is begging to be taken. I doubt alien males are wired differently. All men are the same, no matter where they are from. They might not go for Sia; not sure aliens can cope with all that ice any more than humans can. However, there is no comfort in that. My turn will come soon. We are nothing – all four of us.

"You seem sure they are hostile. Why?" asks Sia, as calmly as ever. Her lack of fear pisses me off even more. Maybe unlike me, she does have value, and she knows it.

"Because I saw how their leader looked at me," I say without being able to stop. My nails dig into my palms, and my heart feels like it's going up my throat. "Like he wanted to fuck me. Like he was going to fuck me just because he could. Because he is bigger and stronger, and it's his right to do so." I can feel their eyes on me like I am crazy. Yeah, let them know what's coming. Let them know we have no value.

"No, no, I can't let them do that to me, I'm a virgin," cries Natalia, pulling at Sia's arm.

"For fuck's sake! Who the fuck is still a virgin at nineteen?" asks Jade.

"I can't let the monsters touch me like that."

"Who knows, a monster cock might cure your monster fear!"

"Enough, Jade!" says Sia with a calm but firm voice.

"You are not my boss, *Elsa*. I don't take orders from your famous, skinny ass!" She gives her a nasty look, then turns towards me.

"How furry and how big are we talking here?"

"I don't know. Who cares?" I say. "It's more like hairy, not furry, anyway. They have long, wild-looking hair and big beards. Their skin is covered in short hair, and there's more on their chest and abdomen, going down... well... you know..."

"Shit! Were they naked?" She asks another stupid question.

"Mostly. Except for some sort of white leather kilt thingy. And some leather coverings for their feet. Boots like, I don't know."

"Did you get all these details from the one who wants to fuck you?" she asks me with a wink, and I have to stop myself from pulling her perfect hair off.

"Fuck you, Jade!"

"Yeah, right back at you, *Blondie*. And how big are we talking?"

"Monsters," says Natalia, making Jade slap her forehead and roll her eyes.

"They are huge," I hear myself talk out loud. "Maybe eight feet tall? Maybe more. They are all pure muscle. Impossible to fight them."

"Wait, was that your plan? Fight some aliens, take their ship and go back to Earth?" asks Jade, giving me a dismissive look.

"I have to fight. I won't let him touch me. I will fight. I will die fighting!" I say, kicking at the furs on the floor. It makes stupid Natalia cry some more.

"Good luck to you!" says Jade. "Not for me! The last time I fought my way out of shit, I got kidnapped by aliens. How is that for fucked-up karma? No fighting for me. Maybe at least I can get myself some monster cock. How about that, Natalia?" she asks with a wink and a disturbing grin on her beautiful face.

"I don't want to die like the girl on the ship," Natalia says unexpectedly, and we all stop moving.

"They killed a girl on the ship?" asks Sia softly.

"Yes," she says through tears. "Her neck made a horrible noise when they broke it."

God, I feel like a bitch for bullying this girl. I slept through all that.

"She was having an asthma attack and grabbed at the monster's robe. He slapped her face, and blood splattered all over him. That made him angry, and next, he broke her neck. It made a horrible noise," she says with a shuddering sob, and Sia gives her a hug and pets her red curls. The *Ice Queen* has more empathy than I do.

"Was it someone we know?" asks Jade, and this time the mocking tone is gone.

"I don't know her name. I think it is... was the pretty Brazilian model. The one with pink hair."

"Yara? They killed Yara?" I ask with trembling lips I can't control. I can feel tears building at the back of my eyes. *I will not cry.* Why didn't they kill me? Why didn't I go before Yara? She was the only thing I had left in this world. She forced herself into my heart, and one day I couldn't kick her out any more. I just wanted a party buddy, not a friend. But Yara was different. She was all sunshine and laughter. Until the day an animal decided she belonged to him and her personal torment reminded me of all the memories I was running away from. Her stalker took her sleep, laugh, and love for life away within less than four months. Her fear was overwhelming. Her asthma attacks were more frequent. He was always stalking and chasing from the shadows. He was everywhere. We weren't talking about it, but life had become a long, terrifying wait for the inevitable: the moment, he would leave the shadows and come for her. Yara had security around the clock, but it didn't do much. Then one day, her dad hired Brian, and things got better. The new bodyguard was different. He was everything I hated in a man. The type women would have no defense against. Too big to fight, too scary, and scarred at the same time. But Brian came with safety and an undeniable feel of protectiveness. He was only paid to guard Yara, but he would always watch out for me, too. She felt safe for the first time. I did, too. Like there was hope... Like we were allowed to break the rule. Reality doesn't work like that.

We are all quiet for a long time. Only Natalia's soft crying breaks the heavy silence.

"Were there any more women?" asks Sia with that calm, cold voice. The more I hear it, the more I find it soothing. How strange!

"No, just us four and Yara. There was also the man, but I think they killed him too."

"There was a man?" Jade asks before we get to. One doesn't have to be a genius to understand why they took five women.

"One of the models?" asks Sia.

"No, it was the big scary guy who followed Yara around."

I stop pacing.

"Her bodyguard? Brian?" I ask.

"I don't know," she says, hiding her face in Sia's white hair.

How much more of this? Why am I still alive?

"It must have been him," I say, feeling rage making my throat close in. "Since her disgusting stalker tried to kill her, Yara wouldn't even go to the bathroom without her bodyguard."

"Did they kill him?" asks Jade.

"He tried to help her," says Natalia, and her big blue eyes seem haunted. "He lost his mind when they snapped her neck. He broke the restraints and attacked them. He killed two of them before they could stop him."

"How? They were huge!" I hear myself ask, but I don't need an answer. Brian is a force of nature.

"He was really, really angry," says Natalia with a small voice. "They couldn't stop him. They kept shocking him with their rods, and he wouldn't stop. I wished he would stop, but he kept going for them. His skin was bleeding from everywhere. I couldn't watch, so I closed my eyes. When I woke up, he was gone."

I don't get to process my pain, my anger, my hate for the world. *He is here.* I know it before the panel by the exit lights up and the slit opens. I know it because the prey can always smell the predator. It just can't outrun it. Despite our differences, instinct takes over, and we scramble together towards the back of the room, holding onto each other, cowering on the floor. I hate myself for doing it, for showing him my fear. These women can't help me. Why am I holding on to them? They all look at him, except for Natalia, who's keeping her eyes closed and covering her ears with her hands, just like a child would. I don't look either. I am sure I don't. I somehow see he is not wearing a kilt any more, but a white shirt like ours and pristine white trousers. He has no weapons. He doesn't need them for weaklings. His presence seems even more overpowering in a room lined with soft furs and frightened women. I don't look, but I take in the details of the largest predator I have ever been around.

Everything about him is oversized and terrifying. From the height to the muscles that never stop moving under his shirt, the huge black beard with braids in and the wild dark hair, streaked with a white lock, the same color as Sia's hair. I don't look, but I know his eyes are on me. Only on me. Sia is the first to stand, and she arranges her extra-large shirt in a very composed and calm gesture. Why isn't she afraid? Maybe because he is not looking at her like she is dinner. Perhaps because his nostrils don't flare her way, like a predator's.

"Is the Human in pain?" he points at Natalia but asks Sia as if she is in charge. His voice is booming, and I try to block it. I can't. It goes under my skin. It reaches every part of my being. It's invading me from the inside out.

"No," she says calmly. "She is only scared."

"No need to be scared any more, little females."

Jade lets out a puffing noise, and he gives her a wary look. Jade is brave. Sia is brave. Natalia owns her fragility. I am just nothing.

"I am the High Commander of the *Blood Fleet*, the elite Warrior force of Tarrassia. We are on our way to Mother Planet. We will arrive shortly, if..." he stops for a second, looking at Natalia, "if we can do the *Jump*, otherwise it will take four spans. The *Jump* can be difficult and scary for those unused to it. Will the small female be able to take that?"

Jade ignores his question and asks her own.

"When are you taking us back to our home? Are we prisoners or something?"

"You are not prisoners, female," he tells her, but his eyes are on me. Always on me.

"The name is Jade, not fucking Female, dude."

"And my name is Zaan, not Dude, female Jade."

She is speechless. Probably her first time. Sia looks from him to me, and then she moves closer to my side in a protective gesture. She noticed how he stares at me.

"You cannot be returned to your planet. It is forbidden. You will be taken to Tarrassia and be safe from harm for the rest of your spans. All the former slaves we rescue make good lives for themselves on Mother Planet. You will be given dwellings, clothing, food, and be assigned jobs," he says to all, but looking at me. Always looking at me.

"What? So, we are slaves. Your people get to decide for us?" asks Jade.

"No, you are not slaves. Yes, my people are in charge of your lives now. You belong to Tarrassia."

Yes, we have no value. They know now what I always have.

"God, that's just bonkers!" explodes Jade, as expected.

"My name is Zaan, not God, and my device can't translate *boncars*."

"What the hell?"

"Enough, female Jade!" He stops her by putting a huge hand up. I don't look, but I can see the claws. I never look.

"When we get to Tarrassia, the Elders will explain everything to you. I am a Warrior. I don't explain things to females."

Of course he doesn't. My dad's rule applies everywhere in the Universe. He eventually takes his eyes from me and points at the table, jutting out of the wall.

"You need to eat and drink, females. Don't your kind eat meat?"

"Jesus! Dude, it's raw!" says Jade, rolling her beautiful eyes dramatically. He gives her a look you would give to an annoying bug.

"My name is not Jesus Dude. It's Zaan. But you can call me High Commander since you don't seem able to remember my name. Do Humans eat their meat alive? We can't provide that on my warship, but there are plenty of live animals to eat on Mother Planet. I will send in some seeds and mountain fruits until then."

His copper eyes stop upon me again. I don't look; I never do. But I can feel the copper turning gold as his stare touches every inch of my skin, of my hair, of my face, of my soul. As he turns to leave, he warns us, without looking back: "You are not prisoners, but I don't want any loose females walking around my ship, disturbing my Warriors. This door is set to respond to my hand only. My genetic code is the only thing that can make it open. So, I suggest you don't try to open it and hurt your tiny hands in the process."

He slaps his massive palm on the left screen, which responds with a bright light, and the slit in the wall opens with a hiss. And then he is gone before we can even process what he was saying or ask questions.

"Well, wasn't that interesting?" Apparently, Jade always has something to say. "I don't know about you girls, but from my first experience ever with an alien, three things have become obvious. He is very black and white, he put the L into taking things literally, and he definitely wants to fuck Gianna."

Her crude words give me the clarity I needed. There are three of the most beautiful women Earth has to offer in this room. One is so ethereally beautiful, she almost looks alien. One is what all men want in their beds. One is so fragile and vulnerable, it would trigger the instinct of all predators. Yet... he wants me. I am the faulty one. My father's rule only applies to me.

"I am escaping. Anyone coming?" I say, walking to the slit in the wall. I know they won't, and I don't want them to. I didn't live fighting. It is really sad for a girl who wanted to become a Marine. No wonder I wasn't worthy. But I will die fighting.

"Gianna, please don't listen to Jade," says Sia. "They look like honorable men... beings..."

"There is no such thing as honorable men," I reply, and my hateful voice is just as scary as everything else.

"True," says Jade. "However, the options are just as grim. Run away where? In space, around the ship? Are you sure you want that thing chasing you around his ship? Leaving this room might lead to immediate death."

"I'd rather that than let him touch me. At least I get to choose how I die," I tell her, and my words give me back some power and control I never had. I realize I do have control over the way I die, no matter how weak I am.

"It doesn't matter anyway; he's the only one who can open the door," says Sia.

I don't answer. I can't admit she is thinking straight, and I am not. I place my shaking hand on the massive panel, fit for the alien's size. It lights up instantly, and the slit opens, revealing the ship's metal corridor behind it.

"Well, what do you know?" I say with probably a crazy look in my eyes. The fact that he lied makes me even angrier. "He thought we were too weak and stupid to question his words. So, are you coming? No? Fine, suit yourselves!" I walk out, powered by all the hate and anger in the Universe.

3

ZAAN

I need to speak to my sire so I don't return to the command room. Instead, I go to my personal quarters, so I can talk to him in privacy. I consider reaching out to his mind, but I don't want him to feel the fire burning my sanity right now. Hollocom it is then. I pace my room, trying to put words together. I am a vexing full! My sire will not like this, but I don't have a choice. No later than at the beginning of this cursed span, he asked me to take extra cautions. The one mission where nothing could go wrong. One look at her, and now everything is wrong.

My Warriors know nothing of the importance of these particular aliens. To them, this was just another rescue mission. We had to get the females before the Noorranni reached their destination. They were going to sell them on Zora 23 in the highest bidder transaction. The Seven Stars' vexing law says we cannot fight them on a planet they legally own. Luckily, we don't have to. My Blood Fleet excels at fighting in space. That is where we break the chains of the slaves and take the lives of the filthy slavers. The Tarrassian Army of Shadows got information on

28

these females. We tracked them over many spans and rescued them. They come from a Red Orbit Planet we are not allowed to interact with, so they cannot be returned. It happens a lot with many of the freed slaves. So, we keep them on Tarrassia. And that is all my Warriors know. They had no idea this was the mission that had our race's future in the balance. According to my father, anyway.

As the Elder of the Healers and member of the Royal Council, my sire dedicated his life to the mission our former Wise King had entrusted him with. My people are hard-headed and too proud to admit we are about to become extinct. Hardly any mated couples had cubs for over a hundred rotations, which stopped altogether eleven rotations ago. No one ever talks about it. It would be like admitting defeat, and that is not the Tarrassian way. My sire spent half of his life span trying to find a solution. He entrusted me with his torment of not finding any. He took it upon himself to save our race. He calls me obsessed with my work and stuck in my ways, but we are both the same. When we get something in our heads, we just don't let go. My father thinks our people are punished for arrogance.

Tarrassians only breed with each other and mainly amongst castes. Almost everyone is paired at birth, and my sire thinks years of inbreeding have weakened our blood. I am one of the very few high-born Tarrassians who hasn't been matched at birth. My parents are probably the only open-minded Tarrassians. They wanted me to make my own choices. I owe them much, and I vexing ruined the one thing my sire ever asked from me. *Find these females and bring them safely to Tarrassia.* That is all he asked.

We never heard of any slaves being put up for such high prices. The credits asked for one are enough to buy a medium-sized planet. My sire saw it in my feed from the Shadows, and became obsessed. Nothing triggers his instincts more than a mystery. Knowing him, he probably hasn't rested, eaten or drank since that moment. These females are a Red Orbit Planet species and no interaction is allowed. I have no idea where he managed to find his samples, but that is what he did. According to him, this is it. *The big breakthrough*, as he called it. He found the one race compatible enough with ours to procreate. I didn't have the heart to tell him; he might be wrong. He needs to rest and let go for a while. Besides, he showed me images of Humans and I had my doubts. How could we be compatible with such weaklings? They look... breakable. But then I saw her, and now it feels like I am the weak one.

My parents were blessed with a strong mates' connection. They treasure each other immensely, despite not having the Sign of our Astrals. Nobody has it any more. Nowadays, there are no symbols on foreheads, no mating marks adorning arms, and no one has their silent heart alive. According to our young King, it's a far-fetched story of the Elders, and no one ever had it. Our King is not one to hold his tongue or his temper. He loves winding up the Elders just as much as he loves taking the heads of our enemies. He may be the former Wise King's son, but wisdom is not a trait he inherited. He could be right about the Sign, but there is no denying we are born with two hearts. I saw my Fleet's Healer and my sire perform surgery on many Warriors. There is the right heart beating in our chests, keeping us alive, but there is also the silent one. My sire showed me when I was only a cub. Inside the open chest of an old Tarrassian male, there was the silent left heart. Much smaller than the functioning one, looking all dried out and lonely. It gave me a strange feeling of longing for something none of us could have any more.

My sire, though, is the biggest dreamer ever. My mother, too. Despite their strong connection, they feel like they are missing something because they don't share our Great Ancestors' mating marks. My sire is convinced we are being punished by the Astrals for our great arrogance. Hence his quest to restore the balance. To make the Astrals forgive us. His research has proven that Humans can bear our cubs, and now he has decided to embark on this foolish mission. There is no changing his mind. My mother and I have tried. There is a chance the other Elders might think his mind is broken, and they will not hesitate to remove him from the Council. It has never been done before, but neither has what he is planning to do.

He wants to present his findings to the King and the Council then give them the solution, in the form of the four Human females we rescued. He wants to prove his theory right, and if it works, then we can take over their planet and together restore our dying numbers. He also plans on asking the King to rule by example and take one of these females as his Queen. Madness! Tarrassians don't breed with other species, never mind such a primitive one.

A niggling thought scrapes at my War Beast, and I can feel my body starting to grow. Muscles spasming, fangs pushing at my gums, claws releasing… No one, King or not, touches *her*! *No, I must control my instincts, and my anger!* There is a reason why I changed my Kannicloth in favour of the casual Tarrassian outfit. It wasn't just to put the females at ease but to stop myself from releasing my War Beast. As if the fear of tearing through clothes could stop it. I try to get a grip on my anger. The King has the other three to choose from and I am just about to deliver the news to my sire. The foul-mouthed one sounds quite appropriate for our King. I can sense a match. I had the honor of fighting many wars with him. Our young King is the kind of male you would want to watch your back in battle. He is loyal and fearless. A highly skilled Warrior. He is also the most reckless and unhinged Tarrassian ever, so I have ended up saving his skin many times. He might have a lot in common with the foul-mouthed Human.

Now I have to brace myself and tell my sire; I will only release three females for the King to choose from. He will be disappointed with my actions, but he will have to accept my decision. Luckily, the Council hasn't taken place yet. Just like me, my sire doesn't leave any loose ends. He wanted to examine the females' blood samples before calling the assembly. He will say he has three available females, and that is the end of it. The fourth one is mine, and there is nothing in this Universe to take her from me.

To be fair, I don't think my sire can convince the King to take any of them. I know Tars well enough. He only wants to go to war and sample all the female pleasures on the Yellow Planets. Killing and fucking are his only interests. Our King is not big on following rules, instructions or traditions. He only does whatever he pleases. And he definitely doesn't want to settle down.

Neither do I, for the name of the Astrals! I pull at my head fur and mess it up with my fingers. A gesture my mother has always tried to put a stop to. I worked so hard to become a Blood Fleet Warrior. That is all I trained for since I could walk. I spent all my cubhood in the Training Pits, training with the obsession and determination that made me the youngest High Commander in our history. My life means battles and space travel. I can't fit a mate in that, can I? Some of my Warriors have families, but they are the ones we normally shelter in battle, and they take leave more often than others. Besides, if she was waiting for me in my dwelling, in between my furs, there won't be a chance in the pits of fire I will stay away. And that is why I cannot risk letting the King see her. Not him, not whoever else the Council decides worthy of choosing a Human. What if her beauty does to them what it did to me? One look at those alien green eyes, one sniff of her scent, and everything changed. Nothing I ever worked for or cared for matters any more. She is all that matters.

Just as I am about to com my sire, the emergency beacon

starts pulsing through the floor, and warning lights are spinning around the ceiling. I restrain my growing muscles because there is no time to change into my Kannicloth now. I just grab my weapons as I make my way to the control room. I wouldn't usually worry. This is a Blood Fleet warship. There are very few reckless enough to attack us. And on an average span, my Warriors and I would welcome the challenge. But this time is different. Our cargo is precious. Nothing and no one threatens my female! My wrist's com device is silent, so not that much of an emergency if my Commanders do not update me on the situation. I pick up the pace because, with every nanoclip that passes, it feels like my chest is about to explode. And it's not the War Beast itching for battle. It's something else – anxiety, fear, madness… all the things I never feel. I learned a long time ago how to control all of those and rule my Warriors by example. Only a leader in control of himself can control others. My emotions are not in any way reassured by the grim look of my Third in Command and Healer of the Blood Fleet. It only takes me a nanoclip to notice the only red panel in the control room is the emergency pod release. One is missing. Unexpected sweat covers my forehead. Tarrassians can regulate body temperature. They can also breathe. Right now, it feels like I can't do either.

"High Commander, one of the Humans escaped." I hear the words that hurt more than a sword going through my skin. I don't need to ask which one. I already know. *Fear.* She put her precious life in danger just to run from me. *Pain.* My chest feels so tight as if someone put stitches on the inside. My female ran from me, and nothing could ever hurt more. *Anger.* She doesn't get to do that. Not without consequences.

"Zaan… I don't…"

The Healer's words are just noise burning my ears. *Efficiency.* That is what I need now. *Planning. Fixing.* I will deal with my pain when the order has been restored. I will deal with her when she is safe. I ignore him and ask the MI to show me all the recorded feeds. Her little form, swamped by my shirt, lingers in the shadows of my ship, tiptoeing on tiny bare feet, avoiding my vexing Warriors. She doesn't hesitate; she doesn't question herself; she just acts. Methodically, efficiently, brilliantly. The Warrior in me feels pride. The male in me wants to kill her. However, the High Commander and the son of an Elder worries. Something in her movements reminds me of our Shadow Warriors. Not only does she seem to know exactly what she's doing, but her little palm opens the security panels, one after the other. They can only open for those with clearance. The most worrying thing of all is she opened the one in the Humans' holding room. That one was programmed to only open for me. Who is she? What are these Humans? My years of training and self-discipline only make my chest tighter. I have to consider, these females may not be as weak as they look. I have to accept they might be an enemy. I have to keep my people safe. That doesn't change the facts. She is mine to keep; she just might not like the keeping terms.

"Put us in standby," I tell Barin who watches me like I have lost my wits. Perhaps I have. "Inform the High General and ask him to remove the other Humans from my ship. Don't beam her pod back in yet. Keep her within range. I don't need to tell you what happens to you if she gets hurt."

I don't wait for him to answer; I know he will follow my orders to the detail. As badly as I want her back on my ship, I need to know what I am dealing with first. She is safe in the emergency escape pod, and she can't go anywhere. There is no way a non Tarrassian can opperate our ships and the MI only activates itself with an identity chip. She is not Tarrassian, so she is going nowhere. I consider stopping by my quarters to change into my Kannicloth. The War Beast is pushing at the fabric of my shirt, and the last thing I want is to tear my garment in front of the females. But then again, maybe that's what they need to see. They need to know who commands this warship and who commands them while they are in my care.

As I walk in and the security wall closes behind me, the Human females huddle together towards the back of the room. The small red female starts making strange noises again and leaks water from her eyes like a cub. I will not be fooled by their fragility again. We have no idea what these aliens really are or who they work for. Even the reckless one seems scared, looking at my growing muscles with a pang of worry in her eyes. However, the white-haired female has decided to come clean, I see. She stands straight as a board in front of them, protecting them from me. Is she their leader? She looks like one. She holds my eyes, and very few can when the white of the War Beast takes over. All beings cower to a Tarrassian War Beast. This one... doesn't. She looks entirely in control, cold and unimpressed by my anger or my growing muscles. What are they?

"Where is Gianna?" she asks me. Her voice is calm, and there is no fear in it.

Gianna. The strange yet beautiful name of my mate. I try not to let it pause my determination or weaken my heart.

"How did she get out?" I ask my own question. I try to control my anger. These creatures may be an unexpected enemy, but they are still females.

"The same way you did," she tells me. "She placed her palm on the panel, and it opened for her."

She is lying, and there are no signs of deceit on her serene face. Does betrayal come so easy to her kind?

"Do not deceive me, female!" I growl, and the small red Human starts sobbing. "This device only responds to the particles in my blood. I set it that way. It only opens for me. Not for my Warriors, not for the Astrals, and not for Humans! For the last time! How did she leave the room?" I will not be able to contain my anger any longer. Did I get distracted by my female's beauty and miss important details? Have I allowed enemies on board my ship?

"You asked a question, High Commander, and I answered," she says, raising her chin high.

There is no deceit and no fear in those frosty gray eyes. I take a deep breath and try to control my physical strength. I could easily break this female's bones with the wrong touch. I grab her wrist with only two fingers and start pulling her towards the slit's panel. She doesn't fight me and follows me willingly. I release more of my pressure as her bones feel fragile and her skin soft under my fingers. I place her tiny pale hand on the screen. Nothing. I try it again. Nothing. I place her right palm. The slit remains closed.

"Ask the females to come here," I tell her, and I can hear the uncertainty in my voice. Something is not right, and my mind cannot process the magnitude of it. My entire body and soul scream at me. Telling me the one thing I am missing. The only one that matters. My brain is not ready to process it. How could it?

The Human called Jade rolls her eyes at me in a strange gesture and tries to bring the little one over. She cries louder, and only when the white-haired female encourages her, she comes forward. The little red-haired Human touches the panel quickly, one tiny hand at a time, pushing up on tiptoes just to reach it. Nothing happens. She scurries back to the safety of the furs, away from me. I don't tell her to, but the silly Human called Jade places her hands over and over on the panel like it's a game.

"*Jesus Dude*, shall I try my feet? What do you think? Left one? Right one?" she asks me, a glint of challenge in her eyes. But I am not getting angry. How could I? Out of all the worthy Tarrassians, the Astrals have chosen me to receive the greatest gift of all. I can't see it, but I know my eyes are swimming in gold, matching the glowing particles under my skin. The white-haired female places herself between me and the reckless one in a protective gesture. She doesn't understand how precious they are to us. I would never hurt them.

"The course of action has changed, little females," I tell them, trying to sound less threatening. "The High General of Tarrassia and his Generals are on their way to collect you. The Blood Fleet has another destination now. They will take you to *Levianha*. They will do the *Jump* and be here in the next eleven nanoclips. Please, don't do anything to put yourselves in danger. You are all precious to us now. Any questions?"

"What is *Levianha*?" asks the calm white-haired female.

"Our Royal Ship."

"What's waiting for us there?"

"Our King!" I tell her, hoping that sounds reassuring enough. Sadly, there aren't many reassuring things about him, but she doesn't need to know that yet.

My Third in Command is waiting outside the Humans' room with dread in his eyes. I already know what he is going to tell me. I need to keep my anger, anxiety, and all the swirls of emotions down. Until she is safe in my arms, where she belongs, I will only allow my strengths to rule me. Not my weaknesses. I will make the best of the qualities that allowed me to become the youngest High Commander of the Blood Fleet.

"I don't understand... I am sorry High Commander, I failed you," he says, and despite the urgency burning in my chest, I stop and place a hand on his shoulder.

"You did not, Barin," I tell him. "I know she managed to launch the pod. You couldn't have overrun her control of the MI. My clearance is higher than yours."

"What are you saying, Zaan? How could she have tricked the MI to think she is you?"

"Because she is my mate. We are becoming one, and our genetic codes have started to intertwine."

"That's not possible; that only happens if…" He stops talking as he understands the magnitude of this. It only takes him a few nanoclips to recompose himself, then he takes a fist to his chest, giving me the Tarrassian salute. He also does it to pledge his trust and respect to me. As my oldest friend, I didn't expect anything less from him.

"What do you require, High Commander?" he asks.

"First, discretion. No one else can know of this yet. Once she is safe, I will deal with whatever the Council or my sire might have to say. Is the High General on board?"

"Yes, High Commander."

"Good, now let's avoid him," I say and take the opposite corridor, Barin quick to follow. He doesn't like the High General any more than I do. I failed in the simple mission of keeping these fragile females safe. The High General doesn't understand failure. He will not hesitate to ruin my vexing span, and I don't have time for that. I also know he would rather avoid me, just like I am avoiding him. Our shared history will keep him away from me. He will probably let the King deal with me later and only retrieve the females for now. I would rather have the King's judgment over his, on any given span. Once he's taken the Humans off my ship, we can easily track the escape pod and bring my reckless female back. When she is safe, I will deal with all the vexing problems, but most of all, I will show her what happens when she runs from me.

4

—

GIANNA

How are these aliens so technologically advanced when they are this stupid? Their security is shit! The ideal plan was to make it to the small pod the Healer and I came in. I knew that wasn't going to happen. He used his palm to open several security access points as we arrived on the main ship. So, plan B was to get caught, grab a weapon, make them kill me, or do it myself. Probably just as stupid as plan A. Yet... here I am. Onboard the same familiar pod I arrived in. All the security doors opened for my palm. It was a stretch to reach some of them but luckily, I am taller than most women so I managed. I can feel that thing I hate the most inside me, and I am quick to crush it. Hope has no place in this. I might have made it, but I will not allow myself to hope any more. It's not like I can make it alive out of this thing. Now I just need to get away from here, away from him.

The airlock closes behind me automatically, which is good because I have no idea how to. I sit in one of the only two chairs in the pod, trying to remember how the Healer engaged the safety harness. I think he just pulled it but trying to do the same almost removes my shoulder from its socket. It doesn't matter. Dead people don't need safety belts. If anything, it will make it quicker. The Healer called the operating system MI. I am positive he did. No idea what it means, but the artificial intelligence of the pod responded to it.

"MI, prepare to launch!" I say, hoping I sound firm enough. Silly, of course. This is a stupid machine. It doesn't care. Only, it's not that stupid.

"Malfunction detected in the voice recognition program. Please present your identity chip, Warrior," says the harsh robotic-like voice. My adventure was very short-lived, after all. For whatever reason, my palm opened all the airlocks on the way here but taking one of their ships away must be a different thing. The control panel is so simple. An oval dark glass shape is surrounded by precisely three buttons and some sort of a lever. That's all. But the worst part is I don't see any of the identity panels around. Put my palm print where?

"MI, where and how do I present my identity?" I know it's a ridiculous question, and this thing will expose me as an intruder. Not that it matters. As the airlock closed behind me, it activated an alarm. They already know I escaped.

"Please press your palm on the mapping screen so I can read your identity chip, Warrior."

Wow, maybe Artificial Intelligence will always be lacking in… intelligence. No questions asked is fine by me. And it doesn't take a genius to know it meant the oval screen. I take a deep breath and place my palm on it. It lights up with a green glare, but then it turns dark again. There is a slight noise of static.

"High Commander, there seems to be a malfunction within the identity system. Please press and hold on the mapping screen, making sure your palm is connected correctly with the identity chip reader."

What? Is the thing broken? Can alien stuff even break? I do

what it says, regardless. I know the airlock will open any minute now. I haven't explored the small supplies area or the little enclosed space, separated by a glass panel. I can tell that's some sort of a restroom. I already know from the previous trip in this pod there aren't any weapons lying around. And would I know how to use alien weapons? I can't even make sense of their stupid MI. It's best to focus my efforts on leaving or dying in the process – ideally the latter. The screen lights up again as I press my palm on it.

"Hanni, High Commander. Welcome on board. The system is rebooting. No further malfunctioning was detected. Awaiting instructions."

Oh, my God! What is this? Did I break it? Instruction for what? I didn't think I would make it this far. The possibility of being successful makes my body fill with adrenaline but also fear. I keep watching the airlock, and I can hear my own heart, beating erratically.

"MI, launch the pod into space."

"I am sorry, High Commander. I do not understand the instruction. Please rephrase."

Shit! What do I do?

"MI, detach the pod from the Blood Fleet."

"I am sorry, High Commander. I do not understand the instruction. Please rephrase."

Perhaps it needs a precise destination. But where? Do I dare hope?

"MI, set destination for planet Earth."

"Planet Earth is part of the Red Orbit Treaty. Interaction is forbidden."

"Really? How the hell do you think I got here?" My outburst gets no reply from the MI, as expected. I am wasting precious time.

"MI, what is the nearest planet?"

"High Commander, the nearest planet is the Orbital Station Rinaae 45."

"MI, set destination for the nearest planet," I say because I am not sure I can pronounce all that. Before I get to think about consequences, fear, or dying, the MI sets the destination, powers the pod, all lights coming on at once, and straps me in the seat large enough to fit two of me. I close my eyes and wait for the inevitable. This cannot work. No way. Nothing is ever that simple or easy. Not for me, anyway. There are no windows in here, and it makes me very anxious. It adds to my ever-present feeling of being powerless. My stomach sinks to my knees as the pod detaches itself from the ship and launches into space. My ears are popping, and it makes the inside of my head feel immense pressure. I try to mimic chewing gum, a trick a flight attendant taught me during my many travels worldwide. It doesn't really work, but it keeps you distracted from pain or discomfort. In this case, both.

"High Commander, you are on route to the destination. Journey span set to seventy-six nano rotations."

The stupid translating device only translates what it pleases. What is a nano? I open my eyes, and I can see the bright light has been dimmed. The so-called mapping panel is a satnav. It doesn't look like anything I've seen before. The screen changes at a swift pace, and there is a tone of symbols, long texts, maps coming and going in a flash. How can they read and process all that, yet they have the most stupid artificial intelligence in the world? For some reason, it thinks I am *him*. I can't even be happy with my escape because this feels like the Universe's ultimate bad joke. Each time the MI mentions him, it's like a slap in the face, reminding me I am not allowed to forget about him and his stupid golden eyes. *Focus, Gianna!*

"MI, convert *nano rotations* to English," I say, not hoping for much. There is static again, and I think it happens when it encounters a problem or a question it's not used to. If this is anything like the smart devices back home, it should learn and adapt as it goes.

"High Commander, a nano rotation is the equivalent of a Human hour. I cannot find its equivalent in English." Is this thing for real? I am shocked to feel a trace of a smile on my dry lips. That suddenly reminds me of reality. I don't even know how long we were kept asleep on that ship or when I ate last. My stomach feels hollow, and my mouth as dry as the desert. Seventy-two hours is a very long time. Am I supposed to be strapped in a chair for that long? I know there are supplies on the shelves by the restroom. Probably raw meat...

"MI, disengage the safety restraint," I say, remembering that's what the Healer called it. Again, another bad joke, since I am so fond of that word.

"Yes, High Commander," says the freaking thing. It puts me off asking anything, and I have so many questions. I get up on shaky bare feet.

Unlike the floor on the main ship, this one is bitterly cold. The temperature feels lower altogether. I try to delay thinking and look through the supplies first – no raw meat, just square pouches nicely arranged by colors. I am happy to see a couple of large furs and an entire shelf of transparent bags with a clear liquid inside. It must be water or something similar. Just looking at it reminds me I am desperate to use the toilet, so I decide to investigate that first. There is no panel or button by the glass wall separating it from the control room. How do I get in? I wave at it, but nothing happens. I slap the glass in frustration, and it opens with a hiss. It takes a lot of hit and miss to make sense of everything. I am happy to survive the experience. I know my little escape will end up with me dying. But I really don't want to know it happened while trying to use alien facilities. There is no running water. The sink, which is really a hole in the metal wall, the toilet, similar to a Japanese one, and the shower, are all operated with steam – a cleaning, fragrant steam which leaves me feeling cleaner than ever before. The problem is, the pressure is enough to cause severe damage to fragile human skin. I just need to mind my angles and protect my most sensitive parts.

My painful stomach reminds me of my other needs. I brace myself while going for a square white pouch. It opens with something similar to a zipper, but sadly there is just white powder inside. It looks just like the one lying around on coffee tables at my wild parties. I hope it's not that sort of powder. Not my thing. It smells really strong, but not in a bad way. It is not a familiar smell, unlike the one *he* left behind him in the room. What the hell is wrong with me? Why did I think of that of all things? I ignore myself and put the entire content of the pouch in my mouth. I don't care if it's poison. I would probably welcome it right now. I choke the second it hits my tongue, as it's worse than poison! The powder expands in my mouth, and it turns solid. An irrational panic takes over and I quickly spit it out. I get the rest out with my fingers, gagging in the process. Some still went down my throat, and probably down the wrong pipe. I have no idea what it is, but it sucks big time. Never mind the texture, the taste is so sweet, my eyes pour down tears, and my mandibula clenches like it has its own sugar rush. What the hell is this? A weapon?

Maybe raw meat wasn't the worst option. No more white pouches, I decide. I go to the opposite spectrum of safe and choose one in a bright purple color. The powder inside is just as bright as the wrapping. I imagine it's purple broccoli, the only vegetable I can stomach, and take a small amount, as I know it will expand. It does just that, and it turns solid enough to chew. So that's what it's meant to do. Unless of course you put the whole thing down your throat like an idiot. Oh, my god! Meat. Smoky, barbecued meat. The taste is so intense, my brain brings up the smell of an actual barbeque. The pouch is slightly smaller than my hand, but

I feel too full to finish it less than halfway through. I try to fold it closed, as I can't afford to waste food.

I have to use one of the furs to aim at a water bag on the top shelf. I am not tall enough to reach it otherwise. I catch it before it smashes onto the floor. There is quite a substantial amount of liquid in the transparent bag. I can see how to open it, but the question is, what do I do after. I can't reclose it, and all the water is bound to spill. There are only six bags of water; I can't afford to waste it. I consider holding on to it, but as I open it, I realize I don't have to. It molds to my lips as I drink and then to whatever shape I give it. I press the ends together, and it reseals itself. They have all these amazing things, yet the stupid MI thinks I am *him*.

I feel better once hunger and thirst have been sated. I wrap myself in one of the large furs, trying not to imagine what sort of animals they came from. I need to think, but I am cautious not to allow myself to hope. There is no such thing, and I find I don't really mind. My fate was sealed the moment I was taken from Earth. Unlike the other girls, I chose to alter it and find death on my own terms. I realize this is the most power and control I was ever going to have. It took an alien abduction for that, but at least I get to die the way I choose. I certainly didn't live that way. For the first time in forever, I am free, and I have a purpose. Even if it's dying. The last few years of my life have been nothing but constant noise and rush. I did whatever I needed to cover the pain. I do welcome this silence and the loneliness. Maybe the world can forget about me, and I can just float in space until I run out of supplies and die. The thought only reminds me, I have a destination to reach. Of course, I don't intend to get to any planet. I don't know if the air will be breathable or if the locals will have me for breakfast. I only set that destination to be able to get away from him and his stupid golden stare. I feel increasingly tired and very cold. Probably to be expected, considering the physical and emotional roller-coaster. There is also this strange feeling of... I don't really know what it is. Like I've lost something. It puts me on edge, and there is some panic building inside me. I don't know why. I've already decided I don't fear death. I grab the other fur and use it as a blanket as I sit again in front of the control panel. I hate talking to this MI person... thingy, but just because I know I will die, it doesn't mean I have to go the easy way.

"MI, why are Red Orbit Planets forbidden?"

"Hanni, High Commander, welcome back."

This fucking thing!!!!

"Red Orbit Planets are primitive. Interaction is forbidden."

I see, I tell myself without being able to suppress the anger. I guess they don't mind fucking primitive species. To my surprise, the MI continues to explain.

"Primitive planets are not aware of intergalactic travel or other sentient species. They have short life spans and no self-healing abilities. They are vulnerable, and interaction with vulnerable species is not allowed."

Okay... if you put it like that, I guess we are primitive. At least my smartphone never thought I was someone else. That's still something. I have to make a decision and change the route somehow. But where to? Maybe a further planet? Until I run out of food and die. It just sounds so stupid. Will the aliens try and find me? They have three other women, right? Maybe they will think I am already dead or something. Despite my determination to forget about *him*, the memory of his stare tells me otherwise. He will not let go because he thinks I belong to him. That's all I am to him. A belonging and men like him don't let go of their property.

"MI, how far are we from the Blood Fleet Warship?"

"The Blood Fleet will catch up with us in the next twenty-four nanos."

What? I swallow hard and pull my fur closer around me. The cold is getting a bit uncomfortable. If a nano rotation is an hour, would a nano be a minute? Twenty-four minutes? That is all I got? I know the warship must be much faster than this pod, but how would they... Stupid! I feel so stupid! How was I ever going to become a Marine?

"MI, can you disengage the pod's tracking device?"

"I am the tracking device, High Commander. Would you like me to disengage myself?"

What now? You have got to be kidding me. That is almost like a low blow. Is this something they do on purpose? I can't let him find me. He will want to make an example out of me. I knew he would hurt me from the beginning; I knew he would bring all my nightmares back and then give me new ones to put the old ones to shame. But now he will make it ten times worse. I know his type, alien or not. I welcome death, just not at his hands. I refuse to!

"MI, what is the fastest speed you can reach?" Static. It finds my question weird.

"High Commander, would you like to activate the *Jump*?"

Activate what? I am sure the device in my ear said *Jump*. Could that be...? The thought makes me want to smile. That is freaking awesome! I remember he mentioned it, and it does sound like teleporting.

"MI, is the *Jump* a form of time travel?"

"I am not familiar with the term, High Commander."

Right, so that is just human sci-fi. *Focus, Gianna!* "MI, what is the furthest distance you can *Jump*?" More static. I am going to give this thing a headache.

"High Commander, the furthest location is Moorra Galaxy in the Eight Quadrant."

"MI, how long will it take to perform the *Jump*?"

"The *Jump* will take eleven nanoclips, regardless of destination, High Commander."

Time to try the impossible. It's not like I have a choice. He did say the *Jump* was not for the faint-hearted. Maybe it will kill me if I am lucky enough.

"MI, *Jump* to Moorra Galaxy in the Eight Quadrant, then disengage yourself." Static. It doesn't like it. Is it because I didn't pronounce the words right, or because I used two instructions at the same time?

"High Commander, the Eight Quadrant is outside the safety zone of The Coalition of the Seven Stars. Travel is not recommended."

Outside of his control? Oh, this is better than I could have hoped for. Not that I hope for anything anymore. "MI, engage the safety restraint," I ask and wait for it to do it. I try not to think much or give my last moments of life too much meaning. "MI, *Jump* to Moorra Galaxy in the Eight Quadrant, then disengage yourself."

5

—

ZAAN

My vexing chest feels like it's about to explode. Nothing like when the War Beast takes over our bodies. This is different. I rub a hand over it, trying to soothe the pain. Knowing your mate would rather endanger herself than be around you is the kind of pain no male should ever feel. For the last two spans rotations, I let anger power my determination. But the longer she is away from me, the less I can put anger at my foremind. Worry for her safety overpowers everything else. She is all alone out there and must be terrified. I know she is alive because I am still alive. I watch the mapping screen the same way I have for the last spans. No sleeping, no eating, no drinking… I won't last long this way. My training tells me I need to make sure my body is strong enough to fight. But how do I take my eyes off the screen? What if I miss something? Part of me wishes I would have accepted Barin's offer to accompany me. Or at least take one of my Warriors. But this is a personal matter and I couldn't involve anyone else. I may be a vexing fool about to be stripped of all the achievements I worked so hard for, but I am still the High Commander. I will not risk a single one of my Warriors or the honor of the Blood Fleet. When my infuriating female activated the *Jump*, she sealed both my fate and future.

My orders had been to retrieve the females from the Noorranni and nothing more. However, I know the King would have expected me to track and return the missing one. Not just because the Humans are essential to us, but because she is a fragile female, and our code of honor would demand it. The Eight Quadrant, though? That changes everything. The Moorra Galaxy is not a place where the Blood Fleet can go without special permission from the Council, from the Moorri and their cursed King. A lot of diplomacy and trading would have been required, and I wasn't going to wait for that. And what if the Council said no? Taking risks and forgetting to ask permission might be accepted. Going against a strict order would be treason. So, before anyone could do anything to stop me, I asked Nodric, my Second in Command, to take control of the Blood Fleet. He was not happy with me, but he is a male who is hardly ever pleased with anyone. I took my personal warship to the Eight Quadrant and disabled all tracking and communication channels. I know I won't be allowed to keep my title after such reckless behavior, but at least it won't be treason. I can't be accused of disobeying an order from the King if I never got one. Besides, doing this all alone won't be perceived as an act of war from Tarrassia. My King will not be accused of the actions of a lone Warrior.

The Eight Quadrant are not enemies, but they are not our allies either. None of these nations are part of the Coalition of the Dark Moon. They are not part of any. They only serve their greed. These planets are where the richest, the most deprived, and corrupt live. Yet, we are not allowed to crush them. The laws of the Coalition of the Seven Stars are not something I could ever understand. They enable these planets to thrive because they never displayed aggression. They never took over other species, and they never invaded anyone. In reality, they are just as bad as the Noorranni slavers and the Dark Moon worshippers. Without the Eight Quadrant buying the slaves from the hidden markets, there wouldn't be any slavers. I always knew deep down, our young King felt the same. That is why he would rather go to battle or visit the Yellow Planets than attend the Council. And my vexing sire put an end to that, making him take a Queen.

As if to prove me right, a transport of the Dark Moon appears on my mapping screen, and I quickly cloak my ship and change direction. My chest hurts even more. She is entirely at the mercy of all the scum amongst the galaxies. I pull at my head and facial fur until it stings. *How do I find you? Where are you, my Lorra?* Perhaps I need to rest. I have been injured in battle or during sparring in the Training Pits more times than I can recall. Yet this pain in my chest is excruciating. Like it has expanded somehow. My body demands to rest, and my worried mind needs it even more. If only for a while, I need to forget that she's been all alone for almost three span rotations, and that she ran from me.

I also need to forget I am letting everybody down. My parents, my King... my Warriors. I turned all the ship's communication systems off, but Tarrassians can reach each other's minds. We also have to allow it, and for the last spans, I pushed away all the people I care for. My sire tries almost every nano rotation. My mother stopped a few spans ago. Our females are fragile creatures, and her pain must be too much to bear. On the last span, the King tried to access my mind and not long ago, even the High General. He avoids me like the plague since that cursed span when I saw the male behind the mask. Their constant pressure in my tired mind only makes it worse. Just then, I feel Barin requesting a mind connection, and I allow it. I trust him and Nodric with my life, but most importantly, I trust them with hers.

She is alive High Commander, but that is the only good thing, he starts, and my heart sinks.

Tell me, Barin!

Our Shadows in the Quadrant have news. The Moorri King found a female in his space territory. One he had already purchased from the Noorranni before the actual bidding. Rumour goes he paid for her with enough credits to buy an entire galaxy.

The pounding in my chest becomes so loud it is making me dizzy. I can almost feel his blood in my mouth. There will be no place for him to hide. The Moorri King doesn't buy what is mine.

When did he find her?

Less than a nano rotation ago. But Zaan, please, you can't...

Is she at his Palace?

Yes, but please, you need to listen, there have been many developments on Mother Planet and...

I block his access to my mind, as I know he will offer to send the Blood Fleet next. As much as I need them for this, it will be an act of war if our enemies chose to read it as such. I will not risk my King. I can get her out all by myself. The Moorri King will wish the wrath of Tarrassia upon him, rather than mine. The rush of the imminent fight, the anger, the rage at his filthy hands touching what's mine, push all my tiredness away. I need all my training, my discipline and my strength for this. Love and anger will be dealt with later.

I *Jump* straight to the Moorri arrival pad and ask their vexing control for permission to land and an audience with the King. I know these things take time, but every nano that passes without a reply rips my chest apart. The guilt makes it all worse. I cannot go without saying sorry to my sire. My parents deserve better than the reckless son shaming them. They treasure their connection enough to understand I will sacrifice anything for her. I know they will not judge me. My sire's mind opens for me as soon as I think about him.

My son, finally, he says. I can feel relief flooding his mind.

I don't have long, my sire. I wanted you and mother to forgive me for shaming you.

Zaan, what are you saying? I can feel you are not well, my son. Your mind is… different. And why would you feel ashamed for trying to save one of the Humans? They are precious to us. Now more than ever. Why are you doing it alone? You left your Second in Command in charge? Do you not wish to succeed in this rescue? Are you unwell, my son? Your body functioning seems altered somehow.

My sire is a male of few words. For him to use this many is a great sign of distress.

I know the Humans are precious to us, my sire; I just didn't think the Council would be willing to start a war, simply because those females can give us cubs. I wasn't going to risk her because she is precious to me.

What do you mean, my son? Did you touch this female? he asks but quickly corrects himself when he feels my rage. *That is not what I meant, my son. I know you would never hurt a female. And not because you are Tarrassian or because of your Warrior honor. You wouldn't do that because of the male you are. I meant to ask if you had contact with her skin at all?*

My sire's words don't make any sense, and I am wasting precious time. My permission to dock could be granted any time now. I have so much to tell my parents. I may never see them again.

I haven't touched the female, sire, and I am still not sure I understand. You have to…

No, Zaan, you have to listen and stop acting recklessly. There might be some truth in what you said about the Council not risking a war with the Eight Quadrant. It was my idea to use these females, and it was I who discovered our compatibility. Nevertheless, I would have voted against this rescue. We cannot risk Tarrassia's safety for the chance one female might give us a few cubs. But every single Tarrassian would sacrifice themselves to protect our Sign.

What is he saying? Can he somehow feel she is my mate? I know our people haven't had the Sign in longer than we can remember, but there is no other explanation why she shares my genetic code. Unless she is a Shadow of the Coalition of the Dark Moon, making a vexing fool out of me. Regardless, she is still my female.

Everything is different now, my son. The Council and the entire Mother Planet hold their breath until the missing female is back in our care. Humans are a lot more precious than we thought. They brought back our Sign. The King developed our long-lost mating marks after touching one of the females. So did the Great Warrior. It cannot be a coincidence. Two out of the four females we rescued brought back our Sign and awakened their males' silent hearts. That is why you can wipe the Eight Quadrant off and send it to the pits of fire if you wish. The Council will stand behind you. You just need your Blood Fleet for that, you fool!

She is not a Shadow working with our enemies. She is just MINE.

It is not only two out of four, is it my son? I can feel my sire's emotion in my mind, and it overwhelms me.

No, sire. This female is my mate. The one I have been waiting for my entire life span. I hope you can understand why I had to do this reckless thing. There is no time to wait for my Blood Fleet. The Moorri King has my female, and you know very well his slaves only last a span if they are lucky enough.

My son, don't be reckless again. He paid more for her than for his entire Palace, fleet and slaves put together. He will not just give her up because you asked.

Even scum of the galaxies like him will respect a mated pair. It is the law of all our ancestors.

My son, you are not thinking straight. I know you are like me. That is why I can tell you, obsession can make one achieve but can also lead to destruction. Please, be wise. Wait for your Warriors. King Marud will want to see proof. He will not just take your word for it.

He will allow me to touch her; he cannot deny it, I tell my sire and myself. My plan is reckless, but I will act on it either way.

I worry, my son. We forgot so many things about our Sign. The King and the Great Warrior awakened their silent hearts and developed the mating marks upon touching their females for the first time. Just as our stories tell us. It doesn't explain why your heart came to life without the other marks or touching your female.

I stop pacing the control room and sit in my chair. Of course, that is why my chest hurts. I have two beating hearts now. I was too tired, worried, and angry to even notice. I place my hand over my left heart. It beats for her. It came to life for her. For my Lorra.

This is perfect, sire! My new heart is all the proof I need.

Yes, indeed, my son. You have been blessed. Our entire House has been blessed. However, the Sign seems to act differently in your case. What if you don't develop the marks? The Moorri King can't see your new heart, and I doubt he knows how many hearts should Tarrassians even have.

It is true. Tarrassians are very private and we don't share our history or traditions with inferior species. That gives me an idea. The Mating Bite. It is not a Tarrassian thing, but my people imported the bite from other species in lack of our Sign. Unlike them, we only do it as a symbol – a pledge of our mates' connection. It heals soon after, and it doesn't leave a mark, but he doesn't know all that.

I will give her my bite in front of him. His species practises it as their oldest mating ritual. He won't know Tarrassians don't, and he will respect it.

Zaan of House Marni, you will do no such thing to a fragile Human! We give our bite to our females during the first mating.

That can take their mind away from the pain, and our females can self-heal. Humans are incredibly fragile and easy to break.

It didn't stop her from escaping or messing with my vexing MI. I have to go, sire, I tell him, as permission for both docking and an audience is granted. *Please tell Mother I am sorry for hurting her feelings and that we will always be connected no matter what happens to me.*

Zaan, please... Tell me at least you will bring the Blood Fleet into the Moorra Galaxy.

Yes, sire. I have already given the order.

One more thing, my son. I have a very reckless message from our King. I would rather not repeat it if I had a choice. Between the two of you, wisdom has no chance of showing itself. I believe his exact words were: 'Tell the Moorri fool I beg him to give me a reason to take his head.'

My King's words may seem strange to an Elder, but not to me. There is a reason why every single one of my Warriors would die for Tars. He would do the same for us.

6

GIANNA

A little flashing blue dot came to life on the satnav a while ago. It's a warning. About time. I am surprised I survived for this long. At some point, I lost track of time, and it makes me feel disoriented. I didn't think I could stay alive for this long. I would have remembered some of my training otherwise. The short, painful eight months of training as a Marine, before reality came crashing down. Maybe the bullies were right. I was only good at being the General's daughter. Otherwise, I would have remembered keeping time and staying fit are the first survival rules in captivity. And this pod is no different than a cell in a basement. It is cold, dark, with no windows and no way of telling day and night apart. It feels like I've been here for years. And I've only gone through less than half of the provisions. There goes my hope to die of starvation. I seriously underestimated my eating habits. I know I have an eating disorder. For two years after I left my father's house, all my meals would end up in the toilet. I knew I needed help, but I couldn't manage a shrink taking my life apart while checking the time on his watch. Yara also had an eating disorder, but unlike me, she had professional help. I used all her tips and treatment, and together we managed to heal ourselves. What was even the point? We both ended up victims anyway...

Being a famous model and parading around with hardly any clothes on made me stop my other habit: self-harming. No amount of make-up could have hidden the scratches on my arms. It started with me trying to scrub myself in the shower until my skin bled from its pores. It continued with scratching at my wrists, trying to remove the marks of the restraints. Being in the public eye made me stop. That also didn't last... I feel my raw arms under the furs from all the rubbing and scratching. Somehow, it's not just the old familiar need to self-harm. For some reason, my skin tingles in a very uncomfortable way, and my forehead throbs. Being in space for so long has started to affect my body... I think. I feel lost as if someone took all the sense out of the world. Not that my life ever made sense to me before.

Everything hurts from sleeping on the hard floor or in the equally uncomfortable chair. The worst of all has got to be the cold. I think something is not quite right with the pod. The lights are getting dimmer, and the temperature is continuously dropping. Despite the shower's extreme pressure, I used the steam a lot to keep myself warm. But then, a day or so ago, it stopped. Now there is only steam flushing the toilet. The floor is freezing, so I curl into myself on the unforgivingly hard chair, trying to make the best of my only two furs. The strangest thing? My breath doesn't even steam. Am I already dead? That probably explains my stupid thoughts and needs. The alive Gianna would not wish *he* could find me. The alive Gianna would not hug herself to sleep pretending it was his arms around me. The alive Gianna would not dream of golden eyes and the smell of Sicilian blood oranges. *His smell.* I must be dead.

Another flashing light appears on the screen, but this one is growing with particular urgency, and the entire floor of the pod starts flashing the same yellow color. There is a sudden bump outside the airlock and a humming noise followed by a vibration. It feels as if... the pod is being attached to a larger ship. I wanted him to find me, didn't I? Because I am weak. Because I have no value. I am only defined by the men who want to own me. I stand, using all the little dignity I have left, bracing myself to face the pair of eyes I hate the most in this world.

Only the man coming through the airlock is not him. It's the Devil himself! He walks in, followed by two of his demons, and the pod feels too tight, swamped by their height and bulk. Is everybody in this world bigger than me? The Devil comes closer, and I would retreat if I had space. He sniffs my way, no different than the man with the golden eyes did. Once again, I am prey, property. No value.

"Charming," the Devil says, and I am surprised I can understand him. Would the device inside my ear translate Devil? "Welcome home, my *Special One*."

Home? Does that mean I was always meant to go to Hell?

"You found your way to me all by yourself. The fool slavers took my credits but failed to deliver you or refund me for the loss. For escaping the Tarrassian pest and returning to your rightful owner, you will be rewarded. I declare you my special pleasure slave, and all the other slaves will bow to you. You are now my *Special One*. You may thank me for such preferential treatment."

This is not the Devil. I am sure of it because Satan himself couldn't be so full of shit. This is just another man who thinks he owns me. I don't reply anything as he moves around me in a small circle. I didn't see what the aliens who kidnapped us looked like when they were alive. Only whatever was left of them. Tarrassians look like oversized Vikings with metallic skin but still very much human. In a way, this feels like my first encounter with an alien form of life. He may not be the Devil, but he sure looks like one. His skin is a bright red, probably what an angry tomato would look like. He is bald, which only draws attention to the two stubby horns jutting out of his head. He probably has some of the most beautiful eyes I have ever seen, if red is your color that is. They are rimmed with long black lashes, making the red stand out. He has a huge silver ring going through his broad nose. Maybe he is a bull, not a devil. But then again, he has a thin, long tail, bifurcated at the end. He is currently using it to feel my legs up, under the fur. Really? Am I being groped by a tail?

The two heavily armed aliens behind him look very similar to him, but their skin is a duller shade of red. The one sniffing at me like he's a freaking dog is much larger and certainly much more terrifying. There's a commanding air about him, as if he was born to be obeyed and he knows it. His body is heavily muscled in a work of art kind of way. Maybe the bright red color of his skin accentuates all the ridges, the abs and the pecs. Yes, it must be the color, because I am quite sure the Tarrassians are bigger. He wears tight leather trousers, just as red as his skin and gives the illusion he is naked. His torso is barely covered by a sleeveless leather vest. Once you get over the bright color, horns, and tail, he looks human enough. He reaches out a massive clawed hand and pulls the fur away from my body.

"A Tarrassian outfit on my slave!" he booms, making me want to cover my ears. Without any warning, he rips my shirt apart, and his claws catch the skin on my shoulders in the process. He watches the droplets of blood with anger.

"The Noorranni promised your kind only looked fragile. I see they deceived me. And you will have to fatten up," he says, looking at my naked body with a very displeased expression. "I don't like bony. How long does your species require to fatten up?"

For the first time in who knows how long, I want to laugh.

The hysterical type of laughter. This is real, but it feels like a bad comedy. He likes them curvy, yet he bought himself a high-fashion model with an eating disorder. The joke is on him, I guess.

"I probably should have bought the female with the big tits," he says as if he could hear my thoughts.

Yes, Jade would have been very suitable indeed.

"Too pale for my liking," he explains to himself with an almost human-like eye roll; only his bright red eyes are not exactly common where I come from. "All the pale females looked sick. You will do. I will feed you when we get to my Palace."

With that, he turns his back and disappears through the airlock, down the most ostentatious thing I have ever seen. One of his men, demons, whatever they are, drags me along behind him, like a lifeless, naked, useless doll. The ship we are in screams: *look at me, I am rich and good taste is overrated*. It's enough to give anyone a headache. It's got everything from heavy fabrics, massive pieces of furniture, beds... I was just going to ask myself who has beds in the middle of a spaceship, but then I notice there is a woman in every bed. I think they are women. One of the four creatures splayed on top of the beds is definitely the same race as the men, but the other three... Just when I try to make sense of what they are, I notice the restraints. So, I stop looking. The sudden distress flooding my mind stops me from noticing he has just attached something to my neck. Cold hard metal. A collar. It is not tight, probably the opposite, and I should worry more about the chafing. Instead, my mouth goes dry, my naked body stiffens, and sweat covers my skin, despite how cold I feel. My blood turns into thousands of shards, stabbing me from the inside. He doesn't seem to even notice and just stares at whatever he put around my neck with a satisfied look. It gives him an instant erection. A huge rod starts swelling down his leg, pushing at his leather trousers. He rubs it with a content smile while still looking at my throat rather than at me. Is this a nightmare? God, please let it be a nightmare!

"Beautiful," he says, running a really hot finger across my nipples. "Your fear and fragility make the slave collar look better on you than on any other female. You are worthy of the cage, my *Special One*," he says, and his men take me to a heavily ornated... pen?

It is made of a gleaming, almost blinding white metal, and large red stones decorate the metalwork. It is shaped like a dome, and it is tall enough for me to stand. Other species will probably find this to be very tight confinement, but for a Human it is quite roomy. There are soft furs on the bottom of the cage, and one of the demon aliens puts in a water bowl for me. It is made of the same shiny metal and decorated with hundreds of tiny stones. It looks like a Swarovski crystal pet bowl. I don't say anything. I find that even my mind is blank. I failed at dying just like I failed at living. Maybe I just need to accept this is what women like me get. A shiny pet bowl and a cage. I try to keep my mind empty. *Don't process the reality, Gianna. Just don't!* It works... for a while.

My blank mind allows itself to be filled with images of golden eyes and how they looked at me. No! I will instead let my brain deal with reality. I am a slave in a cage, with a collar around my neck. I am naked, about to be fattened up, then raped by a demon or by several. It is not lost on me that ever since he put that thing around my neck and shoved me in here, all the other aliens get matching erections when they look my way. Yet, reality hurts less than the memory of *his* eyes. The red demon alien keeps talking to me while rubbing the length of his erection. So do some of his guards, and it only makes him laugh. I ignore them. I know I won't last long. These creatures are too strong and brutal. I keep staring at a heavily ornated golden vase with a blue tree growing out of it. Ignoring the world... forgetting myself. *Why am I still alive?*

There is sudden shake in the floor under my cage and an unpleasant pressure builds in my ears. A migraine is building up and my eyelids feel like a curtain of needles over my eyes. Soon enough the pressure stops just as sudden as it started. We arrived on a planet, I think. Hard to tell because from the ship, we walk straight into the most blinding place I have ever been in. Every single surface is decorated with gems. Including the very high ceilings. The light bounces off the precious stones and hurts my eyes. It doesn't help with my headache either. Being naked in such a highly lit place only makes me more aware.

I am still inside my cage, carried by two aliens along the corridors. I feel hundreds of red eyes glued to my naked body as we walk along. They all bow to the demon who put me in the cage and call him King. Aren't I lucky? I am the pet of a King. Probably that's the most value I was ever going to have. Halfway through, he puts a hand through the broad bars of the cage and pets my curly hair. I don't recoil, just like I refuse to cover my naked body with the furs available inside the pen. It makes him smile in approval. Gleaming white fangs. Charming!

We part ways, and I am carried through a labyrinth of rooms and corridors. It goes on forever and I try to pay as little attention as possible. It's best not to look. The extravagant interiors overload my sensory perception. My head is pounding, and my forehead feels as if something is about to grow on it. And then, there are the demons. They all wear rich, heavy fabrics with intricate patterns. Strangely enough, the King is dressed in simple clothes same as his guards. Most of them carry around pets attached to beautifully decorated chains. It is undeniable, all pets are of the sentient variety. Some look like they have been hurt, repeatedly. No, not some. Most of them. Some are males, I think, but most of them are females. Yes, the rule applies everywhere in the world. My father would be very proud to know I finally believe him.

I am taken to a massive pool, cage and all. The demon guards lower it into the water, which is red, of course. I sigh in relief when I realise it is only water and not blood. The color is given by hundreds of red precious stones engraved into the side walls of the pool. Alien women of different species, also wearing collars, wash me through the pen. I don't cover, nor do I protect myself from their intrusive hands. I am scrubbed while being caged, but I just stand there and take it, like a lifeless statue. The men remove the dripping cage from the water and place it back on the rods they used to carry it around. More hands dry me through the bars and replace the wet furs with dry ones. They dress me in something as useless as bare skin. The red skirt made of narrow strips of ribbon is really tight on my waist, then flaring down my legs in a sea of stringy fabric, obviously not meant to cover much. No panties, so each time I move, my bare bottom peeks through the slits. The top is just a bra, only it's not made of fabric. Little chains cup my breasts, and my nipples poke out, most likely part of the plan.

One of the slaves who looks to be the same species as the King takes me out of the cage, and for the first time, I realize it was never locked. Somehow that adds to my humiliation. She pulls me to an area at the back of the room with holes in the floor. She can't possibly want me to… I am so dehydrated I don't even feel like going. Her sharp claws dig into my arm and then twist.

"Do it, slave," she says to me while watching the guards. "You will be in the cage by the King's feet for the rest of the span. If you soil the furs, you will be punished severely. I don't think your species, whatever that is, can take it."

Her words alone are enough to make me feel like peeing myself, so I just do what she advised. Back in my cage, I am paraded around the place once again, then placed by the King's feet. I try to keep my eyes down. There is too much noise and too much light. After being on my own for so many days, this is overwhelming. The room I am in is too vast to even see its ends and the echo enhances the nightmarish feeling. There are hundreds of beings in here. I can see them in the corner of my eye. The noise is deafening. And I am sure there is some sexual activity going on around me, judging by the grunts and moans. My cage is placed by a massive throne made entirely of precious stones. I hope it hurts his ass. We are on some sort of dais overlooking all the audience. The demon king is splayed on his throne like a... well, like a king, while gulping down some deadly looking liquid from a clear goblet. He asks for something, and soon several hands reach through the bars of my cage, placing so many food platters around me that I barely have any space left to sit.

"Finish it all, my *Special One*," he says, petting my golden curly hair. "You need fattening up; my cock is too big for you. I paid a lot of money for you. You have to last me a while."

My brain wants to laugh and scream at the same time. What do I tell him first? Humans eat this amount of food in a month or should I tell him my vagina won't grow bigger, no matter how fat I get. I choose to say neither. I don't really want to eat, it can only delay the death I am so rooting for. I know it is not an option. I will be punished if I refuse. That's going to happen either way once he notices I can't eat all that food. I grab a piece of fruit, or at least I hope that's what it is. I pause at the unexpected taste. Despite my predicament, its taste is like instant happiness. I don't even know what to compare it with, but it does crazy stuff to my taste buds. Maybe I can fatten up after all. Even our fruit is primitive compared to the alien ones.

He pets my hair again.

"You are a very obedient slave. It pleases me greatly. It worries my warriors and guards," he says with a rumbling laugh. "They think I might not want to share you. They are right, my *Special One*. I won't."

"Thank you, my King," I say, surprising the both of us. Survival instinct took over against my will. I know this man is nothing like the rich little boys I had wrapped around my fingers on Earth.

The men I chose to surround myself with were usually in awe of my celebrity status and would have done whatever I said when I said it. Most of them were too drunk or too high to even have sex with me. They either didn't remember, or they were too embarrassed to admit they couldn't get it up. I would always spread rumors about their 'amazing' bedroom skills, petting their little egos and creating the wild reputation that kept me safe. They were happy with that, so never questioned the truth. In reality, there were very few men I had sex with. Not only am I not a sexual person, but I would scratch my skin raw in the shower for days after, having to cancel work and hide my injuries from the world. Regardless of the inconveniences, it gave me the power and control; I couldn't have any other way.

This man is nothing like the type I could easily manipulate. The situation I am in is not one I can control. I know that, but accepting this fate I've done nothing to deserve is too much. Maybe if I fake compliance it would hurt less? It did before. Yes, I can pretend that I love being a king's caged slave. I can pretend I like being hurt. I can convince myself this is a willing game. I look up at him commanding my stiff face to smile. Men on Earth go mad for my smile. The King, however, is not paying attention. He is all stiff, and anger rolls off him like a wave.

"You bring a lot of trouble, my *Special One*, not to mention you cost me a fortune. You better be worth it," he says, while some pompous court attendant announces the visitor.

7

—

ZAAN

The harsh Warrior training I had since I was a child is the only thing that can save my life and hers now. I walk into the Moorri King's court wearing nothing but my Kannicloth and boots. I had to leave all my weapons on my ship. Not that they would have made much of a difference. Despite being a race of traders and merchants, the Moorri are naturally strong and skilled in battle. This is not a fight I could win on my own, so hopefully, I won't have to fight them for her. Once she is safe, I will make him pay for this. My female is the first thing I see when I walk in. I look at her for less than a nanoclip because I have to play my game right. If he sees what she means to me, he will only want her more. Everything is a challenge to the Moorri.

My newly awakened heart rages inside me at the sight of my mate. He put a slave collar on her. Her barely covered body, the bruises on her arms, the cage, him touching her hair... it all pushes the War Beast out for blood. The Great Warrior taught me how to control it when we were both nothing more than cubs. I use all my knowledge, self-discipline, and strength to pretend this is nothing more than a trade.

What I didn't expect or understand, are her reactions towards me. And it hurts! When we first met, she looked at me with hateful eyes, then she stopped looking at me altogether. Later, she ran from me, and there is no bigger offense for a Tarrassian male. She put her precious life in danger just to get away from me. And now, it feels like she put a sword through both my hearts. She was vexing smiling at him when I walked in. As her eyes took me in, the smile changed to anger. Her body is exposed in her pleasure slave outfit but she doesn't seem to mind the hundreds of eyes on her. One look at me, and the first thing she did was to cover herself with a fur. Maybe I deserve this. She was in my care, and now she is in a cage because I didn't keep her safe. I failed her. I will spend my entire life span making up to her.

"What an honor," says the King's mocking tone. "A mighty Tarrassian amongst us, the poor mortals. And not just any Tarrassian. The High Commander of the Blood Fleet and the son of an Elder. To what do we owe the pleasure?" he says, and his Court starts laughing in unison.

"You have something that belongs to Tarrassia, Moorri King," I tell him as calmly as I can.

"I do? Where?" says the fool pretending to look around. "Has anyone seen anything Tarrassian?" he asks his Court, and they all laugh like vexing idiots.

I will not respond. I have a plan, and I will not let my emotions get in the way.

"This female belongs to Tarrassia," I say, pointing at her. My words make her flinch. She has her back turned at me, preferring to look at him instead. Can she even understand what it does to me? Why would she hurt me like this?

"Oh, do you mean the slave I legally bought from the Noorranni traders?" he asks me with a smirk on that stupid red face. I wonder what color his blood is. I will find out soon enough.

"This female was taken against her will from a Red Orbit Planet. It is against the Coalition of the Seven Stars laws and the laws of the Eight Quadrant to interact with a forbidden planet."

"Good thing I didn't do such a thing then," he says, mimicking an innocent look.

"I am happy you weren't aware, Moorri King," I say playing along. "I am here to take her back, and this misunderstanding can be put behind us."

"Hmm, a few problems with that plan of action, High Commander," he says and reaches inside the cage to caress her shoulder. She doesn't flinch at his touch.

The image of his hand on my female burns my brain, and I feel the familiar twitch of my War Beast begging to release itself.

"Firstly, let it be said, it is not my problem where the traders get the slaves from. I only pay the fees requested. We are not a race of Warriors, so it is not our job to restore the order in the Universe," he says with a very mocking tone. "I believe there is a fleet with access to all the funds of the Coalition of the Seven Stars, paid to do just that. What are they called? Oh, yes, the Blood Fleet," he says, and the Court erupts in laughter.

"I am happy you understand why I am here, King Moorri," I say, pretending to miss all the mockery. "As the High Commander of the very fleet you mentioned, I am here to restore the justice and free an illegal slave."

"This brings me to my second point," he says with an evil grin, while his hungry eyes roam over my female. "Since the Humans cannot be returned to their planet, they get to stay on yours. How very convenient, High Commander, don't you think? Rumors travel fast around the galaxies. Apparently, your King and the male your people call the Great Warrior have already taken two of these females as theirs," he says, and my Lorra flinches again. His fingers touch her hair as if to reassure her, and she leans into his touch. I knew my training and self-discipline would keep my anger in control. But I didn't expect she would be the one poking at my War Beast. She will pay for this!

"Tell me, High Commander, why is it okay for Tarrassians to mate illegal slaves, but not for me? At least I paid enough credits to buy a galaxy for her. What did you do? You ran your sword through a couple of merchants and took her away by force. Unlike your people, I don't disguise my darkness behind heroic acts. I own my darkness. Do you?"

His words cut deeper than a blade. Luckily, our Great Astrals have stopped us from shaming ourselves. Without the Sign's reappearance, it might have looked like we were using these females as cub vessels.

"My King and the Great Warrior took the Humans as precious mates for life, not pleasure slaves. They offered them their homes, not a cage to live in," I tell him, and I can see a muscle jump in his jaw. My words cut him just as deep. Sadly, my victory is short-lived.

"You know what, High Commander, you are absolutely right," he says with a smirk. "Perhaps it is time for me to take a Queen. Rumour goes the Humans brought back your long-gone mating Sign. Maybe they are special. Worthy of a King, if I am to believe that wild ruler of yours."

I won't let this throw me back. There were no real chances he would hand her over. I wish she would just look my way. At this point, it doesn't matter if he can see my true feelings for her.

"This female cannot be your Queen because she belongs to me," I tell him.

Diplomacy is over. There's a low hum going through the crowd, but what bothers me the most is her reaction. My words make her move closer to him. Why is she doing this to me? Does she think he is a better protector? *Well, she doesn't have a choice,* my anger reminds me. She is my mate. She awakened my heart without even touching me. That is how strong our connection is. My reckless female will do what she is vexing told.

"And they say the Moorri are greedy," says the fool with a rumbling laugh.

"She is my bonded mate, and that is a connection your species will respect," I tell him, trying to control my burning emotions.

"Well, yes, of course. I would if only I could see it," he says with another mocking laugh. His Court is quick to follow.

He reaches again for her and strokes her face, making my War Beast push at my growing muscles. This time, I do not stop it. I need it. I can hear the noise going through the crowd. The Moorri King watches the changes in my body with a bored expression and a yawn.

"Is this a threat, High Commander, or just a useless display of Tarrassian arrogance?"

"Neither, Moorri King. It is my species' natural reaction when one's mate is being touched by another."

"I see," he says and looks at her with an amused expression. "My *Special One*, tell me, is this Tarrassian your mate?"

"Most definitely not, my King. I have no idea who this male is. He is delusional," she says, and the room roars with laughter.

She made a fool out of me. He strokes her hair with an almost affectionate gesture, but I know it is all to hurt me, only he can't. He doesn't have that kind of power. My female, on the other hand, all she does is hurt me.

"It looks like you are trying to deceive me, High Commander, just so I would give you the Human."

"Allow me to prove it, Moorri King," I say, taking a deep breath and a massive leap of faith. I know she is mine, and I don't need any mating marks to prove that. I do need them to convince him, though. Despite my sire's warning, I will give her my bite. I am not taking any chances in case the marks don't develop. The thought of putting my fangs into her skin seems quite pleasant right now. I can cause pain, too.

"Let me touch her, and if the mating bond doesn't show itself, you can kill me," I say because I know the Moorri like to trade. To my surprise, he just laughs.

"And cause a war with Tarrassia? Nice try, High Commander. I have already been informed twelve Blood Fleet ships wait outside the atmosphere of my planet."

Vexing Nodric! He sure chooses his moments.

"I have a different deal for you, High Commander. I will allow you to touch the female. If you can convince us she is indeed your mate, you are, of course, free to take her and leave unharmed. If you fail to prove it, you will leave unharmed but alone. However, before you go, you will watch me put my cock in her, and make her scream my name. Do we have a deal?"

The need for my sword makes my palm itch. But just when I think nothing could anger me more, I hear her little voice.

"Please don't let him touch me. I will be the most obedient slave you ever had," she says and reaches out through the bars to touch his leg. He watches her with a deeply shocked expression and puts his large hand over hers.

When I think she can hurt me no more, she finds ways to push the dagger deeper and twist until I bleed on the inside.

"Such a strange creature," he says, almost like talking to himself. "Worth every credit. Don't you worry my *Special One*. The Tarrassian is talking nonsense. I will let him touch you, just because he wasted my time enough and I crave some entertainment. I want to see the look on his face when I make you mine."

He pushes her hand away and orders his guards to bring her out of her cage.

"Remove her slave collar," I tell him, and he nods silently towards his guards.

They forcefully drag her out, pull the fur away from her and remove the precious metal band around her neck. As they push her down the stairs of the King's dais, she almost trips over the long strips of her skirt. I force myself to remain still and not reach for her. She stops at the bottom of the stairs, only a nanolength away from me, looking down, her small hands fisted by her side.

"Come to me," I say, reaching out my hand to her.

After chasing her around for so many spans, I need her to choose me. Only, she doesn't. She doesn't even look at me. My anger clouds my mind, and I go for her. *More forcefully than I should have.* I grab her by her wrists and pull her hard against my chest. Then I lift her up by her waist and sink my fangs into her neck. *More forcefully than I should have.* Her sweet blood floods my mouth. *More blood than I should have spilled.* Her beautiful light green eyes go big with pain, betrayal, and fear all at once. As my marks burn her skin, causing even more damage and the Sign of my House carves itself in the middle of her forehead, she goes limp in my arms, losing consciousness. I thank the Astrals. I am no stranger to injuries and wounds. But the pain of the marks is excruciating, as they burn through flesh. What must it be like to her fragile skin? I cradle her to my chest and grab a cloak off the shoulders of the nearest pompous fool to cover her from their eyes.

"My King has taken her planet to protect it," I tell the Moorri King. "Don't expect a replacement from the Noorranni any time soon."

"I have my ways, High Commander," I hear him laugh behind me, but I just ignore him. Let him go after another Human, see what happens. Right now, I only care about taking my female to the safety of my ship and make the bleeding stop. The flesh is wide open where her shoulder meets her long neck, and a constant stream of red blood trickles down my chest. I am such a vexing fool. I control my anger against my enemies but not against my fragile female.

8

GIANNA

The pain wakes me from a nightmare where I was desperately trying to remove some barbed wire stuck in my neck. Only the burning sting doesn't go away when I open my eyes and reality pours into my brain like venom.

He bit me! And I am here alone with him, wherever here is. He is watching me with that disturbing intensity that makes my skin ping with awareness. I quickly take the environment in without removing my eyes from him for more than a second.

This is one of their ships. Not as big as the one I first escaped from, but definitely not a pod. I am lying on something soft enough to be a bed. It's all open space, and I can see a large control room at the far end of the ship, the large glass panel of the cleaning room, and a storage area. Weapons. There are a lot of different types of weapons there. Not that I can reach any. I am too hurt. He didn't just bite me. He burned my skin with something. I don't dare take my eyes off him to get a proper look at the damage he caused. He watches me from a chair at the foot of the bed. Despite the excruciating pain, I pull myself to a seated position and rest my back against the metal frame. I don't want to face him lying down. The movement makes my neck spasm painfully and a warm trickle of liquid goes down my chest.

"You shouldn't be straining your wound like this, my Lorra," he says, and it looks as if he is trying to stop himself from moving closer.

Would he bite me again? He looks strange. Stranger than before, that is. There is a pulsing red mark in the middle of his forehead. It appears to be a little glowing maple leaf. There are bright red and white tattoos on his thick arms and shoulders. They look like vines wrapping around his coppery skin. I don't need to look to know I have them too. My arms are covered by the oversized white shirt I am wearing, but the bright red swirls glow through the soft fabric. The back of my palms shows the same strange pattern I can see on his arms. I feel sick. What sort of twisted magic is this? Are they alien tattoos? I look down at myself. He removed my other outfit, which means I am naked under the huge shirt. The movement causes my neck wound to bleed some more. There is some sort of a bandage there, and I can feel it getting soaked.

"For the name of the Astrals, stop moving, Lorra!" he says with the booming voice I kept hearing in my dreams all those nights and days in the pod. *In my nightmares, not my dreams.*

There is a fur covering resting in my lap, and I grab it up to my chin, like a shield, as he gets up. I try not to cower, but how can I avoid it? He is so big and there is something disturbingly intense about him. His slow movements and unblinking stare remind me of a feline predator preparing to pounce. He stops by the metal bedside shelf and removes a massive dagger from the belt of his kilt. I watch him in dismay as he uses it to cut a deep gash on his forearm. He squeezes the fresh wound above a glass, and it soon fills with a thick, coppery-color liquid. There are hundreds of shiny particles in it. Blood. And he wants me to drink it. I don't know how I know that, but I do. What kind of twisted nightmare is this? He is crazy! I plaster myself to the headboard in a futile attempt to get away.

"I put healing gel on your burn marks, Lorra, but your neck wound needs more than that. Tarrassian blood can heal and avoid infection. Please drink it. I know it may not be pleasant, but you must take it."

"No," I say with a croaky, weak voice that doesn't even sound like me. I stop myself from asking for mercy. Not sure why that came into my mind, anyway. I have begged before, but it never works with men like him. It only makes it worse.

He takes a deep breath, and I can see red dots peppering the gold of his eyes. I am too stunned to react when he pulls me down the bed by my ankles and climbs over me. He kneels on the bed above me, trapping my chest in between thick thighs, which press painfully into my sides. Panic stops me from breathing as I realize he is now using his knees to pin my arms into the mattress. One massive hand comes above my face, and suddenly, there is no air at all going into my lungs as a grip of steel pinches my nose. I open my mouth on instinct, and a thick sweet fluid fills it. The gagging reflex makes me swallow it before I can even fight it. The panic turns everything dark for a brief moment, but then I involuntary swallow just to get some air in. I choke and try to free my hands and kick my legs. His hold of me doesn't allow any movement. I keep swallowing the thick liquid, and eventually, he gets off me.

I pull myself up again, looking down at my body. My blood and saliva, mixed with his copper blood, make my shirt look like a crime scene. His huge frame is facing away and his tense muscles scream their frustration. He runs oversized hands covered in red tattoos through his long black hair, pulling at it with anger. If this happened on Earth, my mind would immediately assume I was the prisoner of a serial killer. He is obviously psychotic. Probably even for an alien. I've been a prey to very evil men before. But nothing compares to this. Panic floods me again, and I start scratching at the red swirls on my arms through my shirt. His shirt. There is something on my forehead too, and I try removing it. *Oh God, is there something growing on my face?* I can't breathe. My chest hurts, my muscles are spasming, I can't swallow, I choke and… *I must remove the marks, I must remove the marks!!*

"Stop it! Lorra, stop it! Why are you doing this to me? Haven't you hurt me enough?"

The booming voice is once again above me. Thick, heavy arms grab me and plaster me to his chest. I push, I scratch, I kick. More blood comes out of my neck wound, soaking both of us. I can't breathe. I wanted to die, didn't I? Why am I fighting it? Why am I allowing myself to gasp for air? He lifts me up and takes my space on the bed, placing me in his arms. Legs as strong as steel tangle with mine, stopping me from kicking. I can't move any part of my body. My face is plastered to his chest, slippery with my blood, and his arms pin mine around my torso, in a grip that makes me think my ribs will soon crack. My weak brain decides it cannot fight someone this big and strong, so it orders my body to go limp.

Strangely enough, as soon as I do that, my lungs fill with air, and the pain in my chest goes away. The grip around my body is not painful; it's… safe. I am completely drained, and my eyelids weigh a ton. I cannot make them stay open.

I used to feel safe like this when I was a little girl, hugging my soft white bunny to sleep. Dad won it for me at a traveling carnival. As expected, he didn't miss a single target that day and won too many toys to carry around. The big white bunny was by far my favorite. I had forgotten how good it felt, that moment when you are halfway between sleep and being awake. In my pink bedroom with fluffy blue clouds painted on the ceiling, surrounded by all the toys Dad kept buying for me. Safe. So, I just let sleep take me.

9

GIANNA

Sadly, I wake from my safe space with a start because my face is so painful. Even opening my eyes hurts, and a few eyelashes pull as I do. Not painful, just uncomfortable. My face is so dry, it feels like I have a beauty mask on. The type you have to peel off when it dries out. The reality comes crashing down on me, as I realize it's my own dried blood. *Not safe. Not a little girl any more.* And the golden eyes I can't escape are still there watching me. He watches me from the same chair as before, large hands resting on the armrests.

I pull myself into a seated position. I am still wearing his shirt, stiff with dry blood. This feels like déjà vu. Does it mean he will make me drink more of his blood? Is that some kind of sick ritual? I suddenly remember the bite, and I touch my neck. No bandage, but I can't feel anything else either. There is too much dried blood all over me. The pain is still there, but it's rather dull, and it feels superficial, like a skin graze. The tattoos, or whatever these things are, don't hurt any more either. How long did I sleep? He watches me with fatigued yet intense eyes. Did he get more marks? His chest is a sea of red, but I soon realize that it is only my blood. It's all dried up in the hair covering his skin. Silly Natalia calls it fur. Maybe she was right all along. Maybe they are monsters. I don't really know her, but my heart fears for her. His King and another Tarrassian took two of the women. It is not hard to imagine, Natalia was the easiest prey out of all. And me, of course, I am always the first to attract predators.

The biggest and the most dangerous one is watching me with that disturbing intensity of his. It makes my skin prickle and it triggers all my flight instincts. By now, I have met quite a few aliens from various species. None of them gave this psychotic vibe. I suddenly remember what happened to Yara, back on Earth. *Stalker!*

He is the alien version of an obsessive, disturbing, and very intense stalker.

"You will not endanger yourself again! That is the first rule," he says with a calm voice. It doesn't fool me. I am quite familiar with that sort of calmness. It's the voice about to give orders that must be obeyed, or else. "You will listen and follow instructions. That is the second rule," he says, proving me right. "You will never run away from me again. That is the third rule. There will be others as we go along. You seem in desperate need of rules. I am trying to keep this simple, so now just remember this: Disobey any of the first three rules, and there will be consequences. You won't like them."

He is crazy! I want to be brave enough and tell him to go fuck himself. Jade would. I find I can't. He scares the shit out of me. I was forced before to follow the ruling of others, just because they were bigger, stronger, and in charge of my life. Even through the worst of it, survival instinct pushes you forward. The pain must end and eventually you will be able to get away. They will get bored and want a new toy, or they will kill you and end your torment. He doesn't function like that. He wants forever! His intense, obsessive stare tells me he will not let go. Ever!

"Good," he says, taking my silence for approval. "Now I need you to listen and please, Lorra, try and remember that is one of the rules," he adds with a sigh.

What an asshole! He doesn't even know my name. Is it like one fit for all? Is that what he called the women before me? Suddenly, my brain fills with thoughts of his hands touching others, and I just want to scream. Kill something. *What the hell?*

He runs clawless fingers over the red marks on his arms, and the tattoos' glowing intensifies. Are their claws retractable then?

"These are mating marks," he says, and there is emotion in his voice. The gold of his eyes shimmer in an almost hypnotic way. My vision blurs with wetness and I try to blink it away.

"This is also a mating mark," he says, touching his forehead. The maple-like leaf starts pulsing, and so does the one on my forehead. Just like his, mine must be lit up as it throws red and white patterns over my body. It feels heavy and throbby on my forehead. I start breathing faster. What did he do to me? Is it another bug, like the one they put in my ear?

"My Lorra," he says with a subtle but firm warning, "please remember the second rule. You must listen!"

I don't care about the stupid rules. But I have to know what is happening. I know nothing, and it makes me feel more vulnerable than ever.

"Good," he says like he's proud of me. He needs a face slap; remove all that smug. I wish I could be brave enough to do it.

"Only Tarrassians are blessed with this mating mark. It is the Sign of the Astrals – our Gods," he continues while staring at me in the same overwhelming way. It makes me want to run and hide.

"My people lost it for many hundreds of orbit rotations. No one really knows why. According to the High Healer, the lack of it, or years of inbreeding made my species infertile. There haven't been any cubs born in eleven rotations. The research of the High Healer has shown your species is compatible with ours. Human females can carry cubs for us. What is more, you brought back our Sign," he says, touching it again with reverence.

"The King and the Great Warrior have also been blessed with it. Obviously, not just a lucky coincidence, but a fact. Mating marks or not, Tarrassians only take one mate for life. In our case, it also means our union was blessed by the Great Ancestors, and we will be able to have many cubs. The Sign enhances fertility. It also shows, without a question or a doubt, that you are mine," he says pointing a finger at his chest.

Is this guy for real?

"What you see on my forehead is an exact replica of what you have on yours. The leaf of the Marni Tree is the symbol of my family. You belong to the Marni House. Your title is High Lady of the Red Forest of Tarrassia, and that is how all beings will refer to you from now on. It is a title that comes with great respect and recognition on Tarrassia and around the galaxies. I hope this helps with obeying rule number three. There is no more running. The mark on your forehead will tell everyone you belong to me. If you have any questions, I will be happy to answer since you listened like a really good female, and I am very pleased with our progress."

He waits for me to ask my questions. *Like a good female,* nevertheless. I feel like crying and laughing at the same time. It has become my thing lately. He more or less laid out my future for me, like I have no say in it. As if I am nothing and he is entitled to decide what's best for me.

Do I have any questions? I have just been told he branded me bang in the middle of my forehead, for anyone to see who I belong to. I have just been told I am quite fertile, and I have to pop out oversized, hairy, coppery babies for the rest of my life. I have been told I am a high-society lady, just like my father always wanted me to be.

Finally, I have been told if I run, I will always be returned to the sender. Owner, in this case. Why would I have any questions?

Nope, I don't have any. Of course, that seems to please him even more. Didn't he tell us on his ship he doesn't explain things to females? This must be the longest he has ever talked to one.

"Good," he says, getting up to his towering height. "You will have plenty of time to ask later. We are returning to Tarrassia, but I haven't initiated the *Jump*. We need to spend some time alone and get to know each other before my family and everyone else wants me to share you with them. Not willing to do that just yet, so we are taking the long way home. We will be there in nine spans at full speed. Now we both need to get clean. Your wound has knitted itself, but the sight of your precious blood makes me sick. Not to mention it brings back the memory of you breaking rule one, two, and three, in one go," he says with a glint of anger in those eyes that never, ever leave mine.

"Come to me!" he says, lifting a large hand, palm up.

At first, I don't really understand what he means. My bed is probably five steps away from where he stands. He could easily reach for me. I guess it doesn't take a genius to know what he's doing. He is establishing the hierarchy of power. He says jump, and I ask how high. Maybe because I am not *good female* material, or perhaps because I am stupid, I keep sitting there like a lifeless doll, waiting for what's coming. I don't know what an alien's idea of punishment is, but it's not hard to imagine. Aren't they all the same? I just wish I didn't feel this choking fear as I watch him lower his hand. He doesn't seem angry, though. Is that hurt in his eyes?

"You don't need to be afraid for not coming to me. That is not one of the rules and it will never be. Time to get you clean and fed now," he says, picking me up from the bed like I am a rag doll, before I can even process his strange words. Nothing he says makes sense, so why bother.

He puts me down on my shaky feet, in front of the steam shower thingy. I stagger, and he keeps me steady for a few seconds before releasing the glass panel, separating the shower enclosure from the rest of the ship. He removes his hands from my upper arms and steps behind me. The wet room is much larger than the one on the pod and somehow different. The high ceiling and the two side walls are covered in thousands of tiny little orifices. The back wall of the enclosure doesn't seem to have any. Three dispensers of soap, I hope, are lined up in the corner. There was no soap on the pod, not that the steam left me feeling like I needed any. He presses something, and I involuntarily gasp and step back, hitting a hard wall of muscles and hot skin.

Oh, my god! This is an actual shower room with running water and I would give anything to get in there. Only, I can't. If the ridiculous pressure of the steam didn't kill me on the pod, this definitely will. The hot water coming from all those too many to count orifices looks like a curtain of bullets, ready to tear my skin apart. It sounds like it, too. The noise of water hitting metal is deafening and I cringe imagining what it would do to my skin. Maybe I should be grateful. This is my chance at a quick death.

"What is it?" asks a strong voice behind me, making my body vibrate. I realize I am still plastered to his front, and I take a step forward, careful not to get into the death trap. Apparently, even taking a shower can kill a Human around here.

"I will take my turn when you are done. You can have privacy if this is what you are worried about," he says with a slight coldness in his voice. Like the thought alone offends him. "I left a clean shirt and a drying cloth for you there," he says, pointing to a neat pile next to the glass panel.

"It's the pressure," I say with a small voice, not looking behind me. "It might crush me, or at least break my skin. I could be wrong, but..." I can hear him take a deep breath behind me.

"No, you are not wrong," he says, his voice much softer now. "I am a vexing idiot for not thinking about it. I am really pleased with you, my beautiful, for respecting my first rule and keeping yourself safe."

I am screaming on the inside! I want to tell him he can take his rules and fuck himself with them. If only I knew he would just kill me and make it quick. That is why I chose the demon king over him. I would choose anyone but him. He doesn't want quick. He wants forever. Unlike all the other men, he doesn't just want to own my body. This one wants to own my soul and mind. It makes him more dangerous than any other predator out there.

For now, I am alone with him entirely at his mercy, so I keep my anger to myself. This is one fight I cannot allow myself to lose. I lost every other battle in my life. I still had my soul and mind left to carry on. There won't be anything left of me if I let him win. I must appear weak and subdued until I find my opportunity.

I take a deep breath as I notice he removed my shirt in one swift motion and now I am completely naked.

"What are you doing?" I hate the shaky note of my voice. I sound weak and frightened. No different than whiny Natalia. Maybe I can convince myself I am faking weakness on purpose.

"You need to clean yourself, and this is all we have available until we get home. I will protect you from the pressure," he says behind me, and I hear myself scream as one huge arm coils around my waist, lifting me up. My scream is covered by the noise of water hitting the metal, like a rain of tiny bullets. Hot water soaks me, going into my eyes and my open mouth. I wait for the pain of my pierced skin to breach my hazed mind, but it doesn't come. I am pressed between something cold and hard at my front and something hot and hard at my back. I feel trapped, I feel… safe?

Soothing water rains over me, taking all the pain away. I go limp in his arms, and he puts me down, my feet finally touching the floor. There is only a tiny space between me and the safe metal wall I am facing. It is enough to be able to look down at my feet and see the water turn red for the first few minutes. Did I bleed that much? Did he mean to kill me? I don't understand. Nothing makes sense. Why would he protect me now when he almost cut my carotid with his fangs? He uses his big body around me like a protective cage to keep the water from tearing me apart. I can hear the drops hitting his skin with a sharp noise. My back is pressed to his front and his large hands rest against the wall in front of me. His chin is lowered over the top of my head in an attempt to stop the deadly stream pouring from the ceiling. His hair and beard fall over me like a curtain tangling with my own locks, and I use my hands to push it all out of my eyes. My shoulder-length bob reaches my elbows when wet. He removes one hand from the wall, running it through my hair.

"Why is it so much longer now?" he asks, lowering his head closer to my ear, so I can hear him over the noise of the shower.

"It is normal for Afro hair. The springs pull and stretch when they are wet," I tell him, and his other arm coils around my waist to pull me up against him. I feel the tendrils of panic again when my feet can't touch the floor, and I am completely attached to his front. My stupid brain decides this is a good time to notice he is just as naked as I am.

His lips touch my ear, and his breath is much hotter than the water.

"I could barely hear you, my Lorra. Tell me again. What is hair and what is Afro? The words didn't translate," he says, and I am relieved to know I am not the only one struggling with the device. It is quite temperamental and leaves certain words out.

I am trying to find my speech again but the hotness of his breath in my ear makes me feel... I don't know what it makes me feel. What is wrong with me?

"This is what we call hair," I say touching my locks with a hand. "Afro is a type of hair and it mainly means really curly.

When you refer to hair, my device just says head fur. Strange, but I understand what you mean, just like I know facial fur must be what my species calls a beard," I say.

I realise it's even stranger we are having a conversation about hair in the midst of all this madness.

"Your skin and hair look different than the other females." He moves his lips over my ear, playing with my ear lobe, and I am doing my best to ignore it. I am trying to ignore a lot of things right now.

"I am a different race than the others. Half, anyway," I say keeping my head down, so the water won't pull my eyes out of their sockets.

"You are only half Human?" he asks, stopping his ministrations for a second.

I would laugh if I wasn't this aware of his presence and what it does to me.

"Humans come in many different colors, body shapes, facial features, and heights. Different eyes and hair color, too."

"That is confusing and different indeed. It is also beautiful, my Lorra," he says, moving his attention from my ear to my neck. He uses his free hand to push my hair out of the way, nuzzling at my skin and placing a soft kiss over the patch he bit. Tore apart, more likely. His movement exposes me for a second to the powerful jet from above, and he quickly pushes me closer into the wall, but without putting me back down on the floor. I am completely trapped.

"I am sorry, are you hurt?" he asks.

"No, it's fine," I say with a weak voice. It's a squeak, really. I am more worried about his lips on my neck than the pressure of the water. Will he bite me again? For some reason, it scares me more than the way he feels pressed against me. There is a very good chance I might not survive sex with an alien cock the size of my forearm. At least that's what it feels like. And from the way it pulses and jerks against my thighs, it's still growing. Sex could lead to immediate death and that is all I want right now. His bite, though? What if he keeps on tearing my flesh apart and then healing me with his blood? Over and over again. I don't mind death. I just don't want the long agony with it.

"I can smell your fear, my beautiful female, and it saddens me deeply," he says with his lips pressed against my skin. "I know you can feel my body's need for you, but I am not a vexing beast. I cannot control my physical reaction to you, nor the pull of the Sign. The mating instinct demands I take you here and now. What I can control are my actions. I will not give into my instinct until you are ready. I don't want your fear. I want your arousal. Now I am going to wash you and you are going to control your fear. It offends me."

Wait, what? Anyone else would assume the device in my ear translates his strange speech into short, clipped sentences, that don't make sense. I am my father's daughter though, so I know what his clipped phrases mean. He is not asking or explaining. He is telling me! He puts me back down on my feet and cages me again between the wall and his body, which only spikes my fear. I know he said he won't act on it, but the way that huge rod presses against my skin is just too intimidating to ignore. And the thing is, can he ignore it? Men don't care about controlling their needs, do they? I jolt when I feel his fingers in my hair, lathering something that smells like... him. Orange blossom and a very particular one at that. My grandparents had never-ending orchards of Sicilian blood oranges. At least that's what it seemed like to my child mind. The fragrant orange trees would spread as far as I could see. My nonna and nonno died when I was too young to remember them, but I still have the memory of running barefoot through never-ending rows of orange trees, with my arms spread around me, pretending I was a butterfly.

My dad's brother took over the orchards when their parents died and we stopped visiting. I never met my uncle or his family.

My dad wouldn't even say his name for whatever the reason. The sweet smell stayed hidden somewhere in my happy memories until I met him. He had to ruin it for me. His skin and hair have no right to smell like my favorite childhood memory.

The shampoo... soap... not sure what it is, goes down my face, and I close my eyes in case it stings. Having my eyes closed only intensifies the other senses: the smell, the pressure of his fingers massaging my scalp, the way I feel both trapped and protected in between his body and the wall. All my senses are assaulted and it is overwhelming. So is the thought of washing with water that touches his body first, dropping gently over me.

"It is a Tarrassian custom to wash one's mate," he says above my head, but his voice is strong enough to cover the noise of the shower. "I feel privileged to wash your beautiful hair. It has the color of Tarrassian eyes when we look upon our treasured ones. Your hair has the color of love, my beautiful Lorra."

I don't say anything, because... he can't hear me, right? That's an excuse as good as any. I feel unsure, shy, and highly inexperienced right now. Only a month ago, I was a famous supermodel, chased by men, paparazzi and hordes of fans.

"I also feel privileged because Tarrassian women have no hair at all. Another perk of having a Human mate," he says, and I can hear the smile in his voice. *What would his smile look like?* What on earth does he mean? Do they shave it?

"Our females are born without any hair. In a way, the exact opposite of the males," he explains, almost like he can hear my thoughts. He lifts his head off mine slightly, allowing more water to fall over me and rinse my hair. When it's all clean, he applies something else and... *Oh my god, it smells like heaven!* No wonder Tarrassians smell so lovely. Is it conditioner? It feels like I dipped my hair in silk. He rinses my locks again, and I close my eyes, forgetting myself for a minute. I feel warm and safe and looked after, which is horrible, really. My idiot body doesn't seem to mind it and goes all soft, leaning into the wall of muscles behind me. It feels as if I am drowning into the gentle touch of the fingers, running over the mark he left on my neck, over the marks he left on my arms, whatever they are, over my hard nipples... I suddenly open my eyes and take a deep breath, which is never a good idea while having a shower, never mind a deadly one.

"This is also another perk," his voice says somewhere in my hair. "Our females' tits only look this large when they are with cub. And never ever as large as the Human's called Jade," he says while running soft fingers over my sensitive buds.

Oh, I see. And here was I thinking he only had eyes for me back on his ship. His peripheral view must be quite something. Not that men ever miss Jade and her boobs. What an asshole!

I move away from his touch, glueing myself to the wall. It's not like I can go far; it's only meant to prove a point. I gasp involuntarily, and water goes down my open mouth. Within less than a second, my feet are off the floor again, a punishing arm is coiled around my waist, digging into my skinny ribs, and a massive hand grabs my neck in a tight squeeze. I choke, mainly because water went down the wrong pipe, and my hands hold onto the fingers encasing my throat, desperately trying to remove them. He releases some of the pressure but doesn't let go.

"Moving away from my touch classifies as running, and you will not do that to me again," he says with his lips against my ear. "Now dry yourself, get dressed, and sit in the control area without touching anything."

With that, he pushes me out of the enclosure and closes the panel behind him.

10

—

GIANNA

He is crazy! This can't be normal behavior on any planet. Idiot! Feeling vulnerable and naked is enough to make me rush. I don't bother with drying my skin, too desperate to cover my naked body with the shirt. Luckily, it is absolutely massive on me and surrounds me like a protective sheet.

My brain calls me stupid to my face. Not only did he change my clothes while I was asleep, but he just petted me in the shower in all my naked glory; misery, more like it. He's already seen all of me. I dry my hair with the strange towel, which absorbs all the moisture from it within seconds. Not only that, but my hair feels like silk. The curls are tight as usual, but there is none of the frizz I struggled with in the past. I've always used the most expensive products available to keep my natural hair in perfect shape. Apparently, I needed the alien stuff all along.

I find myself sitting on a circular bench surrounding a small metal table. Like a *good female*, no doubt. I train my eyes on the large viewing window in front of the control panel. I would have loved to have that in the pod rather than stare at cold walls. I could spend hours looking into the vast darkness of space, waiting for the next splash of light to appear. I wonder what those flashing lights are. Or those traces of color. It's so mesmerizing.

"I am afraid we only have high protein travel rations on this ship," he says somewhere next to me, and I try not to look. It's not like I have to, on a ship where every surface is reflective. Probably on purpose, as they are so in love with themselves.

I wonder what their women look like without hair and boobs. Probably not that enticing. Maybe that's why their men are so full of shit and help themselves to other species.

I see he finally decided to wear decent clothes and drop the stupid kilt. About time as I had enough of staring at all that exposed skin. He wears the same white shirt and pristine white pants as before when he came to see the four of us on his ship. They match the strange white lock in his hair. His stupid golden eyes are on me even as he goes through the supplies, getting things ready for dinner. He never ever takes his eyes off me, and that unsettles me in a way I haven't quite felt before. He lays some familiar by now pouches on the table, as well as glasses. I brave a quick look at him, and the first thing that hits me is how tired he looks. Without my blood all over his face and beard, it's easier to see. A strange thought comes to my mind.

"How long did I sleep for after I... drank your blood?"

"For almost two spans," he says, eyes pinned to mine. I blink and look away. Does he mean two freaking days? An even more disturbing thought comes to mind.

"What did you do while I slept?"

"I watched you," he says, like that is normal. It is not!

"I don't like it," I say before I can stop myself.

"I don't care. You are mine to watch. It is bad enough, I agreed to no mating until you lose your fear. Oh, and Lorra," he says with a hint of a promise in his voice, "that term has a very short expiring span."

"What? What do you mean?" I find myself asking. Not sure why. It's not like I believed his promise to start with. I know he will take his fill when and if he pleases. Not much I can do to stop him.

"I reached out to my parents and asked them to organize our Sacred Mating Ceremony as soon as we return home. I will sadly have to leave you in their care and return to my duty. My King has declared war on the Coalition of the Dark Moon. I will not part without completing our mating bond."

This is actually great news. Maybe I can escape after he leaves? I can fake willing sex, right? I am not expecting much because I already agreed not to allow that treacherous bitch called hope into my life. No idea how guarded I might be or what house of horrors his parents run over there. It is still better than having him stare at me non-stop, like a psycho. I just have to pretend I am weak, quiet, and compliant, the way men like him like their women. I lower my eyes and stare at my fingers.

"I am sorry to leave you so soon," says the idiot, obviously mistaking my reaction for an upset. Soooo freaking full of himself! "My Warriors can handle any fight all by themselves, but since Earth is so precious to us, I know the King would want me on that task," he says, and I lift my eyes to his. He watches me warily, confirming my suspicion.

Oh my god! Are they invading Earth? Is that what he's saying?

"Our King can be..." he struggles to find a word. I have a few, but I also have a role to play, so I am sticking to it.

They say once a Marine, always a Marine. I took an oath to defend my country and having a conversation over dinner or whatever this is with a member of the invading species is making me scream on the inside. I hope he can't tell my rage, but then the stupid marks on my arms start to pulse a deeper red. His too. Can he feel my emotions in his marks?

"You are upset. It is your home, and you have every right to be," he reaches over the table and takes my hands into his. I am shaking like a leaf, and I force myself to stay still. He waits for a second, giving me a chance to decide. There is no decision. Didn't he warn me about pulling away from his touch? I take a deep breath and relax my hands in his.

"Well done, Lorra. I am so proud to see you are trying," he says, and I almost lose it. What the hell? Does he have to praise me like I am five and just ate all my greens? So annoying!

"Our King is not known for his wise decisions. The Blood Fleet was instructed not to harm any Humans; I hope this makes it easier for you."

Yeah, right. An alien invasion will go down really smooth on Earth. They obviously know shit about Humans.

"What is your King known for?" I ask, trying to take my mind off my anger.

"Mainly for removing heads. And he is our King. You need to remember that," he says, rubbing a finger over my wrists. My heart drops, but his eyes are on me. He is not looking at the scars. The marks are faded, but I can see them as clearly as ever. Only then his words register, and I can see he is not joking. God, the King person sounds deranged.

"Do you know which of the women is his mate?" I ask while praying he doesn't say Natalia.

"I don't know; it didn't occur to me to ask my sire. But you mustn't worry, my Lorra. The King would never hurt a female, no Tarrassian ever would," he says, but I can tell his own lie bothers him. Almost like a memory shadows his eyes. I hope the shame is about himself. He tore my throat open and nearly strangled me just now, in the shower. "Besides, my sire assured me not only are the King and Queen really happy, but they are expecting a cub."

What? How long have I been on that pod?

"How is it possible?"

"The Sign can make that happen. I told you it comes with

enhanced fertility," he says, staring at me like I am dinner. "You will look beautiful heavy with my cub."

I want to scream so badly and so loudly, they hear me in every galaxy. Instead, I lower my eyes like a *good female*.

"Once I make sure everything is under control, and vexing Nodric can keep himself in check, I will come back to you."

"Who is Nodric?" I ask while munching on my favorite purple powder. God, that sounds so wrong!

"My Second in Command. The most experienced and probably skilled Warrior in my Fleet. Sadly, he has a deep disregard for rules."

"Oh, wow, that must go down really well with the master of all rules," I say like an idiot before I can stop myself. To my surprise, he laughs, and that turns my brain off for a few good seconds. Not because he didn't punish me for talking back, but because his laugh is... I mustn't make him laugh again. I don't want to see it! No man is allowed to have that laugh. Idiot!

"Talking back or being snarly is not part of the rules, my Lorra," he says with a smile. He shouldn't be allowed to smile either. It's blinding!

"I wasn't snarly," I say, trying to blink repeatedly and remove his perfect smile from my retina.

"Yes, you were, but I quite liked it. Our females are very delicate, softly spoken creatures. Most hardly ever talk or look up from the floor," he says, and I have to stop myself from commenting. "As if that is not bad enough, they go to Etiquette School for all their cubhood, where they learn how to be even more quiet and invisible," he says with a sigh.

Doesn't he like that? He makes no sense!

"You don't agree?" I say casually.

"No. It could be because of my upbringing. I grew up listening to my sire encouraging my mother to have a voice," he says, shocking the hell out of me. He is full of contradictions.

"Did it work?" I ask, and I quickly regret it because it makes him smile again. I don't want to see that smile. I really don't. It makes me want stupid things. *Please, stop smiling!*

"It worked indeed. My sire once said: If you turn a Tarrassian female on, you can't turn her off again. My mother can even boss my Warriors around. The shock on their faces is priceless. The best thing, she does it all with the sweet smile she was taught at Etiquette School."

There is so much longing and love on his face when he talks about his parents. Isn't it great? Even aliens have better parenting skills than my family.

"Now, my beautiful, if you are done playing with your food, you can have more sleep. We will revisit your poor eating habits when we wake. This will not do for me," he says, pointing the finger at the open purple pouch. I haven't even realized I only took a bite or two and used the rest of the powder to draw shapes in. Damn him! Why is it his business? He stands at the other side of the table.

"I have to instruct my Warriors, check in with my sire and the Council. You may go to sleep now or look around the ship, get to know where things are. Don't touch the weapons! I will join you when I finish," he says and already turns his back to me, opening some device that looks similar enough to an electronic tablet.

Maybe I should scream out loud, after all. He just barks orders and rules at me. What if I don't feel like sleeping or looking around? What if I feel like touching the weapons? Let me guess, I won't like the consequences. Besides, does it really matter what I do? He said he will join me to sleep shortly, which means only one thing, no matter the galaxy. He also said he will not act on it as long as I still fear him. What if something goes wrong with his nose and he decides my fear smells like arousal? I need a better bargaining chip than the way my body fluids smell. Ugh!

Despite how long I slept, I still feel tired. All the torment of the last weeks has caught up with me. Sleeping doesn't feel safe enough. I hate admitting it to myself, but that is not the case with him around. God knows why I feel safe, especially when he does this annoying staring at all times. Didn't he say he needed to call people? Instead, he sits in the main control chair by the ship's operating systems, watching me. I ignore him and go to what they call the cleaning room; the only place his disturbing stare cannot follow. Unlike the pod, where everything was out in the open, the facilities are at the back of the room, sheltered by the non-see-through glass. *Good God!* I whisper as I take it all in. Everything in here is covered by wall-to-wall mirrors, including the ceiling. They really do like to look at themselves.

My own image startles me, as I don't recognize myself. Freaking glowing tattoos! I look like a character from Yara's books. She is... was obsessed with fantasy novels. She was all about fae shapeshifters and mythical creatures. Yara probably would have loved all this. I've always looked like a stranger to myself in the mirror, so at least now I have a reason. My mom was black, my dad was white, yet in the mirror I could only see a brown child with golden hair and strange lime-green eyes. Most likely, that is not a problem for the millions of mixed children out there. It was for me because my parents hated my other heritage. My mom referred to me as black, my dad as white, and I felt like neither. The woman staring back at me from the mirror is even less familiar. I can't deny the beauty of these things glowing on my skin. The red leaf on my forehead makes the strange color of my eyes appear like green fires. I look eerily beautiful, and whatever was in that alien shampoo has made my hair look like a golden fleece. It catches all the light around me. I am a freaking glowing walking stick in an oversized shirt! His shirt. And, of course, it smells like him. I can't get away from him anywhere on this ship! I finally decide to leave the safety of the washroom, only to find him waiting outside the glass panel. Is he for real? Does he want to watch me pee now?

"We will sleep now," he says, and I really wonder if he understands I am an actual person. I can't sleep, walk or sit, whenever he tells me to.

He takes my hand and pulls me towards the bed. I allow it because I don't have a choice. My throat feels dry, and there's not enough air going in. He suddenly turns to watch me. He wasn't joking; he can smell my fear. He seems hurt by it. I flinch as one large hand touches my face.

"I am very tired, my Lorra. I haven't had much sleep since you ran from me, and then I had to watch over you for the last two spans. Emotions overpower sensible decisions when one is this tired. We will rest now, but you will tell me why you are afraid of me when we wake. I only exist to keep you safe. There are no reasons for this fear. You will also explain why you keep hurting my feelings."

"I don't want to sleep with you. I mean, mate or whatever it is you call it," I say before I can think any better.

I hate myself for my lack of self-preservation. I am entirely at his mercy. I can't survive the horror of another man taking me against my will. I've always hated sex more than anything else in the world. Somehow, if I pretended to want it, I could survive it. It allowed me to go to a safe place where my mind was empty. How am I going to fake it now? I've just cornered myself.

"Sleeping and mating are two different things. Which one is it you don't want to do with me, my Lorra?"

His golden eyes watch me with the usual intensity. The hurt in them is undeniable. I never hurt anyone before. I tried to, but it just didn't happen. It took me a long time to understand it was because no one cared enough. But he does. So, I hurt him.

"Neither. I don't want to do anything with you," I say and just stand there, with his golden shimmery eyes on me, waiting for the inevitable punishment. There is a slight shake in the big hand holding mine, and the pain in his eyes is like a drug to me. I can feel his torment in my forehead mark and in the ones on my arms. I don't know why I have the power to hurt this huge, scary alien, but I do. He might rape me, bite me, torture me, or whatever the plan is, but it will hurt him just as much. And that is like music to my ears right now. I will probably regret it by morning, but this is my little moment in time, so I will take it.

"I see," he says and pulls me again towards the bed. His touch is gentle, and his voice is soft. His lack of anger scares me even more. His touch on my wrist feels cold all of a sudden, and I look down. My heart drops. There is a very alien restraint on my left wrist. The cuff looks like a bangle, and it feels cold like metal. However, it seems alive. It changes shape and color and becomes tighter when I move. He also has one on his right wrist, and there is a delicate little chain between my cuff and his. *He chained me to himself!* The realization hits me like a train. I am too stunned to react to him putting me to bed like a doll. He removes my shirt but keeps his clothes on. Lays us both on our sides, facing each other, and pulls a massive fur over us. Part of my brain notices stupid details, like the fact he changed the bloodied bedsheets, and I didn't even see. From this close the stark white lock of hair seems softer than the rest of his hair and my fingers itch to touch it.

He pulls me up until our faces are only inches apart. The fingers of his right hand lace with my left hand and the cuffs flick with a green color.

"I don't like restraints," I tell him defiantly.

"You didn't seem to mind the Moorri King's ones," he says with a calm voice. For whatever reason, it scares me more than anger. "I need to sleep, my Lorra," he adds with a very Human-like sigh. "This is only to make sure you won't do anything to endanger yourself while I rest."

"Is that why I am naked?"

"No, that is because you will always sleep naked while in my bed and in my arms."

"But you're allowed clothes to bed, right?"

"No, that is because I can't trust my cock while I am asleep, and you said no mating. Unless you've changed your mind."

My god, he is so crazy! Probably even by alien standards. I close my eyes because I don't want to look at his stupid golden stare any more. I don't want to look at any part of his perfect face. I turn my back to him, and he allows it. The restraint, not so much. It closes tighter around my wrist, and it's slightly painful. He coils the arm with the matching cuff around my waist and pulls me into him. His lips hover in my hair, close to my ear.

"You mustn't pull at the device with sudden motions. It will tighten itself. It could crush bones if someone was to try to escape the binding. As soon as you relax your hand, the grip will release to a comfortable level again. Now you sleep!"

"Fine," I say, hoping he can't tell I am fighting tears. These stupid aliens are too mighty to know crying anyway. I am supposed to just go to sleep cuffed to him, naked and with a freaking baseball bat pulsing against my backside. Perfectly normal sleeping conditions. What else could go wrong?

You belong to me! You are mine! You must feel that, my beautiful, Lorra.

He says the words inside my mind, as clearly as daylight. There is always room for more things to go wrong!

11

—

GIANNA

I know his eyes are on me, even before I fully wake. A hundred thoughts come to my mind all at once, as if my brain has recovered its functionality and it's eager to show me what it can do. Maybe because I had the best sleep of my life and my brain is fully functioning, or perhaps because I am stupid, considering he can read my mind. I know he said those words inside my brain, somehow. I will soon see, I guess. The last thoughts that came to me as I drifted to sleep are the equivalent of me breaking all his stupid rules. If he doesn't kill me in the next two minutes, it means he can't read my mind, and my brain is playing tricks on me. I would much rather die right now, anyway.

I am entirely plastered to him, and somehow, I know he didn't move me. I am the one who is clinging to him like ivy. My face rests on his chest and his heart, under my cheek, feels like it's about to break his skin and come for me. It honestly sounds like he's got more than one heart. My very naked body is more or less mounting his. My boobs press shamelessly against his naked skin, and my leg is stretched over his body, glued to his junk. So grateful he kept his pants on, even though he must have removed his shirt at some point. I don't dare look at him. His eyes are burning the top of my head, and the stupid Sign on my forehead goes mad when he presses a kiss in my hair.

"I think I like you more when you're asleep, my Lorra," he says, peppering my hair and forehead with kisses. His lips feel firm and hot, and the touch of his beard is like a caress.

I try not to move. I even keep my breathing to a minimum. My body reacts to being touched, being held, and waking up next to a man. None of it happened before, and that scares me more than being forced to do things. What if he can smell it?

"Your body craved mine all night," he says, and once again I wonder if he can read my mind. The arm he holds behind my back wraps around my waist, bringing me closer to him. The huge appendage under my leg grows even bigger and starts pulsing like mad. Surely that can't be a normal cock. And surely, he can't expect that thing to fit anywhere inside me. His right hand starts caressing my side, going all the way down my hip and upper thigh. I suddenly notice, he removed the restraint at some point. The big hand touching my skin moves over my bottom, grabbing all of it in his palm and pulling me above him.

No, no, no, I can't, he said no mating… I invoke all the fear I can imagine. He said he doesn't want my fear, right?

"I can smell your arousal, my beautiful Lorra. I could scent it all night," he whispers with his lips in my hair. "Does that mean we are done playing games? Are you done hating me, my beautiful?"

His hands pull me higher above him until my forehead rests on his. I close my eyes so the light coming from our Signs won't burn them. The touch brings a strange flood of emotions and energy, spreading inside me like wildfire. It is also soothing, making me feel safe, in a way I have never felt before. Like I am inside this bubble where it's just the two of us, and nothing can harm me. What is happening? Why can't I fight it? Why don't I want to fight it?

"Answering my questions is rule number five, Lorra," says the asshole, and it is precisely what I needed to snap out of it. Did he say five? What was the fourth one again? I thought there were only three.

Now that I've been kindly reminded of my rules, my sanity returns. It is quite apparent he can't read my mind. So, it is time I play my cards right. I never had power over anything. Wouldn't it be funny if I had control over the scariest and strongest being I have ever met? Time to find out.

"There is something I want to talk to you about," I say, removing my face from his, so we can have eye contact – big mistake. The gold in his stare is swallowing me whole. He watches me like I am… precious. And this close it is impossible not to feel overwhelmed by his scent, his beautiful face, or the way I feel in his embrace.

"You answer my questions first, Lorra. And this is the last time I will ask nicely," says the asshole, pulling me out of my stupid trance.

"I am not playing games," I tell him, and I hope he can't smell lies. Technically it's not a lie since I am trying to survive here, not have fun. "I am sorry if it felt that way. It will all make sense if you hear me out."

He watches me with those hypnotic eyes, a silent invite in them. "Not here," I say, trying to move away from him, but the cage of his arms won't allow it. "Maybe we can talk over breakfast, and I would like to have some clothes on when we do."

"I agree," he says with a pained sigh in my hair. "If I have you naked in my arms for another nanoclip, I might break my own rules. And I like my rules."

"Yes, I noticed," I say before I can stop myself.

"Snarly," he says with a smile and leaves my side before I can even tell what's happening. That seems to be my state of mind around this man. So annoying!

With him using the wash room and finally away from his prying eyes, I take a moment to brace myself. I can do this. It is my only chance to get away. And that is what I want. I am sure it is. I take a deep breath into the soft foam pillow before pulling myself out of the furs – stupid idea. My lungs fill with his smell, with the heat he left behind. My god, I need to get away from him. I really do! The shirt I put on smells like him; the chair I sit in does, too. I bet I smell like him. He comes with this overpowering intensity which consumes everything around him. I must get away. He doesn't take his eyes off me for more than a second while checking the systems, while reading something on the tablet thingy, he calls a com, while getting breakfast ready. Madness!

"This is a mixture of fruit and sweet dough we usually have for the first meal of the span," he says, offering me a glass with a blue liquid inside. "I noticed you struggle with the texture of the powder. Until we get home and have proper food, you will eat your pouches in liquid form. It is what we give to new-born cubs, to supplement mother's milk." *He wants to give me baby formula?* He takes my hand and wraps it around the glass like I am five years old or something.

"Drink!" He barks the order, and I do because I have bigger battles to win today.

"Well done," he says, leaning in to press a kiss to my forehead. What the hell? He needs a dog, not a wife. I am too angry to even admit, the drink is delicious. It tastes like a blueberry muffin smoothie.

"Talk! I am listening," he says from across the table.

One would think being my father's daughter has made me immune to bossy assholes barking orders. Apparently not.

Maybe, in this case, my weakness can help my case. I am, after all, going to play the damsel in distress who needs a hero. Men like him love that kind of shit.

"I am sorry I ran away," I start, and I really hope he buys it. I am terrible at lying.

"Hmm..." he says with a thoughtful expression. "Why did you, beautiful?"

God, the ways he says that word... I know I am beautiful. People called me that all my life. But when he says it, I almost believe it.

"I got scared," I say, and for once, that is the truth.

"Scared of me?" he asks, and there is hurt in those stunning eyes.

"Scared of everything," I tell him and prepare my next words carefully. "Most of all, scared of what will happen to my little brother in my absence."

There! I said it. His whole vibe changes, and I can see the worry I am faking becoming real in his eyes. I refuse to feel guilty. I really do! He reaches over the table and takes my hands into his, stopping them from fidgeting.

"How old is he?" he asks. Details... Of course, he wants details.

"He is five," I say, looking away from the emotion in his eyes.

"That is very young. Is he with your parents?" he asks, and his fingers run delicate patterns over my wrists. He doesn't seem to have noticed the scars. But why does he always touch me there?

"Our mother died when she gave birth to him, and our father passed last year, after a very long illness," I say, and the emptiness of my voice scares me. They do say one lie turns into many. I can't stand to look at him, but I don't even have to. I can feel his pain in the stupid marks. They actually hurt. My fake pain hurts him for real. A large hand moves to my face, and before I know what I am doing, my cheek leans into his palm. He pulls me from my seat, onto his lap. I cannot look at him. I will not look at him. I close my eyes and hide my face where his shoulder meets his neck, using his beard to hide my shame. Stupid me! Everybody lies to save their skin, right?

"Is he safe?"

"I don't know. I am all he has left. A nanny looks after him when I go to work."

"What is a nanny, my Lorra?" he asks in my hair. I think he likes its texture. His lips always find their way in there.

"Someone I pay to look after him. I don't know if she still has him since I haven't paid her for so long. I think of the worst. Especially now that your people invaded our planet. Maybe she fled somewhere, and he is all alone and scared. Or hungry…"

"Is that why you cannot eat? You feel guilty your cub brother might be starving?" he asks, and I start crying into his skin like a stupid, useless idiot… What am I doing here? This is not who I am. He cradles me to his chest and wipes the tears off my face with gentle kisses. I just want to become invisible.

"You should have told me sooner, my Lorra. You must learn to trust me and just ask me for anything you need. I am here to fight all your battles; you just have to let me."

His words are enough to pull me out of my guilt trip. I don't need a freaking man to fight my battles! I need one who supports me while I fight my own.

"Your little brother will be waiting for us on Tarrassia by the time we get there. I promise you that. I will never have you this worried or pained again. Give me the coordinates of your cub brother's location, and my Second in Command will personally find him."

Shit! I didn't think of that! Of course he could ask his people to do it. *Think, Gianna!*

"No, he is only a little boy," I say with a sniff. "My people must be terrified of yours. We didn't even know aliens existed.

He will run away like I did." He puts a small distance between us to look me in the eyes.

"What are you asking, Lorra?" he says, watching me like he is trying to read inside my mind and soul. If he can actually do that, I am screwed.

"Can we get my little brother together? Since we can now travel to Earth, can you take me there? Please," I say, looking him in the eyes, no matter how hard it is. Can he see the deceit in mine? The man inside him is battling with the High Commander; that much is obvious. I know very well which one will win. Unless… Time to find out what kind of power I have over this man, if any. What difference does one more lie make? I have told him nothing but lies.

"There is something else you need to know," I say and lower my eyes in what I hope looks like shyness. In reality, I can't look at him now. Why do I feel so guilty? He is the enemy, right? "In my culture, a female will only mate for life with the male willing to grant her a wish. So, you see, it's not that I hate you or I don't want to mate with you. It's just the way I was raised. It is the mating ritual of my people," I tell him and hide my face again in his neck. What am I doing? I am so deep into it, I don't even know any more.

"Of course," he says to my surprise. "No wonder the other two females ran from the King and the Great Warrior."

Oh shit! I forgot about the others. He can easily check my story with them. Wait, they did what?

"What do you mean? Are the women safe?" I ask, looking up at him.

"Yes, all the females are safe on Tarrassia now. As you know, the Queen is expecting a cub."

God! I hope it's not that silly little girl. No way a tiny thing like Natalia can birth an alien-sized baby. How did the girls even manage sex with these creatures? He cups my face in between his long fingers and keeps it in place while his eyes seem to search every corner of my soul. I force myself to look at him. Why does he have to be so freaking intense?

"So, if I grant you this wish, I will be worthy of being your mate, by the law of your people?"

God, does he have to put it in that many words? Lies are better when they are vague.

"Yes," I say.

"There will be no more running or hiding, and you will follow all my rules?"

Fuck your rules! What is wrong with him?

"Yes."

"Yes, what?" he asks, and I can hear myself scream inside. What now? Does he want me to say *yes, sir,* after every word?

"My name is Zaan. I want you to say it."

Oh, that... I would actually prefer calling him sir. Less freaking personal!

"Yes, Zaan," I say, trying to sound sweet and stupid.

"Well done, my Lorra," he says, pressing his lips to my forehead and petting my hair.

I swear to God, this man brings the worst out of me. I am so tempted to give up all the scheming and my carefully planned escape just to be able to scratch his face.

"Fine, I will take you to Earth to retrieve your brother," he says, shocking the hell out of me. "Might just as well show face with the Earth authorities, check on my Fleet and all that."

It worked... It just doesn't feel like a victory. I am probably too worried about all the many things that could go wrong. Yes, that must be it. He lifts my chin up to meet his stare.

"Does this mean mating has to wait until I make your wish happen?" he asks with a glint in those beautiful golden eyes.

I know what I am going to answer, but will he accept it? Sitting on his lap is making me very aware of how much his body wants mine. He can easily take what he wants. Why would he stop himself?

"Yes, we can't have sex; I mean mating as you call it. It is important to me, I follow the laws of my people."

"Very well, my Lorra, no mating until your cub brother is safe with us," he says with a deep sigh, pressing his forehead on top of mine.

As before, that gesture does crazy things to me. Is it because our marks touch? It feels strangely like sex, and it should horrify me, considering I hate sex. The arm around my back brings me closer to his chest. His other hand goes down my leg, all the way to my ankle, then back up my calf, my knee, my thigh... I involuntarily move, and that only makes my bottom rub itself on his throbbing erection. He moans with his lips pressed against my forehead. The large hand caressing my thigh holds me in place, stopping me from moving. His lips move down my face, kissing both of my closed eyes, they kiss my nose, they go down my cheek... His beard is so soft, and it smells like orange flowers. *He is going to kiss me.* What do I do? I said no mating, didn't I? Only, he doesn't kiss me and that feels... like disappointment. What is wrong with me? His lips move to my neck and press against the mark left by his bite. I will forever have a scar there. Another one. Is he going to bite me again? Whatever he's doing, it sends stupid signals to the large cock I am practically sitting on. It grows even bigger, hotter, and throbbier. God, I said no sex, right? What is he doing? What am I doing? I feel the strange stickiness between my legs, which is more alien to me than the large alien holding me. I don't ever get wet. I have a feeling that is one of the reasons I hate sex. It really hurts, no matter how tiny the cocks of my former toy boys, as Yara used to call them. Dry sex is painful. How badly would it hurt with someone his size? Does it even hurt if you are this wet? Why am I, though? Is it because of a lack of panties? I hope so.

"Zaan, wha... what are you doing?" I ask with a voice I hardly recognize as my own.

"Sniffing you," he says with his lips leaving a wet trail on my sensitive neck. "Tasting you."

"You agreed to no mating, remember?" I say and squeeze my legs together. God, he won't be able to smell that, right?

"Yes, my Lorra, I did. You didn't say anything about touching or tasting."

"Wwwhat?"

"You need to learn how to bargain, my beautiful."

I don't get to process what he is saying, and not only because my brain doesn't work anymore. He lifts me up in one swift motion, and the next thing I know, I can feel the soft furs of the bed under my back. Panic! Where is it when I need it? What happened to fear? He needs to smell my fear! The strange, unfamiliar pulsing in my core quietens everything else. Is that a build-up to an orgasm? I had a few when I was a young teen and was exploring my own body, before the... the rape. At least, I think that's what they were. Never since, and the thought of one being triggered by a man is... I don't know what it is. His face is above mine, and the curtain of his hair drapes my cheeks. His eyes are glowing, burning mine. There is so much need in them. Like I am all that matters in the world. He supports his weight off me with one hand and uses the other one to unbutton my shirt. Why don't I stop him? He opens it up, revealing all of me to those hungry eyes, but doesn't remove it. Once again, he presses his forehead to mine. Despite the distance he put in between our bodies, his massive erection presses insistently against my thigh. That alone will leave a bruise.

"I smelled nothing but fear and anger on you in my presence," he says with his lips pressed to mine. "Do you know what that did to me, my Lorra? Seeing you smile for others but not for me? Can you understand the pain you caused me? You said no mating, and I will respect your wish. But after so many cursed spans of knowing the scent of your fear, do you think I can stop myself from tasting your arousal? I can't, beautiful. I won't!"

His lips go down my neck again. I tense as his tongue licks my skin and stops to suck where my pulse is. My hips push up to meet his body, and he uses his hand to press them back down into the mattress. I arch again despite the pressure when his hot mouth closes over a very erect nipple. I might not have double anything like Jade and Natalia, but my nipples are in a league of their own, and he seems to love them. He licks them, sucks them, pulling and teasing and... Oh my god, I am so wet, I can smell myself now. Is that normal? I try to squeeze my legs together, but he growls with my nipple in his mouth and presses a knee in between my legs, parting them. I freeze for a second. He wouldn't bite me there, would he? The stupid thought only makes my core throb harder. I push myself against his knee. I can feel my wetness soaking his pants. He growls against my other nipple, and this time I think I would welcome a bite. Anything that can give me some friction or whatever it is I need. My hips are determined to reach for him, no matter how much he tries to stop me. I suddenly realize all my fingers are fisted in his hair, pushing his head down on my sore nipples.

"Zaan, please, I need..."

"What do you need, my beautiful Lorra?" he asks while leaving a trail of hot, wet kisses down my abdomen.

"I don't know," says the whiny, needy voice. It can't be mine, can it?

The hot lips stop over my sex, nuzzling at the soft curls.

"I know what you need, my beautiful mate, and I will always give it to you."

I can't stop my scream, or my hips pushing into him, or the gush of wetness, as I feel his tongue inside me. I never allowed my one-night stands to touch me like that. I couldn't... *Is that me saying his name like a prayer?* I jump as he licks my clit and he stops for a second, almost like trying to make sense of my intense reaction. Then he does it again and again, and I fist his hair even harder when he sucks on it. A large finger breaches inside my tight channel, then another one. Instead of pulling away, my hips push against the welcome intrusion. I want more; I need more.

So tight, my beautiful. So wet for me. Your taste is worth all the pain you put me through. I need you to come on my tongue, my treasured mate. Will you do that for me? Make me forget the pain.

"Yes, Zaan," I say. I don't know what he is asking, but he can have anything he wants. I can't stop it. My body is about to explode or implode; I don't really know. My ears are ringing, my legs are shaking, my eyesight darkens, and I can hear myself, somewhere in the distance, saying his name like a prayer. Over and over again. The fingers inside me touch a spot that makes the world explode in hundreds of tiny shards of light. I feel like falling, and I keep pushing over and over against his touch until none of my muscles listens anymore, and I go completely limp. My brain is empty like I have no will power left. Somewhere in the distance, I can hear my heavy breathing. I feel lifted and moved around like a boneless doll. I wouldn't protest even if I could so instead, I hide my face into the warm chest I am cradled against. Fingers run through my hair, lips kiss every inch of my face, more fingers run up and down my spine. God, what did I just do?

12

GIANNA

I try to keep my eyes closed for as long as possible. I know he's looking at me. Doesn't he always? He pulled me off his chest at some point after holding me for what felt like forever, and now his face is inches away from mine. I can feel his breath on my skin; his golden eyes searching for my soul and every thought I have. This time, I can't blame it on my hyperactive brain. He did talk to me in my mind. I was too overwhelmed by his tongue inside me to even notice at the time. But I know he did. Can he read all my thoughts? He seemed to believe my story. Is he pretending to help only to see if I would come clean by myself? Is he faking everything? The longing, the need, the passion... *He most likely is, stupid woman!* I remind myself. He doesn't even know my name. He didn't even kiss me. He probably thinks it's enough to give me an orgasm to keep me good and pliant. Not that I want him to kiss me. I haven't allowed any of my flings to kiss me. And of all people, I definitely don't want him to do it. He is so freaking intense. He would probably suck the soul out of me. Good thing he doesn't think I am worthy of a kiss anyway. *I must get away. I will get away!* I don't care if he knows about my plan and he's just playing a game. I'll play along.

"We will *Jump* to your little planet, my Lorra," he says with his lips in my hair. "I can feel your anxiety. The sooner I reunite you with your cub brother, the sooner I can see your smiles. After we retrieve him, we will *Jump* to the Red Forest. I want you in my dwelling, I want your scent to fill my home, but I want to hear your laughter most of all. That is the sixth rule. You must let me hear the sound of your laughter every span."

Who has a rule about laughing? Do aliens have personality disorders? I am sure he has several.

He tilts my chin up, and I force myself to look at him. I know he won't stop until I do. This close, it feels like I'm drowning in a sea of gold. It is really distracting. God, so it's the smell of his beard. I can smell myself on it. How embarrassing! This is terrible!

"Say: *Yes*," he nudges me. Yes, to what? Oh, who cares. I need to choose my battles. Getting away from his bubble of madness is the only priority.

"Yes," I say.

"Yes, what?"

Oh my god!!!!!!!!

"Yes, Zaan," I say like a *good female*. Of course, I get the pat on the hair and the kiss on the forehead. I hate him so much!

"A better male would take you to the pressurer, right now," he says, and it takes me a while to understand he means the shower. "I am no such thing, my Lorra. I want my smell on you, just like I don't want to wash the scent of your release off me. I struggle as it is, knowing I will shortly have to share you with so many eyes. I want you to smell like me."

Yes, right. Being covered in bright red marks and having a pulsing leaf on my forehead is not enough.

"Besides, my control is very close to its limits," he says with a smile. Right, I got my release but he didn't. Not sure how that makes me feel. Men can't control themselves like that, can they?

"I don't think I can manage to have you naked against the pressurer's wall and not act on this vexing desire," he says, almost like an answer to my question. Then, he smiles.

That smile... reaches his eyes, and it touches my soul... He is so beautiful, it hurts. Since when do I like big, hairy and intense? *I must get away!*

He helps me off the bed and buttons up my shirt. Takes me by my hand, and I just follow like a puppy. At some point, I can feel some sort of a brush going through my hair. More food in liquid form is brought to my lips... Maybe he doesn't need a wife nor a dog. A puppet would be more appropriate. One that comes with plenty of strings. Yet, being looked after like this feels strangely empowering instead of humiliating. Like I mean everything to someone. Maybe there is something wrong with me. I look away as he swaps his pants for the white leather kilt. He methodically attaches weapons to his belt, while he never takes his eyes off me. He doesn't even blink that much if I think about it. Then he says those dreadful words again.

"Come to me," he whispers, reaching out a hand for me to take.

He is less than five steps away. He is testing me, and he does it in the most obvious way possible. It feels like an insult because of it. Damn be my escape, my life, and everything else! I refuse. I turn my back and sit in one of the chairs by the control panel. I fiddle with the belt, but I already know I am not strong enough to activate it. I am not going to ask the MI to do it. I aggravated him enough as it is. He said going to him when he asked was not part of the rules, and I won't be punished for it. I can feel his pain in the marks on my arms. He presses something on my chair without touching me, and the safety belt zooms in place. There is a button for it?? He takes the seat next to mine and belts himself in, while checking the systems. This ship is far more complicated than anything I have seen so far. No MI at work here. He likes to control his own ship, no surprise there. The lack of reaction to my little rebellion is a surprise, though. He is not angry, just hurt. Why do I have this sort of power over him? Is it the Sign? Do his people respect it that much? Before I know it, the intense golden stare is back on me.

"Like I said, my Lorra, I want to keep it simple so you find it easier to follow the rules. Would you like me to repeat the first three rules?"

He is not joking. I want to cry, scream and slap his stupid face all at once. Instead, I keep my eyes on the prize.

"No, Zaan, I remember the rules," I say.

"Good. Taking my precious mate to a hostile planet is a very daunting experience. Everything inside me screams not to do such a reckless thing. However, your wishes and your happiness will always come first to me," he says, and I look away to an invisible spot on the screen ahead.

He bit you, gave you rules, he pats your head like you're a dog, calls your home a hostile planet, doesn't know your name, and he likes you so much he can't even kiss you, get it, Gianna? Yes, I do get it, and I will repeat all that to myself every time he says stupid things like that. I am also trying to simultaneously think of about twenty escape routes, hoping he won't tell which one is real in case he can read my mind – anything to keep me busy. I will ignore all the things he makes me feel until I am safe and away from him. Yes, that is the best way forward. No thinking, no feeling, just planning like the soldier I wanted to be.

"Do you have a location for your cub brother, my Lorra?" he asks, and I try to ignore the hurt in his eyes. He expected me to say something to his words. No doubt fanning myself for having such *a knight in shining armor* in my corner. Not happening!

"Yes, please. Camp Pendleton, in the San Diego County, USA," I say with a very soft voice. I can't hide how anxious I am, but he might just as well think I am worried about my made-up brother if he bought my lies.

"An army base?" he asks with a question in his eyes.

"Yes, the nanny's husband, mate, is an officer there. I don't know her address, the details were on my phone. He is highly ranked, and everyone would know how to find him."

"Very well," he says, not making any comments whether or not he finds it all a bit strange. He types more instructions into his com thingy at a fast speed. "Prepare for the *Jump*. I am sure you are quite familiar with it by now." He adds the ever-present hint to my escape. He's seen nothing yet. I am done being a victim. Of course, my stupid brain mocks me in the background. It's not like I'm escaping because I am such a strong person or because I can fight an alien twice my size. I can only do it because of the help of yet another man who thinks he owns me. At least my father is the Devil, I know.

Just like the last time I experienced the *Jump*, I feel lightheaded and slightly nauseous. Of course, I don't show any of this as he releases my belt and helps me up, ready to catch me if I fall or something. I don't look at him, pretending to make my oversized shirt look decent. I can feel his smile, then his lips press themselves against my forehead.

"I like your fragility, your shyness, and your wariness. There is a sweet little creature in the Red Forest you remind me of. It is so skittish, it freezes in front of danger, instead of saving itself," he says like a whisper in my hair. "There is no need to hide your true self from me, my Lorra. I like it. It makes me want to protect you and keep you safe from all harm."

He thinks I am similar to a deer?!!! Shy?!!! Fragile?!!! Fuck him! He is about to find out. I steel myself through the embrace he gives me, through the looks I get from his Warriors who come on board to report to him, through the stupid reassuring smiles I get from his Healer. They all look at me like I hung the moon or something. More like it, all they see is the Sign. They don't see me. Well, they obviously love it enough to have invaded a planet for it. I wonder, what are they doing here? Do they take women by the dozen back to Tarrassia? Force them, pay them? What?

"I am so happy to see you are well, High Lady Marni," says the Healer. My stupid brain keeps referring to him as the *kind alien*. Luckily, I don't have to reply as Zaan is in full High Commander mode. That pretty much means he's an asshole, barking orders at every single one of them. If I were in a more reasonable state of mind, I would admit he is not really barking orders. Just being ridiculously specific about his questions and their answers. He asks for the tiniest details to be explained, and he makes them repeat his orders back to make sure they got it right. Jesus! At least I am not the only one who gets his own brand of crazy. We only leave the safety of the ship once Barin assures him – four times – every single Human soldier inside the Camp is compliant and not a danger to me. They know shit about my people! Humans are not compliant. They would fake anything to survive.

He informs me we are about to walk to a secure area and contact my nanny's husband from there. I know exactly where we're going as we follow the corridors leading to the high command offices. He holds my hand in front of his Warriors and all the Humans we run into. He doesn't seem to want to separate duty from his personal life. Not that he has to. Our stupid Signs are there for everybody to stare at. And they all do. The marks on my arms are mainly covered by the oversized shirt, but they can see his and the one pulsing on our foreheads. Some look scared, a few look shocked, but most look disgusted. Their whispers reach me, no matter how far they are... I stop suddenly, and Zaan's eyes, a full copper now, search my face.

"What is it, my Lorra?"

"I can hear them… even whispers. Everything is more intense, I don't know…" I say, and he smiles briefly.

"The Sign has gifted you Tarrassian traits. All your senses will be enhanced. What did you hear?" he asks, looking around with hard, suspicious eyes, at the people passing by. I see he wasn't paying attention.

"Nothing," I lie, and we resume our walk. I've been called a whore many times before. Being called an *alien's whore* makes no difference to me. Right now, I need to focus on what I am about to do. I can feel my hand shaking inside his much larger one, and I almost trip when he lifts it to his lips and kisses my knuckles. Right there, in front of his people and mine. Aliens are strange.

We finally make it to a gigantic office, not far from my father's one. There are no Humans here, only his Warriors who look at him like he is God, ready to spring into action at his first words. Nothing I haven't seen before. His people appear so out of place around the Camp. Kilts and swords are not precisely what one would expect to see.

"Give me his name, my Lorra. I will have the nanny's mate brought here," he says while checking things on the strange device, similar to a tablet. The images on the screen move at a dizzying speed. He seems able to read all that while staring at me.

"It is Lance Corporal Geoffrey Brown, but I do remember his number. I can call him from here if it's okay," I say, hoping he will not question why I can remember his telephone number but not his wife's address. Geoffrey is real, and his wife Brenda is indeed a nanny. She used to babysit me many years ago. No idea if he is still around or if he has a different Insignia. The closer I keep it to reality, the better. I go behind the large mahogany desk and type my father's number into the landline phone. There are hundreds of things that could go wrong, but this is all I have. I just know

Zaan and his oversized minions will not allow me to leave this Camp alone to look for the so-called nanny.

My father's grave voice answers on the second ring. I haven't spoken to him in almost six years, but now is not the time for bad memories. Zaan watches me like a hawk. He is not even blinking.

"Hello, Lance Corporal Brown. My name is Gianna Raymond; you probably don't know who I am. Your wife Brenda looks after my little brother... Oh, you do? That is amazing. Yes, that's right. Such good news, and I am very grateful for keeping him safe. Yes, I am at the Camp. Yes. No, I can't. Yes. Do you think she can bring him here? Oh, that is so kind of you. Your office? Yes, of course, I will wait for him in there. Yes, I know he is scared. There won't be any aliens around when he comes over. Yes, I will explain to him... Thank you. I will make my way there in a few minutes."

I end my fake conversation and watch Zaan with wary eyes. He does the same. I know now he can't read my mind. He would kill me on the spot otherwise. However, he is growing more mistrusting by the second. It is time to up my game, no matter how painful. I give him my famous smile. The one that kept the tabloids buzzing and melted the demon Moorri King. He watches it like his brain is trying to analyze and make sense of every muscle involved in it. I can see the moment he somehow decides that is not a real smile. *Shit!* I wrap my arms around his waist, as far as they will go.

"He is safe. They are bringing him here now. Thank you, Zaan. You have no idea what it means to me," I say with my face hidden into his bare chest. The heart under my ear is so loud. Deafening. *Unforgettable. Mine.* Why did I think of such words? Why am I crying? Why am I hoping he won't buy my lies? Tears can be convincing though, even for aliens who are not used to them. I am definitely not crying because this is my last time in his arms, the last time I can inhale his scent, the last time I... No, not going there. There is no point. I couldn't change anything now, even if I wanted to. I cannot magically produce a younger brother. *Please, don't believe my lies!*

"Don't cry, my beautiful, perfect mate," he says with his lips in my hair, ignoring the fact we are not alone. "No more pain for you. I will not allow it." *You are stupid. I hate you so much!*

"Can I join you when you meet your brother?" he asks, and I snap out of whatever this is. Enough! I have a plan. Well, my father does, but his plans never fail, so that is probably better.

"No, the Corporal said my little brother is terrified of your people. Sorry, he will come around once he understands you are his new family."

"Yes, cubs of all species are resilient," he agrees. "I have many issues to deal with around here. You take your time with him. If you think it's necessary, we will stay here for a few spans; I will arrange safe accommodation for us and the cub. You and everyone you love are my first priority."

Stupid! So stupid!! "Uh... oh, okay, I will see him, and then we can decide."

"I cannot have you unguarded, but my Warriors will stay out of sight and give you privacy once the cub arrives."

"Yes, that is fine," I say because it really is. My father has already taken that into account. He never leaves anything to chance. I am his only failed project.

He places a burning kiss inside my palm, and my marks go mad with color. Not even the fabric of the shirt can hide it. My skin tingles and I just know no water, soap or scrub will remove the mark of his lips from my palm. *I don't want to remove it.* He leaves the room in a rush, almost like he pushes himself to walk away from me. *He is gone! It's over. I will never see him again. I will never...* I stop my thoughts and focus on here and now. I have a plan. Barin was the only Tarrassian who followed him out of the room; all the other eight Warriors are obviously my new guards. One of them can easily take down about fifty of ours. Why do I need that many?

It doesn't matter, my father's plan is perfect. I am the only imperfect thing the Commandant of the Marine Corps has ever created. As expected, he immediately understood the predicament. There was no hesitation. He asked minimum questions and gave me precise details of what to do next. My father's instructions have made another thing obvious. There isn't much compliance at all, and my father seems at the heart of it. He is loyal to his men, and they are devoted to him. They know he chose them over his own daughter, and that weighs heavily in the balance. I might just as well take advantage.

A very young and terrified Marine walks in to hand me a mobile. He tells me my 'little brother' is on the line and he is having some sort of a meltdown. I take the phone and start walking, following my father's directions. I can hear him talk on at least two other lines, giving orders and making arrangements. I can't help the pang of pain and the memories. I used to feel so safe growing up, having a father who could fix all problems and fight all monsters. Until I was the problem he had to fix.

I stroll, ignoring the whispers, the name-calling, the stares. I can feel the aliens walking like huge shadows around me, flinching and occasionally even growling. Their enhanced hearing can tell what I am being called by my own people. One of them asks me if I want anything done about it, and I politely decline. Eventually, I reach my destination. The large conference room is already occupied by both Tarrassians and a few high ranked Marines. One of my guards asks everybody to leave, and I am suddenly all alone. The Warriors assigned to me are all waiting outside for my 'cub brother' to arrive.

I don't risk blowing my cover and talk loudly, pretending to calm the little boy on the other side of the line. My father guides me to a hidden exit leading underneath the building. It is a labyrinth of pipes and narrow corridors. My father's instructions are precise to the detail. He tells me to follow things like a small dent in the wall or a loose pipe. Over ten minutes into my walk, he asks me to pick up the pace. My absence has already been discovered. He doesn't have to tell me what I already know. I can feel anger in my marks. It's more than anger. It's pain, heartbreak and betrayal. I refuse to pay attention. I can't change things now. It's too late. *What have I done?*

I run faster. Luckily, I am more than fit to do that, even while wearing the oversized shirt. I've always been athletic and working out was my religion. Not even the long weeks in the pod could damage my muscles. What is more, I feel stronger, faster and more aware of all my senses. It must be the Sign. My father tells me I am six minutes away from my contact point with one of his men. This place goes on forever. Every two minutes or so, the tunnel spreads into several directions. This place could link the Camp to any location out there. The Tarrassians have no idea what they have got themselves into. Humans don't know how to surrender.

I stop suddenly like I have been punched in the face. My father sent *him.* Of course, he did. Is this a reminder of my value?

"In my defence, I did tell him this was a stupid idea, Blondie," he says with the usual sly smile on. "The Commander wanted the best for the job, and we all know who that is."

I have to order my legs to stay put. My brain is in overdrive. Everything is pushing me back to safety. To Zaan. Away from the man grinning in front of me.

"Oh, I have to say you look quite the picture, Blondie. I can't blame the aliens for marking you. You are irresistible. I know because I got there first, didn't I? Not sure many guys will feel the alien vibe," he grins pointing at my marks. "But I am always available if you want to have some fun. I don't mind it at all. It will be like fucking a little elf fairy," he says, and his fingers run down my cheek.

I feel sick; I think I am about to throw up. My throat is tight and I can't swallow. I brace myself on the nearest pipe, and it makes him laugh.

"You can sure hold a grudge, Blondie. I'll give you that." He touches the device in his ear, and his face becomes harder; the soldier pushes to the front of the monster living behind those chiseled features. "Time to rush now, Blondie. Not sure the Commander would appreciate it if I returned his daughter dead."

No, of course not. The Commander doesn't mind his daughter being raped and beaten. As long as she's alive, it's all good. He reaches for my hand, but I move away.

"Only trying to be a gentleman here and help, Blondie. Chill, okay?" he says, putting both hands up. The hands that took all my innocence away.

"I can run, Lieutenant; I don't need help. You are here to follow orders from your General, not play the gentleman."

"Ouch, you grew guts and a tongue. Actually, you always had a tongue. I still remember the feel of it on my cock," he says with a wink.

I want to hurt him, I want to cause pain to the whole world, but it doesn't work, as always. They can hurt me more. The strange pain in my marks reminds me there is only one being out there I have the power to hurt and break. And I did.

"This way, Blondie, and hurry the fuck up! Thirty minutes till the chopper touches down. It's Colonel these days, by the way. You can always call me Tim, Blondie. You know I have a soft spot for you. Loads of hard things, too," he says with the usual smug voice.

"I need a gun," I say. I know him well enough to know he carries more than one. He was always my father's favorite. He is the son he never had. Part of me will forever wonder if my father knew what Tim and his minions had planned for me. As horrible as that may sound, he could easily do something like that. He wanted me out of the Corps, he wanted me to learn what happens to pretty girls in the army, and he wanted to marry me off to the next guy on the road to the White House. What better way than to encourage four of his favorites to teach me a lesson?

"You're good, Blondie, I've got you covered; you don't need a gun."

"I am perfectly capable of using one," I say, running behind him.

"Oh, I know that. I also know you will use it on me. And Daddy dearest will be quick to cover it up."

"Is that why he made the man who raped his only daughter a Colonel?" I say with a bitter laugh behind him.

"Oh, come now, Blondie, no one raped you. You had the full attention of the hottest four men in the unit. We gave you our special treatment. No wonder you became the Man-Eater. We got you addicted to dick, didn't we?" he asks with a loud laugh. He always laughed at his own jokes.

I ignore him. There is no point trying to say anything hurtful. He doesn't care what I say or do. I felt so guilty after the rape. Like it was indeed my fault. Like I asked for it.

I was just a day over fourteen when I first met Lieutenant Tim Miller. The second I laid eyes on him in my father's office, I had an instant girl crush. All golden hair, bright blue eyes, rippling muscles, and sexy smiles. He looked at me like I had no clothes on, and stupid me thought it was hot, not really understanding the notion of a pedophile. Less than a month after I joined the Corps, I could see him for what he was. A pompous loser with a narcissistic personality. Yes, one hell of a soldier, but only because he loved killing, pumping iron, and hitting targets. Preferably live ones. I refused all his attention, and soon the interest turned into bullying and harassment.

Twenty minutes into a fast-paced run, he turns to give me a sick smile.

"You've got serious stamina, Blondie. No wonder you were such a good fuck," he laughs. "You made quite an impression with the four of us. We are all still single, imagine that. I am looking to settle down if you're interested. And we can always have the guys around at the weekend. You know me, I like to share the joy." His laughter echoes against the empty corridors.

I ignore it; I keep my eyes ahead. The pain in my marks is quite intense. *He is in pain.* I need to focus. After another twenty minutes or so, we finally make it to an exit. We crawl through something that looks like a drain and we come out in the middle of a field. Like he said, a chopper is waiting there, engines on, and we are up in the air before we even secure the belts. Luckily, the asshole ignores me, deciding to chat to the pilot, and I can close my eyes, trying to finally catch my breath. Hundreds of thoughts and unwanted feelings come to my mind. *His eyes, his touch, his pain.* I quickly open my eyes, considering if I should poke at Tim Miller and his bullying tendencies to keep myself busy. I would welcome anything that could get those golden eyes out of my mind.

13

—

ZAAN

Her name is not Raymond. There is no cub brother, and both her parents are alive. There is no Human mating ritual saying the male has to grant a wish. She is not shy, and she is not inexperienced. According to the information in front of me, she is quite the opposite. I have never seen a more embarrassed Shadow Warrior than the one who handed me the report. He was avoiding my eyes. They all do, Barin most of all. His embarrassment is mixed with pain, which only makes it worse.

She has been gone for five spans. I haven't reached out to her mind. I wanted to know all the facts first. Once I did, I wasn't sure I wanted to reach out at all. Humans have proven to be quite resourceful for such primitive beings. We own this planet now, yet it took my Shadows five spans to find her. If there is something I learned from her it is that her species has no honor. It makes them unpredictable, like the Noorranni and all the other scum in the Coalition of the Dark Moon. Why would the Astrals allow such beings the privilege of bringing our Sign back?

I like knowing all facts and details before acting, and I cannot blame beings for the traits of their species. My Shadows looked into the other females who developed the Sign. Just like her, they are very public figures here on Earth, so it was easy enough to find information on them. Despite their beauty and fame, there weren't any shameful secrets to reveal. The little red female I rescued isn't faking fragility. The white-haired one is not faking being a dignified creature. Not even the foul-mouthed one has a reputation like my female. The King and the Great Warrior are fortunate males. I am nothing but a fool. If I ever doubt it, all I have to do is look around. My Warriors pity me. The Humans, too.

It matters not. She is my mate, and we will both die without fulfilling the Sign and its demands. My marks scream with pain as it is. They are dim and faded. The bearers of the Sign cannot stay away from each other. The further apart they are, the more intense the pain. Once the mating has been fulfilled, and cubs connect the two mates, the pull should be less painful. At least that is what the Elders say, but no one knows for sure. Our Sign had been lost for too long.

My hollocom comes to life as Barin asks permission to board. For the last few spans, I commanded my Fleet from my private ship. I refused the accommodation offered by the Humans, and I choose to avoid the main ship. I don't want their stares, nor their pity. Even the Humans talk behind my back. I cannot blame them either. It's best to keep my distance so that I won't kill anyone. Probably an even worse idea to be around her when I am this angry, but she is my responsibility. I will bring my female to Tarrassia and no one else.

"Hanni, High Commander," says Barin with a worried look on his face. Still avoiding my eyes. "Your Second in Command has joined us, and…"

"Nodric can't talk for himself?" I ask.

"A bit too much, if you ask me," answers Barin. "He is not too fond of the Humans, and you don't need his bickering right now."

"Perhaps he is a smarter male than I am," I say.

"Zaan, please... Listen," he says, finally meeting my eyes, "as your oldest friend, maybe you should take my advice. The situation in the Fourth Quadrant is rapidly deteriorating. It is beyond me why the King would think we should take on all enemies at once. I believe it is best if you cover that situation. Your reputation alone could deter the Aleki from picking up a fight. Nodric and me can handle Earth all by ourselves. I will retrieve your mate, take her to Tarrassia, and you can join her later. You know... once you calm down a bit."

"No," I say, and he knows better than to push me when all my limits have been stretched as it is. "My Second in Command will cover Earth. You are too soft, Barin, when females are involved. Nodric hates everybody, especially the Humans. He will not fall prey to their deceiving ways. I need you to cover the Fourth Quadrant. The Great Warrior will be assisting."

"Didn't Nodric just rescue him and his new Human mate from Sketos? Why would he go to war so soon?" he asks.

"I am not the Great Warrior's keeper. No one is. Maybe he can't stand the sight of his mate any more than I can stand mine. On that issue, as soon as I retrieve her and she is safe in between the confinements of my dwelling, I will join you," I tell him as I change into my Kannicloth. "Her sire is one of the highest ranked Generals in the Human army. A troublesome one, I was informed. He is not cooperating and a fight is imminent."

"If the Great Warrior is covering the Fourth Quadrant, maybe I can assist you, High Commander. He can probably fight the entire Aleki army alone," he says with a carefree smile in his usual manner. Sadly, it only scrapes badly at my temper. However, I refuse to take it out against my oldest friend. I will take my anger out on the one who caused it. On the one who turned me into the laughing stock of her people and mine.

"You have your orders, Healer of the Blood Fleet. I expect you to follow them," I reply, already dismissing him. I check in with the few Warriors I chose for this mission. They are some of my strongest, and we fought many battles side by side. They know my orders before I even give them. Everything has been calculated to precision, and every detail has been carefully accounted for. I asked my parents for a few spans alone with my mate on my return, and they were happy to oblige, moving temporarily to our dwelling in the High City. The Red Forest Residence is large enough to get lost in, but I know my mother. She won't be able to stay away and would want to spoil my mate. She will want to show her around or plan our Sacred Ceremony. My parents don't know any better, and I didn't have the heart to tell them the truth. They are both very gentle souls and will not agree or understand. Luckily, as the Queen is heavy with cub, my sire's presence is required more often in the High City.

"I know you are upset enough to put your sword through me, but I will say my piece, Zaan," says the fool. "Your female has been through a lot, and fear does strange things to all beings. She had been taken against her will, not once but twice. As if the Noorranni pest wasn't enough, she had to endure the horrors of the Moorri," he says, trying to plead with me for my own mate, the fool. That is enough to make my War Beast grow, and he is quick to retreat and put his hands up in a peace-seeking gesture.

"I think my mate quite enjoyed the horrors of the Moorri King. He is a much smarter male than I am. Humans are primitive beings with no honor. A cage and a collar are all they deserve. Leave me!" I tell him, and this time he knows better.

My Warriors inform me the other two ships are ready, and that they have found three large clearances in the forest for landing. Separate locations, but close enough to each other. My ship can easily board all the Warriors I am taking on this mission, but I don't want any around after I retrieve my female. No one looks at her, and no one touches her! Not any more. Once I have her, we will *Jump* back home.

My Orbit MI surveyed her location for the last five spans. She is alone with her sire, in a remote dwelling surrounded by mountains and forests. Her sire is one of the high-ranked officials suspected of putting together a resistance. It will bring me great joy to crush them. A harsh lesson is needed. But first, I will let my female have hers. Despite all the anger, wounded pride, and bleeding hearts, I am still not ready to accept her rejection. I cannot do this without giving her the chance to return to me all by herself. Maybe she was just scared and confused. I brace myself for the inevitable pain. All she does is hurt me, but I need to know I gave us one more chance.

The first thing I feel when I reach inside her head is fear. The next one, is hate. Her marks seem even duller than mine, and I can feel the pain they are causing her. She would rather suffer than belong to me.

Come to me. There will be no punishment if you return to me on your own.

I know she heard me, and I can see it's increasing both her fear and hate. Without her permission to open her mind for me, I cannot breach it. I don't know what she is thinking, but she chooses to ignore my plea either way. She pushes me away like an afterthought. Very well then. It has been decided. No more chances.

My ship lands first. My location is the closest to her father's dwelling, and I wait for my Warriors to join me on foot. I cloak my ship just in case. This is a primitive planet, and all their archaic interception systems are under my control. Regardless, I learned long ago never to dismiss an enemy. I teach my Warriors to treat the weakest just as they would the strongest. Everything can become a threat at short notice. The simple fact her sire is alone with her makes me very suspicious. He must have guards, but where?

My Warriors join me soon, and I can see they all have their War Beasts out, and they are ready for a fight. Begging for one, more like it. They are trapped on this forgotten planet without a fight or anyone to kill or fuck. For no better reason than a chance to get their hearts crushed by a species with no respect or honor. I can feel their growing frustration with every span. The only thing keeping them in line at this point is the possibility of finding a Human female. Sign or not, all these females will be able to give life to Tarrassian cubs and save us from extinction. According to my sire, anyway. He better be right because my Warriors are trained to spill blood, not for politics and alliances. They need action and soon. We walk quietly through the strange forest. It's all bright green, like the flocks of the Alini birds. I can smell and hear strange beasts around me, but they are all skittish and harmless.

She knows I am here. My Sign pulses, and my marks have a brighter glow. I can scent her now on the breeze. Fear, anger, frustration, hate. That is all my presence ever makes her feel. I fooled myself thinking her body's reaction to my touch was more than a simple hormone-induced one. How many males have given her that before? Way too many, according to her reputation. Maybe the King is right. Our Astrals are nothing but a bunch of fools.

As we approach the clearing, I allow my Warriors to draw their swords and have their weapons ready. I can now sense the older male. Strong, aggressive, protective and eager to spill my blood. Either way, I am keeping my War Beast under control, and my weapons are still attached to my Kannicloth. I will not harm her loved ones in front of her.

The strangely shaped dwelling seems made of the tree trunks surrounding it.

The front entrance opens widely, and she runs down the stairs in obvious distress. My newly awakened heart beats fast enough to break my skin. Is she coming to me? She stops in front of her sire's dwelling giving a worried look behind her, and then she finally looks at me.

"Please don't hurt my father. I will come with you willingly," she says with an unreadable look in those strange, beautiful eyes. *She was not running to me.*

Her marks are much dimmer than mine and they are bleeding. I can see the shape of her blunt nails imprinted all over her arms. Did she try to scratch at them? Does she hate me that much she would hurt herself just to remove my marks? How dare she damage her beautiful skin? She will learn her skin belongs to me, and she is not allowed to cause any harm to herself any more. Nor is she allowed to expose herself in her ridiculous Human clothing. Her white top is barely going under her perky tits, and her scrap of blue bottoms leave all her legs exposed. I am trying with everything in me not to release my War Beast.

An old and large by Human standards male appears through the dwelling's front entrance. He holds a long weapon aiming at us. I can hear my Warriors chuckling behind me then quickly apologizing. They know dismissive behavior against an enemy is not accepted under my command.

"Dad, you cannot hurt them with that. Please, there is no point. We talked about this," she pleads with her sire, who gives me an evil grin.

"I can hurt them and I will. Get back inside, Gia. I will deal with this," he says.

"Do you have a translation device, Human?" I ask, trying to stay as calm as possible, but such a thing is not easy. Not when I can see her scraping at our mating marks, right under my eyes. She doesn't even notice doing it any more. Hating me and everything that connects her to me is like second nature to her. I can see she is also slimmer. She hasn't been eating properly.

"It is important to understand one's enemies," says the

foolish old man. "You and your men have one chance to retreat before I blow up your ships."

"Your weapon cannot hurt us or damage our ships. Enough of this!" I say, taking another step towards my mate. Both Humans flinch at my motion, and she goes back up the stairs to block her sire from me in a protective gesture. He seems offended by it and pushes her roughly behind him. Her delicate hip hits the open door of the dwelling. Nothing I do or say can stop my body from growing now. No one hurts my female. I growl as I advance on him.

"Take another step, and all your three ships will go up in flames," he says, lifting a hand in the air, higher than the one holding the gun. How does he know how many ships we brought? A small device is flickering in his hand. I can hear its slight hum. It is active. The Human has mined all the clearings. It is a useless act, but I cannot help the respect owed to a worthy enemy.

"You will not be able to call for enforcements either, as all the signals are jammed in this forest," he says, and sure enough, a look at my wrist hollocom tells me it is dead. Impressive. I let him savor his little victory for a few nanos while I reach out in my mind to my Fleet. I ask them to remotely control the ships and lift them to a safe distance from the soil until we return. I also command my Central Space Intelligence to disengage the explosives. Soon enough, the small device in his hand goes dead. To his credit, the old male doesn't even flinch, faking that everything is still going to plan. Vexing Humans, as Nodric would say. Not as harmless as they seem.

Before I even realize what I am doing, I lift my hand, palm up to her.

"Come to me," I say. *Not again, Zaan! Have some self-respect.*

I can hear the weakness in my voice. My Warriors can, too. How many more chances am I going to give this female? She doesn't even look my way. I am nothing to her. Instead, she puts her fingers over her sire's gun and lowers it.

"Please, Dad, there is no point. More will come. This is their planet now."

"This will never be their planet, little girl. You watch your tongue," he says with a snarl. Is this how Humans treat their cubs? She is not his to disrespect any more. She is mine.

Enough of this! I reach her with a few steps and throw her over my shoulder. I don't give the old male a single look as I return to the forest. I know my Warriors have him under control, just like they have everything else.

"Put me down, asshole! I can walk; you are hurting me!" she says, scraping at my back while her head jolts with every step I take. She soon starts hitting instead of scratching, and I have to admit my female can deliver a good punch despite her tiny size.

"You lost the right to make demands. You lost all rights, Human!"

14

—

GIANNA

My insides shake as he drops me like I'm a pile of wood into one of the chairs facing the control panel. He doesn't talk and doesn't look at me as he engages my safety belt. Two of his Warriors followed us on board, and he starts giving them orders about some Quadrant like this is just another day at the office. I am scared to the core, tired, in pain, and maybe a bit more broken than ever. Nothing else can explain why I am determined to act like a fool. I press the release button, and my belt snaps back into the armrest. I stand and face him.

"I want to know what happened to my father," I say with strength I didn't know I had.

It is not lost on me; even his Warriors seem angry at my behavior. He turns to look at me with eyes devoid of anything but anger. The beautiful gold is gone, replaced by an eerie white speckled with red dots. I almost retreat to my seat on my own accord as he moves closer to me. The thing they call the War Beast has completely taken over his body. He looks bigger, scarier, and completely unhinged. I refuse to cower. Maybe if he

135

gets angry enough, he will just kill me. I flinch when his hand pulls me by one wrist to the far end wall of the ship. It feels like my bone will snap under the pressure, but then I notice he is only holding it with two fingers. He pushes me into the wall and steps away, already returning to his Warriors. Before I even understand what's happening, a sharp noise scratches my ears as metal bars release from the ceiling to the floor right in front of me, trapping me behind them. An even louder zing goes through the metal, and little sparks of electricity make the bars look alive for a second. Instinctively, I push myself against the back wall, as far away as I can from the deadly bars. Is this a makeshift cell? A second later, the welcoming idea comes. All I have to do is touch those bars charged with electricity, and all the pain will stop. I can end this here and now. It won't kill an alien, but it will definitely kill me.

Once again, it happens too fast. As if there is a delay in everything I do, and he is always one step ahead of my actions. The bars go back up into the ceiling before I even get to move, and one large hand grabs me by my throat, lifting me up and pushing me into the wall.

For a brief moment, air leaves my lungs, and I grab in panic at his fingers around my neck, my feet dangling in the air like I am nothing but a broken doll. Suddenly, the floor is back under my feet, and air reaches my lungs once again. He grabs both my wrists and pushes them down forcefully into the wall behind me. I don't really understand what he is trying to do, until I look in horror at my hands, pinned by the side of my hips. Restraints! No, no, no, no! I can't have those. Two large metal cuffs emerge from the wall and attach themselves to my wrists. Two more similar-looking devices encase my ankles, pushing my heels painfully into the wall behind me. Everything is so tight it feels like the bonds are trying to suck me into the metal wall behind me. I try to pull, and a sharp pain leaves me breathless for a second. A sheen of cold sweat covers my skin, and nausea makes my stomach roll.

"The more you fight, the tighter they'll get. The cuffs will break your bones, but unlike the electric bars, they won't kill you. I need you alive, but I do not care about your broken bones. Your choice," he says without even looking at me.

As he returns to where his Warriors wait for him, the deadly metal bars release from the ceiling once again. I am frozen in fear. The memory of broken bones and the pain that comes with it hits me like a train. I feel faint, and my throat constricts. He is right. The broken bones of my wrists and ankles won't kill me. I know because I survived that before.

I don't even remember which of the four broke my arm. I wasn't fighting anymore when it happened. After more than an hour into being repeatedly raped and used as a punch bag, there was no fight left in me. It was such a useless thing to do, breaking the bones of someone who wasn't even fighting back. They all laughed when they heard the cracks in my left arm. They high-fived each other when Tim broke my ribs. They...

I snap out of my memories as the wetness on my bare feet brings me back to reality. I somehow expected to see blood, but it's nothing more than my big fat tears landing on my toes. I feel his stare on me and lift my head. As our eyes meet, he turns his back at me once again and continues talking to his Warriors.

Why wouldn't he? I am nothing. I have no value. Maybe it would have been better to listen to my father from the very beginning. There is no fighting this. Would he still be alive, my father? He is all I have left. Mother never cared. For as long as I remember I was only allowed to see her a few times a year. Sometimes she would skip those, too. I know she is probably scared of my dad, but she never even tried to fight for me. She signed my application for the Marines as a lone act of defiance against him. She was wise enough to move to Brazil after. She married some rich guy, and I haven't seen her since. She calls on my birthday and on Christmas Eve and keeps the conversation as brief as possible. I know I probably remind her of him, so I can't really blame her. My father's green eyes stare back at me each time I look in the mirror. Probably not something she can ignore.

I still my movements and close my eyes, trying to stop the tears. I am not pulling at my restraints, but for some reason, they keep on shrinking. I realize it's because I am shaking. Badly. My father is an asshole, but he is all I have. Or had, more likely. I caused his death, I am sure of it. Some of the men under his command may be monsters, but they are the only ones brave enough to resist an alien invasion. My father's death will be a huge blow to the New Resistance, as they call it. My actions will affect many, and it was all for nothing. I knew I could never get away from the Tarrassians. From *him*. Stupid guilt pools my closed eyes with more tears. My chest hurts. Breathing hurts. *I am nothing! Nothing! Nothing! Nothing!*

"Look at me, Human!" he says with a cold voice that feels like a punch to my stomach.

I open my eyes because defiance and hate are all I have left, and I want him to see it. His War Beast has retreated, and the white eyes are back to copper. Whatever little power I had to hurt this man is gone. I can see it now, and for whatever stupid reason, I prefer it this way. Knowing that I could easily break his heart gave me strange thoughts and feelings I didn't want. I would much rather have no control at all. His Warriors are gone, and we are alone on his ship. He comes closer to the electric bars and stares me down with that unsettling intensity of his. I force myself to meet his cold eyes, blocking stupid memories of the beautiful gold that's all gone.

"Let me guess, you have rules for me," I say with a mocking voice. At least, that's what I am trying to portray. All I can hear is anger and hate in my shaky voice. I am too scared to analyze any of my feelings right now, but I know they are all aimed at me even without doing so. I hate myself, and I don't even understand why. I am on a roller coaster spinning out of control. I don't know how to stop it, and it's tearing me apart.

"Having rules is a right, and you have none left, Human," he says with the cold, impersonal voice he used for the Moorri King. The voice he addresses his enemies. I hate it. "You will have food and shelter, but don't think for a single nano they are privileges. They are not! Now pay attention," he says, taking a step closer to stare me down with those metallic eyes.

The scent of orange flowers invades my nostrils, mocking me. Always mocking me. The heat emanating from his body reminds me I am cold. So cold. Always cold.

"We will *Jump* to my dwelling in the Red Forest. From now on, you are not allowed to speak to me or to anyone without my permission. You will keep your eyes down at all times and follow my instructions. I don't want your despicable Human traits offending my people or my family. You will not be allowed to leave my personal quarters or interact with anyone. If you learn to obey and respect me, some of your restrictions will be lifted in time. Continue with your reckless behavior, and you will never be allowed to leave my quarters or see anyone. If I have to, l won't hesitate to remove our cubs from you as soon as they are born. You will not corrupt everything around me with your deceiving ways."

He turns his back at me and returns to the control panels. I am not sure what kind of punishment I envisioned, but this wasn't it. I can survive broken bones, humiliation, rape, and even restraints that take all my dignity away. But no one can survive a lifetime of punishment. He doesn't want to hurt me for a while. He wants to do it forever. Systematically, patiently, obsessively… the same way he does everything else. He is the kind of predator who can never let go of his prey, nor does he kill it. He wants to take my children away. Like my father did to my mom. He is insane!

"I hate you! You are nothing but a fucking asshole using your power against a weaker being! I will always hate you! The Moorri King is twice the man you are!" I scream as loudly as I can and try to push away from the wall. The blinding anger made me forget the bounds. A sharp pain goes up my femur, reminding me of my cursed fragility. I still my movements, but I am too angry and worked up to stop the shaking.

He grabs something from the weapons compartment and returns to the bars of my cell.

"I said no talking, and I meant it, Human. I do not wish to hear your voice," he says with that horrible coldness he saves for his enemies. There is something far more unsettling in his tone, and it breaks me into a million pieces when I understand what it is. Repulsion. I repulse him.

"Do you know what this is?" he asks, opening one large palm in front of me. I look against my better judgment. Whatever it is, it instantly reminds me of the earwig-like device they put in my inner ear. Even though it looks nothing like it shape-wise, it feels strangely similar. He unfolds the metal scroll, and now it looks like a rectangular sheet made of molten silver. As he holds it up in front of me, it starts pulsing and moving, trying to wrap itself around his fingers like a snake. I feel like I am going to empty the contents of my stomach all over myself. I already know what that is. What kind of sick people have organic restraints?

"This device is meant to stop prisoners from biting or spitting poison. In your case, it will prevent talking, the same thing really. It is highly unstable and only used in extreme cases. It will mold itself around your mouth, locking at the back of your head. Every single time you move your lips or try to open your mouth, it will tighten and release a substance that will cause painful inflammation to your tongue. And before you put your hopes up, let me tell you, the device won't kill you. It monitors your oxygen levels and will give you a short reprieve each time you are close to dying. Would you like me to use it?"

He offers his question as if he asked me if I wanted a drink. My eyes are glued to the monstrosity in his hands. It's moving with impatience now as if it's desperate to wrap itself around my mouth. There is no point in answering. I lower my head and close my eyes. I used to be so good at retreating into my head when the pain got too much.

Halfway through being raped and beaten, something happened. The scent of my childhood's orange orchards invaded my body, and I was once again the little girl running barefoot under the Sicilian sun. No one could hurt me there. No one could follow me inside my bubble of safety. In the years that followed the rape, I used that over and over again each time the reality wanted to crush me. Now, I can't, and I hate him for that more than for anything else. The orange orchards don't smell like my safety bubble any more. They smell like him. He can follow me inside my bubble. He took everything from me. And I let him!

My stomach drops as if gravity disappeared for a moment. I quickly still my breath as I realize he initiated the *Jump*. Without warning, of course, since I don't have any rights left. I keep my eyes closed for long after the ship settles, and I feel a small impact, similar to docking. The jolt makes my restraints react, and deep pain goes up in my arms and legs. The bars retreat into the ceiling with a sharp hiss. I don't open my eyes as I feel his body heat near me – his stupid scent. I almost drop to the ground when the restraints disappear inside the wall like they were never there. It takes less than a second before a different type of device encircles one of my wrists. I look briefly only to see it's the one that connects our hands. The chain in between us seems longer than the last time he used it. He doesn't want to be close to me... That makes two of us. My body jolts, and I almost fall flat on my face as he pulls me behind him as one would an animal on a leash.

I keep my eyes down as we leave the ship, but it's not because he said so. I somehow feel like the world is closing in on me. As if I am inside walls that keep on shrinking.

The landing pad, or whatever they call it, is connected to his house by a long, tubular passage. The floor under my bare feet is cool and silky, reflective like the surfaces of their ships. I almost choke when the scent assaults all my senses. Everything smells like him here, and it feels like such a bad joke. I am in Hell, but it smells like my safe place. I try to keep up the best I can with his long strides. His walk is fast-paced, and I think part of it is trying to avoid attention. I refuse to look up; I don't want to have eye contact with all the beings we run into. I can feel their shock, surprise, and sometimes even horror. I can hear their quiet whispers as they ask each other what's happening. Family, servants, guards, I have no idea what they are. I can only see their alien feet in all shapes, sizes, and textures. Some I have no idea what they are meant to be. We walk for what feels like forever. How big is this place? Even though I keep my eyes down, the light around is blinding. Unlike in the Moorri Palace, it's not coming from jewels on the ceiling, but from huge windows that let the sunshine in. I can see in the corner of my eye there are windows everywhere. A bright red forest peeks from behind the glass. I train my eyes on the floor again. I don't want to look around. Prisons have no right to look or smell like this. They shouldn't feel like a home either. I don't even know where that stupid thought came from, but he is quick to crush it anyway. We stop in the middle of a very large room, easy to tell by the echo bouncing off the sparse furnishings. There must be quite a gathering of people, aliens, in here. They are all quiet, but I can feel their curious eyes on me. He pulls roughly on the chain connecting his wrist to mine, and I almost bump into his side.

"This Human female is my mate and the new High Lady of House Marni," he addresses the audience with clipped words as if barking orders to his Warriors. "She is a prisoner here until I say otherwise. Unless you have been instructed by me to do so, no one is allowed to interact with her or offer their assistance. I will only say this once. Anyone willing to help this female against my orders will be forever removed from Tarrassia. My sire will not keep you safe from my wrath. Have I made myself clear?"

They all reply individually, to my shock, and we stand there waiting for every single one of them to answer his question. Just how crazy is this man? It takes a long time before they all pledge to treat me like the nothing I am. Each new voice feels like a punch. My knees are shaking. The world is shrinking some more. He waits patiently for the last answer before pulling me behind him for another fast-paced walk. Even though I don't look, I know we reach his personal quarters, whatever that means. *The rooms I am not allowed to leave for the rest of my life.* The smell of Sicilian oranges is much more intense – that and a general feeling that he lives there. Like the air is saturated with his presence. I can't breathe in here. This is worse than physical torture.

I close my eyes when he comes close enough to remove the restrain from my wrist. I don't want to look at him. I don't know if it's because I hate him so much or because I can't stand to see the gold in his eyes is gone. My body tingles with stupid awareness and something else when I feel his fingers on my skin. On my wrists, on my ankles... what is he doing? I open my eyes curiously and look at... jewelry? Two beautifully carved wide bangles adorn my wrists. Similar-looking anklets decorate my bare feet. As I try to imagine why a prisoner would need jewelry, they all flash a bright green light before looking once again like innocent pieces of adornment. What an asshole!

"Just how many restraints can one person own? You are sick!" I tell him, damn be the consequences.

"Did I say you were allowed to talk?" he asks, looming over me, and I mentally brace myself for what I know will come next: pain.

"Fuck you!" I tell him, and I am proud of myself when I don't hear any fear in my voice. I have most likely lost my mind.

"Yes, we'll get to that part shortly," he says, watching me with an intensity that feels like a kick to my knees. "These are tracking devices. They are programmed to respond to a numeric code, not my genetic one, so don't even bother to remove them. One thing you should know about me, I never fall for the same trick twice. You are free to walk around my quarters," he says, pointing without looking at the lavish golden bedroom around us. "Step one foot outside the safety perimeter, the tracking devices will become restraints. You will get a single warning from the MI, then the two anklets will glue themselves together. Only when you return to the designated perimeter will they release their hold. Walking back with glued legs and broken bones might prove difficult, so it's best not to try it."

As he talks to me about all the crazy things, I am not sure I fully understand, I take an involuntary step back. I hate myself for it. I don't want to feel fear, and even less to show it. His body is definitely getting bigger as he approaches me with a predatory stare in his copper eyes. *Please, I can't take that again! Not from you!* The large muscles under his shimmery skin seem to grow, his shoulders are broader, and he looks taller, like upgrading from huge to giant. Even his beard and hair seem to come to life. The War Beast… Do they just call it that, or is it like a different entity taking over? I don't know, and I suddenly realize I don't know much about him or Tarrassians. I know more about the Moorri Royal Court and their customs than I do about the man who calls himself my mate. All I got from him was a stupid set of rules.

My eyes drop to the large hands removing his weapons methodically. I wish I didn't look, as the huge erection tenting his kilt tells me exactly what will happen next.

His forehead Sign and the tattoos on his arms light up, and I am happy to notice mine don't. He is very aware of that fact, and a fleeting shadow of hurt goes through his eyes. Was I supposed to enjoy rape? Is that what he thought was going to happen?

"Remove your garments, Human," he orders, and for a stupid brief moment, I feel like I am going to cry. This man is nothing like the one I woke up next to on his ship. Did my actions cause the change, or was he always like this? Is my lack of compliance what brought the real him out? Are they all the same? Why couldn't he be different? *Please be different!*

"I will not make things easier for you, asshole! Every little thing you want from me, you will have to take it by force," I tell him, and my anger feels like a drug. It builds and builds, and it takes the fear away, even if it's only for a short while. I know I won't be able to keep it up. Not when he rapes me. I know I won't. *Please be different!* "I hate you, Zaan of House Marni! I hate your stupid mating marks; I hate even the idea that you exist in this world. I will not fake compliance just so you don't punish me. Do your worst and deal with the knowledge that I hate you more than anyone else in the entire world!"

For a brief moment my words feel like a drug. I was never this brave before, and here I am doing it in front of the biggest predator of all. Only... it doesn't last. It never does. My power, my control, my choices are always fake. *Please, be different!*

"Force it is then. Females like you don't deserve anything else," he says, lifting my tank top over my head and throwing it randomly behind him. Not only did he move so fast and unexpectedly, but I was too stunned by his words to even notice how close we got. I ignore my first instinct to cover my exposed chest. What is the point? He's already seen it all before.

"Females like me?" I ask, standing straight as a board as his fingers unbutton my daisy shorts. He is not looking at what he's doing or at my naked body. His intense stare is glued to my eyes

145

like he is trying to burn my head from inside out. "You know nothing about me!" I tell him with a small voice. I somehow know what's coming. I just don't want to hear it. *Not from you. Please, don't say it!*

"Oh, but I do, Human," he says, pushing my shorts and panties down my legs. He throws them away with an obvious gesture of disgust. "Everybody knows since you never made a secret of it. I have an entire folder of vids and reports about the kind of female you are. Sadly, my Warriors are also aware, and now the interest in taking a Human mate has lost its spark. That is why you will not be allowed to leave these quarters until everyone forgets about your pitiful existence. Until my Warriors can only remember how dignified the other Human females are and how worthy of our respect."

It feels like his eyes are about to dig a hole into my face. I tell myself it's the intensity of his stare that makes my eyes water. *I am not crying!* I am trying to find words that can hurt him back, but there aren't any. I can take his violence, his punishment, but not his disgust. He knows nothing! He has no right to judge me! No one does! I can't do this. I can't take his words or his disgust. He is too full of himself to notice he left the thing they call a fire blaster within easy reach. He will have to find himself a dignified woman because this trashy one has had enough of living. My wild emotions and searing pain give me strength and speed that surprises both of us. I reach the weapon first, only I didn't expect it would be so heavy. I know exactly how to use it as my father put together detailed manuals for his men about most Tarrassian weapons. I spent my time at the cabin devouring all the valuable information I could find. Too bad my father had no idea about their capacity to communicate telepathically. I don't doubt it any more.

His hand grabs my fingers holding the gun, just as I desperately try to point it at my chest. As he snatches it off me, I let go the trigger, and a laser-like hiss cuts through the air. I wait for the pain, but it's not coming. Maybe death is meant to be painless since life is nothing but excruciating. There is no pain but there is blood. Hot, rusty-colored blood, trickling down from his upper chest.

Did I do that? Did I just...?

"Zaan? I... do you need... are you...?" I can't finish any of my words as he grabs my wrists and brings them together behind my back. Something like a small electric impulse prickles my skin, and I realize the cuffs are now attached to each other in the tightest of binds. The more I try to release my hands, the more painful the hold becomes. I scream as one large hand grabs my mandibula and squeezes. My brain informs me he is about to break my jaw, and it will hurt. Only, he doesn't.

"That was a big mistake, Human," he tells me with a calm voice. His lack of anger is terrifying. He picks me up with a painful grip and lays me on a soft pile of furs. A bed, I realize. *No, no, no!* I try to kick with all my might, but he easily grabs my legs apart and positions himself above me. My hands are bound behind my back, and they hurt like mad because of the pressure of both my body weight and his, resting on top of them.

"I hate you! I hate you! I fucking hate you!" I scream, and I can hear my voice choked by tears.

"I know!" It's all he says as he removes his kilt. I can feel his huge, throbbing rod touching my skin, pressing into my inner thigh. What am I doing? I can't fight him. I was meant to pretend I wanted this. Like I did with the Moorri King. Like I did with all the other men on Earth. If I fight it, it means it's rape. Is it?

No, of course it's not rape. They are just trying to scare me. Tim is a loser, and so are his three little minions. My father is their superior. Surely they can't possibly think they can get away with it. Any minute now, they will stop and crack one of their stupid jokes nobody laughs at. I can hear the loud noise made by tearing clothes. The air conditioning of the storage room touches my skin. Am I naked? This can't be real. Is this a prank? I am underage, my father is their General, I am... Pain explodes behind my eyes. Did one of them just punch me in the face?

"Gianna?"

Is there something wrong with my eye? I can't open it any more, and the throbbing behind the socket makes me dizzy. I am trying to touch it, but I can't lift my hands. Is that blood I can smell? Whose blood is it? It can't be mine, right? A cold, painful chain digs into my skin. I open my mouth to tell them to stop, but cruel laughter erupts around me as one of them stuffs something into my mouth, telling me to suck it.

"Gianna? Gianna, open your eyes! Gianna!"

There is sharp pain in every part of my body. It hurts even more on the inside. They broke something on my right side. Is it a rib? One of them takes my hand out of the chain. Is it over? He kneels on it, and then he snaps it like a little twig. It sounds like one, too. Crack, Crack – more laughter.

"Please, please open your eyes! Breathe, my Lorra! You are safe. Please, come back to me!"

Is someone calling my name? Who is Lorra? Do I have two names? Are they here to save me? But then again what from? I am in my grandparents' orchard. I know because the smell of the orange flowers tickles my nostrils. There is no reason to be rescued. I like it here. It is safe, and I can pretend I am a butterfly, chasing the petals blown around by the soft sea breeze. Why do they keep calling my name? I don't want to leave my orchard. Am I lying on the grass? On the ground? Whatever it is, I don't want to leave it. It's warm, and it smells like oranges. I rub my face into it. It feels so safe, and it has a soothing beating like a heart. It is not the one in my chest, yet it is mine, just the same. A heart that only lives for me!

I open my eyes and take a deep breath. His scent fills my lungs. His heat is all around me, his lips in my hair, and his arms are rocking me gently. Where am I? What did he do to me? I don't move; I barely even breathe, trying to assess my predicament first. We are not on the bed any more. I think we are sitting in some sort of large chair. He is, anyway. I am straddling his lap, my front pressed to his, my legs dangling over each side of his thick thighs. I lift my face off his chest and look down. Naked! We are both naked, and his huge erection is trapped in between our bodies and…

"Lorra? Look at me! Eyes on me, beautiful!" he says, and his hands leave my waist to encase my face and keep it still. Golden eyes stare at me, and something breaks inside me. I can hear it so loudly, as if the entire world snapped in half. I don't know what to do with myself when the gold is gone. Now it's back I don't want it to ever go away again.

"Nothing happened; I didn't touch you, do you understand?" he says, searching my eyes.

Actually, I don't understand what he is saying. Is he lying? Did he put that big thing inside me? I wait to see if I can register any pain, but I don't. There is blood, though. A lot of it. Why is it copper? I am sure mine is red.

"I will get dressed and get away from you as soon as you understand you are safe. As soon as you breathe normally. Please, Lorra, can you try that?"

I am not entirely sure what he means. Am I not breathing? I nod in agreement, nevertheless, and take a deep breath of air. I only end up inhaling him since we are so close. It still works, and the pain in my chest subsides. Then I do it again and again until my brain feels less subdued by fog and my breathing evens.

"Well done. Good listening, Lorra," he says, and all of a sudden, I remember how much I hate him. His stupid rules, silly praises, the smell of his skin, the ridiculous golden eyes, his obsessive behavior, his smiles… I hate all of him. It probably shows on my face because his eyes fill with pain as he looks at me. Good! I want him to suffer!

"I will leave now and send someone who can help. It will be a very gentle and trustworthy female, is that okay? She won't hurt you. No one will ever hurt you again, my Lorra, do you understand?" he asks, and I nod just because I find it easier to agree to anything right now. "Before I go, I want you to tell me who it was," he says, and his fingers force my head up so he could look me in the eyes. I don't want to look at him, but I can't fight him. I can't fight anyone. "Who was it, Lorra?" What does he mean? Why is he so angry? It scares me! I try to move away, but he won't let go of my face. "Was it the Moorri King?"

He is crazy! What does he want from me? The Moorri King didn't hurt me. He saved me from him before anything happened. Did he forget?

"Humans. It was the Humans!" he says and gets us both up.

He wraps my naked body in a large fur and places me gently on the bed, lays a kiss on my forehead, then steps away. I hide my face into the soft, scented pillows, but I can hear him getting dressed, collecting his weapons then leaving the room.

15

—

GIANNA

"Will you please have something to eat, my Lady?" asks the alien woman yet again. She is like a broken record, her high-pitched voice grating my sensitive ears.

Everything about the world seems painful and extra sharp – the light, the scents, the touch of the soft bedding, like sandpaper scraping me raw. I just want to sleep; unfortunately, my body has had enough of that. That is all I have been doing for... not sure for how long. Two days? The room around me kept getting light, then dark, then something in between. I've been up a few times, with the help of the strange alien woman. Or girl, not sure about that one either.

She seems awfully young to me. She shouldn't be here, looking after a broken soul. She shouldn't see what that looks like. She helped me use the facilities, ran me a couple of baths, I think. At least that's what she called it. To me, it looked more like a pool than a bathtub. The water had a purple tint, and it smelled like the orange flowers of my childhood, of course. Why not? I refused food after each bath and rushed back to the safety of my bed. *His bed.*

Once again, I refuse to eat— not sure I could, anyway. I keep my head covered with a fur, not just to block her out, but to block everything out. The beauty of this room, the mesmerizing colors of the purple sunset, the new world around me trying to pull me out of my darkness. No matter how much I want to go to the large windows and look out, I won't allow it! This is not a holiday in a place that looks and smells like Heaven. This is a prison, and the shy alien woman is nothing more than a warden. I mustn't forget reality.

My brain and my wounded soul feel betrayed by my stupid body and its pragmatic needs. My stomach growls, and it hurts. It's squeezing and twisting, almost like it's trying to eat itself.

And then, there is that one pain I can't ignore. The mating marks hurt! Just like they do each time he is too far away. It is humiliating and cruel, reminding me I am forever connected to him. My body screams with the need to get out of bed and pace the floor. Anything to distract me from the dull pain in the marks on my arms and from the throbbing Sign on my forehead. I hate him so much! He hurts me even when he is not near me. I take a deep breath and pull myself up into a seated position. I am wearing a nightgown, but I had more decent outfits on during a lingerie photoshoot. The white robe-like gown is entirely see-through, and I don't understand what's the point of it. Unless you're meant to be a sex toy, of course. Stupid aliens! I pull the fur covering up to my chin and give my prison warden a stern look. Her long blue lashes flicker like mad over gorgeous purple eyes, and she looks like she is going to faint. Is that... fear?

"Do Humans eat Garrii?" she asks in that high-pitched voice. What? What does she mean?

"What's Garrii?" I ask, forgetting my self-imposed silence. I am shocked to hear my voice, it sounds broken and rough. My throat hurts a bit. Was I screaming in my sleep? No, I realize with dread. It wasn't in my sleep. For the first time, I had a nightmare while being wide awake. *Oh, no!* The memory of what happened comes crashing down on me. I gave him front seats to my tormented past. Is that what stopped him from raping me? Was it the thought that others got to do that first? Is he even more disgusted with me now?

"I am a Garrii. It's the name of my species, and I am quite sure I don't taste good," says the alien girl, pulling me out of my thoughts.

I watch her beautiful alien face, and I am sure I would probably smile if my face didn't feel as tight. She is terrified of me. She calls herself a Garrii, but my brain screams *Elf! My prison warden is an elf!*

Maybe that's what Garrii means. She is as tall as I am, equally willowy, but that's about all we have in common. Her skin is pinkish, no, peachy, maybe blueish? I stop wondering, as common sense tells me it is neither. It changes with her emotions, going through a hue of pastel colors. It's not very obvious; the change quite subtle, but there is nothing subtle about the glow. She glitters like freaking Tinker Bell. Looks like her, too. God, Yara would have loved this alien girl! I push the painful memory of the only friend I ever had away. The girl's bright blue hair reaches under her bottom in a sea of soft waves. It's beautiful, just like the rest of her. She's got the most perfect pink mouth, turned-up nose, and enormous purple eyes. She looks very much like an anime character except for the elf ears. They are really long, pointy, and stick out through the mass of blue hair. Even those strange appendages look beautiful on her.

Something uncomfortable makes my heart squeeze. He must have noticed how stunning this woman is. I quickly ignore where my mind is taking me and look around the room for something. Yes! I can see my tank top and daisy shorts nicely folded on a chair made of purple wood... Glowing purple wood. I ignore that too and stand up to retrieve my familiar clothes. My only belongings. I stagger a bit, my muscles weakened from too much sleep and hunger. I put my clothes on and curse when my shorts catch on the stupid tracking devices on my ankles. Couldn't even take them off during bathing. I was hoping the water would break them, but they still flicker green every so often. They cause chafing, but then again, maybe they are meant to. He wouldn't spare me any pain.

"My High Lady's dresses are..."

"Not interested!" I stop her with a snappy voice, and she takes a few steps back.

Let her wear pretty dresses, it's not my style. I briefly look at her lean, willowy body, showcased by a stunning blue dress. The corset hugs her small round breasts and tiny waist, then flares into a myriad of flowy fabric all the way down to the floor. A multitude of slits reveal stunning long legs with every step she takes.

He must be so pissed his gods paired him with me when something like her was on offer. I ignore the twist in my heart and focus on the one in my stomach. I hate the thought of food, but I don't think I have a choice.

"So, where is my meal?" I ask her, and a warning in my brain tells me I am acting like a proper bitch. I don't care!

"You don't mean me, do you, High Lady?" she asks, taking another step back.

Jesus! This again? I take a deep breath and return to my bed as I feel dizzy again.

"No, Humans don't eat people, so you are safe," I tell her with a mocking voice, but her obvious relief makes me feel guilty and stupid. She is not the enemy. I doubt she can be anyone's enemy. This girl is way more fragile than I am. Good to know it can even happen to the aliens.

Once her fear is gone, she leaves the room but returns quickly with a tray. I am grateful when I don't see any of those horrible things they are so keen on. Raw meat and chewie powder... ugh! A beautifully decorated bowl contains a thick steaming broth. Slices of warm bread, I hope, are neatly arranged around the bowl. The broth is blue, the bread is yellow, and I decide it is wise not to ask any details about the ingredients. I feel hunger and disgust in equal measures, but I have to eat. I don't really understand why. Wouldn't it be better if I die sooner? I mix the feather-light spoon in the broth and take a sip, trying to avoid the bits of meat inside. I am not vegan or vegetarian, but I don't think I want to eat blue meat either. Despite my hate relationship with food, my taste buds explode with pleasure. I get braver and try the bread. It is a bit sweet and spongy, but something is comforting about its texture – a bit like sourdough bread.

"My name is Ollianna," she says, watching me with wary eyes. I don't care about her name, so I ignore her. "You are very beautiful. Are all Humans beautiful? Well, I haven't seen the Queen, but people say her hair is made of light and her eyes are as gray as the Still Waters."

Great, I get a chatty prison warden! Just my luck! Her words finally sink in. Does she mean Sia? Is that who the King went for? Poor guy. She'll freeze his ass off.

"I am so happy you are eating, my Lady," she continues, utterly undeterred by my grumpy silence. "The High Commander said I must make sure you eat plenty. He will be very pleased with this."

And just like that, my appetite is all gone. I have had enough of eating, and I have had more than enough of her chatter.

"Should you be talking to me?" I snap, and she takes a step backward. "Didn't your precious Commander say those who interact with me will be punished, sent off Tarrassia, or whatever?"

She lowers her lashes over those beautiful eyes and looks a bit embarrassed.

"Well, yes he did, but you are his mate and our new Lady. We have to look after you. He will appreciate it when he calms down. Males say a lot of silly things when they are angry. Especially Tarrassian males. They have a bad temper," she says and gives me a small smile.

What is she saying? Will she or any of these people be willing to help me? Are they not afraid of him, then? I remember he mentioned his father and warned them not to seek his help. Maybe his father has more power than him?

"What happens if he finds out? He said you will be sent away. Is that not a bad punishment?" I ask, trying to wrap my head around it but careful not to give myself any false hopes. She takes my tray away with a sigh.

"Being sent away from Tarrassia is a very bad thing, my Lady," she says after placing it on a small wooden table. "Except for me and only a few others, there is no home to return to for most of the servants and guards. And the former slaves who still have a home planet left, are too scared to return. Others are simply too grateful to leave the Tarrassians."

Did she use to be a slave? I refuse to feel guilty for snapping at her. She is not my friend. I remember he explained about the slaves who couldn't be returned to their homes, so they were given jobs on Tarrassia.

"So, you do have a place to go back to," I say against my better judgment. I somehow know I don't want to hear her reasons for staying.

"Yes, my planet, Garria, is safe and under Tarrassian protection. I visit my family quite often," she says with a gorgeous smile full of love. Her canines are pretty long, but she even makes that look adorable.

"Why are you here then?" I ask because I am stupid like that.

"I want to serve the High Commander, of course. I could never leave him," she says, and her eyes glow with an intense purple.

There you go, Gianna. Now you know! She could never leave him. Stop asking stupid questions and focus on what matters! I admonish myself, ignoring all the things her answer did to me.

"Are you telling me you are willing to disobey his orders to help me?" I ask, and her skin starts flashing strange pastels.

"Well, there is no need to put it in that many words. Things don't have to be one thing or the other. They can be somewhere in the middle. My people don't like extremes much. That is a Tarrassian thing. Maybe Human, too," she adds, watching me warily.

Her preaching annoys the hell out of me. Isn't she Miss Perfect? I try to control my anger before I talk. I need allies, and I have to play my cards right. I have very little to cling on to here if any.

"Aren't you worried he will punish you and the other servants if you break his rules?" I ask as calmly as I can fake. Could they help me escape?

"No, not really," comes the unexpected reply. "All the servants and the guards in the Red Forest had been saved from slavery by the High Commander himself, at some point. He spilled his blood for us and even went against the Council's orders to save some of us. It is very unlikely he will send us away after all that trouble. And we don't follow the Commander's rules out of fear of punishment, High Lady," she says in an almost patronizing way. At least that's what it feels like to me.

"Oh, really? Is there any other reason why people follow rules?" I ask her with less contained anger.

"I don't know about other people, my Lady, but here we follow the rules because they keep us safe," she says, and I am honestly speechless.

I have to give it to him. This is priceless. So, half of these alien races, like the Noorranni and the Moorri, have slaves, the other half, like the Tarrassians, have paid servants. And then, there is him who has brainwashed minions, ready to do his bidding because he keeps them safe. Amazing stuff!

"Since you are not scared of him, would any of you remove my tracking devices?" I ask. No more crap!

"Oh, those are to keep you safe, my Lady. Some of the most vicious wild beasts of Tarrassia live in the Red Forest. At times, they are fearless and come close to our gardens," she tells me, and her face scrunches with fear.

"I see. Do you have tracking devices, Ollianna?" I ask her with a mocking voice, but I can hear the shaking in my speech that typically leads to crying. I won't do it in front of her. No more crying in front of any of them.

"No, my Lady. I never ever break the rules, so I don't need any."

That's it! I have fucking had it!

"Good on you, elf girl! Now get the hell out of my room and don't return until I say so. If you do, I will eat you, and I will start with your ears. They look delicious. Humans' favorite food is ear soup!" I shout, and she runs out like a blur, nearly tripping over her stupid dress.

That felt good. Petty, but good. I guess nobody is coming to the rescue – time to save myself or die trying.

16

ZAAN

"Enough!" I shout, and the anger in my voice makes the bickering stop. Finally! My Second and Third in Command have been at it for the last ten nanos since I returned to my ship.

"I say, vex the Humans!" starts Nodric all over again. "I hate the conniving little creatures! And what is all the fuss about their females? I find them very plain," he adds as if anyone ever doubted his dislike of the Human race.

"Yes, we know, Nodric. You are not one to keep a secret," replies Barin in his quiet, good-natured way. It drives Nodric mad, but he ignores his comment and tries to plead with me instead.

"High Commander... Zaan, listen to me, please! You cannot turn yourself in. The vexing Elders will make an example out of you. Think about your sire. He will have to vote against you. Do you know what that would do to him? The King said not to harm any vexing Humans. And you killed four of them. This is treason; you will get exiled! Please, let us cover it. Go to the Fourth Quadrant battle; they are in desperate need of your leadership. The Great Warrior never made it there. Probably that's too far from his vexing Human! Let me deal with this. I don't care if I have to kill all the Humans who witnessed it."

"Can you even hear yourself talk, Nodric?" asks Barin shaking his head. "There is footage of the incident. Humans all over the planet have seen it. He cannot hide! The sooner he faces the King, the better. There won't be an exile; Zaan has the Sign. No Elder would dare condemn someone who has our sacred mating marks. As for the King, he will never exile one of his Warriors."

"Vex the marks! The Sign must be cursed since it's the Humans who brought it back. And you need to remember I am your superior," says Nodric pulling his sword at Barin.

To my surprise, my usually good-natured and overly patient friend does the same.

"Out! Both of you!" I say and open the airlock for them as an invitation to obey my orders. I am too tired to argue with them. And my stupid wounds are taking forever to heal. Our blood can only speed up the self-healing process while we sleep, but I have hardly had any since I left her side. How could I, while those males were still breathing? Now, I can finally sleep. As soon as I do right by my King, that is. And get rid of these two.

"Second in Command, you will stay on Earth and carry on with the negotiations." I address Nodric with the tone he knows better than to challenge. "I want all the Resistance under control. There is a dangerous spike in the places called Russia and Australia. No punitive measures will be taken without consulting the King or the High General. I mean it, Nodric. You will keep your dislike of the Humans out of it!"

"Why can't Barin do it? Or anyone else who doesn't want to feed on Human blood," he says with a grunt.

"Because I said so," I tell him, and he takes a fist to his chest, pledging his obedience. He knows me well enough to stop before it's too late.

"The American Resistance is run by my female's sire," I tell him with a warning in my voice. "No one is to harm him. He is under home detention and not allowed contact with his people. If he gives you trouble, you will only ask my sire how to proceed. Not the King, not the Council. I want the Human General safe. Is that understood, Second in Command?"

"Yes, High Commander!" he says without any further comments.

"Healer." I address my oldest friend with a pained heart. This might be the last time I see him. "I want you in the Fourth Quadrant by the end of this span."

"Yes, High Commander!" he says, taking a fist to his chest.

I can feel his pain, mirroring mine. Nodric's one, too. They leave my ship quietly, trying to make it easier for me.

There is nothing easier about any of this. I look down at my body covered in Human blood, as well as my own. Time is of the essence here, and I can't pause for a proper clean. Still, I can't present myself like this in front of the Great Warrior, especially not in front of his Human mate.

I get under the boiling water for less than a few nanos, just to let the blood run off my body. My wounds will heal better if they are clean. The ones I got from the Human males are minor and have already started to knit. Vexing cowards, they are only able to cause damage to weaker beings. The injury my female caused will need a Healer at some point. Seeing it bleed every so often makes me feel better. I deserved it. And anyway, I would take anything she is willing to give me – even a chest wound. I press my throbbing forehead against the back wall of the cleanser's enclosure. My mind fills with the memory of having her in my arms, washing her soft body, her beautiful golden hair. Smelling her arousal for the first time. The way she was shaking with a desire; I thought it had been one-sided.

Despite how angry and betrayed I felt after she deceived me

yet again, I was never going to force myself on her. Not only because it is not the Tarrassian way, but because I knew consent was never going to be a problem. Her body would have reacted to my touch, craving it the way she did when we were last in this cleanser or when she slept in my arms.

Whatever reaction I expected, it wasn't that. Her screams, pain, and utter fear, while trapped in her head, will stay with me for the rest of my spans. I had seen it one too many times before. Many of the slaves I saved had been through that kind of abuse at the hands of the slavers. Most have never recovered, their minds broken, their souls shattered. What must it have been like for her, suffering that at the hands of her own kind, under her sire's care?

I considered killing the old Human male, but I could tell letting him live was a far greater punishment. I am no better than he is. I judged her when she needed trust and acceptance; I humiliated her when she needed to be cherished; I rushed her when she needed patience. It feels like I am getting all of this wrong. Even now, I am missing pieces, and I don't know where to find them. Perhaps I cannot fix this. My beautiful female hates me; she would rather see me dead than give herself to me. I would gladly give her what she wants, but I cannot. No matter how much she hates me, her life is connected to mine. If I die, she dies; if I am too far away and for too long from her, the Sign would eventually kill us. That is why I cannot let the Elders exile me for my mistake, worthy of an untrained Warrior.

I let my rage blind my better judgment. I am not sorry for killing the Humans, and I am most definitely not sorry for doing it in such a gruesome way. I used to wonder why the King would cause unnecessary carnage on the battlefields. It gave him the fierce reputation that freezes the blood of our enemies. However, to me, it seemed like unrequired violence. I understand now that rage is both consuming and liberating, and I do not regret my actions. I only regret not paying attention and not planning any of it, which is very unlike me. And to make matters worse, the vexing Humans had what they call *press people* around for a briefing.

Barin is right. The Council will not exile someone who has our long-lost Sign. They will just take the command of the Blood Fleet away from me. And as much as that pains me, my Lorra is my first priority. My only one! However, I don't think my mating marks and Sign can convince the Elders. Something is not right. The pain is expected when the mates are too far away, but this feels different. Like the life inside them is dying. I don't know what it means, but I know someone who might. He is also the only one who can help at this stage. The Great Warrior is my only chance, so I set my ship to *Jump* to the White Palace, in the Purple Forest of Tarrassia.

After landing permission on the Palace's pad is given, I wait impatiently to be escorted. The Great Warrior does not enjoy having visitors. He enjoys talking to them even less. My only hope is that things are now different since he is mated to one of the Humans. One I rescued. I hope that will weigh heavily in the balance. That and the other favor he owes me. I also hope it is the white-haired female who bears his mating marks. Reasoning with the foul-mouthed one might be a challenge.

The High Keeper welcomes me with a grunt and a look that tells me I am not welcome. I doubt anyone ever is. There is no coincidence the Keeper of the White Palace is just as grumpy as the Great Warrior. It is probably why he got the job. Kayon is a Neflay, and his species are known for their fierce loyalty and skill with weaponry. I've known Kayon ever since I was a small cub training in the Pits. If I remember correctly, he was never one of the rescued slaves. The Great Warrior's grandsire saved his son from the slaver's fighting pits when he was nothing more than a cub. Kayon and his family pledged their life to the Oria House in gratitude, and they have all lived on Tarrassia since.

His position is highly respected and revered by my people. He is the High Keeper of our sacred Oria birds. The white flocks live in the Purple Forest, and they choose our Elders at birth. Kayon also helps the Great Warrior train all the young Warriors. I still remember his harsh discipline. The two of them and my sire's guidance made me the Warrior I am today.

Kayon gives me a stern look that tells me he is both suspicious and wary of my dishevelled look and unannounced visit. As he escorts me to a private room, I try to keep my War Beast under control, as I can feel it lurking under my skin. I cannot fool Kayon. No one can. By the time we reach the large parlor, I have not one but seven large Palace Guards flanking me. I must look worse than I thought. Either that or news of my actions have already reached Tarrassia.

Kayon informs me I will have to wait as both the Great Warrior and his High Lady have not returned yet from a visit to the forest. It is strange, considering the late hours. He gives my weapons a wary look, but he knows better than to ask me to hand them in. I am still the vexing High Commander of the Blood Fleet, so he just excuses himself instead and leaves me alone with my torment.

It is not lost on me he referred to Tannon as the Great Warrior. Perhaps there is no hope here, and I should have gone straight to the High City, handed myself in.

Tannon is only seven rotations older than I am. Still, he taught me everything I know about fighting and especially about controlling my War Beast. He is the strongest and the most skilled Warrior I know. He is also the only Tarrassian who prefers to fight alone. He belongs to no unit and only follows the King's orders, if any. He is more than able to take down entire armies by himself. His many scars speak of his bravery. Sadly, they also put most Tarrassians off, especially the females. My people are obsessed with beauty and perfection, and Tannon is neither. The scars are a trademark of the Warriors, and I am no stranger to them. But when you fight all your battles alone like Tannon does, one tends to accumulate a lot more.

I know he hides behind them, just like he hides behind the wild head and facial fur he never trims. He is Tarrassia's only half-breed ever, and his story is one of pain and injustice. Not something my people are willing to face or accept too often. Tarrassians would rather pretend misfortune and sorrow never happen. Tannon's mother's story pains me now more than ever before. No female should have to go through that, and unfortunately, it happens all too often and in every galaxy.

The High Lady Oria was kidnapped and raped by a former slave. My predecessor had rescued Tannon's sire, if he is even worthy of that title, from the most ferocious fighting pits. He was a massive beast-like creature who couldn't talk, and the rumor goes he wasn't entirely sentient. By the time they found him and killed him, the poor Lady Oria was already heavy with cub. The brave female lived long enough to give birth to him, then she took her own life. The pain broke her sire's mind, and he chased his end in reckless battles. His mate and Tannon's grandmother died of sorrow soon after. Left at such a young age without a family, Tannon was raised by his aunt, the Queen, and the White Palace servants.

Considering all the unfortunate circumstances of his upbringing and how our people treat him, it is no surprise he refused his rightful title. Tannon was chosen at birth by the Oria birds to become our High Elder. That is the highest position any Tarrassian can ever have. The High Elder is one of the three Astrals, a god. His powers are far greater than any other Tarrassian's, and his ruling is above the King or the other Elders. His voice is above all our laws. Yet, Tannon refused to take his seat in the Council. He even refused the title of High Master, even though he is in charge of the Training Pits. I am not sure he ever officially accepted the Great Warrior's title, which is not even a Tarrassian thing. He earned it in battle, and that's how all the galaxies refer to him now.

It is very unusual for Tannon to stay on Tarrassia for more than a couple of spans and even less usual to stay away from a good fight. Now he is doing both, so I was hoping things might have changed. Sadly, Kayon did not refer to him as the High Elder. At least my visit here won't be in vain. Whoever his mate is, she will protect my female.

17

—

ZAAN

I pull angrily at my hair and beard, and then I pause, realizing I called them as she does. *Hair. Beard.* Time is running out on me and I need to hand myself in. My sire won't live with the shame otherwise. Just when I am about to lose all control over my temper, I can feel the vibration of the Great Warrior's steps. He is angry. I cannot blame him. He will get even more enraged when he hears what I've done.

Despite all the torment inside my mind and pained hearts, everything else disappears for a few nanos. Not sure what surprises me most as I try to understand what I am looking at. Tannon's skittish mate hides most of her tiny body behind him, only peeking at me from the shelter of his wide arm. Huge cub-like blue eyes watch me warily, and one little pale hand pushes stubborn locks of red hair out of her face. Is this his mate?

Tannon is the biggest and scariest looking of all Tarrassians. Yet, he is paired to the tiniest and the most fragile of the females we rescued. That doesn't make much sense but mated indeed they are. It is not only because of the bright pink marks on their arms or because of the identical Signs on their foreheads but because of how they interact. There is no hiding a connection that strong. They remind me of my parents and of everything I will never have. The fact they both smell of each other's mating fluids only makes it more obvious. It is no wonder Tannon looks like he wants to kill me, considering I most likely interrupted a very intimate moment. Also, he must know I can smell it on her, which triggers all the protective instincts of a Tarrassian male.

"Is Gianna safe?" the female asks straight away, her voice just as cub-like as the rest of her. Her distress makes him react as expected. I hope he doesn't kill me before I even ask my favor.

"Yes, High Lady. She is on Tarrassia," I rush to reassure her before he takes my head off.

"What is the meaning of this, High Commander?" Tannon asks in his usual gruff voice.

I wish I could have the time to ponder my words and act wisely. My mate's life depends on this, so I don't hide behind polite words. He will be angry, but he will understand.

"I once saved the life of a Garrii female you treasure very much, Great Warrior. I believe she is mated to your Healer," I tell him, but I curse myself as I hear my words out loud. I hope he knows me well enough to understand this is me asking a favor, not making a threat.

Our dated laws do not allow Tarrassians to mate for life with other species. At least that's how it was before the Humans. Our harsh laws also say no other species are allowed to procreate on Tarrassia. All the former slaves are fitted with devices that stop them from conceiving. Here, in the Purple Forest, both laws are ignored. Some mated servants have cubs, and the Tarrassian Healer is mated to a Garrii female I saved. They also have a cub of their own. Except for Tannon and his loyal people, Ollianna and I are the only ones aware. Ollianna, because she is the sister of the Healer's mate and me because I saved them both from certain death.

"You said my bravery on that span was worthy of a favor, and I shouldn't hesitate to ask for it," I add for good measure, but I can see he never took my words as a threat. His mate did. There is a worry in her eyes, so she must also be aware of what's hiding in the Purple Forest.

"Ask, High Commander," he says while hugging his female closer to him in a reassuring gesture.

"I did something vexing stupid, Great Warrior," I start, pulling at my head fur as if that could stop my torment. "I am not sorry for what I did, and I will not apologize to anyone for it. I am only sorry I've done it in the open. With witnesses."

"What did you do, Zaan?" he asks with a sigh. The coldness in his voice is gone, replaced by the care I had the honor to experience many times. Even though he is only a few rotations older than most of my Warriors and me, Tannon is like a sire to all of us. Maybe because he is an Astral after all. He can't help himself from being protective.

"I might have killed a few Humans," I say and tense as I hear his mate gasp. He pulls her even closer, bends down to reach her forehead, and places a reassuring kiss on it.

"In battle, High Commander?" he asks.

"Not exactly... There is no official battle happening on Earth. On paper, they signed their surrender. In practice, I don't think Humans have a clue what surrendering means. Anyway, I killed those males for personal reasons. As you well know, the King said no Humans were to be harmed. I disobeyed my King and the Council, and I returned to Tarrassia to accept my fate."

He runs his fingers through his head fur, no different than I do.

"Zaan, you should have known better. You are the most disciplined Warrior. It's your high ethics, strict rules, and discipline that keep in check the unruly Blood Fleet. You are the only Commander who has ever managed that, and you are nothing but respected by everyone. The King's rule was there for a reason. The best way to prove we are not invaders is not to kill anyone. How many witnesses were there?"

"It was shown on something they call *Fox News*," I say, and his female gasps again, covering her mouth with her tiny hands. She knows. Of course she does; she is Human.

"He means everyone on Earth has seen it, more or less," she explains to him with a skittish voice.

"I will speak to the King and ask for clemency on your behalf, High Commander. I think you know well enough, the King will be on your side, but that will not help much. The law is there to be respected." He tells me what I already know.

"The King's will cannot change the Council's decision on this matter," I tell him, and I can feel his tension. He knows what's coming, and he is not happy about it. "The Elders will vote against him, my own sire included. I shamed him, and he would not hesitate to choose his duty as an Elder over me, no matter his pain."

"Yes, they will vote against the King, Zaan," says Tannon, "but I will help you build a case for yourself. Perhaps your remarkable achievements and your service to our Mother Planet will be enough to avoid exile. However, you will lose your title as High Commander; you will lose your Warriors and everything you fought so hard for."

"Right now, I don't give a vexing thing about my title, my Warriors, my reputation, or my life, Tannon. I only care about my female," I tell him, and this time I cannot control my rage. Tannon doesn't react; he knows very well my anger is not aimed at him. "If they exile me to the outskirts of the galaxy, I won't be able to protect her."

"Protect her from what?" asks the little female, and I look at her with tormented eyes.

"From herself…" I tell her the truth.

"Zaan, is the Human female hurt? Your marks are faded, and they shouldn't be if she is on Tarrassia, as you said."

Tannon's voice has an unmistakable accusatory note. So, he noticed. Of course he did. His own marks are full of life, and his Sign speaks of the blessing of having a willing mate.

"She is not hurt," I reply with a sigh. "She is in my father's house, in the Marni Forest. It's best you hear from me, Tannon. She is there against her will." It feels like my newly awakened heart is bleeding. No male should ever have to say those words.

"Why is that, Zaan?" asks the little red female, her round blue eyes watching mine closely for the truth. So, I give it to her.

"She won't do anything I ask willingly."

"Did you hurt her?" she insists on hearing all the cursed truth.

I watch with a heavy heart how she laces her tiny fingers with his and leans on his arm for comfort. *Willingly.*

"I did not hurt her physically if that is what you mean, High Lady," I tell her and lower my eyes because I can't bear to look at them and their happiness any more. "She is hurt because my existence alone is what hurts her the most. If not for the Sign, I would have removed myself from her life already. She wants nothing more than for my life to end, and I would happily give her that. Because of the Sign, I cannot. If I die, she dies. If they exile me, the Sign will slowly kill us both. That is why I am asking for your help, Great Warrior. The King's ruling cannot outvote the Elders on matters of our Sacred Law. The ruling of the High Elder can." I hold my breath as the silence in the room feels like it could crash the walls in on us.

"You are turning into a very reckless male, High Commander," Tannon tells me with a cold voice, the friendly tone all gone. "You are talking about things that are not yours to talk about. And you do it in front of my mate, without even wondering if she is aware. I could easily run you through my sword, for that alone."

I am a vexing idiot! I never make mistakes like these. I never forget myself, I always think about the details, I always… I've messed up everything!

"It is okay, Zaan," says the female with a kind voice. "I was already aware; no harm was done here," she adds, looking at Tannon with an accusatory stare. She pulls her hand out of his and takes a few steps away from him.

"I cannot help you, High Commander," says Tannon trying to reach for his female, but she pulls away. His torment mirrors mine, now. "There is no High Elder on Tarrassia, and there won't be one until the Oria birds choose again," he says to me but without taking his pleading eyes off his female. It is strange to see a male feared by all beings looking so vulnerable.

"I am sorry, I thought perhaps…" I stop myself as there isn't anything left to say. His determination tells me this subject is closed. His female gives me an apologetic look, and her big blue eyes water as she looks at me. It reminds me of what I have to do next.

"My apologies, Great Warrior, I meant to cause no inconvenience. I am just trying to keep my mate safe. I know you understand," I tell him, and he silently nods. "Can I please ask for a favor from the High Lady, Great Warrior?"

"Please call me Natalia, and of course you can," she replies before he gets to. She ignores his growl and refuses to look at him.

"Can you please allow Gianna to come live with you? She hates living in my house, anywhere near what's mine…" I take a deep breath, trying to push the pain away. "I am afraid she will do something silly and endanger herself again, just to get away from me. The Purple Forest has always been a sanctuary for those in need. Please offer her the protection of House Oria."

"Of course, we will shelter Gianna," she says with glowing eyes full of care. This time she does look at Tannon, and he nods in support of her decision.

He asks her to retreat so he can talk to me about a private matter. As Natalia says her soft goodbye to me, she looks like she wants to give me a hug, and I pray to the Astrals she doesn't. He will kill me over that! Luckily, she just hugs him instead, which is enough to make all his tension and anger over my actions dissipate. What would it feel like to have my female hug me like that? *Willingly*. I will never know...

"Your marks are faded, Zaan, and they shouldn't be. You are not that far away from your mate. The Elders will not like it, and that is the only defense you have," he says after she leaves. Always a straightforward male.

"I do not know why, Tannon. Other than she hates me, of course," I add with a bitter sigh. "Is that enough to dim our mating marks?" I ask without expecting an answer. However, to my surprise, I can see on his face he knows why. Just as I am about to ask, he stops me with a warning look.

"Leave it with me, Zaan," he says and places a heavy hand on my shoulder. "What you must do now is travel to the High City and hand yourself in with honor. I will have the High Fortress Healer waiting for you. That wound needs to be sealed properly," he says, pointing at my chest. "Is that from the Humans you killed?"

"No, it is from my female. She used my fire blaster," I say, and I can see the surprise in his strange purple eyes. No other Tarrassian has eyes that color, and his were the same as mine, last time I saw him.

I hope he doesn't ask about my female's reasons. But of course, he does.

"What did you do?"

"I tried to force mating, and she wasn't willing." I tell him the truth because he deserves to know.

"And did you?" he asks, and I can see his muscles starting to grow and his eyes turning white. His War Beast is about to tear me apart.

"No, I did not force myself on her. And it was not because she had injured me," I reply and allow his eyes to look into mine and see I speak the truth. His War Beast slowly retreats.

"I will travel to the High City on the next span," he says with a sigh. "I will explain to the King, and you should prepare for his wrath. Once that's over, he will give you his full support and enrage all the Elders in the process. That is why I will have the High General deal with your case instead. He is your direct superior, so that makes sense anyway."

Sadly, Tannon is not aware of the personal history I share with the High General, and I can't tell him either. It is not my secret to share. This is probably the best chance the High General will ever get to silence me forever. I am the only one who knows what kind of monster hides behind the cold, polished appearance of Tarrassia's most honored General.

"Thank you, Great Warrior," I reply instead. "Please, look after my treasured mate," I say, and he silently takes a fist to his heart as a promise I know he will never break.

18

GIANNA

The pain wakes me up from yet another nightmare. They had stopped altogether during the last couple of years only to come back with a vengeance after being taken from Earth. Especially after what *he* did to me. This time, the nightmare seemed a better escape than a reality where everything hurts. The stupid marks on my arms give a deep-bone, dull kind of pain. I suspect this is what severe rheumatic pain might feel like. The cursed thing on my forehead gives me a constant migraine. But the most intense pain comes from my bloodied ankles.

After the stupid alien woman had made herself lost, I decided to see for myself how effective these devices were. I expected the heavy wooden doors of my bedroom, *his* bedroom, to be locked, only they weren't. There were two huge guards outside my door, and I could see two more down the corridor. They are all absolutely identical, like clones, their appearance only adding more layers to the confusion inside my fuzzy brain. Maybe they are clones, but I was more worried about their size. They are not Tarrassians, so must be former slaves, I guess. They have large gray wings folded behind their wide shoulders, deadly-looking horns pointing forward, and the biggest, ugliest feet I have ever seen. They all looked nervously at each other but unanimously decided not to stop me. They didn't even break position, and that should have been warning enough for a wiser woman. I kept walking with my head held high all the way to the end of the corridor. My wrist devices started to constrict even before the MI gave the warning. That fucking asshole! He said I will be warned before the trackers turn on me. By that, he meant the stupid cuffs on my ankles went for blood while the MI was still talking. My feet got pulled against each other like magnets and I more or less jumped back to the safety zone.

I need to plan better. I can't walk around with broken bones. Luckily, I didn't get any last evening, but by the time I made it back to my room, I left a long trail of blood behind me. The cuffs broke my skin, and since I am a useless Human with no self-healing powers, now I woke up to the consequences of my actions. A bath would have helped last night, but I had no idea how to make the pool fill with water, and I refused to ask the alien *Pageant Queen* for help. God, I sound like Jade!

I couldn't use the shower either, because it's a death trap and reminds me of other things I hate even more than death. So, I went to sleep in a puddle of my own blood, hoping I would get better by morning. I guess having Tarrassian mating marks is not enough to make me one of them. Or maybe things like self-healing only happens after sex, mating, whatever. Well, that didn't materialize, and I stupidly wonder what stopped him. Did my trip down memory lane remind him there have been others before? Or was it all the crap he read about me? I must be out of my mind wondering what stopped an asshole from raping me. *Way to go, Gianna!*

It is early morning. I know by now, the sunrise bathes everything in a bright purple hue. I can hear birds and a multitude of strange animal noises from outside the large open windows. A soft lilac glow comes from the furniture in my room. I think it's fluorescent, and it was obviously carved from the trees outside. The same glow comes through the windows at night. Why do I care? Once again, I chastise myself for thinking about the beauty of this place. This is not a holiday. I don't care what's outside or how beautiful this room is, or what it smells like. This is a prison!

Despite my poor-quality sleep, I obviously need better-trained senses. Someone brought a tray with fresh food, and there is even a long flowy Tarrassian dress prepared for me on a nearby chair. I wish I'd had scissors to show my appreciation for the dress. At least I put the fear of God, or Astrals, whatever, in the *Pageant Queen*, and she has kept her distance.

I force myself to eat a sickly-sweet piece of fruit or alien spiky cucumber, not sure what it is. There are plenty of other foods on the tray, but my stomach twists with anxiety, and I pass everything else. My daisy shorts are really loose on my waist, which means I've lost weight. I probably look like a bag of bones. No wonder he didn't want to finish what he started. Maybe I can die of starvation after all.

I clean myself the best I can with water from the huge sink. My white top and shorts have bloody fingerprints all over them, most likely from my earlier failed attempt at an escape. Who cares? There is no way I will wear a Tarrassian dress. I know these are his quarters, and there will be plenty of those oversized shirts in his wardrobe, but I would rather walk around naked. They will smell like him, feel like him... Ugh, just no!

I should probably clean my sore ankles, and the dry blood in between the cuffs and my raw skin. What if that triggers them to constrict? And why does it hurt so much? It's not a broken bone type of pain. Could it be an infection? Who does this to someone they are meant to be mated to? I hate him so much!

I suddenly realize there is more pain in my arms besides the one caused by the marks. Unknowingly I have started scraping at them. Back to square one. Everything I fought so hard to overcome is returning. The nightmares, the anorexia, the self-harming. But the worst of all must be the tears. That never happened before. I just don't cry! I don't ever feel lonely, I don't ever wish to be held, I don't ever want to be loved! Before I get to think about it, I pull the large glass doors open and step outside. I need air! *I mustn't think!*

The sun is blinding at first, and I blink, trying to adjust my eyes. Strangely enough, the weather is far from hot. It feels and even smells like a warm but crisp fall day. I remember it used to be my favorite season. There is a small terrace edged by beautiful ornamental plants, leading to large stairs. Just like the house they are made of smooth silk-like metal. Everything reflects in their mirror-like surface and as the breeze moves the trees around, the stairs look alive. They go down to a narrow strip of garden that wraps around the residence as far as I can see.

I can't call this place a house or even a mansion. It's too large for that. I don't really know what it is. The garden ends abruptly where the forest starts, but there is no hedge or fence between them. What happened to the supposed dangerous beasts that live in the woods? Shouldn't they be kept away? These aliens are full of shit! There are, however, guards. All the same species as the ones outside my bedroom. They line the edge of the forest, as far as one can see. Haven't these people heard of fences?

I go down the stairs, and my ankles start to bleed again. I wait for the MI's warning, but that's not it. It's only the chafing of the cuffs against my raw skin causing more bleeding. I keep going until I reach the narrow strip of garden, taking one careful step at a time, waiting for the devices to kick off. The winged guards look at each other, but they don't try to stop me. Right, that's why I am tagged like a criminal; they don't even need to intervene. I ignore them back and focus on the house instead.

I can't see much of it from this close. Is it all made of… metal? It looks exactly like the material their ships are made of. It is smooth, reflective and it has a coppery glow. It mirrors the sky and the forest and… it's beautiful! Like a mirage. It makes me forget myself and my circumstances for a while, and that is refreshing. I take a few steps back, tilting my head and trying to see what I am looking at. I think there must be at least one other floor above my rooms. The ceilings are enormous but surely not enough to… I keep walking backward, trying to get a better view of the house.

The sharp voice of the MI seems to be coming from everywhere, including my own body. It all happens too fast, and a deep pain goes all the way up, deep into my hips, taking my breath away. I command my legs to move back towards the house, but the pain is overwhelming, and it feels as if someone has taken a baseball bat to my ankles. Too late. I can't return to the safety perimeter. There is no point fighting the pain, or my circumstances. I wonder why I keep doing it. Why don't I just let go? I collapse to the ground covered in soft reddish grass that matches my blood.

Suddenly, there is a lot of noise and activity around. I look up in fear. A massive… orc is coming down the stairs from my bedroom. He looks vicious. Huge. Menacing. Entirely clad in a tight black leather outfit, with spiky shoulder pads and large black boots. His big head is bald and shiny, and his larger than life body looks humanoid despite the Hulk-like size. The orc face, however, is as alien as it gets. He is mesmerizing and terrifying at the same time. Two large tusks tremble with rage as he runs down the stairs.

I realize with relief his anger is not aimed at me, but at my guards and even at the *Pageant Queen* who is running all flustered behind him. Is she glowing yellow? I hope that means she is sick. The orc man, alien, whatever he is, grabs me in his arms and runs back up the stairs, depositing me gently on my bed. For someone that big and scary, his touch is almost feather-like. I don't know why I expected pain. He also smells incredibly nice. Like pine and fresh grass and there is something weirdly comforting about his proximity. He pokes gently at my ankle devices and turns an angry face towards Ollianna. He growls at her, and she covers her ears, letting out a sharp noise. I would probably laugh if not for the excruciating pain.

"Take them off, female!" he shouts at her, and her body starts flashing shades of blue.

"I don't know how to, High Keeper. Only the High Commander has the combination," she tells him from the furthest corner of the room. She is terrified of him. Maybe elves and orcs don't get along. I am not even sure I am awake. This new alien world still feels like a long dream I am yet to wake up from. The throbbing pain in my ankles tells me this is all very real. Did I break a bone this time? It is hard to tell. The pain is everywhere.

"High Lady," says the orc person crouching next to my bed so I can look him in the eyes. They are a bit beady and pitch black, but not that alien. However, those tusks so close to my face... not sure about that. "I am the High Keeper of the White Palace, the Oria birds and Master of the Untried but you can call me Kayon. I am here to take you to the Purple Forest. You have been given sanctuary by the Great Warrior and his High Lady. You are now under my care, and no harm will come to you," he says, shouting the last part in anger, but I realize he has already left my side and is yelling at the *Pageant Queen*. She looks about to faint, and I hope she falls flat on her perfect face.

I am positive the Great Warrior is one of the two Tarrassians who mated with one of the girls. Am I being rescued? Has one of the girls managed to convince her man to help me? This orc man, alien, must have power. We are surrounded by guards, but none followed us in here. Not to mention, they all look terrified of him. Maybe he can get me out of here.

"You are a Garrii," he points out at her, and it almost sounds like an insult. "You can reach the minds of all beings."

"Yes, that's right," she says with a shaky voice. "No need to get upset now. I will reach the mind of the High Commander and ask him for the combination," says the *Pageant Queen* with a shaky voice.

"You will do no such thing, female," shouts the orc again. Kayon, I correct myself. I know he is my only hope right now, but I find him really scary. Using his name might humanize him a bit. Oh, what am I saying? He's got tusks... This is bad. I don't like tusks. I am losing my mind. I think the pain makes me feel funny. My vision is a bit clouded. Am I crying? God, I hope not.

"Why not? You said I could..." starts Ollianna, but he interrupts her with a terrific growl.

"You will not disturb the High Commander. He cannot accept any form of communication right now," says Kayon with another shout. I think he likes shouting.

"What does that mean? Where is he? Is he okay?" she asks the same things I want to know.

What do I care? I don't! And what business does she have to be worried about other women's men?

"Not your problem and stop wasting time, female. The High Lady is bleeding, and the devices must come off now!"

"But what can I do?" she asks him, looking at my bloodied ankles with a look of sorrow on her beautiful face.

"The High Commander would have shared important information such as this with one of his Warriors," answers Kayon, who looks like he's thinking out loud. "It is a rule installed by the High Commander himself. All vital information must be shared with at least one other, in case of an emergency," he says.

I see I am not the only one at the receiving end of Zaan's

stupid rules. And what does Kayon mean by emergency? Could it be that the injury I caused him...? *No! I do not care!*

"Shall I reach out to the Second in Command?" asks Ollianna with a small voice and eyes cast down.

"Commander Nodric would gladly get rid of all the Human females if he could, I doubt the High Commander would have shared this with him," says Kayon.

Tarrassians are so charming. Nodric sounds like a total gentleman. I realize I think of stupid things to stop myself from a full-on panic attack. I know the devices are not constricting any more, but it sure feels like it. *I want them off! I want them off!*

"I know, my Lady; they will come off shortly," says Kayon with kindness in his voice. Did I say that out loud?

He turns the kindness back into growling and shouting when he addresses Ollianna.

"Reach the mind of the Third in Command," he barks at her. "The Blood Fleet's Healer is the High Commander's oldest friend. I trained those two vexing fools ever since they were cubs, and even then, they were inseparable."

"No!" comes the unexpected answer. The shrieking answer, to be precise. What does she mean no? Is the mask off? Coming clean about how much she wants me out of her way, I see. Her precious High Commander is all hers, for what I care!

I can see Kayon advancing on her like a predator, and my protective instinct kicks in, no matter how much I dislike her. It was the main reason I wanted to become a Marine, to protect the weak. Little did I know, I was the one in need of protection. I was the weak one. My heart squeezes when he grabs her by her upper arms and lifts her up, smashing her against the wall. Her feet dangle in the air, and she makes strange noises of distress.

"Put her down, Kayon. Now!" I say firmly, despite the choking pain. To my surprise, he does.

Ollianna runs away from him and comes near me as if seeking my protection. Great!

"I am sorry, High Lady," she says with a voice full of pain. She keeps twisting her long fingers like a stress-relief gesture. "I can't reach out to him. Anyone but him, please don't make me. There must be some other Warrior who knows the combination," she says, and her body flashes so many colors it's giving me a headache.

Is she talking about Barin? The only nice alien in this entire freaking world? Why would anyone try to avoid Barin?

"I am sorry, High Lady," says a very determined Kayon, approaching Ollianna again. "I know Human females are fragile and don't like violence. The Great Warrior gave me a task, and I will not fail because of this silly Garrii. She will do as she is told! You can look away if it makes it easier."

I try to sit up and give him a piece of my 'fragile human mind', but a sharp pain in my ankles makes me scream before I can stop it.

"Oh, no! I am so sorry," says Ollianna rushing to take my hand in hers. Her skin is cold and soft, and it has an instant feel of comfort to it. "I will do it, my Lady. I won't let you suffer like this."

She closes her big purple eyes, but I can see her pupils moving and twitching under her eyelids. Her body glows like I haven't seen it before, and the most beautiful shade of gold takes over her skin. Her long fingers keep pulling at each other, and I watch, fascinated by how close they are to tearing her skin open. Is she in distress? Eventually, she opens her eyes but doesn't look at any of us. She starts enumerating a series of letters and numbers to Kayon, and he quickly releases my torture devices from hell. The skin does look infected, especially on my left ankle. I don't get to think much about it as Kayon lifts me back into his arms, and I carefully observe the spikes on his shoulder pads. The last thing I want now is to lose an eye.

"Do you need to pack anything from here, my Lady?" he asks me, looking around.

All I have left in this world are a cropped top and a pair of frayed shorts, both covered in my blood. No, nothing here belongs to me. As he takes me out of the room, I look at Ollianna, wishing I could stop acting like a bitch for a moment. Her eyes are still cast down, and she seems just as broken as I feel.

19

—

GIANNA

Every minute in Kayon's presence makes him less alien. Something about him. My brain almost says fatherly, but then again, I wouldn't know since my own father never quite fit that description. He takes me to a ship that looks nothing like the ones I've seen before. He calls it a low-flying craft. It is probably the closest thing to a flying saucer. Only space for two chairs inside the shiny interior. There is a hard floor, but other than that, all the external walls and the ceiling are made of glass. Probably a good thing as the view distracts me from thinking. The pain does too.

"The White Palace's Healer will take care of those wounds, High Lady," says Kayon without even looking my way. He pilots the craft manually, and his eyes are focused on the navigation panel. Kayon is very intuitive. Not the first time he has noticed my discomfort.

"Please, call me Gianna. The pain is not that bad," I lie, but he doesn't say anything. "Is it far where we're going?" I ask without purpose. I don't really care. After the first rush of hope,

I remembered there is nowhere to go. I am marked as property of the High Commander, as he once kindly mentioned. Always to be returned to sender. Owner, in this case.

"Just over a nano rotation away, or a Human hour, as the High Lady of my House would say," he answers.

That confirms what I already knew. The Tarrassian they call the Great Warrior is mated to one of the girls. Is that a willing thing, I wonder? For whatever stupid reason, I would have liked it to be Sia, the one waiting for me at the White Palace, but I already know she is mated to the King. Maybe because I am more familiar with her than the other two.

Whoever this woman is, would she have any power to help me?

"Is your High Lady... doing well?" I ask a stupid question. I'd rather pass for foolish and harmless. Kayon is fiercely loyal to his master; that much is obvious. Until I know what I am dealing with it is best to play it down.

"The High Lady is doing well, just causing a lot of vexing trouble, as usual," he says, and his tusks tremble with indignation.

Definitely Jade! At least I don't have to wonder about the consensual part. If it comes with a dick, then Jade is willing.

I didn't really expect a white palace, but that is exactly what I can see ahead. It is huge and blinding white. Unlike everything else I've seen around, it is made of gleaming white stone. It stands out like a diamond in the middle of that alien forest. There is no other name to describe the gigantic trees or how their purple canopy reaches out deep into the violet sky. Despite the alien look here there is no high-tech or even modern feel about this Palace. It seems as ancient as the world. Despite my determination to not get impressed with my prison planet, there must be some wonder on my face, as Kayon feels the need to explain.

"The Purple Forest is sacred to the Tarrassians," he says with pride in his strong voice. "It is the home of the Oria birds.

They choose the Elders as soon as they are born. Somehow, they know who will be worthy; they can see the future. The Oria are wondrous creatures, and I am their Keeper," he adds, which explains why he is so proud.

I don't say anything because I don't care about any of it. This is not my home, nor is it a holiday. It's a prison!

On one side of the Palace, the wall looks like a flower growing huge petals. As we approach, I realize they are landing pads. One of them moves out, further than the others, and becomes larger and larger the closer we get. Tiny yellow and green lights turn the floor of it into a sea of color before the underbelly of our craft shadows it. There wasn't even as much as a jolt as Kayon landed. I would give anything to learn how to do that. The freedom that may give one… Not that I will ever know. Here women only pop oversized furry babies and wear stupid flowy dresses. Oh, and follow the *rules*. Let's not forget about that. On second thoughts, maybe Tarrassians are better than my people. At least the aliens say it like it is. They don't pretend that women have rights or power just because there is a quota or they have to be politically correct.

I refuse Kayon's offer to carry me. My ankles' skin is completely shredded and swollen, but no broken bones, so I will walk. The pain was never a deal-breaker for me. Lack of control is, so there is no way some big alien is carrying me around like a damsel in distress. Kayon doesn't ask again. Instead, he gives me what I think might be a smile. As if he approves of my stubbornness. Hard to tell with those tusks. For whatever reason, I feel at ease around him, just like I did with the Blood Fleet's Healer. We walk for a while, and I am trying to keep up with Kayon's long legs. I can tell he is slower on purpose, but my feet are not doing great. I also have to make sure I don't slide in my own blood. Why is there so much of it? A good excuse to look down as we encounter many curious eyes. Kayon growls at most, and they scurry away. It is not lost on me; some leave a slimy trail. And here I was, worried about my bloodied footprints making a mess.

We enter a huge dining hall; not sure since I am trying not to look much. The smell of food, the clatter of dishes and cutlery seems to indicate breakfast is a big deal. There is a flurry of activities; I can hear and feel many beings around. I can tell there is a very lively feel about this place, even without looking.

I stop dead in my tracks as I hear the child-like voice, dipped with a slight Russian accent. Natalia! Just great! How is she going to help me? She probably hopes I am here to save her whiny ass. Only, I can't. And if that creature standing next to her is her mate, no one can save her. He is bigger, scarier, and more scarred than all the other species I've encountered so far. The first word my brain forms is *Monster*. And I thought my Karma was shit. Little, terrified-of-monsters Natalia, got paired with one. Their bright mating marks and the identical Sign on their foreheads confirm he is indeed her mate. Or jailer. An angry-looking bite marks her tiny shoulder.

She wears one of those ridiculous Tarrassian dresses, just as pink as her Sign. I swear to God, these dresses look like they were made for slutty princesses if there was ever such a thing. Her large boobs are pushed to the brim into the very low-cut décolletage. The pasty and slightly freckled shoulders are also exposed. He must be very proud that anyone can see his fangs' mark on her delicate skin. Why is she holding his hand like that, leaning into him? It almost feels as if she is more scared of me than she is of him.

"Oh, Bozhe… Gianna, I am so sorry. I didn't think there would be blood. The Healer will see you shortly. We prepared a beautiful room for you. It used to be Tannon's mother's room, and you will be very comfortable there. No one will hurt you anymore," she says with a voice already trembling with tears.

Her big blue eyes stare at my bloodied ankles with a look full of sorrow and despair. Why does she care? She doesn't even know me.

"It doesn't look to me like you are that safe, either," I say, my accusation aimed at him. Somehow, it just came out bitchy, and she shrinks even more next to her giant, her freckled cheeks flashing pink.

He leans down, like a lot, and places a soft kiss on her forehead. Strange. The alien they call the Great Warrior wears the Tarrassian white leather kilt and black boots, which makes sense since he's... well, a warrior. He has no weapons, not sure this one even needs any. All these alien men, males, whatever, are huge, but he is in a league of his own. Which, of course, makes me wonder about sex. Surely, he can't possibly... That can't work, can it? Not with tiny Natalia. He has the same shoulder-length dark hair and bushy beard as the other Tarrassians, but that's about the only similarity. His strong facial features remind me of a werewolf, and his barrel-like body is definitely furry and not hairy. I remember Zaan said the Great Warrior is Tarrassia's only half breed. Well, now there are two of us. As for his purple eyes? It is hard not to stare. They have a strangely hypnotic quality, and they are absolutely stunning. He watches me with an intensity very different from Zaan's. It is unnerving but without the crazy. Is he trying to read my mind? Can he do that?

"Oh, this is just a mating bite. I rather enjoyed it," says Natalia with a giggle and loud enough that a servant drops a tray somewhere behind her. By my side, Kayon makes funny gurgled noises, and his tusks start shaking. I have to fight a smile. This girl is as crazy as they come. I push myself to remember I am not here for fun.

"Look, Natalia," I say, pointing at the table behind her. It looks as if they were waiting for me to join for breakfast or something. "I appreciate the help and all this, but I really just want to be left alone. I don't want a healer either. I bet on the freedom I don't have the healer is a guy, and I don't want any of those around if that's okay."

"O… okay," says Natalia, who once again looks like she is close to tears, fidgeting with her hair and clinging to his arm. Never seen anyone go through emotions like this girl. "I will only send female attendants to your room, and you can eat in there. You can do whatever you want or feel comfortable doing," she says and hides her face into his forearm, like a child. Jesus! It's like a live lesson on Stockholm Syndrome.

"Is there a lock to my room?" I ask even though I know it's stupid. These aliens could push the wall down with a finger, never mind a door. At least my question bothers them, and they look a bit offended. Natalia, most of all. God! Is she crying now? Her big alien doesn't necessarily look angry with me but definitely out of patience. He leans down again and presses a reassuring kiss on her forehead. His intense purple stare stops on my face. I must have lost a lot of blood. There is no other explanation why I find understanding in those alien eyes.

"What do you need to feel safe, Gianna?" he asks with a booming voice, quite appropriate for his size. It's not bossy, not intimidating, nor patronizing. It's the voice of someone who treats everyone as an equal. And because his question was straightforward and no one else bothered to ask that, I give him an honest answer.

"A weapon would be nice," I say, holding his eyes.

"Very well, what kind of weapon would you like?"

I wait for a few seconds before replying, expecting some mocking joke. But it's not coming.

"Really? You would let me have a weapon?" I ask and mentally curse myself for the flicker of hope.

"If that's what it takes to make you safe, why not? What weapon would you like?"

I look with wary eyes from him to Natalia, to Kayon. No one is laughing. Not only that, but he asked me to choose a weapon. And he means every word of it.

"I would like a sword, I guess, but Tarrassian swords are too big for me, and I haven't used one since I was a teen. A knife would do," I tell him with honesty I didn't expect from myself. I didn't even tell Yara that I used to be a Kendo champion. But then again, I didn't tell her about the rape either. She knew I slashed my veins at some point, but that's only because she had similar scars. She never asked me why because she didn't want me to return the 'favor'. Now, she took her secret to her grave. Some friend I was...

"I will provide you with a smaller sword we use to train younger Warriors. Kayon will give you all the training you need, and you are welcome to join me at the Sparring Pits in the High City. One of my responsibilities is training and assessing the Warriors. For now, you will also have a knife. Kayon can take you to my weapons chamber. You can choose whatever you want. I trust you know how to keep yourself safe from self-harm."

I watch him, waiting for the penny to drop. Giving me a weapon might not be such a big deal. The training that comes with it makes all the difference. What he offers is not a weapon. It is respect.

"What's the catch?" I ask before I can stop myself. Perhaps I should just return his trust and not question him. *Trust...* I don't even know what that feels like.

"I do request a favor," he says, and I hold my breath. "I want you to see the Healer to make sure your wounds are properly looked after. His female mate will accompany him when he attends to you. To put you at ease."

I try to think of a reply, but I simply don't know what to say to unconditional kindness. Because what he just requested is not really a condition. It's care. Another thing I am not used to. He obviously doesn't want or need anything in return.

I can see they are all waiting for me to say something, but I feel like I might cry if I do. I am tired, hungry, and broken into more pieces than anyone can put together. Kindness is not something I can deal with right now. Nor is the look in Natalia's eyes. She has peace and seems thousands of miles away from the scared little girl she was only a few weeks back. She looks at him as if he hung the moon. Can I blame her? Her alien may look like a monster, but he might just be the only decent man in the entire Universe. Lucky her!

20

GIANNA

Over the last five days, I found out Natalia is more than lucky. She is a force of nature. I feel like a coward for avoiding her, but it's for the best. It is foolish if I think about it. I am surrounded by creepy aliens, red demons, overgrown Tarrassians, yet I am terrified of tiny Natalia. I may have managed to avoid her so far, but I ran out of luck today, as she just invited me to lunch on her terrace, whatever that is. It's her house, so I can't really say no.

Lssta, my personal servant as she calls herself no matter how many times I told her not to, runs that strange thing through my hair. She says it's a detangler; I call it God's gift. It is shaped like a giant slice of orange, the same color but see-through. It lights up and hums slightly while analyzing hair texture. Based on the results, it applies a specific pressure, moisture, heat or cold, while hydrating and regenerating hair. I didn't have enough eyebrows to raise when Lssta explained before using it for the first time. Now I wish they would export this stuff to Earth, to all the black women who have to go through hours of torture at the hair salon.

Even though I inherited my father's golden hair color, it has my mother's afro texture. Only expensive products and experienced stylists could deal with it back on Earth. Maybe because I didn't go the easy route. I refused to have a relaxer since that's what my dad wanted. I refused to have braids or a weave to rebel against my mother, and her perfect African Barbie looks. I decided bold, natural curls like a hallow of light around my brown face was my own style. It was different, unique and the high-fashion industry went mad for the afro bob look.

It was not easy to maintain my style, and I could have done all my life with this little device. Now, my hair hangs in soft yet tight curls, looking much longer since the springy texture has been tamed. It reaches just under my shoulders, and I can't stop myself from touching it every so often. I can feel it catch all the light around me like a halo. And it's ever so soft.

I try to avoid the mirror as I don't fancy looking at the dying Sign on my forehead, or at the faded tattoos on my arms. They don't light up any more. I don't really understand why it scares me. If the marks die, I die. Isn't that what I wanted? Maybe it's because this is yet another thing he controls. He's decided to stay away and let me fade to a slow and painful death. Because these freaking things do hurt indeed. Me scraping at them probably doesn't help the matter. The swirls around my arms ache even in my sleep. I don't have enough strength to lift my arms or brush my hair, so I just sit here pretending I love to be pampered by an alien woman with a forked tongue and a scaly scalp.

What I struggle with the most is the irony of it. I can now use a weapon and I am allowed to train, but I don't because I can barely do anything. Kayon let me choose not one but several knives. I was half expecting him to mock me, but he showed great interest in my selection and even praised me for it. Yesterday he brought me the most beautiful sword I have ever seen. It is half the size of the Warriors' ones, still, I couldn't even lift it. Kayon looked at me and my fading marks with a mixture of pity and curiosity but didn't make any other comment.

Now that Natalia has changed the law and the non-Tarrassian species are allowed to procreate, Kayon introduced me to his daughter's family. She is his youngest child and sadly his mate died giving birth to her. His daughter and her mate used to hide their little boy, deep into the Purple Forest, as it was illegal for them to have children. He is the fattest, cutest, cuddliest toddler orc. I've completely changed my mind about tusks. I now find them adorable. Sadly, I couldn't stop the sharp pain in my heart, watching Kayon interact with his daughter. He looks at her as if she could do no wrong. What would it be like to have a father as devoted and warm-hearted as Kayon? It is strange to see how functional alien families are compared to mine. Not sure why I assumed otherwise. Aliens are just people, after all. Sadly, they all keep rubbing their super paternal instincts in my face.

The Tarrassian Healer who lives in the forest not only brought his mate each time he checked on me, but he also brought his daughter. He is completely smitten with her. The little creature is charming, and I tried to ignore her looks. It's not the child's fault her skin glows pastel colors, her hair is bright blue, and pointy ears stick out of it. At least she inherited her father's copper eyes. But then she looked at her parents with adoring eyes, and they changed to gold. Ugh! I hate golden eyes! But I am not going to hold that against her. Also, it's not her fault she's Ollianna's niece.

Why are all these people related? No wonder their fertility sucks. After laying eyes on the Healer's wife, I honestly considered asking him to stop bringing her. He is grumpy as hell and... a man, but that's better than looking at his perfect little elf. According to Gaella, she is a good few years older than Ollianna, but they look almost identical to me. And my God! This one can talk! She hugs me every time she comes and goes, something she learned from Natalia, of course. I thought Gaella had a girl crush on me or something, but she soon explained the mystery of our *instant sisterhood.* She owes her life to the *amazing High Commander,* and I am her new favorite person by proxy. Luckily, my ankles healed quickly enough, and I didn't have to put up with too many visits. I fucking hate elves! Big fan of orcs, though.

Natalia's favorite alien and the real boss around here, despite what Kayon may call himself, came to collect me for the dreaded lunch. Homma is as scary as aliens can get, but maybe I look equally strange to her, so I try not to stare. She is at least a head taller than I am, relatively wide, or maybe a bit chubby. She has really furry hands but no hair anywhere else. Her head is covered in sharp needles that occasionally click against each other and rattle. Her eyes are two moist, dark holes, her scariest feature without a doubt. Her mate, the same species as she is, laughs a lot and keeps joking about everything. Homma doesn't share his easy-going character and invites me to follow her with a bossy gesture that won't allow any comment. I haven't been here long, but I know she is fiercely loyal to Natalia. They all are. The former slaves are grateful for the right to mate and have families like everyone else. The Tarrassians are thankful for having their High Elder back. Everybody fears and respects Sia, their new Queen, but they all adore Natalia.

Unlike the Marni Residence, where people were ruled and controlled by a certain asshole, here people do whatever they feel like. Kayon growls a lot, Homma's head needles rattle aggressively, but as soon as they turn their backs, there is a chorus of giggles and childish behavior. No wonder Natalia fits here.

Lssta is really big on gossip. To be honest, I think that's a very loved alien trait. I am not that keen on her need to inform me of everything. Still, I found out a lot from her constant chatter. Despite my aversion to everything Tarrassian, I have to admit some of the things Lssta says are fascinating. Also, distracting, and I could do with a bit of that.

I can often see the beautiful white birds flying above the forest, and indeed they must be magical, no matter how hard it is for my human brain to grasp that. I was told they can feel when an Elder is about to be born and fly above the birthplace in a single line. It must go on for many days since there are thousands of them. However, when the little Oria birds fly all at once in a swirling flock above the home of a newly born, it means they have chosen a High Elder. Such a position can only be given to a member of the House Oria. It is not automatically granted to all the babies in this family. It can pass hundreds of years before they choose one. To my surprise, Lssta said the High Elder is much more than the ruler of all Elders. He can change or decrete a new law without anyone's approval. He is even more powerful than the King himself. But the most important thing about a High Healer is that he is not even a Tarrassian. He is an Astral. One of their three Gods, or whatever they call them, but with flesh and blood. I guess a bit like Jesus, and for whatever reason, when Lssta explained, all I could think of was Jade. She would mock them dry for ages. The girl never misses a chance to bully people. God, these aliens are so weird!

Then, Lssta told me Natalia's giant mate was the High Elder, and suddenly, it all made sense. I have only met him once since I avoid Natalia like the plague, and those two are glued at the hip. However, it was enough to tell; he was special. Somehow, he seems better than all of us. Clever birds. I think the ones in charge of the Sign must be the other two Astrals. The ethereal Gods, as Lssta said. Those two can drop dead for what I care and take their shitty Sign with.

It turns out, Tannon refused his birthright, and I have a guess or two about that. Because of my biracial heritage, I probably understand his reasons more than most.

Then, along comes little, whiny Natalia, who discovers all the hidden secrets of the Purple Forest, makes him accept his position, and changes a few ancient laws previously set in stone. Kayon said he would rather fight all the notorious beasts of his native planet than tiny Natalia. The Healer is convinced she is poisonous, and Homma's mate thinks she brainwashed Tannon. Charming! I really can't blame myself for wishing I could skip this stupid lunch. All I want to do is sleep.

Somehow, the nightmares are gone. Now, there is just this cold darkness I sink into as soon as I close my eyes. Being awake feels the same: a cold void that grips my new reality. For a moment, I consider grabbing a fur, but I don't want to appear weak. I'm wearing one of the silly dresses Sia sent me, and it is as flimsy as it gets. Obviously, this is one of her own, as it still smells like her. Lavender and something else. Probably icicles. My cropped top and daisy shorts were covered in blood, and they disposed of them without even asking me. So, stupid dress it is. It has slits in the long flowy skirt, all the way to my hips, exposing my legs when I walk. Yet, *he* frowned at my daisy shorts.

I decide to attach a massive curved knife to my belt for good measure. Not like I have any strength or energy left to use it. I am such a joke!

Natalia waits for me on the terrace of her sleeping quarters, as they call them here. I wonder if she can tell it still smells like sex in here. Ugh! This is a very surreal new reality indeed. A few weeks ago, crazy Jade told Natalia some monster cock would cure her fear of monsters. Jade might be a loony, but an educated one.

I still my face refusing to take in the beauty of the alien forest. The terrace is at the very top of the Palace, and the white stone platform reaches out into the Purple Forest, edged by its canopy like a cocoon. A soft breeze moves the oversized purple leaves, revealing hundreds of beady blue eyes. I've never seen the Oria birds this close. Beautiful but a bit creepy! Their blue eyes are so assertive it makes them look sentient, somehow. They are the size of a robin but have at least a metre-long feathery tail trailing behind them. There are too many of them to count amongst the branches, their stare following Natalia's every move.

Her beautiful Tarrassian dress has the same colors as the sky. An ombre of pink and purple matching her vibrant mating marks and her bright red hair. Who would have thought pink works so well on a redhead? Natalia looks as magical as everything else around us. Maybe it's no wonder she has her giant wrapped around her little finger. Her taste in pets is no better than her choice of men. The hideous thing she refers to as Oliver watches me with threatening red eyes. I don't have a great history with that eye color, and I involuntarily touch my knife. The fluffy creature ignores me and cuddles up closer to Natalia's feet.

"That is a very ugly pet you have there, Natalia; I hope you don't mind me saying," I tell her as I sit across from her at the table Homma set for us.

"I know... poor Oliver," she laughs. "He is so ugly; it makes him cute."

I tell her she does have a point. The little thing is a mixture of chihuahua, guinea pig, and cat. Add red eyes and a swirly pig tail. What could possibly go wrong with that?

"Is this tomato sauce with the meatballs?" I ask, helping myself to a tiny portion compared to hers. She is so small, where does all that food go? Probably to her boobs.

"Sadly no, but it is the closest you would get on this planet. Same goes for the meatballs. I made the sauce from a local fruit called huja and like everything else on Tarrassia it is overly sweet."

"Yes, I've noticed," I tell her trying to make polite conversation. She is up to something, despite being her usual child-like persona. "It's okay, though. It goes with the bread. Homma said you baked it yourself," I add and even force a smile. I can make polite conversation, not a problem. "The servants... attendants, not sure what to call them, told me what you did for them," I say, and this time, my smile is genuine. "It is crazy to imagine such a law was in place."

"Yes, the cruellest thing ever," she says. "Stupid, arrogant Tarrassians thought that was perfectly normal."

I watch her without being able to hide my shock.

"You don't like the Tarrassians?" I ask, genuinely surprised. She seems so happy here.

"They are hard on the palate, you know?" she tells me while piling even more food onto her plate. "They are overbearing, bossy, interfering, prone to violence, growling, and they love telling everyone how to live their lives. I don't like growly people."

I shock myself by laughing. Haven't done much of that lately.

"That is the most accurate description, if I ever heard one," I agree, but I do wonder. "Rather strange, considering you are about to marry one of them. Willingly, may I add."

"Oh yes, very willingly," she tells me with a loud happy giggle that makes her big blue eyes shine.

"Yes, I think I heard that willingness one too many times," I tell her with a smile. It's all rather shocking to me, considering this is Natalia we're talking about here. She was a freaking virgin only a few weeks ago.

"Oh, Bozhe… That is terrible. I do get a bit excited, sorry."

"You don't have to say sorry, Natalia. This is your house," I reassure her.

I eat quietly for a while, listening to her chatter. The girl loves to talk. She explains about Tannon being only half Tarrassian, hence less crazy. She tells me about his other heritage, a species of gentle giants with purple eyes who excel at kissing and lovemaking, apparently. This girl is nuts!

"In the name of fairness," she continues, "Tarrassians are also loyal, protective, and never hurt weaker beings. Not even in self-defense."

I can see she wants me to agree, but that's not happening. I play with my food, pretending not to see what she is trying to do. Has she forgotten what my ankles looked like when I got here? Or the scar on my neck?

"Anyway," she carries on, "there are only two Tarrassians in the Purple Forest, so no need to worry about all that. Tannon is only half Tarrassian, as for the stupid Healer... well, I try to remember how much I like his mate to make the sight of him more bearable," she says with a cute smirk. She is not wrong, though. The Healer is not big on her either. Apparently, she made his elf faint a few times while trying to interrogate her about Tannon's secrets. Typical Natalia.

"You do seem comfortable amongst these people; there is no denying that. Not to mention they worship you," I tell her with a soft smile, but then she shocks the life out of me.

"Yes, we have a connection," she says. "Just like most of them, I was born a slave. Same as all the women in my family I was the property of a human trafficking organisation," she explains, and there is a slight tremble in her plump lips.

What does one reply to that? I hardly ate any of the food, but I feel like I am about to regurgitate it all. My mind takes me back to that storage room, and all the memories flood me at once. The tiny ounce of empathy I must have left pushes it all aside. This is not about me. This is about Natalia.

"Your... monsters," I say, suddenly understanding.

"Yes, they were real," she says with a quiet voice.

"Did they... touch you?" I ask before I can stop myself.

"No, I was rescued before it happened. It was too late for my mother and sisters, but not for me."

She gives me a small smile, then carries on eating with one hand while petting the ugly pet on her lap with the other. No tears, no screaming, no traces of childhood trauma on her face. Despite all that, she is still the same cute, fragile young girl any of these aliens could crush with a finger. Only, they don't. They follow her around like oversized puppies. When we were held together in that room on the Blood Fleet, I thought she would go down first. She is no fighter material, and she's not afraid to show it – a red flag to any predator. And yet, all predators seem to bow to her.

I feel lost for some reason. Like I am missing the big picture and have been walking on the wrong path all my life.

"How was Earth?" she asks, pulling me out of my thoughts.

"Invaded," I say with a shrug. What else is there to say? These assholes took a planet because they needed available wombs for their copper Viking babies. "Nothing will ever be the same on Earth. Even if things settle down, it will never be the life we once knew," I say out loud.

"Would you live there again?" she asks, bringing my anger back.

"How could I, Natalia? Look at me!" I say, pointing at my marks and Sign. "I got back to Earth on impulse. To prove a point. I forgot how judgmental our kind can be. I was quickly labeled as the *alien invaders' whore*."

She avoids my eyes, but I am not angry at her. She can't understand. She was always the cute girl next door, the one people want to marry their sons, not the one they shame and judge.

"So, will you be happy to stay here, on Tarrassia?" she asks, and I know she is trying to change the subject. Only this topic makes me even angrier.

"Does it look like I have a choice?" I ask while rubbing roughly at the marks on my left arm. "I am in fucking pain because of these horrible marks as it is."

"Oh, do they hurt?" she asks, watching me closely.

"Of course they do; he's not around, is he?" I shout at her making her stupid pet hiss at me. "But I tell you what, I would rather lose sleep at night because of the pain in my marks than see his stupid face. No doubt he went to some ridiculous battle on purpose, just to show me how much pain I'll be in without him," I tell her, but I don't know why I bother. She will never understand. Her guy worships her, and I don't expect anyone to care enough to put themselves in my shoes.

"Oh no, he hasn't gone to war," she says with a rather unassuming tone. "He's not around because he is in the High Fortress. That's what Tarrassians call their jail. Would you like some lassi fruit? Tannon has it delivered freshly every day for me. It is not as sweet as the other fruit Tarrassians love so much, and it tastes like vanilla ice cream."

I can't fully process what she is saying for a few good seconds.

"Since when?" I ask, even though my brain is telling me not to. *Not your problem, Gianna. You don't care, remember?*

"The day before you arrived. He came here first to ask Tannon and me to look after you. Then he went to the High City to hand himself in."

She arranges a few slices of fruit on a small plate, then offers it to me. I want to shove it down her throat! I want to shove her pet down her throat! I am so angry; I feel completely out of control. The rage is choking me, and I stand in an attempt to breathe better.

"Why would he do that? And why the fuck would they imprison him? He was injured; couldn't they see? He needed a doctor, not jail! Couldn't you see his wounds? Couldn't Tannon? You let him leave like that?" *I don't care! I don't care!*

"Please sit down, Gianna, let me explain," she says without even looking at me. I take a seat only because I feel sick again, and the world seems a bit fuzzy. "Tarrassians can self-heal," she explains like I am a bit dim, "and yes, I could see his scars and the still-bleeding wound in his chest. I already know from Tannon what their injuries look like in different stages of healing. Zaan's were not that bad. Tannon assured me he got the Fortress Healer to him as soon as he was taken there. Please, don't worry about that."

Is this girl stupid? And why is his wound still bleeding? Did I hit an internal organ? Why is he not in a hospital or whatever they call it here? And what does she mean by wounds, as in plural. He only had the one I gave him. *Who cares, anyway? I don't!*

"Who the hell said I was worried?" I scream, and her pet spits a disgusting red blob of saliva on my foot, hiding quickly under the table after. I stand, slap my hands on the table, and lean towards her. "Not only do I not give a shit about what happens to him, but I am proud to inform you I caused the biggest of those wounds. With his own gun, by the way," I add with a grin.

"Would you like to try some fruit?" she asks with a sweet smile. I am so tempted to use my knife on her. She is infuriating!!!!! Instead, my brain seems to go quiet as other instincts take over. Anxiety and pain shadow the anger. *Don't ask! You don't care! Don't you dare ask, Gianna!*

"Why is he in jail, anyway? I thought he was their pride and glory, or something like that," I say, while my fingers scrape at the mating marks. I can somehow see the horror in her eyes. I never self-harm in public, but I just can't stop it.

"He killed some Humans back on Earth," she says, watching me closely.

Really now? I let out a laugh. It scares me as it sounds proper manic.

"There goes their peaceful invasion, I guess," I say mockingly.

"This had nothing to do with the invasion; he said it was personal. Nevertheless, he will be punished because the King's rule was not to hurt any Humans. To make it even worse, the four men he killed were some high-ranked, decorated Marines." She says the words like they are nothing. They are everything to me. They crush whatever was left of me. I let myself drop back in my chair, as my legs won't hold me up any more. Why? Why? He had no right! It feels like the worst kind of betrayal for reasons I can't even think of.

She reaches out over the table, trying to take my hands into hers, but I push her away. I don't want anyone to touch me or comfort me. Not now, not ever! My tears run down my face, and my whole body shakes violently. I can't cry in front of her like this!

"I hate him so much! He had no right to do that. I hope they lock him up and throw the key away! I hope they kill him, even if it kills me too, because of these stupid marks," I hear myself say. *Did I say that out loud?* My nails attack the swirls on my arms with a vengeance. I can feel blood within seconds. I want them off. I want him out of my life!

"Yes, I know you want out of this, and luckily, there is a very easy fix," she says, stroking Oliver's fur. "The mating marks can be rejected."

What? Is there a way out of this nightmare? "They can?" I ask.

"Oh yes, Tannon and I are the only ones aware of this. We know because my friend Leo, who is a Sphinx, told me so."

"Your friend Leo is a what?" What is she saying? Is this another one of her crazy stories about monsters?

"He is a Sphinx. Not like a stone one; he is a real lion monster sort of thing. But really, he is just a man. A crazy one, but most men are that way, and... Sorry, I always talk too much. I will tell you about him one day, just not now, because I feel guilty leaving him behind. He had a crush on me, but I love Tannon and..."

"The marks, Natalia! Tell me about the marks!" I shout, getting up to my full height, trying to look as menacing as I can.

"The mating marks will choose the most compatible beings in the Universe and bring them together. Two halves to create one perfect entity. However, Leo assured me that all the marks have one thing in common: they respect free will. If someone doesn't want them, they won't develop at all. Not sure why they have in your case. Maybe they just took you by surprise. But you can still reverse them."

"I can?" I inspect my arms like they are a foreign body. The marks look ominous now, all covered in scratches and fresh blood. *Did I do that?* "How?" I ask.

"It looks like you are already doing the right thing. I mean, not the scratching," she says quickly. "Please don't try that. All you have to do is keep thinking how much you want them off, how much you hate Zaan, how much you want him dead. You know... things like that. They will most likely be gone by morning. Which is good, because his trial is in the morning. Perfect timing to cut all your connections to him."

She pauses to give me a chance to reply. But her words don't make sense. It takes longer for my brain to process anything right now. A massive headache makes my forehead throb. The air around heavy, the world's sharp edges closing in on me. She looks briefly at my face, then averts her eyes. Can she tell my head is pounding?

"Tannon said the Sign is the only thing that can save Zaan now. As you know, it is sacred to Tarrassians, and they will not exile someone who has it."

"Exile?" I ask slowly.

"Well... yes," she says while feeding her small pet chunks of fruit. "That is what they call it, but Tannon said exile means certain death. They lose their powers if they are away from Tarrassia for too long. They become prey for the Noorranni and all their enemies. I know it sounds cruel of me to say this," she continues without looking at me, "especially because I owe Zaan my life. Sia saw what happened to the Human slaves who couldn't be rescued. It's just horrible. But still, you come first, Gianna. Humans have to stick together, right? This time tomorrow, you will be free of your Sign, free of Zaan, and you can go back to Earth and forget this ever happened."

This girl is strange. She always says the most nonsensical things, but I should still be able to understand some, right? My brain is empty; I can't make it function. Now, even my eyes hurt. There is too much light around. She looks at me with a strange smile. Like she just won a game. Why do I feel like a puppet and she holds all my strings?

"I promised Tannon I wouldn't tell you about the marks, and I wouldn't give you the only weapon that could destroy Zaan. I do feel bad about it, but it's for the best. I don't think Tannon paid attention to Zaan's words the evening he came here. He doesn't care about losing his title, honors, or even his life. He only cares about you. If you reject him, he will most likely welcome the exile, anyway."

She doesn't avert my eyes any more, and her smile is full of triumph. This was a game and she just won it. There is blinding red light around me for a few seconds, throwing patterns of color and spooking the birds watching us from the canopy. They all take off into the purple sky, their long feathery tails trailing behind them. My ears are popping, a bit like they do after the *Jump*. The world constricts then expands around me. A high-pitched bark makes my ears depressurize, bringing me back to reality. I don't need to look at my arms to know what I will see. The swirls are brighter than when they burned my skin for the first time. Maybe I should kill her! Wipe that innocent, unassuming smile off her lips.

"I hate this fucking place, and I hate you, Natalia! You better stay the hell out of my way! And I hate your ugly pet dog!" I scream at her because blinding rage is making my blood boil. I almost run into Homma and her deadly head needles as I rush back to my room. I don't know the meaning of all this, but I need to get away from all of them. My brain decides this would be an excellent time to function again and explain what's happening: *Your mating marks are alive and well, and this time they didn't choose you. You chose them! You chose HIM!*

21

—

ZAAN

The security panel of my holding room removes itself inside the walls with a zoom. I expected it would be the King. He has been my only visitor over the last five days of my confinement. At least he should be pleased with my glowing arms. My King seemed more upset about my dying mating marks than he was about my actions. He accepted my refusal to explain myself. As soon as I said it was a matter of honor involving my mate, he asked no further questions. However, he did ask loads about the state of my marks. Not only because they are my only protection against the Council's ruling. He seemed scared somehow, and my King is a male who doesn't know fear. He thinks it might happen to him, that much was obvious. He wanted me to explain, but there was nothing I could say. There is no explanation for this. Other than she hates me, of course.

That seemed to put his mind at rest, as the Queen's love for our King has become legendary. She raised an army on Sketos to save his life. She made the Elders and everyone else refer to him as the Brave King, and she is heavy with his cub. He has nothing to worry about. Besides, he should be really pleased with my Sign now. It came back to life on the previous span. I still don't know what any of this means, and I'm not even sure if it's a blessing or a curse. My dying marks caused pain, tiredness, and lack of energy. As if life was draining out of me. Now, I feel stronger than ever, my former strength and abilities enhanced by the Sign. It brings a different kind of pain. My mating instinct and my body only want one thing: HER. Exile doesn't feel like such a bad thing right now. Only, I can't. That would mean her death, and I won't allow it.

I see it is not the King who has come to accompany me to the Trial. It is the Great Warrior. I trained my emotions and reactions for many spans; I know better than to show my surprise. The large male who enters my holding room is not exactly the Great Warrior. Not any more. The white tunic he wears has the map of our solar system engraved with an intricate platinum ore thread over his large chest. There is only one being amongst the galaxies allowed to wear that symbol – the High Elder. I take a fist to my heart but also bow my head in respect. Everything else about him seems different than the last time I saw him, which was only five days ago. My training and self-discipline will not allow me to question him, but luckily, he will explain.

"Not sure if I mentioned before, but my tiny mate is quite fond of scheming," he says with a warm smile. His purple eyes glow at the memory of her. "Natalia asked for a favor only the High Elder could grant. Which, of course, had been part of her little plan all along. I had to accept my position, in order to grant her wish."

"High Elder, please tell me she didn't ask you to intervene for me," I say because I know what that would look like to the Elders.

"No, High Commander, she did not. My mate might be a scheming little Human, but she is also very caring and protective of me. She knows my honor wouldn't allow me to ask the Council for a personal favor."

"Neither would mine, High Elder," I tell him, and he nods in agreement.

"Let's hope her other successful scheme will be enough to convince the Elders," he says, looking at my vibrant marks.

Only then do I realize he wasn't surprised to see them. I don't ask because I know I won't like the answer. The High Lady of the Purple Forest has somehow convinced my female not to kill our marks. It angers me more than being taken to trial like a common criminal in front of my sire.

"Control your anger, High Commander. I want none of it in the Council," he says with a warning voice. "I also don't want to be reminded of the state in which your female arrived at my house, with her feet leaving a long trail of blood."

I watch him in stupor and it feels as if he hit me in the face. I don't understand at first. When I do, I ignore all Tarrassian codes of conduct, and I turn my back at the High Elder, facing the wall instead. My scalp is on fire under my head fur as I angrily pull at it. The magnetic restraints! Vexing idiot! I forgot all about them. Did she try to run away, or did it happen when they took her to his house? I forgot to ask the servants to remove them, and once I got here, no communication was allowed. Not that I remembered anyway. No wonder she hates me. I am not worthy of being her mate or protector.

"It is fine, Zaan. You punish yourself too harshly. You always have," he says, placing a hand on my shoulder. "My Natalia taught me we have to be kind to ourselves in order to be kind to others."

"Were there any bro... broken bones?" I ask with a heavy heart.

"No, just a deep flesh wound. Andrac and Gaella took care of it. Your mate has fully healed."

"Thank you, Tannon," I tell him, too distracted to remember using his title.

"Now, we must hurry, and you have to brace yourself, Zaan. You have only two defenders in that Cave on this span. The King and your Sign. I will refrain from voting altogether. I am sure you can understand."

"Yes, of course, I do, and I respect your decision. Tarrassia needs unity," I tell him. I hope the King won't defend me either, but he does whatever he wants. The Elders should be used to it by now.

"You will have to speak for yourself I am afraid, as there won't be a defender," he says, a shadow crossing his face. "On the last span, I joined the High General in his dwelling, leaving my precious mate alone for nothing, as it turns out. The plan was to put together a defense plan with him. I will not lie to you, my friend, vexing Larrs brushed me off. He said his Warriors are his responsibility and none of my business. I am very close to losing patience with him, the vexing fool."

"Please, don't do it on my behalf, High Elder. I am not worthy," I tell him, trying to avoid his curious stare. I know he can read my mind, no matter how much I block it. He is an Astral. Luckily, he is too honorable to do it.

"I will not have you talk like that about yourself. As for the High General, I am not a fool. I know something happened between the two of you. Is there anything you would like to say to me?" he asks, observing me.

"No, High Elder, I have nothing to say. My actions shamed the High General, and I respect his decision. I will defend myself," I tell him, and he accepts my explanation without any further questioning.

As we walk towards the sacred Council Cave, I still my emotions, my War Beast, and regulate my breathing. The very male walking by my side taught me how to do most of it. The rest was span rotations of self-restraint and training. If only I knew how to control my need for her.

The Council Cave inside the High Palace is an exact replica of the Sacred Cave hidden deep into the Spark Mountain, where our first ancestors were born. The Palace is an extravagant display of Tarrassian technology and luxury. The Cave is nothing short of austere. The rock inside here was brought from the Spark Mountain, and it smells of old. The red gaar oil drips from the torches aligning the walls, the only light allowed in the Cave.

All the Council members are already here, and they stand and bow to the High Elder as we enter. They take a seat in order of their ranking. First, the High Elder, then the King, followed by the fourteen Elders, the High General, the two Low Generals, and finally the High Commander of the Royal Ship. He is only covering the empty seat of the Middle General. The male who inherited that position was chosen by the Oria birds to become the Elder of the Fields, instead. He only sired a daughter, so there is currently no Middle General on Tarrassia. The rules of the Council Cave are stricter than my own. It is no wonder someone as untamed as our King is more comfortable on the battlefield.

By the end of the Council table, I stand in the spot dedicated to the ones on trial. The failures. I wish I could avoid my sire's eyes. I am a bad son, but I will never be a coward. He meets my stare from across the table. He looks tired, tormented, and much older. I did this to him. Our eyes communicate all the things our minds can't. Mind talking is not allowed during the Sacred Council.

The Elder of the Caves stands and looks at me with accusatory eyes. It is not a secret he dislikes my sire, the King, the Blood Fleet, and... well, everything else. He is not a pleasant male. Before he gets to open his mouth, the High General stands, and I can feel the Elders cringe. He has that effect on all beings.

"High Elder, my King, I ask permission to speak," he says,

completely ignoring the Elder of the Caves who got up first and is obviously fuming. An angry Elder is a rare sight, but the High General can easily make that happen. Even now, his arrogance defies the Elders' authority and the Council itself. He is a cold, calculated, highly intelligent male and a Warrior with flawless strategy and skill. To everyone, he is the high-born, outstanding Tarrassian citizen. He makes no mistakes and doesn't tolerate failure. He is perfect, from his well-kept appearance to his emotionless understanding of our rigid social conduct. For thousands of span rotations, my people considered lack of emotions a symbol of strength, mandatory for males. As we evolved and learned from other species, showing emotion became less frowned upon. Yet, my people still look up to the High General, and his complete lack of empathy appeals to most. I know what's hiding behind his mask of perfection. And this is when I pay the price for knowing.

"Proceed, High General," says the King, who gives the Elder of the Caves an almost evil grin.

"High Elder, my King, Elders, Warriors," he starts with the usual introduction. "We have gathered here on this span to waste my vexing time!" he says, and all the Elders gasp, including my sire. The King is as happy as a cub, the High Elder sighs, but everyone else is shocked. Cursing is not allowed in the Cave. The rumor goes that rule never stopped the King. The High General ignores all the reactions and continues with his usual cold voice.

"I have an army to command; I have not one but eight open battles to cover. Yet, I have to stand here and listen as your incompetence judges my worthiest Warrior. He went against the King's ruling and killed four Humans. Is that it?" As he asks a question no one really wants to answer, he uses his com to send info to all the other Council members. I can see their screens lighting up, but I don't know what they are looking at. My sire's eyes start glowing, full of hope.

"The High Commander did not kill four Humans, but four members of the group known as the New Resistance. You will find on your feed all the information you couldn't be bothered to look for yourselves. The Earth Protection Treaty doesn't extend to traitors. They will always be hunted down and killed, and the Human leaders agreed to those conditions. And now you can thank my High Commander for defending Tarrassia and for putting up with your ungrateful ways. My King, will you excuse my Warriors and me from the Council? Unlike some, we have actual work to do."

As soon as he finishes speaking, both the King and the High Elder stand and take a fist to their chest, pledging their respect to me. All the Council members follow shortly, and I watch the life returning to my sire's kind face. I return his smile, even though I am not entirely sure what just happened. The High General is more confusing than my female. And that says a lot!

22

GIANNA

I am on my way to meet Kayon and start my official training with him. I don't have any hopes about that. It will most likely consist of learning how to look pretty while spinning around a kiddy sword. My biggest hint? I am expected to train in one of Sia's pretty dresses. The most aggressive thing one can do in this outfit is throw flowers at people. It's still better than hiding in my room. I have been doing just that since yesterday and my chat from hell with Natalia. However, this morning I woke up like a different person.

I am not sure if it's down to the Sign rebuilding my strength. The thought of the four men who can never hurt anyone again might be the actual cause. After moving to New York, I thought being miles away from them was enough, but apparently not. At the back of my mind, I knew they were always there. Living their lives like nothing happened, piling up military honors, and most likely abusing other women. That was like a chain around my throat, and I didn't even know it. Now they are gone, I can breathe again. The thought *he* is the one who made it happen is all sorts of wrong. I refuse to let it spoil my first good day in a very long time.

Kayon is waiting for me in what they call the training pit, which is exactly that, a huge outdoor enclosure, like a training ground from a gladiators' movie. Kayon said the High Elder prefers the old ways, but most training facilities on Tarrassia are very high-tech.

I surprise myself by taking a detour through the massive kitchen. Natalia loves cooking and chatting with the workers in the morning. I am only trying to say hello and show her I don't really hate her. I am not here for any other reason. I do not care about the trial, and I will not ask her. She looks like she was expecting me and gives me a hug, almost knocking me over with her large boobs. Who would have thought those things could be dangerous? I hate this hugging crap she does. I am sure all the aliens around here share my feelings, except the elf girl, but there is no escaping Natalia's hugs.

"So happy to see you looking better," she says with a loud giggle, clapping her hands. Her freckled cheeks are as pink as her Sign, and she has bright yellow flour all over her nose. Nobody does cute like Natalia.

"Yes, I do feel better today and just wanted to say... you know, say good morning and stuff," I tell her, refusing the large yellow bun she offers me. I already had a bit of fruit in my room for breakfast, and that is all I can manage right now.

"Yes, I know you are anxious about the trial, and I was going to find you shortly, tell you the outcome," she says, and I honestly want to do all sorts of violent things to her.

"I am not anxious, and I do not care about that," I tell her as calmly as I can. "I stopped by to... say hello."

"So, you don't want to know? Okay, then. Hello to you, too, Gianna. I hope you have a lovely training session with Kayon today," she says with a beaming smile.

Why did I cringe at the thought of being kidnapped with Jade and Sia? This one right here is the only one I should have worried about!

"Sorry," she says quickly with a shy smile. "I do enjoy scheming, as you know, but not playing silly games like that. Even though you don't want to know, let me tell you everything went just fine. The trial happened at sunrise, a Tarrassian custom, I think, and it lasted for like five minutes or so. Tannon said the High General, who is my friend, even though I don't like him much, defended Zaan. It turns out the men he killed were members of a dangerous human resistance group and, therefore, traitors. The High General made the Council thank Zaan for what he did," she says with another giggle. "I would have loved to see that! Jade did, though. I mean heard. She is soooo crazy! She hides in a secret passage and listens to everything they do in there." Another giggle and Homma, who passes by just then, sighs dramatically. "Only the King and Tannon know about Jade, of course. Because of the Sign, they have increased powers and senses. They can smell her in there, you know?" More giggles. "You must make sure you keep it a secret, though. The High General is not too keen on Jade's antics as it is. Sia said he locked her in the High Fortress' dungeon the other night. But she's okay, no harm done. Sia didn't even get to intervene as the High General got her back out half an hour later. Apparently, Jade was flirting with the guards." A whole plethora of giggles this time, and she finally takes a breath of air.

Wow! Just wow! How can quiet, stern Tannon put up with her chatter? I can feel a headache coming. While I am still speechless, she pulls me into the large dining hall, and a servant hands her a folded pile of strange-looking leather clothes. Her tiny arms are swamped by it, so she quickly places them on a nearby chest.

"These are for you," she says with a shy smile. "They are a gift from Gaella. She ordered them for you from Garria, her homeland. Luckily, you're so famous, and finding your exact measurements from Earth's Internet was easy-peasy." She waits for me to say something, and I wish I could be less... bitchy, for once! Wishing doesn't work.

"Yey! Pretty elf clothes, so nice of her," I say with a mocking voice. Natalia just giggles instead of getting upset.

"I have no idea if they are pretty or not because I don't even understand how they are meant to work. You can probably figure it out as you used to wear all sorts of high fashion. And Gaella can help if you need her. Now," she says with a cute, complicit smile, "we thought you couldn't train in a Tarrassian dress and I'm not sure you should wear a Kannicloth. That's what they call their kilts." Once again, she laughs, and I involuntarily smile at that. Yeah, I can picture that. Topless, with a kilt...

"Gaella had a brilliant idea. She wears dresses here, but that is not possible on Garria, her planet. They live in the canopy of their giant trees. Too many dangerous creatures live on the ground, she said. I always wanted to visit, but I think I won't now that she mentioned that. Anyway, you can imagine, living in the tress means they need comfortable clothing. So, Gaella ordered this for you, but Homma made some adjustments after snorting at the clothes. She said it was not bad for tree climbing but awful for a Warrior. So, there you go!" she says, pointing at the pile. "You take your time changing and all that. I've asked Kayon to move the training for after lunch."

I don't know what to say. I haven't been very nice to any of the three women. Yet, they did all this for me. I wish I could stop being a ball of anger all the time. I just don't know how to do that.

"Thank you," I say because... what else can I do? She accepts it with a gracious nod, Sia's style, then sneezes loudly when her hair ends up in her mouth.

"I have an even better surprise for you, Gianna," she says with a smile full of hope and... love, maybe. She comes closer and takes my fingers into hers. I try not to flinch or pull out. God, her hands are so tiny, and she smells like cakes and babies.

"Brian is alive," she says like a whisper, watching my face closely. The information doesn't register for a good few seconds. Maybe because hope has ruined me before, and I am in no rush to cling to it.

"My Brian?" I ask without even knowing why I chose to call him that. She nods again, and I close my eyes, emotion making my knees tremble. There is maybe a reason why I thought of Brian as mine. Especially here, galaxies away from anything familiar. He is all I've got left from the only friend I ever had. Not only that, but Brian means safety, and I need as much of that as possible.

In the two years he was Yara's bodyguard, I hardly ever spoke to him. He was gruff and on the quiet side, but he was never offensive or rude. That's just him. A loner and a grump.

He was paid to watch Yara, but his protectiveness would often extend to whatever girl or woman was around. How many times did I notice him keep an eye on the girls' drinks at parties, making sure nobody spiked them? Or arrange a safe ride home for them. After a while, I started to let my guard down around him. It was hard not to. His eyes always stayed on mine when he addressed me, instead of checking out my body. In my book, that's worth my trust. And I absolutely miss the way he called me *lass* with that lovely Irish accent of his.

"How? You said he was almost dead and badly hurt back on the slavers' ship," I say, trying to understand. Natalia won't be that cruel to give me fake hopes.

"Oh, he was hurt a lot more than that," she says, and her big blue eyes fill with tears. "Sia found him on Sketos," she explains. "That is the planet where the two of us ended up after we had escaped."

"So, you two did run away," I say with a smile. I almost feel proud of them.

"Yes, well, that was not the brightest idea we ever had," she says with a cute, mischievous smile. "However, things happen for a reason. While there, Sia freed the planet and returned it to its rightful owners. You may find it hard to believe, but they are Angels of Snow; that's what Sia calls them anyway. They keep the balance of the Universe, but please, don't ask me to explain. They somehow absorb all the toxic gases in the world and release clean, purified air back. The Noorranni enslaved them for hundreds of years and used their planet as a slave market. In time, they had forgotten about all their powers and abilities. Sia made them remember, and she turned them into an army of angels or something. They saved the King's life."

"How did she do that?" I ask, but really, I want to ask a hundred questions. Nothing feels real.

"A long story, but guess what? The Ketosi think Sia is their lost Goddess of Snow," she says with a giggle.

"No surprise there," I smile back. Sia is just… Sia, on any planet. A shadow of sadness crosses over Natalia's face, and she seems lost in thoughts. She is miles away. It is my turn to reach for her hand, very unlike me.

"Is that where the Sphinx guy lives?" I ask, and it feels strange to hear myself say such things. I mean… a Sphinx, really?

"Yes," she says with her eyes cast down. "I always believed something good comes from something bad, like what happened with the Ketosi, or Tannon and I bonding over that horrible experience of being stranded in a dangerous place. I just can't understand the point of Leo's suffering. He is all alone, one of only five Sphinxes left in the Universe. The Noorranni damaged their wings and posted them as guardians on the planets they enslaved. They broke the wings of the Sphinxes many times when they were cubs. They never healed enough for them to be able to fly in space. The Sphinxes can never leave their prison planets or mate… And Leo got to witness Tannon and I falling for each other. Then I left him behind, and now he is all alone for eternity."

I surprise myself by giving her a hug. I've lost my mind, no doubt.

"Tell me about Brian," I encourage her, trying to change the painful subject.

"Yes," she says with a smile while wiping tears away. "That's another good thing that came out of our silly escape. Sia and the King freed the slaves they found hidden in the tunnels under Sketos. Brian was one of the very few still alive. Sia said a Human woman was long dead, and another one escaped somehow. But you know... it's an Ice Planet. An escape doesn't mean much. The other slaves were not Humans, and they were all returned to their homes."

"Is Brian here? Can I see him?" I ask, all giddy, a bit like her. I think it's catching.

"Yes and no," she says with a sigh. "Brian had been badly tortured. For days and nights without a break, they hurt him so much; it's a wonder he's still alive. Sia doesn't want to talk about the state she found him. She's too traumatized by that image. Brian has been in a healing pod ever since, and he still has a couple of months or so left. It is some alien medical technology that can restore broken bones and damaged organs. I didn't visit him because Sia said the pod looks really scary. Brian is submerged in some healing glittery gooey stuff. And... you know... naked. Sia asked us to give him privacy and stay away. It's not like he can tell we're there anyway. Of course, try to say it to Jade. She visits him whenever..."

"Can I go? I promise I won't look at his junk," I say, and she just giggles.

"You will have to ask Sia; she is very protective of Brian. Well, everybody treats Brian like a national treasure because the King has a strange obsession with him. The rumor goes

Brian is the reason why the King decided to invade Earth," she says, confusing me even more. "It turns out, our King was so impressed with Brian's resilience, honor and strength, he decided Humans are worth protecting against all odds. The Tarrassians think the Human Spirit is an actual thing and a special power. Imagine that."

What a strange thing indeed. I mean, Brian is the best Human I know, but to invade a planet over that? One with compatible females, nevertheless. A bit convenient if you ask me. I don't say it to her because she trusts these people and refers to their King as hers. She's made a home for herself here, and I will respect that.

"Everything will be okay, Gianna, you will see. Just one day at a time," she says, and here comes my anger again.

"Sure, it's great to give advice from where you're standing, Natalia. You have a place to call home, an army of aliens who follow you around like puppies, a man who fights Sphinxes and changes ancient laws for you, and even a freaking pet, no matter how ugly."

"Yes, it is true. I am so blessed; I will never understand what I've ever done to deserve it," she says, and her big blue eyes fill with happy tears.

Her answer is like a slap in the face. I am such a shitty person! Keep forgetting this girl was born a slave. She grew up watching her mother and sisters being passed around men, wondering when it would be her turn. She was kidnapped by aliens, just like I was. Despite all that, she has never lost herself. She is laughter and love and tears. She is a fighter without pretending or wanting to be one.

"I am sorry," I say, trying to at least fake some decency.

"Oh, please don't. I want to ask you something if that's okay," she says and looks shy and embarrassed. I nod and encourage her, even though I am terrified of what she might ask.

"Actually, it is more about the questions I want you to ask me," she says, and now I am really confused. "I put two and two together, and I think part of your anger is not knowing much about... things." She invites me to take a seat, and I do, simply because I am curious. Her strangeness is weirdly appealing to me.

"Tannon thinks the same and helped a bit with my little investigation."

"What is it with you and being in everybody's business?" I ask, but she just laughs as if it is a compliment.

"Look, Gianna," she begins with an embarrassed smile, "I have a feeling Zaan didn't tell you much about things, like the Sign, the mind connection, the bite..."

I get all tense at that, and my fingers go involuntarily to the little scar on my throat. I can see her bite has fully healed, with no mark left. I don't need to ask why. She is fully mated to Tannon, which means she has Tarrassian traits, such as self-healing. Besides, I saw the bite when it was fresh. It looked more like a bedroom bite than one done in anger. He obviously controlled himself. Meanwhile, Zaan... I can still remember the hanging bits of flesh. Maybe that's why the Warriors still have scars, despite their healing abilities. Big wounds do leave marks, no matter what.

"Of course he didn't tell me anything, Natalia," I say with a smirk. "He told us from the very beginning he doesn't explain things to females. Don't you remember?"

"Well, yes, I do. That's why I thought I could help a bit with that."

"Are you a relationship counselor these days?" I ask, but she just laughs.

"Look, I have to say, I was quite upset about the scar on your neck. It's obvious you and Zaan didn't have... you didn't..."

"Have sex?" I say the words she can't.

"Yes, that," she sighs in relief. "So, there shouldn't have been a bite."

"I am afraid you've lost me, Natalia," I say with a dull look. I wish I could be out there with Kayon. Not to mention I am so curious about the new clothes. I am desperate to get out of this ridiculous dress.

"As you know, Tarrassians lost their Sign and mating marks for many hundreds of years. They adopted the mating bite, a tradition of many other species, just to feel some sort of connection with their mates. In lack of any other sign of recognition, the Tarrassian males give the bite as a pledge of love to their forever mate."

"Charming. Haven't they heard of a wedding ring?" I say, and she just giggles again. I can't even upset this silly girl.

"Anyway, the bite is only given once, during the first time the couple… you know…"

"Have sex?" I offer, and she nods gratefully. What is wrong with her? Can't she tell we're all aware she can't keep her hands off her man?

"Yes. It hurts less during… you know, and the woman would be distracted. I mean, I sure was," she says with a giggle, and I roll my eyes.

"I am happy for you, Natalia, and for all the other women worthy of such special treatment. My bite, in case you are wondering, was given in a less intimate moment. We actually had quite the audience. Oh, and did I mention the hanging flesh? Like literally."

"I am sorry. It must have hurt," she says quietly.

"Well, it did, but then the marks and the Sign burned my flesh alive, so that kind of felt less painful. I would say Zaan is quite the charmer. He sure knows how to woo a girl."

"He did what was necessary to save your life; he just should have explained. Please, let me finish," she says as she can see I am about to leave. "He did it for you, Gianna. As you know, Tarrassians have two hearts and…"

"They have what?" I ask.

"Oh, Bozhe Moi, he didn't even tell you that?" She continues when I don't answer. "They have a functioning right heart they are born with. All males and females also have a silent left heart. It only comes to life when they touch their fated mate. The Sign, the locks on the arms, the left heart, all come to life with that one touch. At least that's what the Elders say. Zaan's silent heart came to life when he was looking for you after your escape. No one really knows why that happened before you two touched. I think it's rather romantic," she says with dreamy eyes.

I ignore her silly remarks because I am too stunned. He has a heart that came to life for me. It beats for me – a sudden memory of waking up with my face resting on his chest. The beating of the heart under my skin in my daytime nightmare… I remember it felt like it was mine. Because it is.

"Anyway, because of the anomaly of the situation, Zaan feared the Sign might have chosen a different way of showing itself. He knew his only chance of getting you alive from Moorra was to convince their King of your bond. It turns out even the worst of these aliens respect the connection of true mates. The Moorri couldn't see his new heart, and Zaan feared the Sign might not spark, so he gave you the mating bite in front of everyone. The Moorri is one of the species who have it, and it is sacred to them. I hope you understand now why he did it."

"It still doesn't explain why he had to tear my throat open," I say because I refuse to be reasonable.

"I think this is something only he can explain. But I can tell you a fact I noticed on my own if it helps. None of these aliens expects Humans to be as fragile as we are. It comes as a big shock to them, and it takes a while for them to learn how to touch us without causing damage. The King broke Sia's ribs, just by bumping into her."

"Oh my god, that's worse than a bite; what the hell is wrong with these people?"

"It's okay, she healed quickly as he gave her his blood."

"Yeah, I know a thing or two about that one. Zaan shoved his blood down my throat while kneeling on top of my pinned down arms," I tell her.

She gasps, and her eyes go wild with shock. Oh, well... join the club.

"Let's not mention this to Tannon. He will kill Zaan," she says, looking really worried.

At least she agrees that's not normal behavior. Not even for an alien. As it is, I have had more than enough of this conversation. "I don't know if this is one of your little schemes, but I appreciate what you are trying to do," I tell her, hoping to avoid any future couple counseling from her. "I know it's difficult for you to understand because Tannon calls you his gift, and that's exactly what you are to him. I have eyes, you know. The man worships you. Zaan and I don't have that sort of relationship. He might have been pleased with the Sign to start with because it's sacred to their kind. Since then, he's heard a few stories that I am sure made him feel like he drew the short straw."

"Gianna, he almost lost everything for you. He killed for you," she says with a pleading voice.

"It must be the Tarrassian code of honor or something because I don't think the man even likes me too much. For God's sake, Natalia, he doesn't even know my name, calls me this stupid Lorra thing, probably the name of a delicate and well-behaved former ex. Oh, and did I mention he didn't even kiss me once? That's how much he likes me!"

"Oh, Gianna... you two really need to communicate more," she says with a soft smile. "I don't know why he calls you Lorra, but Tarrassians don't kiss, honey. Not like us, anyway. Tannon kept kissing me everywhere except on my mouth," she says with a giggle. "After I told him about it, he wanted me to teach him. Me, a virgin, right?" she giggles again. "Tarrassians and most other species out there don't kiss. It might have to do with the strange appendages some aliens have inside their mouth. Ugh! As it turns out, Tannon's Purpurri ancestors were also big on kissing. Sadly, they are extinct now, and Tannon is the only one left. Did I mention Tannon can kiss the brains out of me?"

"Once or twice," I say and can't help laughing. This girl... How is that easier to say than the word sex?

"And I need to tell you something else," she says with a shy look. "Probably not very nice of me, but I wanted to make sure you were safe with Zaan and all that after he acted like a possessive, unhinged loony." That's one way of saying it. "So, I might have tried to interrogate Tannon when he wasn't paying much attention. I mean, you know, he was... I was..."

"Shit, Natalia!" I say, quickly covering my ears. "I don't need details. I really, really don't." She giggles, of course.

"Tannon thinks the world of Zaan and respects him very much. I am really not worried about him ever hurting you. But Tannon said something I think you should know. Just please, don't tell on me to Zaan," she begs like a child trying to avoid the teacher's wrath. "He will not be happy, male pride and all that." I just roll my eyes. Does she think Zaan and I are chat buddies?

"They have these Yellow Planet places," she starts again, rubbing her fingers against her bright pink dress. "They call them pleasure planets, I am sure you know what I mean."

"Yes, I do, and I am really not interested," I snap quickly. I don't want to know some morbid stories about Zaan and his exes. If she is trying to give me leverage over him, considering he knows my reputation, I don't want to hear it! I push away the vivid images inside my brain. Him touching other women, his lips... He gave me my first and only mind-shattering orgasm within minutes. He must have quite the experience. There is no stopping Natalia, though.

"Tannon had to drag the King off those planets, one too many times," she says with a giggle. "I think he was like part of the furniture in there before he met Sia," she adds, and we both laugh at that. "On this particular occasion, Zaan was already dragging out our 'slightly intoxicated' King when Tannon arrived. He offered to take over so the High Commander could return to his... well, you know." *No, I don't want to know!!!* "It turns out Zaan was only there to haul his own rowdy Warriors out. The two of them had a rather extensive conversation while waiting for both the King and Zaan's Warriors to sober up. You know, bromance sort of thing. I mean alienmance." I laugh again because this girl says the craziest things!

"It turns out, not only was Zaan not a regular there, but he'd never been with a woman at all. He told Tannon he would not touch any female until he found the special one. Only the one he wants to keep forever would be allowed to touch him that way. You know what I mean. How sweet is that? Gianna? What's wrong? This is good news, right? It shows how special you are to him."

I get up and push down the tears. *I will not cry!* "Of course! It is fucking great news, Natalia! It explains why he was cleared this morning but didn't come for me. Men like him want perfect women. Like you or Sia. I am the Man-Eater, remember? The party girl with the worst track record. Nobody saves themselves for damaged goods. No wonder he didn't come for me."

Natalia's pretty mouth opens in a perfect O, and I grab the pile of clothes, ready to make my exit. I almost run into Homma, who watches me with suspicion.

"My Lady," she addresses Natalia, "the Elder of the Healers and his High Lady are here and kindly request a visit."

"Oh," says Natalia, her lips parting into a bigger O.

"Thank you for my clothes, Natalia. You too, Homma, it was very kind of you," I say, and the alien woman nods. "I will let you attend to your guests and catch you later," I add, grateful for any excuse to leave.

"I think you should stay, Gianna," she says, looking a bit overwhelmed. "They might be here for you and not for me. They are Zaan's parents."

23

—

GIANNA

Great, just great! What else could go wrong? I just want to be alone with Kayon in the training pit. Maybe he will let me throw some punches at a tree or something. I am considering running the opposite way, but of course, it's too late. For a good few moments, I just stare. Luckily the unusual couple is busy greeting Natalia, who has taken over as a super-hostess. I know she is giving me time to pull myself together. Or stare, in this case.

The Tarrassian men I have met so far don't look too… alien, so this is a big shock. The old man throwing curious glances my way is what an Elder should look like. I think so, anyway. How old is he? He looks ancient! His skin is not copper any more but almost translucent, with visible blood veins underneath. His completely white hair reaches well under his waist, and his beard spreads all over his chest like a white blanket of snow. Intricate braids and tiny metal beads swirl around his hair and beard. He wears a long white tunic and loose white pants underneath. No weapons that I can see, and he has a beautiful pendant around his neck. It has the same symbol as the one engraved on my forehead. The Marni leaf. Despite his age, his body is packed with solid muscles, and his face is beautiful in a very regal way. The resemblance to his stupid son makes me observe his wife instead. Only, she looks even more like Zaan.

When he said Tarrassian women have no hair and no boobs, I wasn't sure what to expect. It wasn't this, though. This woman is beautiful! Strange, alien, but stunning, nevertheless. She is obviously not a young woman, but she has that sort of look that stays young at all ages. Baldness works really well with this kind of flawless features. Almost as if the hair would have masked all that beauty. Her head is perfectly rounded, covered by glowing rose-gold skin. She has no eyebrows, but her forehead almost mimics the presence of some. I think there are two delicate hairless ridges above her eyes. She does have eyelashes. Beautiful, thick, and long, adorning those amazing eyes. Much lighter copper than the men. They are slightly turned up and absolutely huge. They are so big, they appear made of glass. Real-life doll eyes. Her face is just as stunning as the rest of her, with sharp bones and elegant edges. I wondered at the shallow-cut Tarrassian dresses when their women are almost flat-chested. Not only does it work, but I can see the appeal. Her elongated neck looks like a work of art. Skinny shoulders should be a must because she makes it look fabulous. And she may be flat-chested, but she is not boobless. Two barely-there swells enhance the low-cut décolletage. There is an unmistakable hint of pointy nipples under the delicate fabric of her golden dress.

Just like the old man, she keeps looking my way, and finally, Natalia moves, allowing them to come closer. The woman holds on for dear life to the man's hand with her very long fingers. She is nervous, and in a way, it makes me feel more confident. They both seem overcome with emotion as they approach me. To be fair, I am not immune to the intensity of the moment either.

He starts to say something, but she makes a choked noise and covers her mouth with trembling fingers. They both just stare at me like they've seen a ghost. Or an alien. Is everyone intense in this family? They are all big on staring, that's for sure.

"Diran, her eyes!" says the woman as if I am not there. I don't get offended because whatever she sees in my eyes causes her great emotion.

"I am sorry, my daughter," says the Elder, and I almost tell him off for calling me that. *Aliens, Gianna,* I tell myself. *Different people, different customs, be open-minded.* "My beloved and I have forgotten our manners. We don't mean to make you uncomfortable, but this is extraordinary."

I am happy for the distraction offered by the servants, who come in with refreshments, because this is highly embarrassing. Do they find my eyes that alien? They've seen Sia, right? Yes, I know they are unusual. It's really the way they stand out against my dark skin. I have the same eye color as my dad, which is light green. On me, they look lime green because of the contrast. Is green an unusual color for aliens? I don't know, and I shouldn't care! Just when I thought things couldn't get any weirder, the couple come even closer, and the alien woman takes my hand into hers. Her skin is scorching, and she smells so nice. Orange flowers, of course, but there is also a hint of vanilla and rose water.

"I know we are acting a bit strange, but that is because we didn't expect the color of your eyes, my daughter," explains the woman with a very soft voice. Her smile is blinding this close, fangs and all, and I can almost feel her emotion. "The Astrals work in such mysterious ways. You must forgive our astonishment. Please, allow me to explain. When Zaan was only a little cub, we took him to planet Wallani for a trip. No beings live there as it emits poisonous gases every other few span rotations. In between, however, it has plenty of visitors. It is a thing of beauty. Wallani is a tiny planet almost covered by moving waters. It has the biggest moon in the known galaxies. At night, when the moon reaches its full cycle, the planet glows with light. Green light," she says, pointing at my eyes.

"It is really the color of the moving waters reflecting into the moon and making it appear green," says the Elder.

"Oh, Diran, must you spoil everything with science? It is a green moon, now let it go!" she tells him with the sweetest smile.

"Yes, my beloved, the moon of the Wallani planet is green."

I can hear Natalia giggling from the sofa as she watches us with amused eyes. I am happy she is entertained because I am more uncomfortable than ever.

"As I was saying before I got interrupted," says the alien woman still holding my hand, "we took Zaan there to see the phenomena. He became obsessed with that planet and its moon. Even after he became a Warrior, he would often stop there between assignments. He would just sit by the moving waters, staring at that green moon. Now, we understand why," she says, her voice trembling with emotion. "Somewhere, in another galaxy, there was a beautiful female with eyes the color of the Lorra moon. And our great Astrals brought her to him and gave her his mating marks!"

"Oh, Bozhe Moi, this is so romantic! That's why he calls her Lorra. I love it!" says Natalia like an excited puppy. At least it makes the woman let go of my hand to join her on the sofa.

"Isn't that so, High Lady?" she tells Natalia. "That is why Diran and I are so overcome with emotion. Now, come, my daughter, sit with us," she tells me, and the Elder directs me towards the sofa facing her and Natalia. I keep quiet because... well, my brain is frozen, and I am grateful if it stays that way. Right now, I don't even want to meet Kayon in the forest. I just want to go to my room and cry myself to sleep. I guess crying can happen to anyone living with Natalia, so that wouldn't count. The Elder, sitting next to me, seems a bit nervous, and his next words explain why.

"We are here to take you home, my daughter, as our son instructed," he says, and I swear to God I am going to punch something after all.

"Zaan instructed no such thing, Elder of the Healers!" says his wife with a very harsh voice. To my surprise, the southern debutante smile is still on. Smiling and snapping at the same time must be a skill. "Zaan only instructed us to ask you kindly to come home with us. Of your free will, that is. He was very particular about that part," she adds, giving him another overly sweet smile that could kill.

"Yes, free will would be appreciated, but it is not a requirement. She is coming home with us regardless," says the Elder next to me. "The New War in the galaxy is coming closer to Tarrassia every day. My son needs to know his female is safe, in his dwelling."

Zaan's mom ignores him and makes him swap places with her instead. He gives Natalia an apologetic look as he sits next to her. Just when I felt more at ease, the woman takes my hand in hers in a motherly gesture. At least that's what they make it look like in the movies. Not something my real mother would do in real life.

"You will have to excuse my mate, sweet youngling," she says, giving me a look full of love. Her eyes instantly turn to gold, and I feel like running away once again. "The males in my family tend to be a bit controlling, overbearing, annoying, obsessive, and ridiculous on any given span. At least Zaan doesn't have temper tantrums," she adds with a snooty look towards her mate. Natalia covers her mouth with both hands, trying to block a giggle, but I am not sure I can stop mine. I can see what Zaan meant when he said once you turn a Tarrassian woman on, you can't turn her back off.

"It is best if I talk for both of us," she adds, giving him another one of 'those looks'. "My sweet daughter, we are here to escort you to the Marni Residence and reintroduce you to everybody in a more… normal way, perhaps." Her eyes can no longer hold mine and the Elder looks downright murderous, but I can tell it's aimed at his precious son, not me. Perhaps bringing your fiancée home in chains is just as unusual on Tarrassia as it is on Earth. I don't say anything because… well, because I am not Natalia or Jade. Despite my wild reputation, I am the quiet sort, and I need to know if this woman is an ally or an enemy before I react.

"First, we will make sure you are comfortable in your new home," she continues, but with less confidence. Did she expect me to be jumping up and down with joy? "Afterwards, Diran and I will be returning to our High City residence. The King wants his High Healer close to the Queen and the unborn Royal cub. I couldn't be any happier as I love the High City and I am especially fond of the Human females. I have never been able to bond with my Tarrassian peers, you know? Some of them say I talk too much and I don't know my place. Can you imagine that, my youngling? Me, talking too much! I would never!" I involuntarily look at the Elder, and he just shrugs. Natalia looks like she's about to choke, trying to stop a giggle. I can totally understand why my new 'mom' gets along with the Humans.

"Anyway, as I was saying before Diran was shrugging; the Marni Residence and the Red Forest belong to you now. All its inhabitants, beasts, lands, and the sacred Marni Trees are now under your care and command."

What on earth?

"Oh, that is never a good thing," says Natalia looking really embarrassed and about to cry. She obviously wants to tell me in private, but the Elder asks her to explain. Now, it would be rude not to.

"Well, that's what Tannon, I mean the High Elder, said to me before he left me. Gave me his Palace and all that comes with it," she says with a small voice.

"Tannon left you?" I say, and I am not sure I can believe my ears. He worships her.

"Yes, long story. It feels like it happened in another life. I promise I will share when you have some time," she says softly.

"My dearest High Lady, of course, the High Elder was not going to leave his true mate; that just doesn't happen. The Sign won't allow it!" says Zaan's mom with that insane smile on. "In Tarrassian culture, the dwelling and all the riches that come with it belong to the female. If a male upsets his mate, he is invited to leave the residence. Most will remove themselves before even asked to. A matter of honor. That is what the High Elder was trying to do. He must have done something to upset you, so he removed himself."

"Oh, Bozhe," screams Natalia and claps with excitement. "Does that mean I can kick Tannon out when he annoys me?"

"Yes, of course, High Lady. So can the Queen. The Palace belongs to her, and if the King missteps, she can…"

"That is enough, Talla!" says the Elder, and we all startle at his tone. That was not a suggestion. His wife can tell she's probably gone too far, and within seconds she transforms into the demurest creature I have ever seen.

"My darling daughter," starts the Elder watching me with intense eyes, "my reckless son has been shamed enough in the eyes of all Tarrassians. Please, take your rightful residence and don't add to his misfortune. Besides, I would love to have a wise female in my family. We obviously need one of those," he says, and Natalia can't hold that giggle back any more. "My son asked me to inform you, he will not bother you with his presence. Also, he wanted you to know all your arrangements with the High Keeper can carry on as planned. I hope you know what he meant as he did not explain to me. I hope this arrangement is suitable, and now you will allow us to escort you," he ends, giving me a reassuring smile.

"Gianna?" says Natalia, asking for my attention. Her smile is soft and cute as usual, but the baby blue in her eyes looks fierce. "Before you make a decision, I want you to know you will always have a home here and a protector in the High Elder. You don't have to do anything against your will. Never again and definitely not under my watch."

I lean back against the foamy fabric of the sofa, a big smile on my face. Something clicked, just not sure what. Layers of pain, the memories, and the past altogether have somehow shrunk. Like they are part of me, instead of being me. I feel lighter.

"*Merida*, is that your new Tarrassian personality?" I ask with an unfamiliar playfulness in my voice.

"I am afraid that's my old Russian one," she says, and we both laugh. I haven't in so long. Diran and Talla seem a bit lost over our exchange but incredibly happy as I politely accept their offer. At least I get to be Ollianna's boss.

24

GIANNA

Unlike her sister, Ollianna is quiet, and after two weeks, I decide I like having her around. She just brought me a Tarrassian flower tea, as she calls it, and made herself lost, without any other words. She brings me breakfast and dinner in the form of a smoothie. I only get solid food for lunch, and it is cut in ridiculously tiny bites. For whatever reason, that makes it less threatening, like finger food. It does work; I have to say. I am still willowy, but no sticking-out bones, and that is… different. I don't dislike it. I have more energy, and despite the constant pain in my mating marks, I am okay, I guess. The pain itself is rather dull and definitely not excruciating like before. Maybe it's so familiar by now, I don't notice it any more. Which, of course, is a problem in itself.

I have no idea what to do with myself. I spend most of my time inside my bedroom, and I only explore the garden, especially in the evenings. Despite my resolution to dislike my new home, I cannot ignore the purple sunset. It is glorious. As if someone sets purple fires to the entire planet. But even when I do that, I don't go far and stick to the narrow garden strip that's right outside my bedroom. For some reason, my mating marks are always brighter in the evening. I do know the scary forest beasts are real, as I can hear them at night. I have no intention of flashing them like a bright red beacon. After all, keeping myself safe is one of his rules. It feels silly following his instructions when he is not even here to see it, but I am doing it anyway.

I am not a prisoner, and I can go anywhere I want but instead I stick mainly to my quarters. I wish I could be like Natalia.

Go out there, dig for secrets, explore, make friends, be... normal. I almost feel watched at all times, and my paranoia keeps me away from everybody. These people, aliens, whatever, must think I am some pretentious bitch. They probably hate me because they used to have a very caring family to look after, now they have me. I wonder if this place was this quiet when Talla and Diran lived here. There is no noise outside my bedroom. All the servants tiptoe around – unlike Natalia's house, where even the furniture seems alive. Ollianna is polite but distant and somehow sad. I try not to remember it's most likely because she misses Zaan. She must hate me but keeps that to herself and looks just as broken as I am.

Talla and Diran didn't joke when they said they only wanted to reintroduce me to the Marni House people, then move on to their new residence. They were here for about an hour before they returned to the High City. I won't hold it against them, as their crazy King called for Diran every ten minutes or so. He wants his High Healer as close to Sia as possible.

How strange, but I think I would have liked them to stay. Talla said I must call her if I wanted company, but I haven't. I do see her daily on this thing they call a com. It's a bit like a live hologram. I keep it short and polite, but I am left feeling empty. I promise myself, next time, I will say a few more words or ask her to come over, but I don't. I never do.

That also goes for my interaction with the girls. They added me to their group chat on my first day back at the Marni

Residence. It is the craziest group chat ever! Or maybe they are meant to be this way. I've never been part of one. I was home-schooled, so I never had any friends growing up. After I left home, Yara was my first and only friend. Texting her wasn't that much fun and we were always together anyway.

Meanwhile, this chat... Well, Jade is on there, which of course brings it to a whole new level of fun. And crazy. I read everything like an addict. I only text if they ask me a direct question, and of course, I keep it to a couple of polite, meaningless words. They don't complain, giving me time and patience. It's so strange to have friends and be part of a little tribe. Not to mention, so much fun.

Well, it's mainly Jade texting crazy things and Natalia encouraging the madness. There is a naughty streak to her and Jade always brings it out. Sia is more reserved, not always able to reply or chat much. She apologizes, blaming her busy Royal schedule. Jade always responds with a sex-related comment about her and the King going at it like rabbits. To my surprise, Sia just laughs it off. Occasionally, she uses the chat to tell Jade to back off or stop misbehaving. Apparently, she usually causes a riot around the Palace. Going where she's not meant to, swearing, biting random aliens, breaking every rule they have, flirting with everything attached to a dick, you name it. But Jade makes me laugh, and that's pretty much all I have going right now.

The chat is jam-packed at the moment, as Natalia told us her news. I should have known her idea of *news* puts mine to shame. First, she is pregnant and I had no choice but to reply to that. My strange, overly polite congratulations felt cold and stupid compared to the girls' reactions. Natalia also told us she would get married in a month. She wants it like yesterday, but Tannon is an Astral, and the date has to be special. Once a year, due to extraordinary cosmic phenomena, Tarrassia has three moons instead of the usual two, one for each Astral.

Natalia wants to combine Human, Tarrassian, and Purpurri traditions for the wedding. On that note, Jade and I are meant to be her bridesmaids. Sia and the King are their *soul witnesses*, whatever that means. I wish I could have an excuse and just disappear on that day. I am still trying to find a reasonable reason for not showing up. I am turning into a recluse, and for once, I am not sure I want to. I just don't know how to reach out.

I surprised myself by refusing Kayon's offer for training. What is the point? I know he is just trying to indulge me the way one would a child – that and because Tannon told him to, no doubt. I am many things, but spoiled brat I am not. My father wanted to cultivate that image, but it never became me.

Kayon is a busy man. Not only does he look after the Oria birds and the White Palace, but he also helps Tannon train the real Warriors. The ones that have an actual purpose. Not to mention, he has a family of his own. He has better things to do than train me. I know now there are no Warrior women on this planet. Tarrassian women are wallflowers. Talla is the only one with a 'wild reputation', and she couldn't fight a cricket. Or whatever similar thing they have around here. Some of the former slaves do come from places like Earth, where women can be soldiers. Here though, they just wear pretty dresses and look after households or the High Ladies. As I said, training is useless. It's not like I even need the cardio. The more I live here, the stronger I feel. Not to mention the Sign enhances everything. Such an irony. It hurts, yet it makes me stronger.

Technically, I could go for cardio if I felt like it. The one place I did explore was the training quarters. I expected an old-fashioned gladiators' pit, but instead, I walked into something as alien as it gets. The place is the size of a soccer stadium, split into different levels. I could never have imagined anything like this. What we call a treadmill here is actually an entire room with a moving floor. I saw one of the guards in there. It left me with my mouth wide open for a good while. As he activated the floor, the entire room changed into virtual reality. Not only did the scenery turn into some red desert planet, but it looked and felt like the guard was running in sand. There is even a swimming training room. Only the pool is something that looks like a deadly vortex. So, yes, plenty of stuff to use for staying fit in there or for killing yourself. I might explore option one at some point, for fun and to forget the boredom for a while. I'll do it whenever I bring myself to try on the clothes from Gaella, that is. She has sent three more outfits since I left, all adjusted by Homma, I have been told. For now, I am wearing these ridiculous dresses.

At night, when I go to sleep, and there's no one around to see, I wear one of his shirts. Not only does it help me sleep for a straight eight hours, but it makes the pain in my Sign less intense. It is stupid, I know. He's obviously moved on, mating marks or not. For my first few days here, I expected him to show up and give me a dozen rules to follow. Now, I know he won't. He doesn't want me anymore. I try not to obsess over what happened or over what he may think of being mated to someone like me. I try not to think of why I convinced myself to hate him or why I ran away. I instinctively knew he was too good for me, so I've done everything I could to prove myself right. To leave him before he left me. The more things I learn about him, the more I think maybe he is too good for anyone. Perhaps that is why not even beautiful, perfect Ollianna can have him.

A few days ago, I decided not to analyze, think or feel. Now I do something worse. I pretend. I use my imagination to survive reality. I go to sleep in his bed, wearing his shirt, surrounded by his scent, and I pretend he's holding me. It's pathetic, but it works. It really feels like he is there, watching over me as I sleep. I haven't had any nightmares since I came here, and I rest peacefully through the night. It keeps me going, and I find myself counting the hours until I can go back to sleep and pretend. Not sure how long I can carry on like this.

A loud knock at my door pulls me out of my self-pity party. Obviously, not gentle Ollianna. One of the many identical guards informs me the Healer requests an audience. He doesn't say which one, and it's really confusing how these people use job descriptions instead of names. He is waiting for me in the Sacred Garden. I had no idea we even had such a thing. This visit could mean all sorts of bad things, but a break in the maddening routine of my new life is more than welcome.

The huge winged, horned guard escorts me to a piece of heaven. This has been here all this time, and I had no idea. I think we are somewhere in the house's center, as everything seems to be built around this garden; as if the house is nothing but a shelter meant to protect it. It reminds me a bit of the indoor Moroccan gardens, but on a much larger scale. It is huge. The enclosure is an explosion of color, water features, and various species of small shrubs. It's overwhelming but in a subtle way. In the center of it all, there is a massive tree. It looks ancient. A Marni Tree. It's so beautiful, that I forget to breathe for a moment. It feels alive. No, that is a silly thing to say, of course it's alive, it's a tree. It feels... sentient. *Or maybe you need to see more people and get a life!*

Its wide trunk is glowing violet, and its red leaves are a replica of the Sign on my forehead. It is so tall it reaches up into the purple Tarrassian sky, way higher than the wavy copper walls of my house. When did I start calling it *my house*?

Barin and his usual big smile welcome me from behind the giant fern-like plant he's been staring at. At first, I am relieved to see it's him. He will always be my 'kind alien'. Despite his usual easy-going smile, he seems troubled and on edge. He wears his Warrior kilt thingy, the massive Tarrassian sword at his waist, looking even more menacing in the peaceful garden environment. After all this time here, I still find it strange to have a normal conversation with half naked men. Not that I am looking, but they are so huge, it is kind of hard not to ...see things.

Barin seems a bit dishevelled, and maybe his beard could do with a brush. There are some fresh wounds over his wide pecs and toned abs, all in various stages of self-healing. Have they been in a fight? Is that why he is here? Zaan can't be hurt! I think I would know. I am sure I would. He follows my eyes and gives me a reassuring smile.

"My wounds are almost healed, High Lady. Nothing to worry about," he says.

"Please call me Gianna. At least when we're alone," I say, as I am now aware of all the stuck-up Tarrassian protocols. We sit in large stone armchairs, facing each other, and luckily a servant comes with refreshments I should have asked for. Yes, I am definitely no Natalia. I have no hosting skills, and I am a social disaster.

"How have you been, Barin?" I ask, and I feel like groaning. I am so out of my element. The thing is, I don't even know what that is. I was always what others expected me to be. Do I even have an element? Do I know who I am meant to be?

"Very challenging times, Gianna," he says and waits for my next question. Great!

"Is the... Blood Fleet okay?" God, someone give me a brain!!!

"As in the main ship?" he asks, and I can't blame the guy. Not my smartest moment.

I take a deep breath, and I ask the one thing I feel like asking. Damn social rules!

"Why are you here, Barin? Is everything okay?" *He can't be hurt. Please, don't be hurt!*

"Yes, Gianna," he says, but once again, he looks pretty nervous. *Please, don't be hurt.* "As much as I would love to stop by uninvited and check on you whenever I am around, it's not exactly wise. Unmated males don't pay friendly visits to mated females. Not without chaperones, that is."

Oookay, now this is strange. I take a sip of my flower tea,

hoping it is not what it tastes like: gin. I have been living on this stuff, so it better not be. I give it a few seconds, hoping I don't have to ask again. The guy is a pack of nerves. Oh my god! Is he going to confess a secret crush on me or something? No, no, no! I am desperately eyeing the exit.

"I am here to see Ollianna, if you don't mind, Gianna," he says, avoiding my eyes.

It takes a while before my panicked brain registers his words. He wants to see Ollianna? I am surprised but too relieved to wonder about his strange request. I could get her called here, but after the rush of adrenaline, I am happy to go get her myself. I honestly feel like I dodged a bullet.

After I excuse myself, it takes a long time to find her, despite the help I get from my winged guard. Different servants keep sending me on a wild goose chase. What is going on? Twenty annoying minutes later, I find her in my own quarters. I seriously want to shake the life out of her. Was she hiding in here? Her beautiful skin flashes all sorts of colors, more intense than I have ever seen them. Is she having the alien version of a panic attack? She runs to me and grabs my hands with those beautiful long fingers of hers.

"Please, my Lady, don't make me see him. I know you don't like me much, but please don't force me," she pleads, and something amazing happens to her face. Technically, she's not crying, but her eyes swim in moisture, and they keep flickering like they are on fire. The wetness makes them look like precious stones.

"Just to make it clear," I say with a soft voice, "we are talking about Barin here. That's who you don't want to see, right?"

"Yes, yes, my Lady," she says quickly.

I suddenly understand a few things, such as why she didn't want to reach out to him and ask for his help with my restraints. That was not about her wanting me to bleed to death.

And she is definitely not after my man, I realize with relief. *Stop calling him that, Gianna!* I admonish myself. He doesn't want to be anything of mine.

"But why, Ollianna? If you don't mind me asking, of course. Barin is so… nice," I say, and I do mean it. Not just compared to the other Tarrassians. He would pass as a decent guy on any planet.

"He is no such thing. He is a coward!" she says with a fire I didn't think she had. And she obviously believes it.

"Can you explain? But before you do, let me promise you no woman, female, I mean, in this house, does anything against her will. If you say you don't want to see him, then you don't!" My words make her relax instantly, and her beautiful glowing shoulders slump. She doesn't look any happier, though.

"It is not much to tell, my Lady," she says with trembling lips and cast-down eyes. "I have his heart, and he has mine. His is not worthy, though. Like I said, he is a coward. My sister and I were saved by the High Commander from a horrible place. Please, do not ask. I do not wish to remember. It was a place outside the reach of the Coalition of the Seven Stars. The Commander saved us against the orders of the Council. It was a clandestine mission, and he only took the Blood Fleet's two Healers with him, expecting the slaves to be in a bad condition. And we were. Especially my sister. She was barely alive. Two other Garrii females didn't make it at all. It took several spans of hiding and fighting until we could all be rescued by the Commander's Warriors. The five of us somehow bonded during those long spans of darkness. The High Commander will always feel like a brother to me. Andrac took one look at my sister, Gaella, and he knew she was his mate. Signs and mating marks are beautiful, but one doesn't need any of those to recognize their soul's extension. I thought Barin and I had the same thing. The others thought so, too.

"As you know, before the Human females, Tarrassians were not allowed to mate for life with other species. What is more, only Tarrassian couples were allowed to procreate before the High Elder changed the law. That did not stop Andrac. He is a strong, loyal male and a good mate to my sister. He left his Warrior rank and his family behind, just to be with her. The Great Warrior, I mean the High Elder, gave them sanctuary in the Purple Forest."

She seems lost in thoughts, and I just let her cling to my hands and listen. No one ever confessed anything private to me before. Not even Yara. I am not sure what I should do or say. So, I just listen. Part of me still can't believe aliens are so…normal. They feel loss, love and…I am not sure why I expected anything different. They are just people.

"Barin and I were also offered sanctuary so we could be together. Sadly, I was almost an orbit rotation away from legal mating age. The High Commander was very strict about that and said we must wait. He didn't even allow us to be alone together, without supervision. Andrac took Gaella to the Purple Forest, and I came here and waited. And waited… I have been here for six orbit rotations," she says, and I direct her towards a fluffy armchair. I don't think her legs can hold up for any longer. I pull myself a violet wooden stool next to her.

"Did he say anything at all? Did he explain?" I ask, feeling some anger of my own. Men are such shitheads – even the nice ones. My brain is not getting the feminist vibe, though. It reminds me of men like Brian, Kayon, Tannon, and the crazy Tarrassian King who treats Sia like the jewel in his crown. I don't even add Zaan to that list of non shitheads. He is too perfect to be on any list. Why on earth would any Gods think I could have a man like him?

"He sent me a com text the day I turned seventeen rotations, the legal mating age on Tarrassia," Ollianna says, pulling me out of my thoughts.

"Please tell me he didn't break up with you in a text."

"That is exactly what he did, my Lady," she says with a broken little sigh. "By then, he wasn't just The Fleet's Healer but the Third in Command. He said his responsibilities couldn't allow him to have a family. By that, he meant he wasn't going to leave a life of honors and adventures to hide in the Purple Forest with me for the rest of his spans. I was only a youngling, but I was smart enough to understand his meaning. Never heard from him again. He often came here with the High Commander, but I always stayed in my room when it happened, and he never asked for me. He is only doing it now because it is convenient."

I am about to ask what she means, but I remember the circumstances have indeed changed. Now he can marry her, whatever they call it here, and even have kids with her. No need to hide, and he can keep his precious job. I am only holding down the anger because she needs my care now. It may not be my thing, but I am not that heartless either. I give her a hug, and she doesn't pull away.

"Do you still... love him?" I ask.

"He will forever have my heart, my Lady. I did not return to Garria, as my sire would have wanted me to mate with one of our people. I could never do that. I only belong to Barin," she says with a determined look on her angelic face. "It doesn't mean I will be his afterthought. I am no one's convenient choice. Real love requires hardship, not convenience!"

I watch her with envy; I cannot help it. Just like Natalia, she appears fragile and clueless. In reality, they both own who they are, and they are in charge of their lives. What am I missing here?

"Please don't worry, Ollianna," I tell her with what I hope looks like a kind smile. "I will tell him you won't see him, and we don't have to talk about this again unless you want to."

25

GIANNA

I am trying to contain my anger as I return to the Sacred Garden. It is mainly because my huge guard has picked up on it and thought it would be a good time to inform me of his orders. It turns out Zaan has instructed the guards to kill anyone who angers me, Tarrassian or not. Such an idiot! Doesn't he know everybody angers me? I have issues, don't I? So, I pretend I am not fuming hoping my guards won't kill the stupid Healer.

Barin looks even more dishevelled than before. His eyes search behind me, and his normally serene smiley face flashes anger for a second. Are his shoulders getting wider? Really? The War Beast thingy should scare me, but it only annoys me more.

"Keep it together, Barin, you have no right to be offended or angry with her," I tell him with a quiet voice before all the guards barge in.

"I know that. I am here to ask for her forgiveness. I was wrong," he says, and he looks so broken, my anger vanishes in no time. "I know I am not worthy of her, but she is mine, and I am hers. I will spend the rest of my life span becoming the male she deserves."

"Oh, Barin," I sigh. "I do believe you, but I can also understand why she doesn't. It just feels so convenient that you are here now that interspecies relationships are allowed by law."

"Cursed fires, is that what she thinks?" he says, pulling at his long black hair in a very familiar gesture. Zaan does that a lot. The pain in my marks intensifies, and I am cold again. I feel for Ollianna and even for this tormented man in front of me. I just wish they would all go away. I only want to be alone and have an early evening. In his bed, wearing his shirt, pretending he is here.

"Of course she does," he says, answering his own question. "This is all just an unfortunate coincidence. I do not care about that law. If she wants me to leave my position, my title, even my Mother Planet for her, I will. We can live on Garria; we can go wherever she chooses. She must let me explain. Please, Gianna! I didn't leave her because I feared our laws."

"I am afraid it is not my call, Barin. And your timing is very bad indeed. Do you mind if I ask why you left her?"

"I was only appointed Third in Command a few span rotations before her birth span. I was the Healer of the most powerful space fleet amongst the galaxies. My Warriors needed me; my Commander needed me. I thought it was wrong to leave my duty and follow my heart. It felt like a weakness. Zaan told me at the time, a male's first duty was with his mate and his family. He said for every Warrior that leaves or dies, there are hundreds more to take his position. But there is no one to replace us in the hearts of our loved ones. I was angry with him. I told him he was only saying that because it was not his choice to make.

"And now that it has been his turn to make that decision, he did not hesitate to act like a strong male. He put you first, and nothing else mattered. Not his Blood Fleet, not his King, not even his honor. That is what has changed for me now. I watched my oldest friend do what I couldn't. I am deeply ashamed, and I will spend the rest of my spans asking for her forgiveness."

I need to be alone. I can feel tears coming, and I must be on my own. I hug myself in an attempt to stop the cold in my bones. I push away the desperate need to scratch at my skin. Zaan doesn't like it when I hurt myself, so I don't.

"High Lady? Gianna? Are you well?"

"Yes, Barin. I am," I lie the best I can. That is what I am, isn't it? A liar! "Like I said, Ollianna won't see you, and there is nothing I can do about it."

"So, you won't mind if I take my mate with me?" he asks, and I have to pause for a good minute. Maybe the fricking translation device has malfunctioned. But the determination in his eyes tells me I heard that correctly.

"Excuse me? Which part of NO are you not getting, Barin?" I raise my voice, forgetting about my own pain for a while.

"Willingness would be appreciated but is not required," he says, and I wish I hadn't left my knife in my room. Sooooo infuriating! Diran said the exact same thing. Tarrassian men are top dog in the asshole league.

"Ollianna lives in my house, under my care, and I say you cannot take her. Would you like to go against me, Healer?"

"I do not have a death wish, High Lady. My female needs me alive," he says, and his sadness takes my anger away once again. "Zaan would take my head off even for causing you this upset. I am just desperate. If she won't let me explain and make amends, what else is left? Are we both to live with this pain forever? What do I do, Gianna? She won't take my calls or read my com texts. I can't reach her mind as she's not Tarrassian. How do I explain? How do I ask for her forgiveness?"

His sincere questions and desperation make me forget I wanted to kill him a second before. He may be an asshole, but there is no denying his feelings for her. Everybody makes mistakes. I know that better than anyone.

"Sadly, I don't know. I am the worst person to give relationship advice," I tell him, and I really wish I could help. I can't even help myself. I am no master of schemes like Natalia. Wait!! I can hear the little wheels inside my brain spinning. Yes, that could work.

"However, I do know someone who can help," I tell him, and his copper eyes ignite with little golden specks. God, I hope I am not sending him on a wild chase. I know hope can hurt like a bitch!

"I suggest you talk to the High Lady of the Purple Forest. I strongly advise you to ask permission from the High Elder first. I am sure you don't need me to explain why. Let's just make this clear: whatever she advises you and whichever action you may take, fucking kidnapping is not an option!"

Cursing feels good. No wonder Jade is always happy.

"Thank you, Gianna," he says and takes a fist to his chest in the traditional Tarrassian salute. Is he leaving? Why won't he say anything about him? *I need to know. Something. Anything.*

"Barin?" I stop him in his tracks. "How…? Is Zaan doing well?" I ask before I lose my courage.

"I don't really know, I am sorry," comes the unexpected answer. How can he not know?

"What do you mean, Barin?"

"This is my first stop on Tarrassia in many span rotations, and I only had time to come here. I still talk to him via com, but he would only answer battle-related questions. He never replies to the more personal ones."

I know he just explained, but I don't understand a word.

"How can you not know, Barin? Are you not always together, fighting with the Blood Fleet?"

"You don't know," he says with a sigh. I let him continue, as I am too scared to ask. "Zaan is no longer the High Commander.

Nodric refused the position as he is not keen on rules or discipline. I am the Fleet's High Commander now, and Nodric is my second. Which is vexing painful, if you ask me. No idea how Zaan managed to control that male for so long."

"I don't understand, Barin." I know I sound like a broken record, but it makes no sense. "I thought the Council didn't find him guilty. Why would they take his Command away?"

"They didn't," he says with an embarrassed look on his face. "Zaan gave it up on his own."

"Why? He worked all his life to achieve that," I say, and this time I can't hold my tears back. I just can't.

"Being the Commander of the Blood Fleet involves a lot of traveling and staying away from home for long periods, especially now, with the New War upon us. Without consuming the mating bond," he says, avoiding my eyes, "the Sign would give significant pain. If the mates are too far away from each other, the marks may cause burning and skin damage. Zaan is a Warrior used to pain, and our species' self-healing abilities can help ease it. You cannot do either. So, he gave up his Command and stayed on Tarrassia to make sure you won't be suffering."

26

GIANNA

Two days later, I have no tears left. Unlike Natalia's, mine don't have a steady flow. Pretending he never left me doesn't cut it either. My imagination still works; that's not the issue here. I can almost feel him with me every night. Almost is not good enough anymore.

Ollianna has been watching me pace the floor of my bedroom for the last hour or so. She looks worried, but she keeps quiet, except for the times when I ask questions. And I have been asking her a lot since I decided she was not the enemy.

"Can Tarrassians only communicate silently with their own kind?" I ask without stopping my agitated walk.

"Yes, Gianna," she says. "I am not sure about the High Elder. His mind feels different to me. Well, he is an Astral, so who knows what he can do? And I think once Tarrassians are mated for a long time, they can talk to their betrothed, no matter their species. Andrac can reach Gaella's mind, even though they don't have the Sign."

"I see," I say, lost in my thoughts. "Does it mean Tarrassians can also read each other's minds?" I ask, even though I know they can't. He couldn't tell I was lying to him. I wish he could. I wish he had stopped me.

"Mind talking is no different than verbal talking. If you ask me something and I do not wish to reply, there is no conversation," she says, pushing stubborn locks of blue hair behind her pointy ears. Sometimes, it's easy to forget I live in a world where I chat with elves and orcs. "One can start the conversation inside the mind of another by asking a question. Or greeting them," she explains. "If they don't acknowledge you, that's the end of it. It is forbidden by all the laws of the stars to breach a mind. Most won't even be able to do it. As cubs, Gaella used to do it for fun. Other cubs, too," she says with a sweet smile on her face. "As they grew and understood the dangers of breaking the laws, they have lost that capability. Not sure about my sister, though. Gaella can be naughty." She giggles, and for a moment, I wish I'd had a sibling to share my pain and laughs.

"Can I reach other Tarrassians' minds?" I ask, fiddling with the slits of my long skirt. Better those than picking at my skin.

"Yes, of course, Gianna, I will teach you. It takes a bit of practice, but you can try it with your Human females. The mated ones, that is. The Sign gave them Tarrassian abilities. I am a Garrii, and my species can reach all minds. Once you let me in, we can talk that way."

"Yes, that's good," I say without paying much attention. "Do you know where *he* is?" I ask suddenly, and she looks like she is about to faint. Now that I know her heart belongs to another man, I don't jump to silly conclusions, as before. I think her species is very nonconfrontational and easily distressed.

"He is in the High City, my Lady," she says with eyes cast down and not using my name. She only does that when she hides things. And my god, this girl sucks at lying. I let it go because I could very easily find out. I am his mate, and I am sure his location is not meant to be a secret. I am just as certain he would come home if I asked him. I've been here for long enough to know Tarrassians are loyal and respect this Sign thingy more than anything else. And in moments such as these, when I miss him more than I miss my next breath, I am tempted to do just that. Ask him to come home.

He lost everything because of me. His job belongs to another, he avoids his friends, I kicked him out of his house. Not sure he even sees his parents. Talla is a chatterbox. She would have let that slip during our conversations. Yes, if I ask him to come back to me, he would in the blink of an eye. I am his first priority because I have his Sign. Like all the other Tarrassian males, he is loyal, protective, and caring of his mate. He also chooses to stay away. The message is clear, and I don't know if I am desperate enough to ignore it. Should I swallow my pride and ask him to come back to me, regardless? It's not like I don't deserve the cold shoulder or his disgust. Maybe in time, I can make him like me? I know he did in the beginning. Before my lies and before he knew...

It's not like he will go with another woman. He only wanted me, even before he met me. He chased all his life a moon glowing the same green color as my eyes. His silent heart started beating for me before we even touched, right? Unless he is with me, he will never be with any other woman. Maybe that's the way I have to look at this and ignore my pride. Women like me shouldn't wish for more. True, I will always have to live knowing he took me back because I asked him to. What do I do? I miss him so much! My marks look as bright as the day I got them, but I am dying on the inside. I would do anything to get him back.

A loud knock pulls me out of my tormented thoughts, and a large winged guard announces the High Elder. Ollianna's eyes go big, but mine go bigger. Shit!!! Is he here to kill me? If stupid Barin approached Natalia without asking permission first, I am dead meat.

I meet him in the Sacred Garden, as apparently that's where all the visitors are welcomed. I stop suddenly, as the image in front of my eyes leaves me breathless. It feels like I am interrupting a sacred moment. The High Elder, looking bigger than life itself and not just literally, has his forehead placed against the Marni Tree's huge trunk. They are both glowing. There is no other word for it. The High Elder has his eyes closed, and his huge hands rest on the violet bark.

The tree looks like it's being X-rayed. I can see red sap going up and down, glowing with thousands of shiny particles. It goes all the way up to the top, as far as I can see anyway. Some of the lower branches reach for the Elder's body, trying to touch him. They go around his large body as if trying to embrace him. It's beautiful; they are connected and obviously communicating to each other. In that special moment, I realize I am indeed in the presence of an alien God. And my friend is mated to him. And I heard them having sex. It's just crazy. Way crazier than talking to elves and orcs.

Eventually, he removes his hands and forehead, and the tree trunk becomes solid again, the intense glow gone. The branches release their hold on him and he turns towards me with a smile. He looks very different from the first time I saw him. He was still the Great Warrior that morning, wearing his kilt and his battle scars like a trophy. No weapons today, but do Gods even need them? Not to mention, he is large enough to kill any creature with his bare hands. He wears a white tunic with a beautiful golden pattern over his large barrel chest. I think it's a constellation, or a map of some kind. Crisp white pants and golden foot coverings complete the look of someone who is as alien as it gets. His Purpurri legacy makes him look more wolf than humanoid, and those stunning purple eyes are as hypnotic as ever. His large beard and shoulder-length hair look more tamed than the last time I saw him.

Once again, a servant beats me to my perfect hostess game and comes with refreshments. I sip my flower tea, thinking the Elder doesn't look too angry. This might not be about Barin after all. Maybe a bit tired? Do Gods get tired? Probably the ones mated to Natalia do.

"It is pleasant and refreshing to have a moment of peace, such as this," he says, and I struggle not to laugh. I was spot on. Poor guy... "Natalia is a bit too excited with our Sacred Ceremony. I should perhaps make such traditions illegal," he says with a sigh, and this time I do laugh.

"I know I should probably offer to help her," I say, feeling genuinely guilty.

"No need to encourage the madness, Gianna," he smiles. "She has plenty of help. The Oria servants are completely out of control trying to please her, there is a steady flow of Tarrassian High Ladies coming and going, Natalia's two mothers are on their way from Earth, and the Diri pest pet attacks my Guards. My beautiful Lia says he has *anxiety*, because there are too many people around."

God, it does sound manic. I would like to think that's the cause for his tired eyes. But no, my instinct tells me that's not it.

"Natalia doesn't need help, Gianna, but I do," he says, watching me with those strange eyes.

Sure, I help the Gods all the time. I totally kick ass! I don't tell him because, well, I'd rather listen than talk.

"As you know, Gianna," he starts talking with a calm yet booming voice. He even sounds like a God! "the New War is upon us, and life as we know it changes rapidly."

Great! Maybe this is something I should mention. I have no idea what he is talking about. It makes me feel like shit because it reminds me people don't really tell me much. Like I am fragile or something. Such a joke, considering I am the only one of the Humans who wanted to be a soldier.

"Oh, I see. You don't know," he says, and it is not a question, just an acknowledgment of my complete lack of information. "Tarrassia and the Coalition of the Seven Stars have been protecting the galaxies since the beginning of times. We helped the weak, found new, sustainable planets for species in need of one, contained the Merchant Quarters' greed and stopped the slavers from preying on the lower species.

"We grew strong and arrogant. We thrived on helping the weak without noticing the strong were being the target. Under our very own eyes, sacred species like the Sphinxes were decimated. Red Orbit Planets were being enslaved, and the Coalition of the Dark Moon was growing bigger and stronger. We were blind, hiding behind our superiority, rage, and pain – all excuses, in the end.

"The Humans changed all that. And I am not talking about the reappearance of the Sign, nor about finding compatible mates. The Human male known as Brian has been part of that change, as much as the females we saved. Our Brave King started the New War because that male inspired him to."

I listen carefully and refrain from asking questions. I need more information, and for once, someone is giving it to me. Not to mention, this is all fascinating, like a strange story that belongs to a different world. Only, that is now my world. However, I do struggle to keep a straight face. An alien God, who talks to magic trees and could kill Godzilla with a punch, thinks Brian is an inspiration. As someone who knows him personally, I can vouch for him as one hell of a guy. Brian is loyal, protective, and definitely stronger than most other men on Earth. In this alien world, he is nothing but a Human trapped for many months in a healing pod – someone who can't even self-heal. I hope the Tarrassians and their Coalition have better plans when it comes to saving the world, than Brian O'Connor.

"I spent long spans trying to understand. I could feel things before, when I was only the Great Warrior," he says, and he definitely seems guilty. "Once I accepted who I was, that feeling grew stronger and stronger."

"What feeling is that, High Elder?" I ask just because I don't want him to think I am not paying attention.

"Please, call me Tannon when we are alone," he says. "It is perhaps not related to the New War. Our Warriors can fight and win wars. That is not it. I can feel a blanket of sorrow, despair, and darkness spreading over the galaxies. I don't know what it is. It has no shape yet; it's building up with every nano that passes. How can we fight something with no shape? Something we cannot see or understand? What I do know is the Humans are the key to this mystery. The Marni Tree agrees. The Sacred Cave, the rocks in the Spark Mountain, the Sacred Water in my forest, the Oria birds, and the Still Waters, they all whisper the same thing. The Humans can stop the blanket of darkness I see in my mind's eye."

The moment feels charged, and my skin prickles with strange awareness. There is one question I must ask.

"Have you spoken of this with anyone else, Tannon?"

"No, Gianna," he replies with that tired look in his eyes. "I do not like hiding this from my mate. She will worry, and she will be scared. Despite her little schemes, Natalia is fragile. Especially now, with our first cub on the way. I want her to have peace. I want her to have the Sacred Ceremony she deserves. I will tell her after. I must also inform our King and the Council. I just don't want our enemies to know I am aware. Not yet. I need more answers. My people would want some reassurance. They expect Gods to solve problems. I don't think me telling them I am clueless would go down easy."

"How come you can't tell the future, Tannon? Shouldn't Gods be able to do that?" I ask, and luckily, he doesn't laugh at my silly question.

"Gods know the past, the present, and if they are worthy enough, they can feel the changes yet to come. The future belongs to the beings' free will. It changes all the time, and Gods have no control over it. No Deity should tell beings how to live their lives or what kind of future they should have."

"I see," I tell him, trying not to freak out. The more I know him the more humbled I feel in his presence. "Why are you telling me all this before anyone else?"

"I need your help, Gianna, and I wanted you to fully understand why," he carries on with the cryptic conversation. "I spent many span rotations trying to make sense of all this. Humans are the key, and I think one of them more than others. There is an invisible link, somehow, somewhere. It has started to work its thread from the moment we rescued the first Human. It is all connected. There are too many coincidences to keep calling them that.

"Our King was lost to his rage before the Queen came into his life. There is no random coincidence Natalia and Sia escaped to Sketos, of all places. It was there that the link became stronger. I don't really know what it means, but I know it is part of a larger scheme. Sia showed the King a truth none of us could see. Under our careful watch, planets were taken, Sphinxes were being crushed, angels were hiding in the mist and the Universe's course was changed forever.

"The Queen restored the balance on Sketos, freed the slaves, and helped the Ketosi regain their lost powers. Back on Tarrassia, she did the most astonishing thing of all. My cousin, the King, was nothing but an angry, lost soul before her arrival. She found the real him underneath all those layers of madness. The Queen gave us the Brave King when we needed him most."

I wonder if he knows what his story does to me. I still my face and keep listening. Trying to do the right thing, for once.

"I don't need to remind you of what Natalia did," he says,

and this time his eyes glow with love and pride. "She also found me underneath all my layers. I was nothing but a coward before she came. Hiding in my own pain. Running from my past instead of being who I was always meant to be. And the law she asked me to change? I don't know how, but I think that will play its part in our future.

"The Human male's courage and strength reminded us of what we lost. Our spirit, as the Humans call it. We have many enhancements, special powers, and abilities that make us stronger, faster, and more intelligent than most beings. Because of all that, we forgot our stories in time, forgot how to cry, how to hope, and even how to love. The Humans reminded us of what really matters."

Good thing I am not a talker because I wouldn't know what to say. It is crazy but humbling to hear such words of praise for my species from… well, from an alien God. If Jade was here, she would probably say the guy thinks with his dick. Even his own people say Natalia brainwashed him. As for me, I am not so sure. He might know what he's talking about. That could be because I've just seen the guy talk to a freaking glowing tree. Anything goes, right now.

"How can I help, Tannon?" I ask. Best to keep it simple.

"Some of the five Humans on Tarrassia have already done incredible things. Some may still have a big part to play in what is yet to come," he says, observing me. "One of you more than others, but either way, you are all a link in this thread. You all have a role to play."

"I am not too sure what Brian did to impress the Brave King," I say, trying to keep it together. "No one can question how special Sia and Natalia are; we agree on that one. But before you ask for help from this Human," I say, pointing at myself, "let me remind you of something. I robbed Tarrassia of its most honored Commander. I left the Marni Residence without its rightful owners. Should I even mention I gave a massive blow to the Human Resistance? How is that for special?"

"True, at first it may appear you are more trouble than Jade," he says with a grin, and I just laugh. I didn't expect him to have a sense of humor. He is so serious, mature and... godly. At least I feel better about my shitty self. "However, you are the only one who can help with my problem. One of them, anyway," he says, and I go back to listening. Dying of curiosity by now.

"This is not a new issue, by the way," he says. "As you know, the Tarrassian army is male-only. My species is very protective of females. We treat them like fragile flowers as soon as they are born. We have been doing so since the beginning of time. As more battles were cast upon us and we had to fight many species, we encountered some problems. Tarrassian males would not harm females. The Noorranni soon exploited that, and they enslaved many species with female warriors. My people were living targets, so we had to adapt and find a solution.

"The Coalition of the Seven Stars was created with that purpose in mind. Most of the species who joined the Coalition don't mind fighting females, not to mention they have their own female warriors. It is not enough. It never was, because the only Warriors strong enough to keep the Coalition of the Dark Moon under control are still the Tarrassians. We need female Warriors amongst the Tarrassian army. On the Blood Fleet, in the Army of Shadows, in all the units that form our great force.

"A high-ranked Commander has already tried changing the mind of the Council. He failed, as you can tell. The Elders raised their shoulders, pointing out it was not against our laws for the females to join the Warriors. None of them would do such a thing, though. Not when all they are taught from birth is to smile, look pretty, and not talk unless asked to.

"I only need one to convince the many. It may not be any Tarrassian females joining the Warrior Training Pits to start with.

It would at least encourage the former slaves who live amongst us to step forward. Many come from Warrior backgrounds and would welcome the invite. I just need one brave enough to do it first. I need a female to walk into the High City's Training Pits with her head held up high and start training with the Warriors. I believe that female is you, Gianna."

He wants me to say something. I mean, obviously, this is intended to be a conversation. Should I tell him I am not great at those?

"I am hoping you will say yes, so I can be on my way," he says with a small smile. Tarrassian men can turn smiling into the finest art. Even scarred Tannon looks handsome when he does it. "I am a male of few words. This was probably more talking than in all my spans. Please do not mention to Natalia I have this many words. She will have expectations."

I find myself laughing. Tannon always says the right things to put me at ease. Right, so he wants an answer now. Before I even get to think about one, there is something else I need to get out of the way. I can't do this behind Zaan's back. This is definitely not about being the meek woman who has to ask permission. I remember Ollianna's words about the Marni people. She said they respected his rules because he kept them safe. I didn't understand then, but I do now. Zaan has their obedience because he has their respect and love. He has mine too, so I won't do anything to upset him. Not any more.

"I am a mated woman, Tannon," I tell him. "You, Tarrassian males, can be a bit… protective, jealous and intense. No offense."

"A very accurate description. Natalia would just call us crazy," he says, and we both smile.

"Well, yes. I am not sure Zaan would appreciate me spending my days in the Training Pits with a bunch of males around." Actually, would he even care?

"I wouldn't have come here without asking permission to

visit from your mate, Gianna. It is not something Tarrassian males do," he says.

Oh my god, so this is a big thing around here. Barin is such a loose cannon! God, I hope he asks for permission before he sees Natalia. He obviously didn't bother to ask Zaan when he came here. He'd better not get me into trouble.

"I also had to explain the purpose of my visit. I only kept from him my worries about our future. I did say you were the first one I shared with."

"And Zaan agreed?" I ask without believing my ears.

"Yes," he says. I wait for details, but that's all I get. What does it mean? Is Zaan trying to tell me he doesn't care about me anymore? *Of course he doesn't; he is not here, is he?* I put the matter to rest and focus on my other questions. This is just too painful to deal with now, in front of happily mated Tannon. I'll cry myself to sleep again tonight, looks like.

"I thank you for the vote of confidence, Tannon. I really do. And because of that, I want to point out a few things. I would hate to let you down, but that is bound to happen," I say. "How am I ever going to learn how to fight? Sparring by yourself doesn't work. I am a female; no Tarrassian male would even lift an arm against me, never mind a weapon."

"I know," he says with a sigh. "I thought about it. Kayon can help you train with the younger Warriors. He doesn't mind fighting females." No, indeed. He put the fear of God in poor Ollianna.

"The Palace guards also train at the Pits, and they will spar with you. There will be many classes involving learning, battle tactics, studying our enemies. To start with, sparring will be less present in your schedule. I am hoping to gain us enough time. If your presence there encourages other females to come forward, then you can train together and spar each other."

"*If*, being the great denominator here," I say with a sigh.

"So, will you be that one female brave enough to start an army?" he asks. Of course he does. There is a reason why he is their High Elder. He knows how to play ball, hard. He dangles at me the greatest challenge of a lifetime. I wonder if he can see inside my heart when he stares with those strange purple eyes. Because if he can, he must know he has already won. This girl loves a challenge!

"I know, both you and Kayon have plenty of other responsibilities. Would I still be able to go to Warrior training when you two are not available? I really don't fancy judgmental looks or comments from males less keen on change."

"Kayon can only attend the Pits every other span. There will be theory classes on the other spans, anyway. As for me," he says, looking almost amused, "I won't be attending at all. Being an Astral is a full-time job these days. I wish they told me that before I took the position."

I smile at the joke meant to put me at ease, but it really doesn't. It sucks! It's one thing training under the supervision of open-minded Tannon or protective Kayon. The Tarrassians are stuck-up, and the new High Master of the Pits will freak out to see a woman there. I've been in this position before, and mind you, on a planet where women in the army were not a one-off. Can I put myself through that again? Can I cope with more bullying?

"I don't know, Tannon," I say with a small voice. "The new High Master might not be too keen on having women around."

"The new High Master of the Training Pits is the same former high-ranked Commander who tried to introduce females to the army many orbit rotations ago," he says with a kind smile. "I can promise you he is one of the most open-minded Tarrassians. Of course, that is when he doesn't act like a fool and send his mate to my house, all bleeding and frightened."

He stops talking to give me time to react or say something.

Over five minutes into a painful silence, he gets up to leave, as if my silence is an answer in itself. I find myself escorting him out, while trying to make my mouth work again.

For some stupid reason, my frozen brain can only form one question.

"Which part of our conversation is one of Natalia's little schemes?" I ask, looking very high up to meet his eyes. He sighs and shrugs. He doesn't even seem surprised by my question.

"I would like to believe none of it, Gianna. However, as with most things, there is always a doubt. She likes putting thoughts in my head, and I like pretending they were my ideas to start with," he says with a smile that makes him look young and very much in love.

"When do I start, High Elder?" I ask him.

"Kayon will pick you up at sunrise, Warrior. Make sure you are ready on time. The High Master has a very strict rule in place regarding tardiness. He is known to like his rules."

27

—

GIANNA

"You look beautiful, Gianna," says a sleepy but highly excited Ollianna. "It feels like you are one of my people, even with all the changes Homma added to the outfit."

Great! Now I can't even say anything offensive about the outfit. Not without being rude to her people. I mean, what the hell? What is wrong with these creatures, aliens, whatever? Aren't you meant to cover most of your skin when you go to war? I can't wear this!!!!! I beat myself for not trying the clothes on yesterday. Or maybe it's for the best. There is no way I would have survived the night without changing my mind. I am only here getting ready just before the sunrise because I refused to think about anything. I decided I was doing this, and then I went to sleep. No thinking! It was the right decision. But, good grief, this outfit... Zaan is not going to like it. He'll probably tell me to go change, in front of everybody. They are all going to stare and laugh and...

"Gianna? What is wrong? Is it not comfortable?" asks Ollianna with a small voice.

No, it's perfect. Slutty fairy-alien-cavewoman-nympho-Warrior Queen; was totally what I was looking for. Kayon will be here any minute. Shall I just not go? If Natalia can have her moms brought here, maybe I can order something from Earth. Combat pants and a baggy T-shirt, maybe? A nun outfit? Anything normal, really. A freaking bikini would look more decent than what I am wearing. But then again, it means I won't show up today. What would that say about me? Shall I wear one of the Tarrassian dresses? Maybe cut it shorter? That's just as revealing, anyway. Fucking aliens!!! There's no winning this.

I ignore Ollianna, who looks like she's about to faint. The girl cannot cope with stressful situations. I attach the sword Kayon gave me to the wide golden leather belt on my hips. I mean, what freaking animal has golden skin, right? It sure doesn't look dyed to me. The sword reaches all the way to the soles of my boots. Despite that, this is most likely a sword they give to toddlers. As for the boots... I laugh at myself in the mirror. Ollianna gives me a wary look. I know I sound hysterical, but where I come from, these babies are called hooker boots for a reason. I am surprised they forgot to add the high heels. How could they possibly leave the stilettoes out of this outfit? The black leather boots are made of the softest leather, I will give them that. They are flat and slightly pointy on my feet, molding around my calves, knees, and lower thighs like a glove. The leather is somewhat stretchy, making the boots relatively easy to pull on. Once they make contact with my skin, they seem to hold on. These freaking things better not be organic or something. The side of my slutty leg-coverings is beautifully decorated with swirls of golden thread.

And then... there's the kilt. Because, of course, there is one. Natalia and I were joking about that, but now the joke is on me, I guess. I know this white leather kilt they call Kannicloth is their traditional Warrior outfit. But, hello!! I'm a girl! I don't have thick hairy thighs nobody wants to look at. I mean, I did look at Zaan's, and I might look again, but that is not the point! I am not even sure the kilt is the worst part of my outfit. It's got to be the body because that's precisely what I am wearing. My torso is encased in this soft white leather garment. I could have easily worn this on any catwalk. Ridiculous! It's so tight; it has a corset-like quality to it, yet, easy to put on. There are no strings, zips, or fastening. It is contact with my skin that makes it mold itself to every curve. It's squeezing my tiny waist, then envelops my rounded hips like a second skin. This was so not the right time to develop curves. Those freaking smoothies! I know whose idea that was! Luckily, my average-size boobs didn't get any bigger. That's all the luck I get, though, because the leather of the body pushes them all the way up into my neck, in a sweetheart-like cut.

I mean, come on, who wears that to war? Jade would, but that's only because her weapons are very different from mine. I prefer the sharp sort. My shoulders are almost bare, but hey, I've got long sleeves. That's something, right? They reach down to my hands, edging on the back of my palms in a spear-like shape. Can't even say thank you for the small mercies, as the sleeves are cut out at regular intervals, showing my glowing mating marks and... well, a lot of skin.

I should probably be grateful for the kilt. The body fastens itself in between my legs, obviously to make going to the toilet easier. Ollianna said, just press the leather together and it will seal itself. Pull it open when I need to. Simple, right? All my human brain can think of is a possible wardrobe malfunction. I am supposed to be active, and what if it opens by itself and I get to flash the Warrior mob? At least I have the kilt in front of it.

Unlike the male variant, my one doesn't go all around my body. Oh no, no, no! I have two long stretches of white leather, one covering my front, the other my back – they end somewhere under my knees in the same spear-like shape as my sleeves. The narrow strips – like really, really narrow – are attached to the wide golden belt, sitting low on my hips. The side of my thighs and my hips are completely on display. So are my bottom cheeks under the kilt. One move, one gush of wind, and hello mooning!

"You look beautiful and fierce and so... alien!" says Ollianna. "Is it not comfortable, then? Why else wouldn't you like it? And why does it make you aroused?"

"What? Oh my god, you can smell that?" I more or less scream, making her shrink.

How much worse can this be? I mean, yes, it's freaking comfortable since the leather moves with my body. No fastenings imply a lot of freedom. But having leather rubbing against your clit? I don't care how soft it is; that is still a no! I already know from the girls' chat that alien women don't come with a clit. None of the species does. Me, though? Every step I take, this thing rubs. And it rubs... And the timing sucks since I am a horny sizzling mess as it is. I would like to blame it on the pull of the Sign and all that. But really, it's just stupid little things flooding my memory on repeat. His skilled tongue inside me, his body pressed against mine in the shower, his throbbing length pushing against the small of my back...

"Oh, is it getting worse?" she asks, and I take a deep breath, trying to calm the hell down. *Stop thinking about him!* If she can smell it, everybody will. Freaking aliens! What else could possibly go wrong?

Ollianna points out my com is still buzzing, and the High Lady of the Oria House insists I take it. Yeah! There is always room for worse. I don't want any girl chatter now. I am a packet of nerves as it is. I only allow it in case it has something to do with Kayon. I cringe even more when I notice Ollianna opens up the video feed.

It's still difficult for me to get used to the full-body hologram-like image of the person on the other line. It's almost like having them in the room with you. Natalia looks sleepy, and that's expected as the sun is not even up yet. She is pregnant; shouldn't she sleep in or something? What is she up to? Her red mane is a mess of tangled curls, and her big blue eyes look heavy with sleep. Of course, she makes it look damn cute. Her child-like face is a shocking contrast to her feminine body, which I try not to look at. Natalia wears one of those ridiculous sleeping gowns that show more than they hide. She doesn't seem to mind and instead gets overly excited about my outfit.

"I love it, I love it!" she says and claps. The motion makes her boobs jump up and down under her see-through garment.

Oh, Lord, I don't need to see this first thing in the morning.

"Natalia, I really have to go now. It's my first day, and I can't be late," I tell her, hoping she gets the hint.

"Yes, of course," she says, blowing a stubborn red curl out of her face. "I just wanted to wish you good luck and say I am delighted your marks and Sign don't bother you too much."

"What?" I ask stupidly because... honestly. What the hell does she mean?

"Yes, Tannon said they looked bright and glowing last evening, and I can see he was not wrong," she explains, but I am far from getting what she's trying to say.

"And? Your point?" I ask, getting more annoyed by the minute.

"Oh, it's nothing," she says with a big bright smile. A bit like Talla's. Creepy! Those two should not hang out together. "I am just happy for you. When Tannon left me, my marks were very painful and started to burn my skin. He was only in the High City, and the White Palace is much closer to the capital than your house. The distance affected both Tannon and me badly. I am happy to see your marks don't react the same. It's almost as if you guys managed to trick the Sign, and there is no distance between the two of you. Now I will let you go. Tannon needs me. Have fun at the Pits. Love ya!"

The video com ends with a sharp hiss, and the silence left behind is crashing. *What was that?* I look at Ollianna, who's staring at her golden sandals, her blue hair like a curtain hiding her face. For some reason she looks guilty, but maybe she is just embarrassed for my species. I doubt there are any aliens as crazy as Natalia out there. I have no idea what just happened, and luckily, I have too much shit to deal with to care. I know Tannon worries about the fate of the Universe and all that. Maybe he should focus on his loony wife instead.

The guard who will escort me to the Training Pits alongside Kayon informs me it is time to go. I look one more time at the strange reflection in the mirror. Not only do I not look like me, but I don't even look like anything familiar, or human for that matter. Despite all that, I can finally recognize myself. This woman looking back from the mirror is not a stranger anymore.

My golden hair looks like a hollow of light around my face, thanks to the alien magic brush. The tight yet soft curls bounce with every move. My dark skin has a healthy glow, probably because I am not starving myself for a change. It looks much darker against the white garment, and I suddenly regret not wearing more white clothes before. This is definitely my color. It also enhances my eyes, the light green looking as alien as the glowing red leaf on my forehead. I look... beautiful! But most of all, I look like me. This was the image inside my brain, but the mirror never reflected it. It sure does now. I don't know what feeling comfortable in a slutty fairy outfit says about me. For once, I do not care. Deep down inside, I know he will not question my garment or my looks. If he can tell it makes me feel safe, then he will allow it. I know that because Zaan is perfect. I may not deserve perfect, but then again, nobody does. It might just as well be me who gets to have him.

Kayon gives my outfit an appreciative look and says I look fierce, like one of the Neflay warrior females. Okay, maybe aliens have different standards when it comes to body image. Then he has to spoil it by telling me Zaan might kill both Homma and Gaella. He doesn't seem too sad about that, either.

During our low flight over the planet, I let him chat with Helaff, my winged bodyguard. I hope he doesn't expect me to tell him apart from all the other forty Helaffs back at the Marni dwelling.

The High City is closer to Natalia's home than mine, and the flight should take almost two hours. That's a lot of traveling I am looking at. And this aircraft goes really fast. I wonder how big Tarrassia is. Despite the speed, I can still see beautiful forests, mainly red and purple, a red dessert, and there are huge mountains everywhere on the horizon. The strangest things are the lakes. They look weird, almost artificial. Perfectly shaped large expanses of gray waters and very much like Sia's eyes, if I think about it. Kayon confirms they are indeed lakes. He calls them the Still Waters of Tarrassia. He says they are sacred and people are not allowed to bathe or swim in them, but he has no idea why.

I officially stop pretending to be unimpressed when I see the first glimpse of the High City. It doesn't look real, not to my Human mind anyway. The Palace dominates everything by far. It is built from the same copper-like metal as their ships and their swords. I think they call it *Platinum Ore*. It is smooth, shiny, and completely mirror-like. It reflects everything around it, creating the illusion that it is not really there. How come ships or birds don't fly into it? The roof is one continuous wavy structure, pulling itself up to the highest point, like a vortex. Because of the reflection, it looks alive. We fly somewhere to the left of the Palace, and I see what they call the Warrior Training Pits. There is an entire field of buildings, similar to the Palace but on a smaller scale. I can see five large Pits, identical to the one in the Purple Forest. At the back, there are massive fields with rows after rows of perfectly docked ships and smaller aircrafts. In the distance, there is another training facility. Something about it feels more high-tech and less traditional. Kayon tells me that's where the most skilled and worthy Warriors train. They are the ones selected to become part of the Blood Fleet. He also says behind it, it's the Shadows training facility. I point out there is nothing there, and he just replies with: "Precisely". It takes me a good few minutes to understand what he means. Wow! Now that is impressive!

By the time we land, I am considering begging him to take me back home. I am shaking with... I don't even know, other than I am a mess. I find myself taking a deep breath of air once we are out of the ship. It smells wonderful! So different from a human military camp, yet the same. This is so familiar, I forget all my apprehensions. I can smell fuel and sand, gunpowder, metal, leather, dust, sweat, blood, and a lot of testosterone. Trust me to scent that. Everything is different but deep down, the same.

I follow Kayon blindly. He walks with determination, and I appreciate he's not slowing on my account. My fast walk is more like running. All the Warriors we pass by defer to him with respect. To be honest, I expected a lot more people around. Needless to say, they are all men. Not a single woman in sight. I was hoping there would be some. I don't know, doing admin jobs or something. But no such luck. Some of the men are of other species, mainly similar to my guards and Kayon. Some are too scary to look at. The majority are oversized, hairy, copper Vikings, otherwise known as Tarrassians. I am trying not to gawk much, but come on! They must have ugly men on this planet, right? I wonder where they keep them. They all seem a bit on edge as we run into different groups. I don't know if it's because of me since they don't even see me. Like I am invisible. Okay, if that's how they want to play it, fine. Probably a lesser evil than staring and laughing at my outfit. I can't help the feeling they are scared, especially the younger ones.

"Are they offended by my presence? Is it because I am a woman?" I ask Kayon politely, trying not to make a big thing out of it.

"No, they are just worried they might look at you by mistake, and the High Master might take their heads off. Also, by mistake," he says, and his tusks start wobbling. He is laughing! How is this funny?

"Who am I going to train with if they are too scared to even look at me?" I ask, feeling my anger level rise.

"We have simulation dummies," Kayon says, and now Helaff joins in with the laughter. Maybe I will use his extra-large winged ass as a dummy. Idiots!

We pass by one of the larger Sparring Pits. The ground around it shakes with energy, the air is filled with the metallic scent of blood, and the noise makes me want to cover my ears like Natalia does when she is scared. There's growling and grunting, and it is all terrifying. The level of aggression is shocking. It doesn't feel like training. More like they are fighting to the death. This is not what I expected, but I won't let it put me off. The first day is always the worst. Maybe I can learn how to use fire weapons and avoid sparring all together.

My forehead Sign starts pulsing, and little sparks of energy go through the swirling tattoos on my arms. All at the same time, the scent of orange flowers fills my world, and my heart turns into one of the smoothies I have been living on. Zaan approaches us, flanked by two older and rather stern-looking Tarrassian Warriors. It is not lost on me, their swords are dripping with blood. I invoke all the courage I have to look up at him. His eyes are a solid copper, and the few specs of gold are not enough to hide he is not in a jovial mood.

"You are late, Warrior," he says with a voice so stern and cold that I instantly feel like crying. "Make sure it doesn't happen again, or you are out. Kayon, help her choose her unit, then come find me. We have a situation," he says and moves on, followed by his Warriors, without another look my way.

What the hell? I most definitely didn't expect or want preferential treatment, but this? I am almost happy for the reminder he can be such a bossy asshole. At least I don't feel like crying anymore! I am fuming, and I need one of those dummies as soon as.

We reach some sort of a crossroad, and Kayon stops to watch me closely.

"Who do you prefer to train with, the Cub Warriors or the Untried Warriors?" he asks. Is he serious? He wants me to train with children. Really?

"How old are the cubs?" I ask since this is an alien world. Cubs could mean elderly people, for what I know.

"Some are as young as seven and some as old as fourteen rotations," he says, and I am too shocked to be offended he wanted me to train with kids. I know they are a Warrior race, but seven?

"The High Master started training at five, so don't look so shocked," he adds with a shrug of his spiky shoulders.

These people are strange, yet they call us primitive. This shit would be illegal on Earth. "What are the Untried Warriors?" I ask.

"They passed cub age, and they are in intensive training. They are taught by Scholars as well as by Pit Masters. There are levels within this unit, and only when they master the last one, can they be called Warriors. They will choose a Unit of the Tarrassian army to continue with specialized training, and they will be allowed to mate."

"What? Are you telling me I get to choose between children and hormonal teenagers who are not allowed to mate? While wearing this outfit?"

"I am not responsible for your garment," he says, looking increasingly out of patience.

"Is there a third option?"

"Yes, the Marni guard can take you back home," he says, giving me a challenging look.

"Fine, Kayon, I will join the Untried," I say, trying to hide my disappointment. This is a shitty first day.

"Good choice, Untried Warrior. While we are here, you will call me Pit Master. I train your Unit." Well, there is at least that.

28

GIANNA

Day two, three and four, are just as shitty as day one. As I travel to the Pits, I have no better expectations for day five. Kayon is flying the craft today, and he is just as bad at it as Helaff. I watched Zaan like a hawk while piloting his ship manually, plotting to learn something useful. That didn't happen as it looked like actual rocket science. However, I am ready to bet my life Kayon and his buddy have no idea what they are doing. I have no doubt Zaan could make this thing go faster.

Four hours of traveling each day have already started to get to me. It adds to the feeling of being a fish on dry land. Everything is wrong about this, except it feels right. That is why I am still doing it. It doesn't make any sense, so I try not to split hairs here. Instead, I keep going. One more hour, one more day. That alone feels like a victory. Part of me wonders if I keep getting up every morning before sunrise just because Zaan is there. Just to be close to him. Which, of course, is silly considering I am as invisible to him as I am to the other Warriors. I hardly ever see him, and when I do, it's just brief glimpses around the Training

Pits. It is still better than nothing. Who knows, maybe that's why I am still here, watching Kayon fly this beautiful thing as if it were a sloth.

I can't even enumerate all the reasons why I should stay the hell home and learn how to cook bright yellow Tarrassian bread. Too many issues to count.

The theory lessons are most likely amazing. However, I wouldn't know. The Scholars prefer to write on their coms and send us the info that way. In beautiful Tarrassian writing, that is. The ear implant only translates spoken words, not written language. It explains why Talla only calls me on video com instead of texting. I am sure the bastards know I can't read that. Or maybe, they don't. As it happens, Sia is already fluent in Tarrassian, and that includes writing. Back on Earth, she was what we call gifted. Here that's just normal. Maybe they think all Humans are that smart. So, after a long day, I now come home and refuse to sleep until I put in at least two hours of learning Tarrassian. It's gibberish, really, but I keep on pushing.

My Unit uses the Sparring Pits twice a day. I just watch, and not only because no one would pair with me or because my sword looks like a back-scratching device compared to theirs. I know my way around a sword.

My father enrolled me in Kenjutsu classes when I was six years old. Two weeks into my training, the Sensei said I was more suitable for Kendo. I wasn't sure what the difference was, but my father snickered and said Kendo was for wimps. He quickly added that was expected since I was a girl. I felt quite betrayed by the otherwise friendly Japanese Sensei. He took my real sword and gave me a bamboo one. A month later, I was in love with my shinai. Unlike Kenjutsu, Kendo was not about aggression or building pain tolerance. I wanted to be a kick-ass future Marine, but Kendo was all about peace. I thought I would hate it. Instead, my shinai and I became one. I used to train for six hours, every single day. I won one competition after another until my father decided to take control back. I was getting too good. He put my sword in a bonfire and made me watch until there was nothing left but ash. He said girls have to stick to girl stuff. The week after, he took me on a high-end holiday to the Maldives and spoiled me rotten while we were there. That's just how he understands parenting.

I push my memories away and try to think of my predicament instead. After about five minutes in that Pit, it became clear the so-called Untried Warriors could easily kill the entire Earth army. As for their fighting style or skills, they only have one: aggression! They don't just use those swords. They put all their overgrown muscles, giant height, and some serious anger issues into them. And they are not even allowed to use their War Beast yet. Can I fight them without being seriously injured? They don't use training swords, but the real deadly thing. I have no idea what I am doing, but I am still going back every morning. I keep on pushing.

Yesterday, I thought I'd get a reprieve. We trained with fire blasters and some bigger guns they call chargers. No close contact seemed great, but I couldn't lift the latter and almost killed people trying to aim the previous. Zaan is soon to become only the first of my many casualties. If they let me use it again, that is.

The worst part, though, must be the Unit itself. They are all smarter, faster, stronger, and everything else on that spectrum. The cherry on the top? Teenagers are all the same, no matter the species or the galaxy they live in. Hormones are stronger than fear or common sense. So, unlike all the other Warriors or Guards at the Pits, these guys do stare at me. Like, a lot. I have a boob fan club, a bootie one, a leg one, and then some stare at everything I've got.

My outfit doesn't help; theirs doesn't either. Kilts are not great at hiding erections. It's freaking disgusting! But really, what was I expecting? I don't care what they call the Untried; they very much look like men to me. Most of them don't even have full beards yet, but that doesn't make them ignore women. I feel like a proper MILF around here. They are not allowed to mate until they become Warriors. Kayon said abstinence builds aggression. Charming. And now they have me to stare at all day. I should have chosen the Cub Warriors. At least I am sure those don't train with real swords.

Not long after making it back to the Pits, I find out that is not the case. The little boys train with real ones. I know they self-heal and stuff, but they are not immortals. Why would any parent send their boys here to die?

Today, we are informed by Kayon it is sparring day. Apparently, the Untried are 'lacking', and the 'High Master is vexing pissed'. Kayon said it in that many words. I heard the guys, teens, aliens, whatever, saying the new High Commander of the Blood Fleet will soon come to recruit Warriors. Same with all the other High Commanders, as the New War is taking its toll.

Many Warriors are soon to leave training, and the Untried have to move up ranks and quickly. As with all wars, I guess age becomes only a number when your country needs you. Maybe that is why some more advanced Cub Warriors have been invited to join the Untried today. It's just silly. Two of them are already taller than me, but anyone can tell they are just kids. They should be at home, playing ball, or whatever they do here. The taller ones are both twelve, another one is eleven, and the last one is eight. Really?

The funny thing is the youngest could probably join the Blood Fleet right now. He is a little ball of anger, begging for someone to fight him. His wish might come true as they are asked to pick an older sparring partner instead of fighting each other, as I imagined. I just watch from the side, praying to God they don't pair me with the ninja kid just because he is the only one shorter than me. I think he might be feral. Less than a minute into the session, my stomach turns on itself as one of the taller kids bleeds his guts out. One of the stern-looking older males takes him to the Pit's Healer. And by that, I mean he unceremoniously throws him over his shoulder. Fighting carries on like nothing happened.

The other kids seem a bit wary now, trying to avoid fatal blows and not paying attention. Needless to say they get yelled at by Kayon and all the other Pit Masters. The youngest one is not fazed by the possibility of instant death and keeps going at his opponent like a pit bull. He uses all his rage to make up for the size difference. He tries to approach the fight the same way his sparring partner does, with muscles and aggression. Only he can't because he is half the size of the Untried. The kid is already bleeding, and I can tell the older teen is holding back. The feral creature actually shouts in anger when Kayon gives us break time. He should be grateful for the reprieve, the little shit, as Jade would say. I don't really know why I approach him. He growls at me, exposing sharp little fangs. Dear Lord! What are they feeding this kid?

"You are trying to defeat him using his tactics," I tell him, ignoring his little chest-beating act. "You can't. He is taller, stronger, and more experienced. You cannot fight him with your muscles, so fight him with your mind."

He watches me with interest and tilts his head sideways like a puppy trying to make sense of the world. He has beautiful long hair, as black as the night sky. The typical attractive Tarrassian features are punctuated by big copper eyes full of fire and determination. And dimples… Could he be any cuter? He is beautiful, full of life and passion and I really don't want to watch him die today.

"I thought Humans were useless," he says. "How come your people can fight with their mind? And how come you are here? Shouldn't females just look pretty and keep quiet?"

Isn't he a charmer? I ignore his shitty little personality and focus on the facts.

"That is not what I meant. Not literally. You have to use your intelligence. Look for weaknesses, such as the way he favors his right leg. Get him tired, avoid his major blows, deflect, postpone, learn his behavior, think ahead of him, anticipate his next strike," I tell him, and he observes me quietly. "You try to power your sword with the strength of your entire body. That won't work because he is bigger. Don't go at him with force; go with skill. You have to use your wrist more, and you have to aim low. You go up trying to match his height, but that wastes your strengths. Follow the natural fight position required by your height and weight ratio. See?" I ask him, lifting my sword up with both hands. "My body is now focused on fighting up there, and I leave all of me exposed. And look how unnatural it feels. And if I do this?" I ask him, lowering my hands and pointing my sword somewhere above the ground, "I block myself and close my body into another unnatural stance. It doesn't matter where your opponent is. It only matters where you want them to be. Where your body is comfortable to fight them. Do you understand, Cub Warrior?"

"Yes," he tells me with a vicious little smile. The kid can make feral look cute.

"Good, now go and become one of the Untried." I return his smile, hoping I don't get to see this brave little boy die in front of me. I try to return to my watching position by the Pit's edge, but I walk straight into Kayon. Did he just hear all my mumbling?

"You know the ways of the sword," he says, watching me with curious pitch-black eyes. His huge tusks look menacing this close.

"I did say before, but nobody listened," I tell him, hoping I didn't overstep or something. I look over my shoulder at the kid who unlike his people turned out to be a great listener. He owns this fight and takes full advantage of his larger opponent's stupor. He draws blood, like a lot, and soon enough, the older teen has to visit the Healer. The kid gives me a beaming smile and this day officially changed from shitty to extraordinary. Well, except for Kayon, who is still staring.

"I want you to tell the others what you just said to the Cub Warrior. Teach them this mind fighting," he says with a shake of his tasks.

Oh, for God's sake! These freaking aliens! There is no mind fighting!!! They will laugh at the tiny Human's preaching, they will stare at my boobs while I talk, and they don't need my silly advice. That's what they have War Beasts for. But it doesn't matter. I am here to stay, so I push through. I make it another hour; I survive another day.

"Yes, Kayon, I will teach them," I say with all the confidence one can fake.

"Thank you, Untried Warrior. Will you spar with me?"

What? I mean, that is why I am here, what I wanted, but that was before I saw how these aliens train. That's not really the word for it. They fight for real, and the swords are deadly. Being seriously hurt would be inevitable. Zaan's first rule says I have to keep myself safe. And I intend to do just that.

"I respect your ways, Kayon, but I expect your people to respect mine, too. Accommodate them where possible," I tell him. "Humans have very fragile skin, and we don't self-heal. My people train with blunt swords and body armor. It is all about gaining the skill, not about causing damage. I understand how things are different here. Blood and wounds increase aggression and determination. I respect that. Maybe we can find a way to accommodate both. Especially now that females and younger cubs have to prepare for war. Some can learn with strength, some can learn with skill."

I am surprised to hear myself talk. Here I am nothing but a puny Human, one with rules to follow; let's not forget that. Yet here I feel free. I can be me. My Sign starts pulsing with awareness as I understand why. I can be myself because I am safe. Zaan makes me feel that way. I can do anything, and I can be anything because I know he has my back. The strangest thing is, I don't find it humiliating. I should be my own person, fight my own battles, be the empowering woman I was thriving to be. Yet, I only feel like I matter because I have him. It is wrong, and maybe my father was right. I find I don't care. My feelings for Zaan are the best part of me, and I don't want to feel guilty about the one pure thing in my life. I push down the stupid emotion and the longing, trying to remember he's still a bossy asshole who can't even be bothered to say hello. I need to focus. I am in a fucking Pit, talking to an orc.

"Yes, describe these useless swords to me, and I will get them," he says.

Wow, aren't aliens charming? Kayon leaves the Pits in the care of other Masters, then helps me access the net on the central Unit com. Human search engines come up within seconds, which is rather funny. There was hardly any reception at my father's cabin, yet I can easily log in from another planet.

I show Kayon what the Kendo swords look like and describe the bamboo's properties, hoping to find something similar. I expect a comment about useless Humans and blades made of bendy wood. Instead, he just watches me with something very similar to amusement.

"High Lady of House Marni," he says with a glimmer in his beady eyes, "you have just described the Marni wood."

"Have I?" I ask in surprise. I suddenly remember Tannon's words. *Too many coincidences to ignore,* he said.

"Yes," confirms Kayon. "The wood under your family's care is essential to Tarrassia and to many other planets around the stars. It only grows here, though. The Marni wood is strong yet bendable and easy to carve. It resists extreme high or low temperatures, it doesn't burn, it doesn't get wet, and it gives a soft glow in the dark, making it ideal for our dwellings. And we have plenty of it. I will commission the swords with the Weaponry Masters, and they will be ready by the next span," he says, looking pleased with himself.

"Yes, that sounds very efficient," I say, but I can't help the strange protective feel I have over the Marni forest. "How would that affect the trees, Kayon? I mean cutting them down to make swords. It sounds like there is a lot of demand for the wood already."

He gives me a questioning look. As if surprised, I don't know. Why do all these people assume Zaan tells me shit? I don't know anything!

"The Marni wood regenerates itself, Gianna," he says with a smile. "Every branch we cut, it grows back within a few nano rotations. The sap of the trees has healing properties. It is what we use inside the healing pods. It is also the reason why the Oria birds only choose the Elder of the Healers from the Marni House."

I can't help touching the glowing red leaf on my forehead. Not sure what I have ever done to deserve such honor. The Marni is sacred to these people, yet I am the one to have its mark on me. Would they resent me for it? I am a foreigner and I wouldn't blame them if they did.

I leave Kayon and the Scholars behind to gather all the information they need for the High Master of Weaponry. I really wish these people would use names instead of pompous titles that are a mouthful. I walk back to the Pit, hoping my feral little Tarrassian is still alive. Or perhaps I should worry about his opponents.

I struggle not to laugh as all the Warriors I run into try to make themselves invisible. Some go to comical extremes. There is a breeze today, and my kilt doesn't do what it's meant to: cover my booty. Instead, it's free flowing in the wind. I keep a straight face as I make it back to my horny teenagers. I am too focused on trying not to gawk at all the perfect abs around, so I miss what's right in front of me. I just freeze, and my neck starts constricting itself. The red demon has stopped, too, watching me with glowing red eyes. I can't swallow my saliva, talk, and ask for help; I almost feel the cage around me. *Slave, pet, trapped...* *No value.*

"Let go of your breath, Gianna. You are safe. I am here. Nothing can hurt you. Breathe out!"

I do what the voice close to my ear tells me to, and exhale then inhale fresh air. My lungs fill with the scent of orange flowers and the other intoxicating perfume that is all male and all him. I can feel the heat of his body behind me, very close but not quite touching. His head is lowered over my shoulder, trying to whisper words of comfort. Black soft hair brushes my collar bone, and the single white lock in all that darkness falls over my cheek briefly. I am breathing him in again, like a drug. Safe. I am safe. He steps from behind me, and I feel his eyes on my face. The need to see the gold I missed so much gives me the strength to peel my eyes off the red demon ahead and look at Zaan instead. It feels like I haven't looked at his beautiful face in ages. He looks tired, but he watches me with the same gold intensity I used to find disturbing. Now I want to soak in it; I want to absorb it and never let it go. My reckless behavior didn't kill the gold. It's still there.

"This is Mirri, who lives and works in the household of the High General," he tells me with a quiet voice, pointing towards the Moorri woman. "She asked to join the Untried."

She is a former slave who lives and works on Tarrassia. She has no connections with her species and hates the Moorri as much as you do. They sold her to the Yellow Planets because she refused to mate the male chosen by her family. She would never hurt you, but I will send her away if her presence triggers bad memories. It is your choice, Gianna.

I keep looking at him like a stupid teenage girl with a crush, and it takes a while to notice he said the words in my mind. I don't really know how to reply. Ollianna taught me, but when he looks at me like this, my brain goes Jell-O. I use all my willpower to peel my eyes off his and look at the Moorri woman or girl. She looks pretty young. She watches me with wary red eyes, and I can see the disappointment on her beautiful red face.

"I understand, High Master. I am sorry I caused such a reaction. My people normally do, and I can't blame anyone. The Moorri are scum," she says, and I take a step forward despite my fear.

"Hanni, Mirri," I say, using the Tarrassian greeting. "You have no idea how relieved I am to see another female," I tell her, and it is nothing but the truth. Finally, another pair of boobs for the teens to stare at. Unlike the Tarrassian women, this one has a decent set on under her tight leather outfit. She is also very young, so more suitable for the teen squad to crush on. Her cat-woman outfit looks similar to what Kayon wears. Needless to say, it looks better on her than on him. I would actually love one for myself. Unlike my slutty outfit, hers covers every patch of skin, only her beautiful red face and upper neck exposed. She has the most perfect curvy body, so tight one could bounce pennies off. Long dark hair is pulled into some fancy ponytail, enhancing the beauty of her horns. Never thought I would say such a thing. Even her thin and long forked tail adds to her beauty. As I've already noticed in my short time on their planet, the Moorri are very Human-like. As long as you get past the bright red skin, glowing hellish eyes, tail, and horns, that is. Size too. Okay, maybe not that Human. They are just as big as the Tarrassians, and this girl is no exception. She towers over me, and her muscular, solid frame tells me she could easily kick my ass. But then again, so could anyone here, except the Garrii people. Elves are not exactly Warrior material.

"Welcome to the Training Pits, Mirri," Zaan says to her, but his eyes are still on me. "Untried Warrior Gianna will take you to your Unit's Pit Master. He will explain the rules."

"Thank you, High Master," says Mirri, who's more excited than a puppy. She reminds me of my young, stupid self, joining the Marines for the first time.

Zaan nods and then just leaves. I try not to stare after him, but most of all, I try to push away the feeling of loss. He takes away with him his scent, his body heat, and my personal safety bubble. But his eyes were gold again when he looked at me. I try to focus on that and ignore the rest.

29

GIANNA

I am a packet of nerves wrapped up in a slutty alien outfit. I know Kayon said the swords would arrive today, but I didn't quite believe that. Who crafts hundreds of shinai swords overnight? And my God! They are beautiful. The Weapon Masters have followed the feedback, and anyone familiar with Kendo on Earth would recognize the similarities. There are also many differences. For one, they are violet. And probably they will give a faint glow in the dark. They do bend and flex, but there is an undeniable hardness to them. These will cause more hurt than I would have imagined, but I try to keep in mind the men's size. They can't exactly fight with needles, can they? The shinai are much bigger and definitely heavier than what I am used to. Yet, when Kayon and the Scholars ask, I tell them they are perfect. Maybe I am losing my mind. I spend too much time around Natalia.

Luckily, we don't get to use them, not yet at least. To my surprise, the High Scholar says we need to learn everything about the swords' history before we are allowed to use them. A matter of respect, he said. I hope it's all good things they are all learning about my people because I still can't read Tarrassian. For what I know the Scholar could be teaching the origins of anime.

A few minutes into the lesson, while I daydream in my com booth, Mirri starts messing with my systems. Within seconds, all the monitors around me light up in English. I give her a smile and a thank you because I know how to be a good loser. She also tells me *asking for help doesn't make you weak*. Great. Why do I get all the wise-ass women around me? I need to see Jade more often. Restore the balance. There isn't a single wise bone in Jade's body.

Mirri is nice, despite being a Moorri. She is a bit reserved around me because everyone is aware of my little adventure in the Moorra Galaxy. Maybe she thinks I hate her, but I know better than to paint an entire species with the same brush. Her young age is showing and she is a bit overwhelmed with the male attention; the guys are not exactly subtle. Perhaps because she is not mated and a teen herself, Kayon has threatened them at least five times since morning. It must be something I am missing because I don't see them being aggressive or anything like that. They just stare at her like a bunch of horny puppies.

She prefers to stick with me throughout the day, like glue. To my surprise, so does my little feral Tarrassian. I asked him his name, and he growled and snapped his fangs at me. I wonder if they have psychopathic disorders on Tarrassia because the kid fits the bill. During the mid-break, the three of us keep away from the rest, roaming around the camp on our own, and I wonder if I am officially part of the geek squad or something. I was home-schooled my entire life and never got to experience it. I really don't want to start at twenty-three. I am too old for this crap.

A faint but familiar scent envelops me as we reach the front gates of the camp, and the next thing I know, I am watching Talla stroll towards me. She is alone, with no chaperone in sight, which I am sure is frowned upon on Tarrassia. Did she just walk here? Her beautiful, serene smile shows perfectly white fangs, and her copper eyes turn golden when they stop on me. How can she love me after such a short time?

"My beautiful daughter, so happy to see you are well and full of happiness," she says, and I just stand there, not really knowing what to reply. She does talk strangely, though. It's either nonsense from the Etiquette School or a tornado of words breaking a hundred rules per minute.

She hugs me, and I allow it because this is my people's fault. Before freaking Natalia, nobody was exchanging germs around here.

"I was in the area visiting an old friend," obviously a lie, "and I thought it would be appropriate to visit my beloved daughter. How are you, my beautiful youngling?" she asks, petting my hair and fiddling with invisible threads on my outfit. Hers is a beautiful peach-colored dress flowing in the wind, making her look terribly out of place in such a masculine environment. Something about the way she smiles, talks and moves makes her look like an alien Scarlett O'Hara.

"You will get in trouble with the High Master," snarls the feral child at me. "The rule says no visitors, and he likes the rules. Nobody brings their mothers around. That's so sad! Did she bring you fresh fruit and cakes? Do you want her to give you more hugs?"

Before I get to tell him off, Talla points a long skinny finger at him and gives him her brightest smile. Oh, I know that one. It's lethal.

"Hush now, little Ronnin. Just because Commander Nodric is your uncle does not mean you have to be as barbaric as he is. Have some manners, will you?" she dismisses him with an elegant gesture and ignores his loud growl. "My dearest Mirri, how have you been, my youngling?"

Does she know everybody? It sure looks like it. Mirri gives a polite but cold reply, while her red eyes are cast down.

"So, my beautiful daughter, I was thinking…" she doesn't get to finish, as the air charges with hostility around us and my flight instinct tells me I should disappear about now. Mirri retreats to a safe distance, and Ronnin gives me an evil little grin that says *I told you so.*

"What is the meaning of this, Untried Warrior?" Zaan asks me, ignoring everyone else. He is angry, and it's not fair. I didn't do anything! He looks down at me from his towering height, waiting for an answer I don't have. I hate to see him like this. His eyes are copper, no traces of gold left, and his beautiful face looks stern. It reminds me of painful things. Memories that can break me. That's how he looked at me when he found me at my father's house. After I lied to him, after I ran from him. I lift my eyes to meet his gaze, but no words come. My stupid lips are trembling. My chest hurts and I pray to God I am not about to have a panic attack. He watches my lips, my eyes, my face, every single detail of my face, then turns to Talla.

"You know the rules, Mother. No visitors," he tells her with a polite but stern tone.

"Well, yes, of course. It never stopped me before. I remember visiting you quite often when you were just a cub. Like this cute little one," she adds, and she pinches Ronnin's cheeks with affection. The kid growls at her, and I honestly think so does Zaan. I can see Mirri by my side, trying to stop herself from laughing.

"Fine, Mother, now you've seen her. Time for you to go," he says, and asks one of his Warriors to escort Talla back to the High City.

"Of course, I'll be on my way now – no need for an escort. I will walk back with the Queen. It was charming seeing you again, my daughter. Please do come and visit our High City dwelling, one span after training. Especially if you are tired and would like to stay overnight. We live a few nanos away. And from here, you can always walk to the High Palace and visit the Human females. The forest path is only a short stroll away." She points with her long alien fingers towards the treeline outside the gates.

"Mother?" Zaan interrupts her tirade. "Why would you walk back with the Queen?" he asks and looks over Talla's head at the strange party approaching the gates.

All at once, Mirri groans, Ronnin starts laughing, telling me I am the most entertaining female, and Zaan looks at me like I am dead meat. What the hell? How is this my fault? Talla's cheeky smile tells him what her lips don't: *See? Other people visit, too.*

The gates open all the way to allow the large party in. I take everything in as quickly as my brain allows it – Jade, and a more alien-looking than ever Sia, stroll in. There is a small army of some of the biggest Tarrassian Warriors I have ever seen behind them. Even I know who they are. The Queen's Royal Guard. I think there are twenty of them. On top of that, she has about a hundred of the scary winged guards. She does complain about it, especially since there is no such thing as a King's Guard. Tarrassia is safe, and it feels extreme, to say the least.

Today, she only has the Tarrassians in her guard trailing behind her. The Warrior by her side must be the one in charge. The guy is... Wow, just when I thought I'd seen enough gorgeous men to last me a lifetime, this guy shows. He put the H in handsome, and he knows it. The guy is obviously a charmer. He is all bright smiles and sunny disposition, unlike the other surly Tarrassian men.

Jade comes strolling through the gates, with her beautiful kohl-lined green eyes trained on every guy in sight. Some things never change. If not for the boobs and the bright red lipstick or stain as they call it here, I wouldn't recognize her. Her hair is so dark it shines green and blue under the golden hue of the Tarrassian sun. It looks like her natural color. The chocolate-mahogany locks she sported on Earth must have been some fancy dye. Her pitch-black hair makes her marble-white skin look even fairer.

I can finally understand the inside joke I've been failing to get so far on the girls' chat. There are some not very discreet Snow White hints from Natalia. I guess what goes around comes around. The Tarrassian dresses are made for a body like Jade's. Her boobs are practically spilling out from her bright green dress. Her tiny waist is squeezed tightly in the corset, making her already round hips and booty flare provocatively. She sashays rather than walks, no doubt to make her curvy thighs peak through the slits of her dress, with every step she takes. The levels of testosterone in the camp have risen to alarming highs. I can feel it in the air. Jade must love Tarrassia.

Sia is just Sia. She will always stand out on any planet, and I think she has managed the impossible. She looks more alien than all the aliens. Her Sign is beautiful. A tiny light blue water lily pulses gently on her forehead. Her long delicate arms are beautifully adorned by swirls of white and lavender blue, matching her dress. Her hair is as white as ever but longer and shinier. It looks like a cape of light and silk around her willowy body. Her big gray eyes seem more silver than I'd noticed before, and a beautiful smile softens her glacial face. She looks like a real queen – a silly thing to say since she is one.

"My Queen," says Zaan giving her the Tarrassian salute by pressing a fist to his chest. Everybody else around me does the same, and I feel a bit stupid. It never occurred to me to ask how to greet her in public.

The handsome Tarrassian, undoubtedly the High Commander of the Queen's Guard, replies to Zaan's accusatory look with a blinding smile and a shrug of his wide shoulders.

"Not my fault, High Master," he says with unhidden amusement. "What the Queen wants, the Queen gets. The Brave King's orders."

"Oi, *Pretty Boy*, you make her sound like a bitch," says Jade shocking me to the core. How does she get away with this?

The Commander gives her an annoyed look, proving what everyone knows. Jade is a massive pain in the Tarrassians' butts. Maybe it explains why she is still single on a planet with men desperate to get themselves a fertile Human.

"Jade, please don't. And no more nicknames, please," says Sia in her posh British accent. There is, however, a hidden warning in her perfectly composed voice. She greets Talla and Mirri in Tarrassian, I think, because the device in my ear starts to translate.

"This was indeed my idea, High Master, and my Commander said it was not a good one. I simply wanted to say hello in person to Gianna. She's not easy to get a hold of," Sia says, giving me an almost mischievous look. Very unlike her composed icy self.

"So, we ambushed her instead," says Jade, making the High Commander of the Queen's Guard roll his eyes in a very Human-like gesture. One he probably learned from her.

"The Warriors are not allowed to receive visitors, my Queen," says Zaan with a polite but very stern voice. "This is a training camp, not a socializing parlor."

"*Jesus Dude*, take a chill pill, lad!" says Jade, and because it was so unexpected, I burst into laughter. It was an idiotic thing to do since no one else laughed. True, only a Human would get the joke out of us here, and Sia was never that human to start with. That doesn't stop Zaan from looking at me, probably pissed off by my crazy reaction. I just haven't laughed in so long... Jade tries to give me a high five, but I am in enough trouble as it is, so I pass. The woman is crazy, and I missed that so much. Jade will always remind me of Yara, simply because she used to laugh herself to tears at the foulness spilling out of Jade's mouth.

"I am sorry, High Master," says Sia, "I was not aware of such a rule. It will not happen again."

Zaan just nods at her then excuses himself, not before asking her to keep it short and not to leave his mom behind when she leaves. He can be so rude and blunt at times. At all times, really.

"I would like to have a word in private, Untried Warrior. Come find me when you are done with your many visitors and socializing hours," he says as he passes by me, without even looking at me. Oh, so now he gets sarcasm.

"Yes, High Master," I say quietly. Trouble finds me even when I am not looking for it. Dammit!

Sia takes a few steps closer, and like a well-oiled machine, her guards move back, giving us some privacy.

"Can we break more rules?" she asks, putting her arms up. "May I give you a belly hug?" she asks, and only then do I notice the bump. God, this is so surreal. Sia is already four months pregnant. And she wants a hug... The Ice Queen...

I allow it, and her beautiful scent of lavender and fresh snow envelops me. Maybe I do like hugs. It is nice to have people you can call your own.

"My turn!" says Jade pulling Sia off me. "Time for a boob hug!"

I laugh myself silly because, my god! Her boobs are out of this world. Why is she still single?

"Can I have a boob hug, too?" asks the feral kid, his arms already wide open towards Jade.

"No offense, *Karate Kid*, you're a bit young for me," she says with a smirk.

God, he looks genuinely heartbroken. We are all trying to keep a straight face, not to add to his sorrow.

"How about you return to training, Ronnin? Give us some privacy, please?" I say, and he growls at me, making Talla jump.

"You are not my Pit Master, and I don't take orders from females," says the feral little thing. "I might take orders from her," he points at Jade, "but not from you. You are too skinny for my liking and you are already taken."

What? He did not just say that! The kid has no shame.

"I am sure you won't mind taking orders from your Queen, would you, Untried Warrior?" asks Sia. Her voice is soft, but her usual glacial powers work their magic on the kid. For the first time since I met him, he looks scared. He takes a quick fist to his heart, bows his head, and disappears like a blur.

"What can one expect from Commander Nodric's flesh and blood?" says Talla.

"Not much indeed," agrees Sia, and they all exchange a knowing smile. I feel a bit left out. I never know what people talk about, always the last one to find out about everything. But I do think I am to blame for it. They all walk on eggshells around me, waiting for me to reach out instead.

"You look absolutely beautiful," says Sia taking my hand in hers. Her skin is cold but so soft, and her touch is soothing. "I am very proud of you, Gianna."

"We all are," says Talla unexpectedly. "You are the change Tarrassian females have waited for so long."

I don't reply because what is there to say? Do they see any Tarrassian women around? Do they see anyone else other than Mirri? Maybe they are just trying to be polite.

"Please come by the Palace one day after training. We need to catch up, and Natalia wants to go through some details about her Sacred Ceremony. Maybe you can stay overnight?" Sia gives me a pleading look, and I just nod in agreement.

"Lovely! I won't keep you now; I am afraid I've already caused you some trouble," she says and looks as if she is trying to choose the right words for whatever comes next.

"Yara's family were informed about her death, and they had a ceremony for her back in Brazil. I know what she meant to you, and I think we should do the same here. I made arrangements for a resting place in her memory, in the Cave of Souls. It is what Tarrassians call their burial grounds. Somewhere for us to remember and honor her life. I think it will also help Brian with his grief when he wakes."

I don't even fight the lone tear falling down my cheek. Why didn't I think of doing that for Yara? Sia is supposed to be the Ice Queen, yet I am the one who's all iced up.

"There is a reason why she is the Queen," says Jade with a genuine smile. No trace of her usual mocking. Her respect for Sia is evident.

"The best we could have asked for," says a very emotional Talla. "However, there is trouble, my Queen," she adds quickly. I follow her eyes to the treeline.

Is that... a Tarrassian? One bigger than Tannon? After the first shock, I realize he is the average size for a Tarrassian, which is huge anyway. He doesn't even have his War Beast out. At least, I don't think so. He is not wearing the Warrior's kilt, but the more formal white loose shirt and pants. Only his clothes are not that loose. They are about to break at the seams, his War Beast lurking, ready to come out. He has his massive sword in hand and ready to use it. As he approaches us, it is easy to see why I thought he was larger than the other Tarrassian males. His aura is one of pure madness. He is a mixture of rage, unhinged thoughts, and pure violence. The breeze in his hair and bushy beard gives him an even more menacing vibe. He looks like a God of War. It explains why the King doesn't need guards. Who in their right mind would want to fight that man?

I know I keep comparing the Tarrassians to images of the old Vikings from our Earth stories. But none looks the part better than this guy. How is he mated to someone like Sia? Despite their apparent differences, Natalia and Tannon are pretty similar and a perfect match. These two? Far from it.

The King's Sign shines a dark blue, and there are white specs of rage in his eyes. His angry stare never leaves Sia as he approaches us. Her stupid guards walk even further away from her, trying to stay out of his path. This guy is what she needs protection from.

"*Lover Boy* has his chakras misaligned again," says silly Jade. Why is she not scared? Talla is. She steps behind Sia's guards, trying to make herself invisible. I watch Sia warily, but she doesn't seem panicked. She takes a deep breath, folds her hands in front of her, and plasters a serene smile on her beautiful face. She looks as if she is preparing herself to deal with a moody toddler.

"My King," she says in a polite greeting. The man just growls in reply. And I thought Ronnin was feral. He gives her a look that could kill, then to my horror, he turns his eyes on me. I suddenly remember what the guy is most famous for: taking heads off.

"Welcome to Tarrassia, Untrained Warrior," he says, and he is obviously trying to contain his anger when he addresses me. "I didn't get to meet you properly, and I would like you to visit us at some point. I am very honored and proud to have you train as one of my Warriors," he says, and I can see he means it. How strange! He looks like the last man to accept a woman as a Warrior. The rage is back on as he turns to Sia.

"Why are you here, my Queen?" he says, and he is honestly terrifying. Sia doesn't seem impressed, though, and Jade is giggling. Why aren't they scared?

"I was just trying to see Gianna and explain about Brian," she says, then looks at me, ignoring him. He growls again, but she continues to pretend he's not here. Is that wise?

"Brian will wake up soon enough," she explains to me. "The High Healer said his body is fully restored, but we need to tread with care when it comes to his mind. I know he was Yara's bodyguard, not yours, but the three of you were always together. He needs to see a familiar face when he wakes up. I think you should be the only one in the room when that happens." She looks at me expectantly. Yes, it does make sense; I just don't want to get into any more trouble than I already am.

"Yes, I would love to be there for him," I say. "It sounds like he went through hell and back. Of course, I would have to ask permission from Zaan. Brian is a single man, and I don't know if it's appropriate." I can see Jade's shocked expression like I betrayed the entire female gender.

"A respectful Human female. Never thought I would ever get to meet one," says the King staring down at Sia. "Get home! Now!" he booms, and silver fires ignite in Sia's eyes.

"If this is about the visiting rule, I have already apologized to the High Master. I wasn't aware," she says, and she looks like she's about to lose her temper. Sia has a temper?

"I don't care about the rule," he says, bringing his face down to stare her in the eyes. "Zaan has stupid rules about every vexing thing under the sun," he says, and just like that, I decide I like our crazy King. A lot!

"This is about you showing up here, with so many unmated males around!"

"What? Are you serious, Tars?" says Sia, and she goes up on her toes in an attempt to shout in his face. They stare each other down in a battle of wills.

"Are you walking by yourself or shall I...?" he leaves the unspoken threat in the air, a manic grin on his face. Sia takes a big breath as if to calm herself, says her goodbye to me, and starts walking away as straight as a board, chin raised in silent defiance. She is very much the Ice Queen I used to know once again. It rubs her crazy King the wrong way, and he picks her up in his arms like a bride and starts strolling towards the woods. The guards and Talla follow at a respectful distance.

I am too shocked to notice Jade is still here, grinning at me.

"Is she...? Will Sia be okay?" I ask her.

"Oh yes," she says with a dismissive gesture towards the leaving party. "She'll be a bit bruised tomorrow morning, but otherwise, all fine."

"What? Oh, my God! She is pregnant, we can't let him…"

"Oh, keep your knickers on, woman; I didn't mean it that way," she says, giving me a conspiratorial wink. "The Ice Queen likes it rough."

"What?"

"I meant sex, love! Jesus! He will never hit her if that's what you had in mind. He bloody worships her! He is just a bit bonkers in between the sheets if you know what I mean. Lol, I call him *Lover Boy* for a reason. And that's just the way *Elsa* likes it. I tell you, love, it's always the quiet ones. That goes for Natalia, too. Not that she's quiet, you know what I mean, virgin and all that. Those two get all the dick, and us, the Femmes Fatales, get shit. It probably sucks even more for you, no offense."

"If you don't mind, Gianna, I will go back to the Pit. The company is suddenly lacking for me," says Mirri, looking at Jade as if she was a snake.

"What's that, *Ketchup Girl*? Do you want to be bitchy, love? Bring it on, I say. Tarrassian women are fucking sweet and boring, and I have been looking for a bitch to tear into ever since I got here!"

"Enough, Jade! What the hell? Mirri, please go back to the Pit. I will see you shortly," I tell her and turn to Jade after she leaves.

"Hey, *Ketchup Girl* started it, not me," she says, and I have to agree. So unlike Mirri to do that. I guess these people really don't like Jade.

"Anyway, you must go now, Jade, honestly. You are such a troublemaker. More than I am, and that says a lot," I say with a smile.

"Well, I should go, but my legs don't work," she says with a purring voice, her eyes roaming over the Warriors around. And there are many. It looks as if the entire camp found things to do around the front gates. All men love Jade. The rule applies, no matter the planet. Which, of course, makes me wonder.

"Why are you still single, Jade?" I ask.

"Love, forget single. I am not on the market for a bossy mate or crazy glittery tattoos. However, I do demand some dick, and I didn't get any since I got here."

I find myself laughing like I haven't in so long. And it is not lost on me; she is not calling me Blondie or any other derogatory nicknames. The girls never asked much about my past, but I think they put two and two together.

"As much as I feel for you, Jade, please leave and don't cause any trouble. Zaan is not exactly easy on these guys, and they will get punished for staring at you."

"Yeah, no worries. It's hopeless, anyway. None of these arseholes are brave enough to go for me. Brian is my only chance to get my vagina filled. I am jumping his bones as soon as he wakes up, so you know."

"That doesn't make any sense," I say. "Look at them; they act like stupid little boys around you. Who said they won't go for you?"

"The same wanker who put these on. He hates my fucking guts, but he won't allow anyone else to have me either," she says, pulling the slits of her long dress apart so I can see her ankles.

30

—

GIANNA

I take a deep breath, at least I think I am. No air goes in, and my throat does that funny bobbing thing, trying to swallow saliva my dry mouth refuses to produce. It's the beginning of a panic attack.

"Jesus, I am such a cow! Sorry, hun," Jade says while covering her cuffed ankles with her long green dress. "I know what happened to you, but trust me, I am fine. I know the safe perimeter, but most of all, I know how to take them off, lol," she says with a conspiratorial smile and a cute dimple dips in her right cheek.

"Jade, this is serious! You don't have the Sign and haven't lived here long enough to have any Tarrassian traits. These things broke my skin, but they will shatter your bones," I tell her, my fear being replaced by rage. "Which asshole put them on?"

Jade does something really strange. She winks at me, a big sassy grin on her heart-shaped face. Very Jade-like. At the same time, she hugs herself, and her lips tremble, very unlike Jade. It's not fear, though. It's something that looks like pain. The kind you get from a broken heart.

"Look, hun, I am gutted this happened to you, but don't you worry about my narky arse," she says, and despite my anger, I laugh.

"My ear device should translate British because half the time, I have no idea what you're saying," I tell her before I can think any better. Luckily, she just laughs it off, and the cute dimple in her cheek makes her look like a naughty little kid.

"Which asshole, Jade?" I ask again. She obviously doesn't want to talk about it, and I should stay out of it. The old me would have. Yara was my only friend, and I never knew what made her want to die. I never asked any questions, and now it's too late. I don't want to be that person anymore. I just hope not to turn into nosy Natalia.

"The High General," she says and watches me as I panic.

Even I know, he is Tarrassia's Second in Command, after the King. This is a man who has a lot of power.

"Girl, stop fidgeting," she says, untwisting my fingers and keeping them still. "I can take the cuffs off, okay? He has no idea I can. I bribed the alien who knows the code, bit a few others who might grass me up, you know basic stuff," she adds with a wink.

"Is he... are you...?" I ask stupidly and look at her unmarked skin.

"We are nothing," she says with a wink, but Jade is a terrible actress. The over-the-top-diva personality works, no matter how fake. Her lack of acting skills somehow makes it funny and hot. Faking the truth... not so much. "He has a Tarrassian mate, and he will soon have to marry her or whatever the fuck they call it here," she says. "He is also the only arsehole on this entire planet. Tarrassian men may be controlling, over the top, and they can go full-on cavemen at any given time. But as far as lads go, they are as decent as it gets. This guy is crap. He has sex with his own servant ladies as if they are still nothing more than slaves. Ask *Ketchup Girl* who, by the way, is underage by Tarrassian laws.

I guess that makes him a paedo by both Human and Tarrassian standards. She's fifteen, in case you don't know."

What she says sounds horrible, and now I understand at least some of Mirri's behavior. Despite everything, how can I hate the man who saved Zaan from exile? And I don't think Jade hates him either.

"I need to find you a nickname since the old one is not appropriate any more," says Jade, trying to change the subject.

"Gianna would do just fine," I reply.

"Nope, everyone's got to have a nickname, love!"

"What's the High General's one?" I ask. God, please don't let me turn into Natalia.

"He has none. I…" she stops, and I suddenly regret pushing her. I am no Natalia. I have no idea how to deal with my own emotions, never mind someone else's.

"I am sorry, Jade," I say for lack of better words.

"No need to be, Gianna. I don't like lying to myself. Never have. This is who I am and damn proud of it!" she says, giving me a rare glimpse of the real Jade. "The same social rules from back home apply here. No matter the galaxy, I will always be the scrounger, with the skint single mum and an army of half-siblings. You can probably find their pic in the dictionary, next to the word chavs, lol. I think Tarrassians can smell it on me, just like the people back home did."

"Girl, you really need to translate half of what you just said," I tell her, and we both laugh.

"I guess I am what Americans would call trash, trailer-park girl, welfare leech… you know, that sort of thing," she says with a shrug. "My mum was off work all her life, dropping one child after the other, sleeping around, partying, and giving shit to the neighbours. There were nine of us and, of course, no dads in the picture. I don't think my mum even knows who our dads are. You know when people wonder about the sex of the unborn baby?

Well, we used to guess about race. It was anyone's guess what she'd come back with from the hospital. We're like the rainbow family. Most of my siblings are half black, two of us are white, one is half Chinese, and one nobody fucking knows. I used to think he was a leprechaun. Now that I know about the aliens, I wouldn't put that option past my mum. If it comes with a dick, she's jumping it. So, yeah, as you can see, I am not suitable for breeding fine generations of copper babies," she adds with her trademark sassy wink.

I want to tell her how wrong she is, but as usual, my words fail me.

"Right, I'd better let you go before *Jesus Dude* has a temper tantrum," she says, looking up and down every guy who passes by. Crazy Jade is back...

"It's okay," I say with a sigh. "I am already in trouble for having visitors. At least being late for training is something I am guilty of. I am just a coward, to be honest. Trying to postpone the inevitable, like fighting with the Pit Master. Just because I know my way around a sword, it doesn't mean I can fight with an alien three times my size."

"You have to fight? As in for real?" asks Jade, her pretty green eyes going all big.

"God, I am one of the Untried, Jade. What on Earth would I be here for other than learning how to fight?"

"I don't know, I thought girls join the army to be around lads," she says, trying to wind me up.

"Please, just go, Jade, and try to stay out of trouble," I tell her. I am surprised to hear the affection in my voice.

"Always," she says, touching her heart with a dramatic gesture. "Before I go, Natalia asked me to pass on a message. I am to look at your Sign and marks and say: *Oh no, they are so bright! Are they always the same or only when you are in the High City?*"

"What?" I ask in a stupor. Jade's bubbly laugh fills the air, and some of the guys around look short of breath… kind of.

"I adore the bones of that gal but she's really not all in there, love," she says pointing at her head. "Honestly, you shouldn't worry about Natalia. She's bonkers and not afraid to show it. Well, I delivered the message and eyed the lads. Now I am gonna go piss someone else off. Maybe bite some aliens. Show them how it's done in Croydon, lol," she says with a wave and a flick of her stunning pitch-black locks.

Right, I guess I can't postpone it any more. Usually, I would welcome any reason to talk to him, to have his eyes on me again. But this? I already know he's going to give me that look of disappointment. The reminder I am not good enough for him. And it's not fair, considering I haven't broken any rules. Not knowingly and definitely not on purpose.

I try not to have eye contact with Kayon or any other Untried fellows as I walk past the Pit. More people disappointed in me. They probably think I get special treatment because of who I am, and I feel entitled to miss my training. How on Earth did I end up in this position again? Trying to fit in, while being related to the man in charge.

A stern-looking older Tarrassian tells me where to find Zaan, not before giving me a dismissive look and calling over a younger Warrior to help me. This one avoids looking at me altogether and takes me to a building that looks like a dome. It's relatively small, by Tarrassian standards, anyway. As we enter, I understand why. This is only the front chamber, leading into an underground facility. We pass several shiny tubular corridors; some of the walls are covered by screens with live feeds of… fights? Are those happening like right now? I try to keep up with the long strides of the Warrior, but it's hard not to get distracted.

A hissing panel removes itself to allow me into a huge room, covered wall to wall by hundreds of monitors. It's almost overwhelming to take it all in at the same time. My Human brain can't, that's for sure. The tattoos on my arms and the Sign on my forehead ignite with color and make my skin tingle. They always do that at home in the evening for some reason. Here it's probably expected to happen when I am this close to him.

The young Warrior has retreated without a word, and now it's just the two of us. Not that he acknowledges my presence in any shape or form. I stare at his back as he stands closer to the monitors, watching the live feed of some sort of space battle. It almost looks like a computer game, but I know it's not. People are dying as we stand there and watch – his people. Even I can tell it is a Blood Fleet ship under attack. He would be there if not for me. Guilt is my thing these days. Maybe it always has been. I can't be the person the people I love want me to be. I keep failing them.

I don't know what to say or do. As always, I feel like a shy teenager around Zaan. I would rather have his anger and wrath. I would prefer him as mad as the King. Anything but this coldness. I decide to let him talk first, and I just stand there looking at his back. Not that I am complaining. I could look at him for the rest of my life. He is beautiful, and now that I am done pretending not to notice, my hormones are in charge of my brain. He is wearing their traditional white leather kilt, which of course, doesn't cover much. It would be a shame to. His entire body looks like a work of art as if some higher power put a lot of thought into making him.

Zaan is on the tall side, by Tarrassian standards. Giant by my people's ones. Unlike most of his people, he is less bulky, and his muscles are leaner. Most of the Tarrassian Warriors remind me of a straightforward attack predator. Zaan is the stalking predator type. The one lurking in the shadows, learning everything about its prey and planning the attack to the very last detail. He has a born elegance, and if not for his serious face and stern demeanor, one could find him similar to the Commander of the Queen's

Guard. Zaan doesn't care much about being charming, though. Not to me, anyway.

His shoulder-length black hair looks messy, and I already know he must have put his fingers through it over and over again. He does that a lot when he's anxious. Even though I cannot see it from here, I know his beard must look equally messy right now. My fingers are itching with the need to run themselves through his mane, smoothing the wild locks – especially the bright white one.

"Ollianna has a home to return to and a loving family waiting for her," he says unexpectedly. I keep quiet because I really don't understand what he is trying to say. "The Garrii people are very close to their Mother Planet and would never leave unless to follow a mate. If she is here, it only means she wants to be with Barin. You are close to her, yes?"

Am I? I ask myself. I don't hate her any more, and we have an unspoken truth now that I know she's not after my man. I don't know if we're friends. We are both quiet and a bit broken. And for the same reasons. I guess having a broken heart in common qualifies us as friends or something. Did Zaan ask me to come here to play matchmaker? Really? That's a bit cruel. He turns his head slightly to watch me. His eyes are almost copper, and a frown on his forehead makes me want to flee. *I need the gold back. Please, let me have at least that!*

"I asked you a question, Gianna," he says with a stern voice. The one he uses for his enemies, I remember well. He said my name, and the irony is not lost on me. I used to hate him because I thought he didn't know it. Now I hate myself because he may never call me Lorra again. I push the thought away and focus on the present. I do remember this is one of his rules. I must always answer when he asks a question.

"Yes, Ollianna is my friend, High Master," I say, hoping he will ask me to call him by his name. He does not. Instead, he returns to watching the monitors.

311

"Barin acts recklessly, and his death wish overpowers his sense of duty. The High Commander of the Blood Fleet is a liability. His Second in Command is acting on his bloodthirst and need for chaos. He is also a liability. Nothing can be done about Nodric, but he can be kept within the rules under the right Commander. I need sensible Barin back. Tarrassia needs its Highest Commander more than ever. Ollianna has to stop playing games," he says.

Despite everything else, anger moves to the front of my spiralling emotions. Games? Is that what he thinks she is doing? Or is he painting her with the same brush as me? Because that's what he thinks I am doing, right? Playing with his feelings. I choose not to react. Maybe because my sense of duty still works. This is an army base, and he is my superior. I have to keep it impersonal.

"I don't think Ollianna is playing games. She is just hurt and..."

"And you know that because you are an expert in relationships?" he says, cutting me off. *Not fair, please don't go there!* He hasn't even turned to look at me. I hope he doesn't. I feel like crying so badly, my eyes sting.

"No, I am not," I say with a strangled voice, and he looks at me briefly before returning his interest to the monitors. "That is why I've asked Natalia, the High Elder's mate," I explain, "to do something about it. She is good with that sort of thing."

"Yes, I am aware," he says without looking at me. "She is quite skilled at making unwilling females accept mates they hate."

It really feels like he slapped me. Is that what he thinks? Does he believe I stopped fighting the Sign because Natalia tricked me? Maybe she did, but not the way he imagines it. There is no point. This is hopeless. I must get this done and leave before I make a fool of myself and start crying.

"Natalia is getting ready for her wedding, I mean Sacred Ceremony, so perhaps she was just busy. I will remind her.

Anything else, High Master?" I ask, keeping all emotion out of my voice.

"Yes, Untried Warrior, rules must be obeyed, and you just broke one in front of the entire Camp," he says with that impersonal, cold voice that cuts me like a knife. Part of me wants to explain. I had no fucking fault in this. Did he expect me to kick his mom out? Or tell the Queen not to talk to me? Ignore the King? Once again, my sense of duty comes first. Unless asked to, soldiers do not complain or explain. Perhaps I am more my father's daughter than I thought.

"Yes, High Master," I say.

"The punishment for breaking the rule is very straightforward, Untried Warrior. You will have to fight every single member of your Unit and your three Pit Masters."

"I have to do what?" I say before I can stop it, and he turns to look at me. He seems less angry, and there's something else in his eyes I can't quite place. I am not used to copper. I could read everything in the gold. Or maybe that was just wishful thinking.

"You will fight them one at a time, there is no rule about winning, and you can ask for breaks between fights at your own leisure. Not that any Warrior ever does, so you know. Untried Warriors Mirri and Ronnin will face the same punishment."

"Wait, what?" I shout but quickly make my voice sound polite and flat again. "The Untried Warriors just happened to be there when my visitors arrived. They had to answer questions or reply to greetings, right? Not everyone is rude, you know," I say before I can zip it. Maybe I should have. Now there are specs of white in his copper eyes.

"This is my Training Pit and you are all my Warriors. I am the only one who decides what is rude or not," he says with a cold voice. "Interrupting your High Master or raising your voice in my presence classifies as rude. You will now fight your opponents without breaks and if you lose more than two sessions you will be removed from the training programme. Any questions?" he asks, watching me with his usual intensity. As if he is trying to dissect my brain.

Questions? Sure, I have plenty. How about confinement or kitchen duty? What the hell? Fight everybody must be a bit barbaric, right? But winning? It's pretty obvious he just set me up for failure. Well, tough! I didn't go down fighting last time I left a Camp. I am sure as hell going down fighting now. I hear my calm voice break the silence.

"Yes, High Master," I say, and there is definitely a short glimpse of surprise on his beautiful face. Did he think I would crumble and cry? Ask for favors? Nope. Not happening. I will fight. It will probably end with me seeing the Healer within two minutes. And then I will undoubtedly be punished for breaking Rule 1 – *keeping myself safe*. Can't win this, no matter what I do!

"That will be all, Untried Warrior," he says, returning his attention to the monitors.

I should just leave, really. The man dismissed me in the coldest way possible. The message couldn't be any clear.

"I may not have had a choice in breaking the Pit's rules, but I didn't break any of your rules. I want you to know that," I say and turn towards the opening panel of the door.

"You broke one," he says, and I turn on my heels to look at him. His back is still at me.

What is he talking about? How can he say that to me? I respected those rules to the letter. They are all I have left from him. They have become like my Bible. It's not fair.

"Yes, High Master, I will make sure not to attend to visitors in the future," I say like a good little soldier because there is no point fighting this. The man has made up his mind, and that's that. I know how harsh and unreasonable he can be.

"I am not talking about the Camp's rules. You broke one of mine. You may leave now," he says, still without looking at me.

31

GIANNA

Ollianna asks me for the second time this evening what I would like for dinner and if I want her to keep me company. It's silly that she won't have dinner until I come back from training and have my bath. I thought she was just trying to make sure I ate, but now I think she wants my company. We both end up eating quietly, without sharing anything but silence – standard stuff for broken people.

Since I started training, my appetite has grown, and I can manage more than smoothies in the evening. I don't even know who cooks my meals. Still haven't been brave enough to act as the lady of the house and get to know the Marni people. The food is delicious, and I do enjoy it. Tonight though, my stomach is in knots, and not even the long relaxing bath could help with my anxiety. As per usual, at the first sign of distress, my brain tells me: *No food!* I don't think I could eat right now, but not looking after myself means breaking one of his rules. Which, of course, doesn't matter anymore. Not when he accuses me of doing so no matter what. I hate him for sabotaging that for me. His rules were all I had to keep me grounded. To keep him close to me even when he is not.

"Maybe liquid food for this span?" asks Ollianna, her eyes cast down. There is something on her mind. Other than the usual, that is.

"What is it, Ollianna? You can tell me," I encourage her gently. It would do me good to think of someone else's problems.

"I am sorry to bother you with this," she says, watching me with wary purple eyes. After so many days, it's still a shock to the system taking in the beauty of this girl. Her skin has a soft blue hue this evening. It may look stunning, but I know by now it only means she is tired and worried.

"It is regrettable I have to bring this matter to you when you obviously had a difficult span," she says with a cute sigh. "The High Lady of House Oria has asked me to join her at the White Palace. For whatever reason, she thinks I am really good at organizing Sacred Ceremonies. I am not. The High Lady joined a video com I was having with my sister. They both ambushed me and then made me feel guilty for not wanting to help. The High Lady struggles with her unborn cub and apparently needs my help with her Ceremony. This is all very strange, and I don't know what to do. The High Lady cried, and my sister almost fainted," she says with a small voice, her skin flashing all sorts of colors now.

Fucking Natalia! She is not to mess with. And there was a time when I thought she had victim written all over her. It would have been nice if she made me aware of her little plan. I feel sorry for having to lie to Ollianna, but it's for the best. And not because Barin is acting out like a spoiled brat who can't get his favorite toy back. It's because, without him, she will forever be this lost little elf roaming around the Marni house. She can thank me later. Thank Natalia, more like it.

"Oh, I am sorry, Ollianna, I've been so busy and tired lately, I completely forgot. Natalia asked if you could come and help. She is very fond of your species," I say and end up hating my lying self. It reminds me of the disappointment in Zaan's eyes. He also ruined lying for me. Not that I was ever good at it.

"Really? You won't mind?" asks Ollianna, and suddenly her face glows with happiness. Of course, she would welcome the change. Anything is better than spending her time with an equally sad woman. Little does she know, she's about to get ambushed.

I let her change me into one of the ridiculous dresses in my wardrobe, just because she likes being needed. As soon as she leaves for the night, I'll change into one of his shirts, anyway. They did grow on me, the Tarrassian dresses. Especially since I have to wear my slutty Warrior outfit all day. I surprised myself by liking the overly girly outfit when I am at home. It makes me feel like I belong somehow. I involuntary play with the many slits in the soft white dress as Ollianna runs the magic brush through my golden curls. How strange, I think the Tarrassian sun has lightened my hair even more. Funnily enough it's not a hot sun, just incredibly bright. By contrast, my brown skin looks darker against my hair, and my eyes seem downright alien now.

I am happy Ollianna is the quiet type. It allows my own thoughts to run free. Even though I am not doing myself any favors. I mentally ran through the freaking rules like a hundred times since I left him this afternoon. What the hell does he mean I broke one of his? I haven't! Unless I sleepwalk or something. I know I haven't broken any of the major three.

He added a few rules after, and I am trying to focus on those instead. Maybe there is one I missed. And who would have told him about it, anyway? I know Ollianna is loyal. Was it Kayon? Or maybe one of the guards? But which rule? I stare at my reflection in the mirror, so I see the shock in my eyes when I finally get it. *Oh. My God.* I stand to my full height and take a deep breath hoping oxygen can help me think. He is right. I did break a rule. He said I was not allowed to wear clothes when I slept in his bed.

How didn't I think of that? Fucking asshole! Are there cameras in this room? How else would he know?

Another realization hits me hard and I almost laugh. The hysterical sort. This should be my lesson, to never ever dismiss Natalia. Her over-the-top interest in my Sign and what glows when and where was anything but random. She was trying to tell me something. Of course she was. There is always some hidden agenda with that girl. A hundred emotions hit me all at once. Anger, fear, doubt, worry, and the least expected one, hope. *He never left me.* I am not feeling watched because I am paranoid. I don't feel his presence in my dream at night because I've lost my mind. He is not right in the head, and he is such an asshole!!!! *But he never left me.*

"Ollianna, do you mind if you have dinner on your own tonight?" I ask.

"No, of course not. But you must eat, Gianna, please," she says with a pleading voice.

"Yes, I intend to have dinner. Can you please set it in the Sacred Garden? You said the family used to eat all their meals there."

Ollianna watches me with a questioning look, but then her eyes light up.

"What a lovely idea, Gianna! It will do you good to come out of these quarters. The Sacred Garden has healing properties, and many flowers bloom at the beginning of the dark span," she says with a smile.

"Yes, it sounds lovely. Now can you please ask my mate to join me for dinner?"

She is not even trying to pretend. I don't think her species is great with that sort of thing. I am a bit disappointed she kept this from me, but she was loyal to him for many years before she even met me. I will not hold it against her. Good grief, she looks like she's going to faint.

"I am not upset with you, Ollianna, and Zaan won't be either. I will make sure he knows I didn't find out from you," I tell her, and I surprise myself by giving her a hug. She looks even more broken and sad than before. He shouldn't have put this on her.

"Actually, I think you should have some rest, Ollianna. Just ask someone else to serve our dinner. You look very tired, and you have to travel to the White Palace tomorrow. Trust me, it's hectic over there. On second thoughts, you don't have to ask Zaan either. I will do it myself."

"Yes, Gianna," she says without a fight. That's how desperate she is to get away.

"One more thing, Ollianna," I tell her hoping I can keep my rising anger from her. None of this is her fault. She would do anything for the man who saved her and her sister.

"Yes, Gianna?"

"You know that flower tea you've been giving me? The one that definitely tastes stronger in the evenings. What exactly does it do?" I don't really need her to answer. Once again, she looks like she is about to faint, and for the Garrii people, that is an answer in itself. *I. Fucking. Hate. Him!!!* What is wrong with him? Or maybe I am the problem. I am a psycho magnet. There will come a day when I'll think the Moorri King was the most decent guy I ever met.

I try to calm myself before reaching out to him. I could use the com, but I have a point to prove here. Perhaps not ideal to have my first telepathic dialogue with someone who obviously belongs on the psychopathic spectrum. God knows what his twisted brain might look like.

I am trying to remember what Ollianna said, but that in itself is tricky. She said I have to focus on personal things related to the person I am trying to reach. Anything from a scent, a memory, something about the way they look. The more details I can put together, the easier for my mind to connect with theirs. It couldn't be any easier in this case. All I know these days are details of him. How freaking inappropriate to think about the smell of his skin, or those beautiful golden eyes, when I am so angry with him! *Right, I can do this.* I close my eyes, and the scent of orange flowers invades my senses. That and the memory of his tongue inside me. What the hell? Ollianna didn't say I have to remember that sort of thing. The only other person I hate more than Zaan right now has got to be myself.

Gianna? What's wrong? Are you safe?

I force myself not to open my eyes and especially not to panic. I didn't think it would work so easily. It's still overwhelming and a lot to take in. I was shaking my bootie on some catwalk in London only a few months ago. And now I am talking telepathically. To an alien psychopath. It's not something my mind can wrap around easily. His Sign looks strange from the inside of his mind. Everything feels sharp and a bit intimate. And that is the last thing I want to be right now with this jerk.

Yes, Zaan, everything is fine. I was wondering if you would like to join me for dinner in the Sacred Garden. You know, since we share the same house, we might just as well eat together.

There's some strange long pause. Silence is even more bizarre while talking inside someone's mind. Then… a smile. I obviously can't see it, but I can feel it. I am a hundred per cent sure this asshole is smiling right now. Oh, he finds it funny, does he? We'll see about that.

32

—

GIANNA

I am trying to focus on the anger I should be feeling as I walk through the eerily quiet house. Hellaf stomps behind me as if I needed protection in my own damn home. All the guards look like clones, and maybe that's what they are. Despite that confusing little detail, I am quite sure the guy behind me is Hellaf. He looks embarrassed, as if he betrayed my trust or something, which he totally did. They all knew Zaan was living here, and honestly, this thing is getting old. Am I the only clueless person on this planet? Always the last one to know about anything. After leaving Earth, I went from popular to geek in no time. Or maybe I was always a bit nerdy. Hard to tell when you are home-schooled, and there is no one to point out you can't join the cool kids' squad.

I am anything but cool right now. This ridiculous shyness in his presence overpowers any anger. And meanwhile, my reasoning tells me I should feel offended by his creepy behavior; my heart wants to scream its joy from the rooftops. *He never left me. He never let go.* However, being happy over weird stalking behavior is definitely not cool. So, I guess I am not. Cool, that is, because right this moment, I am as excited as I've ever been.

As I reach the Sacred Garden, my Sign decides it would be a great time to ignite with color, and the tattoos on my arms follow shortly. I don't need that to know he's already here. And not just because the scent of oranges is stronger in the air. I feel like liquid on the inside. My stomach is doing somersaults, and my fingers are shaking. I am entirely run by emotions and an overall feeling of vulnerability. Is this what love is meant to be like? Is the Sign messing with me? I am choked by the same fear that made me run away from him twice.

Only now, I understand I am not afraid of him. I never was. I am only terrified of how he makes me feel. He doesn't have power over me because he owns about a thousand organic restraining devices, but because he gives me freaking butterflies. An entire kaleidoscope of them. I've known violence, hate, and pain but somehow managed to survive it all. Love feels different. It strips you of all your power, it takes your strengths away, and it leaves you open to another. They could break you or make you. There is no telling what they could do to you while you just stand there and wait to see which one you may get.

Sharp pain in my chest takes my breath away for a second. Oh, dear God! Is that what he felt like? All of a sudden, I realize this scenario has already happened. He opened his heart to me, and I chose to walk all over it. What have I done? I thought I might have just bruised his ego, but I now understand the magnitude of my mistakes.

"Gianna? You are not breathing properly, again! This nonsense you do has got to stop. Breathe! Now sit!" he says, pointing at a round stone table I haven't noticed before.

I hate his ever-present bossy attitude, but at least it helps with my guilt. He stands by his seat, waiting for me to take mine, looking like a grown-up fed up with a kid's tantrum. A vivid memory of my dad doing the same on many occasions comes to mind. How on Earth did I manage to fall for a guy who is so much like my dad?

"I do not like repeating myself. Breathe! Sit! In that order," he says without even looking at me.

Good grief, he even talks like my father. My only relief right now is that he's not wearing the ridiculous kilt. The less of that perfect body on display, the better for me. His white shirt and loose pants may cover more skin than the Kannicloth, but there is no hiding that beautiful face. I am dying to touch it or run my fingers through his beard. And for whatever reason, I really have a thing for the stark white lock of hair, standing out against his raven mane. All I want is to wrap it around my fingers and pull his face down for a kiss. Oh God, he never kissed anyone before and doesn't even know what it is. This is just ridiculous. Not only do I act like a shy teenage girl around him, but I am just as hormonal as one. I blame fucking Kayon for this. What can one expect after training with a bunch of horny teens all day? Yes, that and the Sign. I am sure they are to blame for my hormonal-induced state of shivers. It's definitely not because I missed him or because he's so beautiful. Or because he smells nice. None of that!

I make my way to the table, trying to focus on the scenery, and compose myself. He'd better not be able to smell what his presence does to my lady parts. Distracting myself from my raging hormones is not that hard because this has got to be the most beautiful place in the entire universe. I've just realised I have never seen it at night. Most of the Sacred Garden is sheltered by the house's walls, but there is no ceiling. The plants, especially the giant Marni Tree in the middle of the garden, reach out into the purple Tarrassian sky. It's all dark now, and the subtle golden light of the twin moons allows the vegetation to give its own glow. The ancient tree looks no different than the other ones in the forest, except for the size. It towers over the house and everything else around. Its trunk gives a soft violet glow, but each time I look at it, I still see the fiery red sap inside it, and I remember how it seemed to communicate with the High Elder. I can't believe I was allowed to witness that special moment.

The dining area is the only bit of the garden protected by a glass ceiling. It is shaped like a dome, and I think the glass might be reflective as it somehow amplifies the soft light of the moons. Hundreds of ivy-like vines hang from the glass dome above the white stone table. They are also glowing with faint violet light. It all looks as if hundreds of candles are lit around, but in a subtle way that doesn't spoil the beauty of the night.

To be fair, after all this time, I still haven't found a single switch to control the lights. I usually ask the MI to do it, and most times, the settings change automatically. One thing I did notice, it is never dark on Tarrassia. There is always some glow, even on the darkest night. It is a strange notion considering the Tarrassians are such a strong species, but I have a feeling they might be scared of the dark. The thought alone is so ludicrous it feels as if someone or something put it inside my mind. Why does it feel like a warning, though? Should I mention it to the High Elder? I ignore it because I have enough shit to deal with as it is. It's not my problem what Tarrassians are scared of.

The round stone table is not as big as one may think, considering the size of everything else around. This is meant to be an intimate place for the use of family and not for entertaining guests. Ollianna did say, Zaan's parents would always eat in here. I take the seat he pointed at, opposite his, and as soon as I do, two tiny aliens start piling food in front of us. Strangely, my brain calls them small, yet they are the same height as Natalia and Jade. I feel guilty for not knowing their names or the name of their species. I need to do better; I need to make an effort. Maybe people don't tell me anything because they think I don't care enough. I can't blame them if they think I am a total bitch.

I take a look at my plate as the steaming food invades my nostrils. The blueish steak, as well as the various types of vegetables have already been cut in tiny bits. Toddler food. God, this is ridiculous!

"Do you always instruct the kitchen staff on how to prepare my food?" I ask. Of all the things I wanted to say that came out first.

"Yes," he admits without even trying to deny it. I finally lift my eyes to meet his. The gold is so intense I almost choke on my own saliva. Despite the intensity of his eyes, the rest of his beautiful face is just as stern as usual. Why do I keep calling him beautiful? I guess he is. That is not the right question. Why do I let it melt me? That is what should worry me.

"Why is that? It's a bit embarrassing, you know? I am given smoothies and tiny chunks of food. Not to mention Ollianna keeps a diary of my meals. Don't think I didn't notice she counts every bite I take."

"Yes, I instructed her to do that," he says like that's just standard around here. Can't he at least deny it? Oh, that's right. He doesn't lie. I am the liar.

"Should I even ask why?" I say, and I am happy to hear the sass in my voice. It's good to know I don't sound as brainwashed as this man's presence makes me feel.

"Of course you can ask, Gianna. It is because you are unable to look after yourself. You are too emotional, prone to self-harming and you don't value yourself enough. Until you stop acting like a cub, you will be treated like one. Eat now. Your food is getting cold."

Say what?!! Oh, why did I ask? I hoped my sass would develop into something more suitable, like smashing the plate or at least stomping my foot, anything really. Instead, I find myself eating like a *good female.* If he gives me one of his stupid praises now, I swear to God I will lose it. Luckily, he doesn't, and we eat in silence.

The soft breeze moving the plants around makes them give a pleasant swishing noise. Like a bamboo forest. I also notice there is a subtle humming coming from the Marni Tree. Strange bird noises pierce the silence from time to time. Add the heady smell of the garden around us, and it all becomes almost hypnotic.

I chew my blue meat slowly, which is stupid considering it's already cut in tiny bits. Maybe I do have an issue with food textures, and that is what caused my eating disorder in the first place. Perhaps the PTSD only aggravated an already present condition. If he keeps staring like this, I will develop even more problems. I know I wished every moment of my new, lonely life to have his eyes back on me. Now that I do, I remember it's not easy to feel watched like you are the freaking dinner. Can't he at least pretend to be normal? Turn it down a notch or something?

"I am listening," he says, looking at me without even blinking.

"Excuse me?" I say because I am sure I missed some part of that sentence.

"You have questions, Gianna. So, ask them. I had been prompting you to do so from the very beginning, yet you chose to act recklessly instead of asking."

Right... so I have. I try not to let his stern, cold voice get to me. If I start crying now, I won't be able to stop.

"Is my father alive?" I surprise myself by asking. I shouldn't care about him, and I shouldn't worry the way I do.

"Yes, he is confined to his dwelling in the green Earth forest. He can only leave for necessities and with a Tarrassian escort," he answers.

"Is he *only* under arrest because he is my father?" I ask.

"Yes. He would be dead otherwise like every other Human proved to conspire against the Coalition."

"Thank you," I say, surprising myself, and he just nods. Part of me would like to ask for a visit or something, but I know he will think it's yet another one of my escape schemes. An even bigger part of me wants to talk about the men he killed, but I really can't go there. Not yet, anyway.

"I am sorry I embarrassed you at the Training Pits. I didn't even think I would have visitors, never mind break a rule," I say, hoping he believes me.

"You only embarrassed yourself, and you are the one to take the required punishment. So, no need to say sorry to me."

Good grief!!!! Must he be such an asshole? I notice most alien species, especially the Tarrassians, tend to take things literally and are very black and white. I am willing to have an open mind, be inclusive and all that. Zaan, however, is damn blunt and freaking rude at all times. In a way, his behavior annoys me enough to ask what I really wanted.

"So, you never left the Marni House," I say, and despite the bushy beard covering his sharp, square jaw, I can see a muscle pulsing in there, like a nervous tick.

"Why would I? It is my home," he says, watching me with even more intensity. It almost feels like a challenge.

"Of course, it is," I say because he does have a point after all. "I just didn't expect it since I am here and all that."

"It is my home because you are here. Where you go, I follow," he says, and now I really feel overrun with emotion.

What is he saying? Is it because of the Sign? Is it a matter of Tarrassian honor, or is it something else?

"Still, it would have been nice for you to tell me," I say.

"You didn't ask, and I am telling you now," he says, again like a challenge. Is he trying to wind me up? Despite feeling like a shy teenager around him at all times, I do have a temper. He really doesn't want to find out what happens when you mix Sicilian and Nigerian heritage.

"You didn't tell me anything, Zaan; I found out by myself!" I tell him, and my voice makes a few birds fly out of a nearby bright yellow bush.

"Gianna, please don't raise your voice," he says calmly.

"That was not in the rules."

"It is now."

"Fine," I say with a shrug.

"Please apologize for raising your voice," he says.

What? I honestly want to pull at my hair the way he does with his. Only I have a feeling he'll make a rule against that, too. *Asshole!!!!*

"I am sorry," I say, trying to choose my battles. Everything feels like one with him.

"What are you sorry for?"

Jesus! This can't be happening! Idiot!!

"I am sorry for raising my voice, Zaan," I say, and I even add an overly fake smile for good measure. A bit like his mom's one. He sees it for what it is but seems willing to let it go. Only I am not that keen on peace any more. The more I think about things the less peaceful I feel.

"Are there cameras in my room?" I ask.

"Live feeds, you mean? Yes, of course there are. They are everywhere you go."

Oh, Lord! He says it like it's nothing. That is even more annoying than the actual offense.

"Does everywhere include the cleaning rooms?" I ask, and he seems to give it a thought.

"If you mean the expelling rooms, no. But if you mean the washing rooms, yes."

"I see," I say with an increasingly angry voice. "Do you watch me while I bathe?"

"Sometimes, when you request Ollianna to leave you alone." He says it like a challenge.

"Is that normal, you think?" I ask, but I do wonder if I am just angry at myself. The thought of him watching me bathe is not as upsetting as it should be.

"For someone who thrives on hurting herself and me in the process, yes, it is normal. If you think I will let you bathe unattended, think again!"

There is undeniable rage in his voice this time. The large hands resting on the table are now fisted, and I involuntarily shrink back in my seat. He observes me, and I can see he is trying to calm himself down. We just stare at each other with matching anger and longing. This is just stupid. Why can't we just talk, like couples do? Like Natalia advised me to. *I missed you so much! I don't want to argue anymore!*

"Do you watch the cameras in my bedroom? When I sleep?" I ask quietly. I think I already know what he will say.

"No, I watch you in person when you sleep," he says, confirming my theory. It explains why he looks so tired. It also explains why I always feel his presence in my dreams. This should be scary. The worst invasion of privacy. Only, it doesn't feel that way. Maybe I'm screwed in the head.

"Why, Zaan?"

"Because you are mine to watch," he says, and the gold in his eyes seems to slip into my veins, traveling straight to my heart. I feel like falling, all my barriers are crumbling, I need something to cling to, maybe some trace of anger... Oh yes. The freaking flower tea!!!

"Have you been drugging me, Zaan? You know, so I won't wake up in the middle of the night and find you doing God knows what to me?" Okay, maybe I shouldn't have added that last bit. He is furious now. I can tell because he is overly calm. Even more worrying, I can see the large muscles under his white shirt starting to expand. Shit!

"The Tarrassian flowers open at the beginning of the dark span almost everywhere on Mother Planet," he explains with that deceivingly calm voice. "They perfume the air, induce sleep and calm the senses. They don't overpower anyone's will but allow our bodies and minds to relax and recharge during the dark span. The Marni Trees are too dense and block the moons' light. No Tarrassian flowers grow in the Marni forest. That is why we buy them and use them in our tea instead. Ollianna was instructed to administer a stronger dose in the evenings because your nightmares needed to stop. You were exhausted, underfed, and with a strong desire to hurt yourself when you got here. That will not happen on my watch. And you should be careful what you accuse me of."

Just as he finishes talking, a servant arrives with my usual cup of tea. Really? Come on! Did they time this on purpose? An idea comes to mind. I just hope I am brave enough to say it out loud. There is still a big part of me who thinks I am not good enough for him. I don't think that will ever change. I may be less than someone like him deserves but it is me who he watches every night.

"I don't want to have the tea anymore. Not in the evenings, anyway, and not a strong dose. I won't mind some tomorrow morning, considering I have to fight *the three hundred*," I say, even though I know he can't get that joke. Not that he can get any. "I want to sleep in your arms instead. Tonight, and every other night. You can keep my nightmares away."

There, I said it! His calm and cold presence seems a bit rattled by my proposal. He'd better not say anything offensive right now. If he mentions my past or my reputation or says this is some sort of a devious plan, I will die. I will break into more pieces than anyone could ever put back together.

"Are you asking me to be a flower tea substitute?" he asks with a faint trace of a smile on his beautiful lips.

"Pretty much," I reply, but unlike him, I allow my smile to reach my eyes.

The gold in his stare flickers as he watches me with an intensity that makes me want to cry. He stands and offers me his hand.

"Come to me," he says softly. I know what his words really mean and unlike in the past, this time I rush to do his bidding.

Now I understand these three words were never about control, quite the opposite. He wanted me to choose him. And now, I do. I go around the table and take his hand with shaky fingers. He completely engulfs my hand in his huge one and starts pulling me towards my quarters. Our quarters. I am happy he's dragging me along, not sure my legs can listen to my brain. They seem so glad to follow him, though. I feel more nervous than ever, and I have no idea what he will do next. I just hope he will stay with me as I asked. Whatever happens next can make or break this relationship forever. I hope he knows that. It's so unnerving not to have any control over such a crucial moment. *Trust*. I have to trust him. Faith. He knows better what I need and admitting it is not as bad as I thought it would be. It doesn't feel diminishing. It just feels right.

33

—

She is conflicted by emotions as she follows me quietly to our sleeping quarters. I am trying to keep my own emotions in check and not just because it is the Tarrassian way to do so. My beautiful, troubled female needs emotional stability just as much as she needs to feel safe. I intend to make sure she has both.

Most of all, I am trying not to think of what will happen on the next span. For the first time ever, I am tempted to scrape off a rule that is not even my own. I know I don't have to worry about the Tarrassian Pit Masters or the Untried. They will simply not raise their swords against a female. That still leaves the four non-Tarrassians in that Unit, who will be willing to fight her.

And although they all know better than to harm my mate and a High Lady of Tarrassia, accidents can happen. She is so vexing fragile. Forget the males; the Moorri young female could easily kill my Lorra without any use of weapons.

I don't care what the King says, nor do I share his obsession with the Human male he rescued. Their species is useless. Not to mention they lack self-preservation since they are entirely unaware of their weaknesses. They seem to believe they stand a chance against much more advanced species. I haven't met the male called Brian. None of us has except for the King. The Human has been in the healing pod ever since his arrival on Tarrassia. I don't think he is any different than the other Humans, and I met plenty of those. The only thing they can do is refuse to comply. Even the strongest species know if you fall in battle, it is safer to stay down. Humans do the exact opposite; they keep getting up each time they fall. The thought is worrying, considering my Lorra might do the same silly thing on the next span.

I am a champion of female warriors. I tried and failed to get the Council to change our old ways and allow mentalities to keep up with the times. I've seen female warriors able to take down males twice their size. It doesn't mean it's suitable for all. Species like the Garrii or the Humans should not let their fragile females fight. And I should definitely find a way to keep my one away from the Pits. I know this is something she has wanted all her life, but the circumstances are different now. She won't be fighting against equally powerless Humans but against species whose cubs alone could easily defeat her. I cannot forbid it out front. She will hold it against me, the way she holds it against her sire. On the following span, she will learn that lesson all by herself. Not only does it not make me happy, but I am terrified she will get hurt. I have to trust my people. They must know if they harm my female, I will end them in painful ways.

As we enter our quarters, she lets go of my hand, and I allow it. The one thing she has never faked is her shyness. I was just a fool not to notice how skittish she was when being touched. I know she needs patience, but she also needs to learn the vexing rules. I am not entirely sure she won't break them again if the opportunity arrives.

"What now?" she asks, trying to fake bravery she doesn't have. "Perhaps we should talk about what happened. I mean about what I did," she adds quickly as if worried I will go near the one subject, I know she wants to avoid. She takes another step back, putting distance between us, then she stops with a worried look in her beautiful green eyes. She is obviously trying to follow my rules, and I refrain from praising her. I know she hates that.

"I wasn't trying to get away just now," she says, avoiding my eyes. "I normally seek distance from people and..." she stops, and a shadow crosses her perfect face. "Probably not something I am famous for, right? Never mind, I can't expect you to believe me," she adds, lowering her eyes. She looks defeated somehow, and I hate I am the one who has made her feel like this. I understand her reasons and actions better than she thinks, and I hate myself for not putting that into words. Not yet and not now. I must be able to trust her fully before I go anywhere near that conversation. It pains me to say I don't know if I can trust her.

"Yes, my Lorra, you will explain your reasons, and we will talk. For now, we just sleep. I want you rested and focused on the next span. Come to me," I tell her, offering her my hand. We are less than a few steps away and to most it may seem like a stupid thing to say. To me, it's the biggest thing of all. Just like earlier in the Sacred Garden, she rushes to take my hand. She chooses me, freely, and I am very tempted to ignore both my rules and my plans for this dark span. And that will not do. I don't know how to function without rules or planning ahead.

"Let's prepare for the night span, my beautiful," I tell her, pulling her towards the chair in front of her favorite mirror. She watches me with unsure eyes as I put her hair detangler in her hand. I know she brushes her beautiful golden locks precisely seven times before she uses the facilities and applies a softening cream to her face and neck and a different one to her arms and legs. Everything she does is fascinating. All her rituals take a precise amount of time, and she has a unique facial expression for each one of them. My favorite is how she bites gently at her plump lower lip while applying softening lotion to those long legs. As if that action requires all her focus. She does it every single time without fail. It makes me painfully hard and chases all my vexing sleep away. It may be torture, but it's my favorite moment of the day – that and watching her sleep. I know how many breaths she takes per nano, I know how often she changes sleeping positions, and I know the signs of stirring before she is about to wake.

Perhaps I shouldn't make her aware of the extent of my obsession. For some reason, it scares her. My mother tried to suggest in her not very subtle ways that I should tone down a bit. Apparently, her friend, the scheming Human female mated to the High Elder, told her my behavior has unpleasant labels on Earth. Good thing we are not on Earth, then. I do not intend to change my ways. I have been waiting for my female for as long as I can remember. On my darkest spans I used to believe my mind was broken. Each time I looked at the Lorra Moon, I could feel a presence. I still remember the exact day and time it happened for the first time. I was sixteen orbit rotation, and it was not long after becoming the youngest High Commander of the Blood Fleet. It felt as if the presence became real and a myriad of invisible strings was connecting us. I have been looking for her ever since.

My people enjoy mating quite a lot. Of course, some more than others. I wonder if our Human Queen is aware almost every female she meets is one of the King's exes. I never had eyes for any and I spent most of my time with the Blood Fleet to avoid unwanted attention from females. I only ever wanted her, even before I met her. It is no wonder my silent left heart came to life before we touched.

"Zaan?" she asks with a small voice.

"Yes?"

"You're staring at me."

"And?"

"You don't have to, okay? I am right here and, I don't intend to go anywhere," she says with a sigh that sounds exasperated.

"I don't do it because I have to. I do it because I want to. Now you get ready for sleep. You are wasting precious time," I tell her, not really able to keep my voice as pleasant as I would like. She can be very infuriating at times.

"You know what? You do whatever. I am going to change in the bathroom, cleaning room, whatever."

"I expect you won't be longer than your usual eighteen and a half nanos," I tell her because I really don't like how tired she looks right now. She needs to sleep. Without the delay of our late dark span meal, she would have been fast asleep by now.

"Say what? Eighteen and a half minutes? You do know I am a real person, right? I am not a freaking pet you time as you please!" she says with way more attitude than I would like to hear in her voice. I am willing to let it go for now. The longer I am this close to her, the more I need to sleep and forget about what I really want to do to her right now.

"I know you are not a pet. Pets are obedient. I don't understand your reasons for being upset," I tell her calmly. "You take seven nanos to moisturize your legs, three for your face and neck, and four nanos for your arms. You take two nanos and a half to clean your blunt teeth, and I added an extra two for using the facilities. This is your dark span routine. How am I the one timing you?"

At first, she laughs. Only it doesn't feel genuine. It is a nervous laugh I don't understand. It must be a Human sign of discomfort. When I don't join in with her fake amusement, her perfect face turns serious, as if she can't believe her ears. Now she looks as if she's about to spill water from her eyes like a cub. She still has to do what she is told, and I choose to ignore her and use the other adjacent cleaning room for myself.

It takes me half the time she requires, and it is mainly because

I rush. I want to wait for her in between the furs and avoid further unnecessary confrontation. Also, I know she is nervous, and the last thing she needs is an eyeful of my erection. Just because I am strong enough not to use it, doesn't mean I can stop it from happening. In between the pull of the Sign and my obsession with this female, that battle has long been lost.

Luckily, most of my clothes are still kept in these quarters, and I choose a pair of sleeping bottoms I didn't even know I owned. I prefer to sleep bare, but it is not advisable right now. I rush to make it under the furs before she returns. Putting the vexing bottoms on with a painful erection is quite the challenge. There is a chance I might not survive this dark span. I refused to allow myself relief ever since I met her. The reasonable part of my mind tells me this is madness, but I have never been driven by reason. My obsessions, my plans, and my self-set goals are what make me function. That span when I first laid eyes on her, back on the slaver's ship, was when I decided: the only times I spill my seed will be inside my female. Right now, that seems like the most vexing stupid idea I have ever had. According to my mother, I have had plenty of those. I know I broke a part of her heart when I decided to join the Training Pits. I was only five orbit rotations and smaller than most other cubs. My mother was terrified and with good reason. I got injured and spilled my blood every single span until one day, I didn't. I defeated Kayon, my Pit Master, when I was eight orbit rotations. That had also been a self-set goal. It was way easier than the current one.

My beautiful female doesn't make it easy. She likes winding me up. Not only is she two nanos late, but she returns wearing clothes. To my bed! True, it is my shirt, and seeing it on her pulls at both my hearts. However, rules must not be broken.

"You are late," I tell her and wait for the inevitable snarly reply. I can see her lips trying to form such a sentence, but she can't. She is nervous and, right now, she looks ridiculously fragile and small. The purple light of the cleaning rooms glows behind her lithe form, making her golden mane look alien yet so enticing. My hands are itching with the need to touch that mass of tight curls. Her beautiful brown skin stands out against the white of my shirt. She twists her fingers then starts pulling at the garment she's wearing, almost as if trying to make it longer.

"Come here," I tell her after I ask the MI to turn off the lights entirely. The soft glow given by the Marni forest outside the windows is enough for comfort. My species can see in the dark, but no Tarrassian seeks to ever use that power willingly. My people are not comfortable in the dark, and we would rather have light around us.

She follows my request and comes to bed, except she is as vexingly slow as a small Raanian beast. At this pace, we might not get to sleep at all on this cursed span. Eventually, she makes it to our sleeping dais and gets under the furs, as far away from me as possible. Like I said, Humans have no sense of self-preservation. I pull her close to me, under the furs, allowing her the comfort of the covers. I remove her shirt in one swift motion before she gets to deny me and I ignore her sharp intake of air. I turn her around in my arms and engulf the back of her with my whole body. Again, a stupid idea, but there is no other way. She is where she belongs. My beautiful female is unexpectedly quiet, stiff as a wooden board, and barely breathing. I still the noise inside my head and the maddening beat of my new heart to assess her condition. I will never forget her pain when my forceful touch pushed her back into her tormented past. I relax instantly when my nostrils fill with the scent of her arousal. She is wary and skittish but not afraid. I bury my nose in the back of her neck and inhale her familiar essence. She is probably not aware, but her beautiful brown skin smells exactly like the leaves of the Marni Trees. The scent of home.

All that happens now is we sleep, my Lorra, I tell her in her mind because this moment seems too precious to waste on spoken words. I am trying to sound calm to help her relax and sleep. Of course, my vexing cock is trying to do the exact opposite thing to her backside. She tenses even more, and I curse quietly.

Ignore it, beautiful. I can't help it react to you, but I can sure stop myself from using it. Sleep! I tell her, and she doesn't reply. She is quiet for a long time but wide awake. For the name of the Astrals! She needs to sleep! I am dying here... I almost wish I hadn't removed her shirt. Having her naked in my arms is too much, even for my well-trained willpower. Me and my stupid rules...

Is there a reason why you don't want to do that? she asks, unexpectedly. Even in my head, her voice sounds small and wary. I am sure I have plenty of reasons, yet none seems important any more.

You have to sleep, my Lorra. We both do. We need a fresh mind on the next span to deal with the mess you caused.

"I didn't cause anything on purpose, this is not fair. But you know what? It's fine; have it your way. I don't want to argue," she says, way too snarly for my liking. Despite her defiant tone she just sounded tired and defeated and because of that I am more than willing to put the matter to rest.

I wrap my arms around her small body even tighter, careful not to apply too much pressure. She is so fragile, and I am quick to push away the memory of her past. Her pain and her sire's words will haunt me for the rest of my spans. I know those vicious males are no more, I know they died tasting pain and fear at my hands, but it still doesn't feel enough. My Lorra's life was known to all, or so I foolishly thought. There was no knowledge of her vicious attack in what her people call *the press,* and my Shadows couldn't find any, either. Her sire was my only option. He didn't even deny being the coward that he was. His Warriors did that to her. He had the power to end them, yet he did nothing. I only let him live because I could see that was the biggest punishment. His inner torment is far worse than death. He gave me their names and their location as soon as I asked. On my way out of his forest-dwelling, he said those words that took the little peace I had left. *Make it hurt*, he said. *They broke her bones.* I did make it hurt. Badly. But that will never be enough to forget the pain they caused or my guilt. I was rescuing other species' females while my own was being hurt. I was protecting strangers while my mate had no one to look after her. I am too distracted by my tormented thoughts to notice she has turned to face me, and I allowed it.

"Fine, we sleep, but there is something I must do first," she says, and before I get to do anything else, she presses her lips to mine. A kiss. Not any kiss, but a Human one. I had no idea what it was when I first met her. Still not entirely sure, but it's the latest Tarrassian craze. The King and Queen are not exactly shy when displaying affection in public, and now that's all my people talk about. If you were to listen to my Warriors, one would think the kiss is more important than the Sign or fertility. Since the arrival of the Humans, Tarrassians have lost their minds, according to Nodric, and right now, I tend to agree.

One of her trembling hands rests on my chest, and the other one cups my face. Small fingers caress my facial fur, that she calls a beard, while her soft lips become more insistent over mine. She wants me to open my mouth, and I allow it – a mistake. Her ridiculously tiny tongue touches mine, and her taste goes straight to my brain, then to my painful cock. Right now, I am not sure which is worse. The need takes over any reason I have left, and I push her shoulders into the sleeping furs, laying her flat on her back. I am careful enough not to crush her as I allow my hands to do what they begged for all this span. My fingers sink in her golden mane, holding her face still, while my mouth devours hers. I don't know the rules of her Human kiss, but they only seem to be one. *Lust.* She clings with both her hands to the nape of my neck, and her body trembles with need. The nanoclip she wraps her legs around me, I pull away, while I still can. She is trying to fight it and keep me close, but that is not a battle she can win. I turn her around in my arms and press her back against my front, the same position as before.

Sleep, Lorra, I give the order inside her mind.

You are a very strange man, Zaan of House Marni, she replies, but luckily, she doesn't seem upset.

That is something both your people and mine can agree on, I tell her before the Astrals take pity on us and let the darkness of sleep take us.

34

ZAAN

"I knew it!" she says with laughter that makes both my hearts flutter like a Donian bird. Never heard her laugh like this for me. The only other time she's done it, it was for her Human friend, Jade. "I knew this ship could fly faster," she explains, but I know what she meant.

"Yes, neither Kayon's nor Hellaff's species are known for their spacecraft flying skills," I tell her with a smile.

I think she likes my smiles. Her fingers fidget with her garment, and she quickly looks away each time I do. A peculiar way to show interest, but Humans are one of the strangest species I have ever met. They are all incredibly individual. To say you understand Humans, one would have to know every single one of them. Maybe that is why the slavers sell them for such high prices. They have no special powers, they are frail, breakable and even the weakest plague can wipe them out. It must be their differences that make them precious. One can't find two Humans alike. They are beautifully different.

It appears my Lorra loves flying and seems fascinated by my

ship. The craft I am piloting manually is not my main ship but a smaller version more suitable for low travel. It doesn't mean it has to fly low or slow. Trust Kayon and Hellaf to do both.

The bright colors of the sunrise paint her golden mane in hundreds of shades, making it throw lights around the ship. My female is painfully beautiful this morning. We might have gone to rest late, but she slept undisturbed in my arms, like a cub without worries. I woke her up with a kiss on her forehead, over her Sign. Our Sign. Then, I quickly retreated to the cleaning room before giving in to what my vexing cock was begging for. Technically, there was time, and she smelled as aroused as I was. I made a plan though, and I stuck with it. I always do. She needs to understand the rules and the consequences for breaking them. *I hate my rules!* I keep telling myself I need to be able to trust her before I let her in. There is more to it, but I push those thoughts away. I do not like complicated things. That is why I have rules. To uncomplicate things. Sadly, my mate belongs to a species whose favourite part about rules is breaking them.

On my return to our sleeping room, I found her already dressed in the ridiculous outfit Ollianna's sister made for her. No doubt to get back at me for being Barin's friend. My Lorra seems to like her new garments, and she looks comfortable wearing them. I just want to kill the entire Camp when she strolls around showing way too much skin, but I am a male known for having control. I will keep it together even if it kills me. I cannot ask for discipline and self-restraint from my Warriors and not practise it myself.

"How can a low-flying ship reach this altitude?" she asks from the seat next to mine. Her beautiful light eyes follow every motion of my fingers. She is trying to make sense of the symbols on my control panel. Tarrassian is a complicated language. All the species we interact with rely on the translating device when communicating with us. All except for our Queen, that is. She is as fluent in Tarrassian as we are. She is a strange creature, our new Queen.

"I am positive the Elder of the Scholars can change the control panel and the travel systems into your language," I told her, watching her like a starved male. I know it makes her nervous, but she is too excited and focused to notice right now. "Once those are in place, I am sure you will easily master flying. Flying has to come naturally. Those who try to bend the elements to their skill will never acquire the skill. Flying has to follow and respect the rules of the environment. The solar wind can be reached at this altitude. It streams plasma and particles from the sun out into space. It acts as a natural propeller for our ship. Other planets could benefit from plasmaspheric breeze. The elements are a Warrior's ally as long as he or she will respect them. I will add the Space Travel Module to your learning pack. It is not an easy one, and once assigned to you, you must pass it."

"What do you mean, Zaan?" she asks me with a trace of doubt in her eyes. Her voice is wary, almost as if she doesn't want to allow herself to believe.

"Would you like to learn how to fly, my Lorra? And I don't mean like Kayon or Hellaf. Cubs can fly better than those two. Would you like to learn how to pilot like a Blood Fleet Warrior?" I cannot help but smile. Her beautiful face is in awe, and her eyes shine brighter than the Lorra Moon itself. The High Elder is right. I was a vexing fool, who didn't pay attention to his mate's needs. I wrongly assumed I knew what she needed. And her being a different species is no excuse. My sire encouraged my mother to be her own person and I should have known better. There is no greater love than seeing people for what they truly are.

"Are you serious? But aren't those like the elite Tarrassian Warriors? They don't even train with us," she says, watching me with hopeful eyes.

"Any of the Untried can become a Blood Fleet Warrior. Their

fighting skills must be as accomplished as the ones joining all other Tarrassian forces. What makes the Blood Fleet Warriors different is their passion for flying and skill for mechanical technology. Although the second can be taught, the first one must be in one's blood. That makes you a candidate."

She watches me quietly and seems genuinely speechless. Again, I can tell she finds it hard to believe. I meant every word I said, but I feel slightly guilty as not all my reasons are honest. Yes, I know she can do it, and I trust her passion for space travel is genuine. If she is to become a Warrior, the safest place would be on a Blood Fleet ship. Some of the most skilled pilots are sheltered from actual fighting, as they are too precious to the Fleet. Of course, fighting is not always something they can avoid, especially in times of War. But I cannot think of that right now. First, I have to deal with this vexing span. The closer we get to the Camp, the more I know I cannot risk her. Not even a scratch. Not happening. I might just as well tell her now.

"I will not allow the fight, my Lorra. There will be no following of the protocol on this span," I tell her without looking her way for a change. My heart is heavy, knowing I will once again shame my sire.

"What do you mean, Zaan? I broke the rule in front of the entire Camp. Isn't the punishment expected?" she asks.

"It is. It doesn't mean I will allow it. I will not risk you," I tell her and hope my harsh tone will end this conversation. Of course, that doesn't work.

"If you think I will embarrass myself by acting like a spoiled little girl because I am related to the boss, think again! No one will ever take me seriously. I might just as well learn how to bake and join the gossip club," she says with a raised voice she must know I will not tolerate.

"Please, remember your rules, Gianna. Do not raise your voice. There is no need for one of your anger outbursts."

"Excuse me? My what? This is so unfair. You just offered to break a rule for me, but I can't raise my voice?" she says, pushing her golden mane away from her face. "I get punished for not following the rules, then I get punished for wanting to follow the rules."

In a way, she does have a point, so I try not to focus on her raised voice. And to be fair, my mother is more to blame for visiting than my female. My sire really needs to stop encouraging her to become the most reckless Tarrassian female ever.

"I will revoke the punishment. As the High Master of the Training Pits, I can make that decision. It will not reflect badly on you," I tell her, trying to keep the hurt out of my voice.

"I know enough about Tarrassians by now. Anything less than perfect will be frowned upon," she says, and unlike me she doesn't keep her emotions out of her voice. "A High Master ignoring a rule to protect his fragile mate will not be accepted."

"Yes, I am familiar with the ways of my people," I tell her flatly.

"Let me guess, you will give up yet another position for me," she says, and I turn my eyes on her. I can see her flinch under the intensity of my stare.

"I would give up anything for you. You always come first. What will it take for you to stop questioning that?" I ask her, and she closes her eyes briefly as if my stare burns her soul. Good! She takes a deep breath, and her slender fingers tremble on her lap. Her strong emotions are the biggest threat to my rules. The two do not match.

"You would give anything up to keep me safe. I know that with all my heart, Zaan," she says, and her flickering eyes watch me with her usual shyness; the defiance is all gone.

"I am more than a fragile Human; I am more than the person you have to keep sacrificing for. I mean, yeah, I am all that; who am I kidding? Everyone around is at least twice my size. I am also someone who has a dream, and now I finally have a chance to reach it. It was taken from me before by people who think they know best what's good for me. It's not just my body you have to keep safe from harm, Zaan. There are also things like my mind, my soul, and my spirit. Those too need looking after, and taking this away from me now will break me. My body may be unharmed at the end of this day, but my spirit may not," she says, trying to convince me to accept this madness.

Humans are obsessed with their *spirit*. A special power according to our King. What is the use of a power no one can see? Is it made up? I already know Humans thrive on deceiving others and quite often themselves.

"You are asking for more than I can give, my beautiful," I tell her with a pained voice – no point hiding it anymore.

"You have to let me do this, please," she says, offering me a shy smile. "I am not stupid; I know none of the Tarrassian males will raise a hand against me. That only leaves Kayon, Mirri, and the two Kartassi Pit Masters. Hellaf already told me what the most sensitive and easily hurt areas of his species are. For creatures that big, they have plenty," she says with a cute grin. "I observed Mirri and Kayon closely and I know their weaknesses in a fight. Mirri makes mistakes out of fear and Kayon out of too much confidence. Please, trust me. I know what I am doing," she says and I am equally shocked and impressed. There is also that little nagging reminder Humans are not what they seem.

"Speaking of the Kartassi, are they clones?" she asks.

"Of course not; why would you think that?"

"Well, they all look identical. I haven't seen any Kartassi women, but the men are perfect copies of each other," she says. I keep forgetting how different Humans look. One would think they are different species. It must be hard for her to understand. Tarrassians look similar enough, but the Kartassi and many other species all look alike.

"No, they are not clones, but I can understand why you would think that. Their females look very different from the males but also identical to each other. Unlike the males, they are very beautiful," I tell her for the sake of information. Still, for whatever reason, she turns the bad attitude back on.

"Are they now? I am happy you noticed, Zaan. You are very observant. We wouldn't want you to miss things like Jade's boobs' size or the beauty of the Kartassi women. Oh, have you noticed the Garrii? They are spectacular," she says and crosses her arms over her chest, like a vexing cub having a tantrum.

"If you keep this up, Gianna, fighting your Unit will be the least of your worries on this span," I tell her pinning her down with a stare I know must be flecked with white specs of my rage. I feel my War Beast pushing at my muscles from the inside, almost like it thinks I am about to join a battle. Everything feels like one with her. "I would ask you to apologize, but I don't even know what for. I have no idea what your latest outburst was about."

"Of course you don't. You are the most black and white person I have ever met," she says with a smirk I so want to wipe off. No wonder Humans can answer the Riddle of the Sphinxes. They make no sense themselves. What is she even talking about? I involuntarily look down at my chest as if expecting to see my skin has changed color overnight.

"Tarrassians only come in various shades of platinum ore. No one in my species is black and white. Do I need to worry about your eyesight just before you are about to enter a fight?" I tell her, and she just slaps her forehead, making my own Sign jolt. Is that a Human gesture, or is she trying to harm herself?

"Dear Lord! Just leave it, Zaan," she says, avoiding my stare.

"Yes, I intend to leave it for now. We will revisit the way you address me later. Now, back to your imminent fight. It is true, the Kartassi have many soft spots on their bodies. That information is useless to someone the size of their cubs. As for

Kayon, his species may not know much about spacecrafts, but they are masters of weapons, skilled fighters, and have no soft spots, confidence or not. Mirri is a female and she may be young and wary, but she is a Moorri. I don't need to remind you how vicious they can be. You have to understand, these are not some powerless Humans you are about to fight," I tell her, hoping she will see the reason for herself.

"And yet… it is Jade's blunt teeth and Natalia's scheming your people are scared of. Oh, and the rumor goes, the Elders are more afraid of the Human Queen than they are of the Noorranni," she says with a smile, and I have no reply to that.

35

GIANNA

I can't believe he did that to me. After he landed his ship down the docking area – on the exact opposite side of the Camp from my Unit, because why not? – he pulled me in for a kiss that left me brainless and breathless. I am sure Natalia got it wrong. This man cannot possibly kiss like that without knowing what it is or serious practice. Right? He doesn't just kiss; he devours. And now he expects me to go kick some oversized alien ass after he turned my legs into Jell-O. As if that wasn't bad enough, just before we parted ways, he reminded me of rule one. I must keep myself safe, or there will be *consequences*. So now, not only am I going to be turned into a human mop by the aliens in my Unit, but I am also going to be punished for it after.

And I had enough of the stupid threats already. I haven't seen any punishment yet, and the longer I wait, the more anxious I get. Somehow, he doesn't seem like the type to make empty threats. Maybe I need to really piss him off, get it over and done with. Perhaps there is some winning in getting my ass kicked and breaking his precious rule, after all.

One look at Kayon tells me I am sure to bite the dust any minute now. He is not a happy orc. And he is equally angry with everybody else.

"You have put us all in a bad position here, Gianna," whispers Mirri near me as we wait in line for the Pit Masters to give us instructions. As expected, the first order of the day is the *reckless Human's punishment*. Yep, Kayon actually said that.

"You were there, if I recall," I snap back.

"But we were not the ones receiving visitors and vexing cuddles, so it doesn't count," interferes the stupid Ninja boy from somewhere behind me.

"Would you like me to add more to your punishment, Untried Warrior?" asks Kayon, booming over the noise of the Camp and staring me down with scary pitch-black eyes. Everybody is whispering and snickering, but of course, only I get called out on it.

"No, Master of The Untried. I am good," I say, and more laughter erupts around me.

"Now, let's get this done so we can return to your learning module. The Scholars are waiting, so, make it quick," he says, obviously thinking there might be an after for me.

"Untried Warrior Gianna of House Marni, choose your weapon. Whatever you decide to go for, your opponents will have the same. Now!" he booms at me when he notices I am not moving.

I somehow make it to the massive pile of shinai swords, because, well, at least I can lift those. All of a sudden, I wish I had taken Zaan's offer. This is beyond madness. It's just plain stupid. My brain only comes back to life to give me a detailed list of why I should have joined the gossip squad instead of the Untried.

You haven't trained with a sword since you were a teen. You don't have the kendogu armor. Nope, not even a pair of kote.

The shinai is way heavier than anything you used before. You cannot self-heal, your skin is soft, you are smaller than anyone around except for the cubs, and they are all pissed with you for whatever reason. This would be a good time to make a run for the Royal Palace and hide under Sia's perfectly stiff dress.

Good thing my brain goes numb again and lets me be. *No more thinking!* I carefully choose a shinai, even though it's stupid. They all look the same. The Tarrassian sun is basking everything in its intense light, so there is no violet glow to the beautiful Marni wood. I can still smell it, though. It smells like home – the scent of the Red Forest that lulls me to sleep every night.

I run my hand up and down over the smooth surface of my shinai. I can't help the smile that pulls at my lips. The people around me must think I have lost my mind. Who smiles before a fight? Ever since I witnessed the little exchange between the High Elder and the Marni Tree, I always smile when I look at my forest or I touch any wood that comes from there. Dead or alive. The image of the glittery red sap, similar to my Sign and marks, has left an imprint on my brain. I touch the shinai and can't help my heart fill with an emotion I don't really understand. Maybe I feel so connected to the Marni forest because of the Sign on my forehead. Perhaps it's something else. All of a sudden, the Kendo sword in my hand feels like an extension of me. I am not doing this alone any more. My trees and I are doing this together. My content smile is still on as I walk to the middle of the Pit and wait for my first opponent. The snickering has stopped for some reason. The air feels charged with something different. Something that won't allow my smile to fade. Are they afraid? Of me?

Kayon invites volunteers to step forward. I can see Mirri in the corner of my eye, pulling silly Ronnin behind her just as he is about to volunteer. She gives him a terrifying red look, and he just growls at her. As expected, none of the other Untried moves, so it is only Mirri stepping forward. There is an apologetic look in her eyes as she chooses her own shinai.

"Don't you dare go easy on me," I tell her quietly as we face each other, taking position. "The punishment for that is immediate discharge. This is your dream as much as it is mine. Please don't let them take it away from you. If you are my friend, you will not make me live with that."

"Gianna, I am stronger than you, and all Moorri females train from very young ages," she says just as quietly.

"I know. Now fight! I will pretend you are your asshole King if you don't. I'll cut your fucking tail off."

As expected, her species' natural aggression takes over, and all charity is gone from her bright red eyes.

I bow my head to her and lift my shinai. My brain impresses me as it starts functioning at full speed. It reminds me of all the forgotten rules of Kendo, methodically, like a school lesson. At the same time, it's telling me which of them I shouldn't apply. The whole idea of Kendo is to avoid causing actual harm and to avoid hitting soft areas in your opponent. My adversaries are fucking aliens, so scrap that. And because my sword is made of wood, it cannot cause significant damage to them. Yes, a blow would kill me, but they can take it. So, they will!

I haven't seen Mirri fight at her full capacity, so my first concern is to learn as much about her as I can. Mirri must like her tail a lot because right now, she is kind of angry. She lifts her sword up and launches my way, hitting at the air, as expected. Why do they barge like that? She is fast though, like, swift. I only manage to avoid her shinai two more times before I have to lift mine to block hers from splitting me in half. The strength of the impact makes my whole body vibrate like a violin string, and the pain in my wrists feels like fire, yet unlike Mirri, I don't drop my sword. It takes a few seconds to register she didn't do that because of the impact. That was probably nothing for her.

Something scared her. Is it the glow of my marks? I can tell my Sign is lit as it throws patterns around the soft sand of the Pit.

"Pick it up, Mirri, I am sure a Moorri of all people doesn't mind a bit of red," I tell her with a smile and lift my sword up in a fighting stance, waiting for her to snap out of it. That is when I see it. Yes, my Sign and marks are probably brighter, as they always are when things get heated. However, the glow doesn't come from them. It comes from my shinai. The wood is suddenly alive, and glittery red sap goes up and down inside as I move it around. I look at Mirri's weapon still lying in the sand. It is as dead as all the other swords lying in a pile of crafted wood. They look nothing like my shinai.

"Pick it up, Mirri. Fight!" I tell her, and she does it almost robotically.

Her attempts are easy to block now, as she is really distracted by my sword, lighting up each time it makes contact with hers. I can hear her rapid breath and the sound of wood smashing against wood, the only sounds left around us. The overly noisy Camp is completely quiet. Even the ever-present Tarrassian breeze has died down, somehow. I could end this fight here and now because she doesn't pay attention.

Kendo is not about aggression, so I don't go on the offensive. Training should be about improving ourselves, not visiting the freaking healers.

"I am not special, and I don't have any powers, Mirri. I am Human, remember? It is the Marni wood that lights up because it likes this. My forest was never meant to become pretty furniture. It was meant for fighting. The Marni wood wants your bravery, not your fear. Get a grip and fight me like a Warrior. Respect your shinai or say goodbye to your tail!"

A flicker of something makes her big red eyes sparkle as she lifts her shinai and the sap inside starts flickering to life. As our swords meet in the air, mine is definitely brighter, and it stays lit at all times. She is still unsure, and the Marni wood takes it as fear. It doesn't like it. I feel empowered and stronger than ever as my sword warms up in my hands every time I lift it against Mirri. I am not stupid, though, nor high on endorphins. This girl's strength is not something I can ignore. My wrists are on fire, and I feel the impact of her blows deep in my shoulder blades. At one point, even though I block it, the tip of her shinai makes contact with my upper arm. Despite the adrenaline running like fire through my blood, the pain reminds me that I cannot hurt myself or get injured. It's in my rules, and I will not let him down. Not again.

I might have glowing tattoos and a sword that borders crazy magic. However, I am still Gianna of Earth, with zero superpowers. Time to use some *deceiving Human ways*, as Zaan so kindly calls them. I don't know if the Moorri have any soft spots on their bodies, but they are a vain species, in love with their own beauty. Probably because they are beautiful. Once you get past all those red horns and forked tails, that is. Speaking of that, Mirri might like hers a bit too much. The only thing holding her back when she attacks is trying to keep it away from me.

So instead of focusing on her blows, I try to reach for her backside with my shinai. It is very risky; it leaves me unprotected for a split second. If she makes contact with my body, the strength of her blow will shatter my bones or crack my scalp. However, the longer I fight, the weaker I'll get. My wrists cannot cope for too long. The risk pays off instantly. She flinches and pulls to the left in a defensive stance, trying to move her tail out of my way. It is so brief, it feels like less than a second, but that's all I need. Instead of going for her tail, as she thought, my shinai makes a full impact with her left side.

Despite their alien looks, my instincts tell me the Moorri have the same anatomy as we do, give or take. I think I might be right. All air goes out of her as my sword hits a lung or several... She drops to her knees, holding her side and gasping for air.

Almost instantly, Kayon's booming voice calls it my win and ends the fight. I know him well enough to hear the relief in his voice. Mirri takes the shaking hand I am offering and pulls herself up.

"I don't think I like the Humans," she says through gritted fangs.

"That's fine by me. I most definitely dislike the Moorri," I reply.

We both share a smile, and she moves back to the line, still holding her side with her hand. I almost laugh as I notice she pets her tail with the other hand. Freaking aliens!

The first of the only two Kartassi Pit Masters of my Unit steps forward. This close, he is scary, and I never thought of his species that way before. Hellaf and all the other Kartassi around my home are there to keep me safe. That made my silly brain put them in the safe category, which of course is stupid. They were used as gladiators for a reason. *Hellaf's list,* as I call it, is my only lifeline right now. I am not here to harm anyone and even less kill a Pit Master. However, he needs to know I can.

Their wings are fragile, and they always keep them neatly folded behind their huge backs and out of the way. This guy is so tall, my head only goes to his abdomen. We probably look like David and Goliath. But today, David's story is about to become mine. From my height, I couldn't even reach his precious gray wings. The thing is, I don't have to. Hellaf said they have something called tassi ridges on both sides of their bodies. They are two horizontal and relatively small dips just above their waist. The Kartassi are not born with wings, which is probably nature's way of keeping those poor mothers from dying in labor. They start growing sometime during their childhood from those same two ridges. Even the slightest pressure on those causes their wings to unfold, and it makes them vulnerable.

Because of our ridiculous height difference, my eyes are

almost at the level of his precious ridges. As we take the sparring position, I keep staring at them, like they are my next meal. He is quick to notice and gets so scared his shinai doesn't even light up when he comes for me. He is also angry with my antics and barges with his sword up high in the air. I don't know who he's looking for, because… hello, I am down here. It's relatively easy to avoid him and squeeze myself past his lifted arms. I touch his left ridge as I pass him. I only allow my shinai to hit it once and relatively gently. Hellaf said, all the blood veins in their wings start from there, and a significant blow can cause serious damage to the wings.

I almost hit the ground face down as a massive wing pokes me from the side. We both quickly turn to face each other, and his stunned expression makes him look so different from all the other Kartassi males. How did I ever think they were clones? His fragile wings may be fully open now, but he is a Warrior and lifts his sword against me regardless. It still doesn't light up, not even a flicker, and it bothers him. Before any of us gets to resume, Kayon's voice calls it my win. It kind of pisses me off because I am not stupid. I know what he's doing. However, I am trying to be reasonable. I did deliver the first hit, and this guy could get in a lot of trouble if I hurt his wings. Hellaf said, once they are open, it takes a while before they can fold them safely out of the way. Yep, maybe I can tell myself Kayon is protecting him and not me.

My second Kartassian Pit Master makes this way too easy. He keeps his huge veiny gray arms glued to his body, trying to protect his tassi ridges. Because of his stance, he holds his sword up with both hands in front of his leather-clad dick. It makes the shinai look like… well, like a dick. There is more laughter and snickering, and this time not just from inside the Untried Pit. We gathered quite a crowd of Warriors outside the enclosure. Kayon is fuming, and he is not trying to hide it.

"Fight the Untried, Pit Master, or move back into the vexing line. We don't have all span," he says, and there is more laughter around. I don't know the name of this Pit Master because aliens are not big on those. They would instead use their titles. This particular one is probably the nicest of the lot, though. That's how I can tell them apart. He always has words of encouragement for those who don't excel. Despite their identical looks, the Kartassi have very different personalities. Kayon needs to chill. I have no idea why he is so much on edge. The Untried must be able to respect the Pit Masters, yet Kayon is turning this guy into a laughing stock. I can't allow it, fuck Kayon!

I lift my sword and pounce on him. The bright red light inside the shinai almost blinds me for a second. I smile to myself. The Marni Tree doesn't only feed on bravery as I initially thought. It also likes kindness. As expected, the Kartassi's male instinct takes over, and he blocks my blow, finally engaging in a fight. I swear to God, that is all he did, but it feels like the impact has rearranged all my internal organs. I suddenly feel nauseous and then something else. My Sign burns with pain. It is a strange thing, as if it's not my own. Zaan. Is he watching this? Stupid question; he always does. And right now, he can tell I am in pain. I lift my shinai again but just when he is about to block my blow, I drop to my knees and push the tip of my sword straight into one of his tassi ridges.

Unlike the last time, I didn't have enough time or space to deliver a calculated blow or reduce its force. Trust me to hurt the only nice guy in my Unit. His wings unfold as expected, but they shake and flutter uncontrollably after the impact of my blow. And of course, now Kayon is taking his time to call it off. I step away from my opponent, and I glare at my least favorite orc. Eventually, he calls it my win and asks who else volunteers to fight me.

Nobody steps forward, as now there are only Tarrassians left to do that. Because they don't fight females, right? The hell they don't! Kayon is just about to step forward when I stop him by putting a hand up. Universal gesture, apparently, as he gets it straight away. I face my Unit, grateful for their super hearing. My voice is not that strong, and I want the little fuckers to hear me.

"You think not fighting females is something to be proud of. Because Tarrassians are the strongest, smartest, and the most advanced race in the universe, you decided to allow yourselves small acts of kindness. *Let's save the slaves and give them a home. Just make sure they are not allowed to procreate. Let's protect the weak females and never harm them. Let's just make sure they have no idea how to keep themselves safe.*" As I speak, I try not to get distracted by the shinai in my right hand. Even though I am not fighting, the wood is lit, and red sap goes up and down my sword, like an electric pulse. The Marni Tree wants me to do this. About time someone does it!

"There is a huge difference between hurting females and fighting females. Mirri and I are not here to get hurt. We are here to fight. By refusing to train with us, you do not protect us. You disrespect us and treat us as inferior beings. Not only that, but all the females graduating from the training course will go to war and not stand a chance out there. Our opponents will fight us and most likely kill us because we had no one to properly train with. You tell me, where is the respect in that?

"I understand you are worried about hurting females, cubs, or weaker Untried. But that is why you have brains. Use them and apply the right kind of force to the right opponents. A training camp is not a fight to the death facility. This is not about showing who is the strongest. This is about learning how to fight as one. Your sword alone cannot win any battle. All of our swords together are a force our enemies will fear. We all matter, and we all deserve to be treated equally. Now come and fight me, unless, of course, you are too scared," I say while my brain screams at me to shut my fucking mouth up. My wrists are on fire, one of my shoulder blades feels like it's sharpening knives for a living, and my nausea is still nagging my gut. Oh well... I can't win them all.

"Get ready to bite the sand, Untried Warrior," says the stupid Ninja kid stepping forward.

Oh, please! What is wrong with this kid? I am tempted to send him back to the line, but that would mean contradicting my own words. Every one of us matters, and all I have to do is make sure I fight him with the right kind of force.

He lifts his shinai but doesn't barge, waiting to see where my own weapon goes first. He is trying to beat me at my own game. His beautiful copper eyes glow with excitement, and as our shinais make contact, they both ignite just as bright. He is not afraid and the Marni wood loves it.

Perhaps I should be afraid. Holy shit! This kid is freaking strong! I didn't expect that, and I almost drop my sword. It takes a few minutes of sparring before I notice. This is it! This is Kendo. He doesn't pounce or come for me with unnecessary force. It allows me to fall into a comfortable rhythm and follow the Kendo techniques I am familiar with. Ronnin follows my lead, learning impressively fast from my moves. After a few minutes, this feels like any other Kendo competition I used to attend. Everything hurts, and the adrenaline has started to wear off. But this feels right, like finding a long-lost best friend. This is not about throwing muscles or dicks around, for that matter. It is about training, improving ourselves, and most of all, about respect. It occurs to me, this would be a good time to take it a step further. Ronnin and I had a good sparring. We don't need a winner. It's not the freaking Olympics.

"Great sparring, Untried Warrior. Your skills and respect for your adversary are impressive," I tell him, and at the same time, I move back and bow my head to him, then take a fist to my heart. Maybe I can show my own respect to my adoptive planet.

Ronnin seems a bit taken aback, but he quickly lowers his shinai and follows my lead replicating my greeting. I might love this kid forever.

To my surprise and Kayon's anger, another Untried steps forward, then another...

They are quick learners, the Tarrassians. Despite me basically calling them a bunch of assholes, they treat me with caution. Still, they don't exactly take it easy on me. None of their shinais is as brightly lit as mine or as Ronnin's, but they don't let it get to them. It's almost as if they want to deserve it first.

There is no more staring at my boobs. Instead, they pay attention to the way I move my wrists, arms, and legs. After my fourth fight with one of the Untried, I start to fail. This is definitely sparring, not fighting, but these teens are twice my size, and my wrists can't take any more. I have a slight moment of panic as yet another one steps forward. It feels like I have achieved something big today. I am too tired and wired up to know exactly what yet, but I don't want to let it go to waste. I am trying to think how best to approach this. I cannot and will not ask for a way out. Luckily, I don't have to – a furious Kayon steps forward, and the Untried rushes back to the line.

"Enough, Untried Warrior," Kayon tells me after he picks a shinai randomly from the pile. "This has taken too long, and we have a vexing learning module waiting for the Unit. I am the Master of the Untried and fighting me will conclude your punishment."

I don't know if I should be grateful or terrified. Why is he so angry?

Our shinais meet for the first time, but there is hardly any pressure into Kayon's blow. There is only a slight red flicker to his sword as he hits mine again. Of all people, I didn't expect that from him.

"Are you scared, Kayon?" I can't help poking at my favorite

orc. I am also getting angry. He better not insult me in front of the entire camp and fight me like I am made of glass.

"What's the matter, Master of the Untried? I thought your species doesn't mind fighting females. According to the Marni wood, you are too scared and angry. It won't come to life for you, as it did for little Ronnin."

My reckless words make Kayon's tusks dribble gooey saliva. He still doesn't put any force behind his blows.

"Do you think I am scared or angry because of a little female with a glowing wooden stick?" he asks, delivering yet another easy-to-block hit.

"What are you scared of then?" I ask, but I really don't have to.

"Him," says Kayon, and his dark eyes look somewhere, over my head.

I turn and follow his gaze to the outside of the Untried's Pit. There is no crowd gathered there. If anything, it looks as if all the Warriors have purposely stayed away from there. Away from him. I've seen Zaan's War Beast once before, at the Moorri Palace. I only looked briefly back then, as I thought he was terrifying. I was just stupid. This man cannot be anything other than beautiful.

The War Beast makes the already massive, bulking Tarrassians look like oversized versions of Hulk. The white taking over their eyes is in a scary league of its own. Zaan has all that going on right now, plus his bonus serial killer vibe. Kayon is not wrong, he does have Zaan's full attention.

"How long has he been there for?" I ask Kayon.

"From the nano you stepped into this Pit," he says quietly. "I am a vexing Neflay. Your glowing wooden stick is not even strong enough to tickle my tusks. He will take my head and everyone else's in this entire camp if you get hurt. I cannot afford to lose any Warriors. Now, you are going to be a good female and apply a blow to my right shoulder. We need to end this before he snaps and ends all of us."

"Why your right shoulder?"

"I have an itch there," he says with a grave face. What an asshole!

I try not to laugh and at least pretend we mean business here. There is amusement in Kayon's dark eyes as I put all my force behind the blow.

36

—

Our flight home is quiet, but I know she is tired. Now that I finally have her near me and safe, I can relax. This was one of the most challenging spans of my life. Not only did I have to use all my restraint and self-control not to kill anyone when she was in the Pit, but it was just as challenging after. All I wanted to do was take her back home. Keep her in my arms, heal her wounds and nurture her to sleep.

There is a slight shake to her body, as her tired muscles desperately need to heal and rest. Her injuries may not be substantial by my people's standards, but she is a vexing Human. There is one sizeable angry bruise on her upper arm and another one on her shoulder. Her outfit may not cover much skin, but I am anxious to take it off her and check for injuries. This felt like the longest span ever. I knew she wouldn't have appreciated any special treatment. I couldn't take her home so I found myself counting every nano until it was time to leave.

She opens her *Lorra green* eyes and watches me from her seat next to mine. Her Human sword, she calls a shinai, is attached to her waist belt instead of the Tarrassian one she had in the morning. The wood is asleep now unlike when it came alive for her. My beautiful female gives me a tired smile that pulls at my hearts.

"Thank you for allowing it," she says with an equally tired voice. I simply nod my head in acknowledgment. I decide then and there on a new Camp rule. After a punishment challenge, the Warriors are entitled to take the following span off. I intend to do the same, even though I cannot add that to the vexing rules. I reach in my mind to my Second in Command and tell him he is to take charge of the Pit. My female needs looking after, and I intend to do just that. Besides, I do need time to come to terms with what just happened.

On this span, something changed the course of Tarrassian history. The High Elder summoned an emergency Royal Council to discuss the events. The King reached out to me to ask for details, and so did my sire. He did not say it in words, but he feels just as guilty as I do. We are the keepers of the Marni Forest, yet we did not know what it could do. The sap inside the trees can heal and regenerate life. Yet, we somehow thought the wood itself was only suitable for making decorative furniture for our dwellings.

My Lorra closes her heavy eyelids again, but there is still a content smile on her soft lips. Her hand caresses her sword gently, and the wood becomes transparent under her touch, allowing me to see the fiery sap inside. How is this possible? What just happened in that Pit? Could the King be right about the Humans? My Lorra is the weakest creature ever to have gone through the punishment challenge, yet she is the only one who did not need to see the healers after.

After I dock my ship, I pick her up in my arms, and of course, she doesn't agree.

"I made one too many compromises on this span, beautiful. I didn't want to treat you like a fragile creature in front of the entire Camp. We are at home, and concessions time is over. Now you only do what I say."

"Fine," she says, hiding a tired smile and a yawn in my shoulder as I carry her out of the ship. "Can we please go to the Sacred Garden first?" she asks, lifting her eyes to look at me.

"You need to rest, my Lorra. We will have the dark span meal in our sleeping quarters."

"That's not why," she replies. Her arms have tightened their hold around my neck, and her cheek rubs against my shoulder, seeking contact with my skin. On her own accord... How many times have I wished for this? For her to seek my comfort and initiate touch, as the mate of the High Healer does, or my mother with my sire. Can this really be the end of pain?

She asks me to put her down when we reach the Sacred Garden. Despite her stubbornness, her legs almost fail her, and I have to keep her steady. Once she trusts herself not to fall, she walks to the sacred Marni Tree, towering over the garden and everything else around. I don't follow; just watch from where I stand. Her arms make an attempt at wrapping themselves around the wide trunk of the Marni Tree, but of course, they don't reach too far. She places her forehead against the purple bark, and I can hear her whispering a *thank you*.

Despite my long orbit rotations of self-control and emotional restraint, I cannot help flinching when the Marni Tree lights up. It only does that for my sire and probably for the High Elder. The bark becomes transparent, making the glowing sap inside the Sacred Tree visible to the eye. At the same time, as high as I can see, all the branches lower themselves to reach for her. They close around her like a cocoon, and I can barely see her from behind the mass of red leaves. That definitely doesn't happen for my sire. The Marni Tree is saying thank you back.

After a while, she steps back, and the branches release their hold on her. This time she doesn't complain when I pick her up. I cannot help the smile as she places her face on my chest, over the heart that beats for her.

When we reach our quarters, I consider if I should feed her first. Her fragile body needs relief from the pain and the tension of her long span, so I decide to deal with that first. The servants have already prepared our bathing pool and added special healing gels to the water, so I take her there instead. This would be easier if she would drink my blood, but I doubt it's a good idea to offer it. Things didn't go too well last time I tried that. Ollianna has gone to the White Palace for reasons I would rather not know about. It is safer that way when the mate of the High Elder is involved. In her absence, I instructed other servants how to care for my mate, and hopefully, they listened. My beautiful Lorra requires a lot of care and attention.

I am clumsily trying to remove her garment and I am never vexing clumsy at anything! How are you even meant to take this off?

"Did Gaella do this on purpose? To make my life hard?" I say out loud, and I am rewarded with my female's beautiful laughter.

"I am sure she didn't. You are her hero," she says while her nimble fingers help me with the impossible task.

"That would be her mate, I believe. Andrac risked everything for her," I tell her.

"As you did for me." She touches my cheek with unsure fingers, and I allow my face to rest against the shelter of her tiny palm. This perfect nanoclip justifies all the pain and all the risks. I would have done it either way without expecting anything in return, because love is its own reward. However, knowing I am finally breaking the walls she surrounded herself with makes it perfect.

Once she is naked and I am satisfied there are no significant injuries other than a lot of bruising, I focus more on keeping it together. This is not the time to go there. Also, I have a vexing plan. And rules, I must remember those. I remove my Kannicloth as quickly as possible. Even though she is not moving away from my touch, she is back to being shy and skittish. Nothing like the female who had the attention and respect of the entire Camp on this span. I am sure the sight of my fully erect cock doesn't help ease her worries, but that is not a matter I can help. The vexing thing has a mind of its own, and since I won't allow it what it needs, it has started to get really uncomfortable, bordering on pain. I ignore it and grab my female once again in my arms. She moans as we enter the bathing pool, and the water soothes her painful muscles. My cock instantly springs out and pokes her in her backside. Luckily, she just laughs.

"No more moaning, beautiful," I beg just as she does it again. She quickly covers her mouth with a hand and smiles.

"Sorry, I just can't help it. The water feels amazing," she says as I move our bodies in a comfortable position. I take us to the shallow end and sit with my back against the bathing pool's stone edge. I place her on my lap, in between my legs, and raise my knees around her body to offer her shelter. Her back leans into my chest, her arms resting on my knees. This is the most comfortable position for her, but of course, it is vexing painful for me. She is practically sitting on top of my cock, and I feel the need to apologize. Again.

"I am sorry, there is no hiding my need for you, my beautiful," I tell her with my lips pressed into the golden curls of her mane. "At least now my cock is trapped and not moving any more."

"Zaan?"

"Yes?"

"I hate to tell you this, but it's still moving. Like a lot..." she says and laughs, so I don't worry much.

"Is the water too hot for your skin, beautiful?" I ask, nuzzling at her neck. I try to push away the memory of the bleeding flesh hanging from her throat. There is only a raised scar now, slightly darker in color than her brown skin. I run my tongue over it, and she shivers in my arms.

"It was never meant to hurt you, Lorra." I give her a long-due apology. "I have never lost control as I did on that span. Fear of not being able to get you out of there got the best of me." And since this is meant to be an honest apology, I have to give her all my reasons. "I also succumbed to my anger and to burning jealousy. The sight of his fingers on your skin made me lose all control. You, smiling for him while not even acknowledging me, took all my reasoning away."

"I am sorry, Zaan. I really am," she says, turning her head to look at me over her shoulder.

"Can I please ask why, beautiful? It is all in the past now, but I would like to know. "

She sighs and rests her cheek on my knee, holding onto my arms linked around her waist.

"Probably for the same reasons as yours, except the jealousy part," she says with an apologetic tone. "I was also scared and angry."

"Am I scarier than the Moorri King?" I ask her gently.

"To me, yes, you are," she says, surprising me. I cannot help the pang of hurt in my chest, but I listen quietly to her explanation. "He was just another slaver, someone who took by force, someone who could have crushed my body and given me pain. I am no stranger to pain. I even took comfort in knowing I wasn't going to last long. He just wanted a body."

Hearing her say such things is enough to wake my War Beast. I can feel it trying to push out of my skin. *I should have killed that fool!* I rein myself in; she doesn't need my anger now.

"You were someone who wanted my soul, my mind, and not only for a while but forever. At least, that is what I was trying to convince myself at the time. Now I know I was scared and angry because you were someone I wanted to give all those things to, all by myself. If you turned out to be nothing but a monster, that would have been my end. Running away from you had somehow turned into the biggest challenge I had ever given myself. I wanted to stop, even as I was doing it. The lying, the running, all of it, I just didn't know how."

I don't often find myself speechless, but her confession empties my brain of words. She wanted to give herself to me from the beginning? Her words are healing balm and poison at the same time. It makes it all feel just a bit wrong, considering I have no intention of forgetting her overdue punishment. I am sure I have good reasons for that; I just can't remember them right now.

"Can you please say you accept my apology, Zaan? I really need to hear those words," she says, and the plea in her voice almost breaks my resolution.

"Yes, beautiful, I fully accept your apology. Let the past be the past," I tell her, and it doesn't feel like a lie. I don't think so, anyway. My people are not as skilled at lying as the Humans. Yes, I do forgive her, and yes, I still plan to deliver the promised punishment. It is not out of revenge, but because she needs to respect her rules. I am sure she will understand.

"Thank you," she says softly, and her lips kiss my left bicep that she is leaning against.

"I am not entirely sure what happened on this span, but you have done really well," I tell her, brushing my hands slowly over her arms. I don't think I am strong enough to touch anything else right now. "I am proud of you as your mate because you kept yourself safe at all times. I am proud of you as your High Master because you are the first Untried to finish the punishment challenge, unharmed. Our King is also very pleased with you," I tell her while nuzzling at one smooth, glistening shoulder. "He is now more convinced than ever, Humans are special."

She laughs softly at my words.

"I think our King is just love-struck. Everything even remotely connected to Sia is special to him," she says, and I can hear the smile in her voice.

"Yes, the King's infatuation with his Queen is not exactly the galaxy's best-kept secret, and until this span, I thought the same. Now I am not so sure. He may have inherited some of his sire's wisdom after all." I can tell she probably wants to argue on that one, but she is too tired to do so, or maybe too relaxed.

I reach over to my wrist com and instruct the Kitchen Master to bring us our meal herself. Without Ollianna here, I wouldn't trust anyone else with my precious mate's food. She struggles with her feeding issues as it is. Not only does my beautiful Lorra not notice when the food arrives, but she doesn't even argue about me feeding her small chunks of Kanni steak dipped in her favorite red sauce. A special recipe the High Lady of the Purple Forest created herself. Her cooking is another Tarrassian craze. It is probably fair to say, my people are obsessed with everything Humans do. More and more Tarrassian females now wear ridiculous red lips, like Jade. I am not one to talk. I have my own Human to obsess over.

I notice her chewing becomes slower with every bite, and even though she has had very little, she probably needs rest first and food after. I only allow us a few more nanos in the soothing water while I rush through my own meal.

"There will be no training for you on the next span," I tell her as I get us both out of the bathing pool. I wrap her in a drying cloth that is way too big for her, and I pat her dripping golden curls with another. It quickly absorbs all the moisture, and then I dry the rest of her. I keep my touch gentle; I learned the hard way how fragile her skin is when I recklessly put my fangs in it. I gently apply her moisturising lotion to her body. It would be wiser to skip this part, but I know this is her ritual and she never goes without it. Maybe Human skin gets dry or something.

Everything is so vexing fragile about them! My brain reminds me my female is the first ever to finish the challenge unharmed. Humans are such a mystery.

I do rush as much as I can, because I am close to reaching my limit now. There is a tremor in my fingers and I pray to the Astrals she can't tell. After I roughly dry myself, I carry her to our sleeping dais. Not only does she not protest, but she pushes her naked chest against mine and wraps her arms around my neck. Her head finds my shoulder, and I almost wish there would be a lengthier walk.

"Why no training tomorrow?" she asks with her lips against my neck.

"Because you had your Punishing Challenge today. The Warriors can take a span off after a challenge," I explain.

"Is that the rule?" she asks.

"It is now," I reply because there is no point hiding it. To my surprise, she just laughs. It is a blessing to see her so relaxed in my presence. *Then don't ruin it, idiot!*

"Will you stay home with me?" she asks.

"Yes."

"Then it is the best rule ever," she says and hugs me even closer to her, pressing her pointy nipples into my chest. My cock slaps her backside so hard it makes her jolt. It is sadly the only part of my body I cannot vexing control. It makes no sense how I can keep in check something as powerful as my War Beast, but my cock refuses to go down when told to.

"Maybe it's about time we do something about *that* situation," she says with a smile hidden in my facial fur she calls a beard. Other Tarrassians have started to call it the same. No surprise there.

I place her on top of our sleeping dais and ask the MI to turn all the lights off. The Tarrassian dark span is more luminous than usual. The glow of our twin moons has grown in preparation for the most sacred event of our Mother Planet. In three-span rotations' time, the Astral Moons will take over the dark sky. A third moon will join ours, and for three spans, they will rein the darkness together. My people call them the Astral Moons, after our deities. One for each of our Astrals. It was expected from our High Elder to have his Mating Ceremony at the beginning of the event. He is, after all, one of our three Gods.

As I place my beautiful female on top of the soft furs, I have to detangle myself from her arms. This is so new and so unexpected. Her willingness to touch me messes with all my resolutions.

"Yes, that situation needs to be solved, just not right now," I tell her as I lie next to her. The same as on the previous dark span, I turn her around in my arms, my body curled around hers, and I press her head under my chin. I cover us with another fur and place an innocent kiss on top of her head. My beard tangles with her golden curls, and somehow that spikes my desire even more. *Act on it, then!*

"Why not?" she asks with an unsure voice. She sounds a bit worried.

"You had a very long and challenging span, my Lorra. This can wait. Your Sign and the healing gels your body absorbed from the water will be enough to fully restore your body after a few nano rotations of sleep."

"Okay, you are probably right. I have to agree I have been... better," she laughs softly. "Tomorrow it is then," she adds between yawns. She relaxes her body even more into mine and rubs her lush bottom against my pulsing cock.

"Keep still, Lorra," I tell her through gritted teeth. "I might die on this dark span if you do that again."

She giggles and grabs at my arm, holding her around her waist. She attempts to move it, and I allow it waiting to see where she wants it. She pulls my arm close to her chest in between her perky tits and brings my open palm under her cheek using it as a shelter for her precious face. Her breathing evens out shortly after, and her body goes all soft in my arms.

Cursed fire pits! How am I going to survive this? A nagging thought tells me this should be the least of my worries. Maybe I should be more concerned about the vexing punishment I still intend to deliver. Does she really deserve it?

37

GIANNA

I wake up, and I almost choke. As if there isn't enough air inside my body because there is no space for it. A very alien feeling makes me think everything inside me expanded somehow. It's overwhelming but so good. Happiness. Contentment. Safe. Valued. I stop myself from adding the L-word into the mix. It's just some resilient trace of cautiousness refusing to go away because, really, there is no denying this man's feelings for me. Yes, his intensity is a bit scary, and the stalking part of it somewhat overwhelming. I have to accept he will always be watching, always in my space, and I will have less privacy than conjoined twins. That is the way he understands love, and I have to accept him the way he is. It is hardly a deal-breaker when all that crazy comes with all that good. His care, protectiveness, how he looks at me with hungry golden eyes, his touches... everything he does screams how much he loves me. He doesn't even need to say it. Maybe I can say it first. The thought alone is ludicrous to the old Gianna. The new Gianna wants to shout it from the peak of the Spark Mountain, or whatever they call it.

I feel giddy and drunk with love this morning. Not to mention horny as hell. Who could blame me? Personally, I would love to blame it on the Sign or on PTSD. But really, must everything be complicated? The hottest man I ever laid eyes on is holding me tightly to his chest and right now, that is more than enough. I can feel the beating of both his hearts against my back, but the one that came to life for me is loud enough to hear it. Not only that, but it matches the beating of my own heart. They move in sync; there is no denying that when we are this close. Yeah, what I have now is more than enough.

I don't think he is awake yet. His face is somewhere in the mess of my hair, and his breathing seems regular enough. That huge thing he calls a cock is wide awake, though. Maybe aliens should call it something less normal since it's far from that. And why is it so hot? I did notice that before when I felt it against me. However, it is almost uncomfortably hot right now. Could it be because this is the first time Zaan has slept entirely naked next to me? Or is he in pain because he has to use it? I hope he does; I need him to. There is a slight element of fear, just because of my previous disastrous experiences with sex. I surprise myself by not even including the rape in that category. Not only because rape and sex are two different things, but because my mind and body have somehow found closure. It could be those losers' death, or it could be that Zaan's love has wiped it all away. What causes the element of fear is my general dislike for sex. I absolutely hated every part of it, despite my reputation. It hurt, it was uncomfortable, it triggered memories of the rape, it gave me a horrible reputation, and I still struggle with self-respect issues after all that. It makes me wonder why I put myself through it all since I hated it so much. No one can punish us the way we punish ourselves.

Maybe his cock can also read minds because it has become even more lively now that my thoughts are in the gutter. It's throbbing and pulsing and... getting bigger? *Oh my god, please don't get bigger!* There is some fear around the size issue, and I would be damn right terrified if I was the first Human woman to mate a Tarrassian. But c'mon, if Natalia can take it, so can I. And tiny Natalia takes it a lot; as her former guest, I should know. Ugh!

I am almost scared to move because of the ridiculous amount of wetness between my thighs. If I start making sloppy noises, I will die of shame. His knee is somewhere between my legs, and I really hope I didn't soak his skin. Only after I'd met him, I started to get wet for the first time. Would he believe me, though? There is this stupid thought going through my mind because I am very good at self-sabotage. My brain tells me he might see my arousal as a cause of my *vast experience*. No, I mustn't go there. He knows about my past, and he doesn't care. I have to stop this. It is no different from self-harming, and I am not allowed to do that.

"Hanni, beautiful," his strong raspy voice says from somewhere in my tangled hair. My bouncy afro and its texture are one of his many obsessions. His fingers always find reasons to touch it.

I turn in his arms and pull myself up to face him; morning breath be damned. I probably don't even have one; he definitely doesn't. The water on Tarrassia is strange. Sia says it tastes like lavender ice cream, and I will have to take her word on that. I am not a Brit, so thank God, I never had to eat lavender ice cream. Whatever it tastes like, it makes your breath smell fresh even after sleep. I do hate to admit it, but there is a reason why Tarrassians think they are perfect. Most times they are. They don't even get morning breath!!!

"Morning, handsome," I say and kiss the tip of his nose. I can see he raises a brow at my greeting. "Handsome means..."

"I know what it means, beautiful," he interrupts me returning the kiss to my nose. His beard is all messy after sleep, and it tickles my face in the most delightful ways. "It is not exactly a term used for Warriors. We're all scarred from too many battles and we can't always be bothered with a trimmed face fur. Beard, I mean. Well, maybe except for Sarrian, the High Commander of the Queen's Guard. He could get away with handsome on every galaxy," he says, and I only allow myself a tiny smile. I am too smart to fall into that trap. There is no way I'll agree with him. Nope, I am not taking the bait.

To be fair, considering Zaan's obsessive behavior, he can control the green-eyed monster better than most around here. Out of the three of us who mated Tarrassians, Sia got it the worst. The King's jealousy borders insanity if you ask me, and her calm temperament is probably the best way to deal with that. Most times, she ignores him, which of course, he hates even more, but at least he forgets about being jealous. It is strange how the King allowed the best-looking guy on Tarrassia to be Sia's shadow more or less. Perhaps Sarrian is not inclined that way. Jade told me there are many same-sex couples in the High City and the Tarrassians don't ever fuss about such things.

"Maybe I can call you handsome when we're alone," I say, running my fingers through his messy beard. Despite how wild it looks, it's so soft. Like silk. So is his shiny black hair and my favorite – the white lock. I wonder if his dad used to have it. Hard to tell now that his hair has turned all white with age.

"I am yours to call me whatever you want, my Lorra," he says. His hand resting on my waist starts moving lower, then his large palm opens up when it reaches my bottom. He grabs it to pull me closer to his burning hot erection. About time he takes this further, fear or insecurities be damned. I need to feel him inside me, badly!

"So," I start twisting his white lock of hair around my finger gently, "it is tomorrow, I mean today, whatever, you know what I mean." God, this man fries up my brain.

"So it is," he says and gives me that deadly hot smile of his. "The light span couldn't come any sooner, my beautiful female. I believe your sweet pussy dripped over my knee for all hours of the dark span. I have had a more relaxing time on the battlefield."

"Oh my god, that is so embarrassing," I say, and I realize I said it out loud. Now that is proper embarrassing.

"Not as much as this," he says, moving his huge cock out of the way in a position where it is not stabbing almost painfully at my upper thighs.

"We'd better do something about our predicaments," I say with a seductive smile; I hope it is anyway. I am surprised at my own courage, considering he always makes me feel shy. The thing is, I am so horny right now; it almost hurts.

"Yes, we'd better," he says and pushes me flat on my back, moving his large body above me. I instantly open my legs to allow him in between my thighs. It is quite a stretch, even for my famously long legs. He may be leaner than most bulky Tarrassians, but he is still huge compared to me. I shiver as his very determined cock goes straight for my slit, but he quickly grabs it to move it up, resting it on my belly. His body pushes it against me, trapping it from going anywhere else. I want to protest because I need it inside me like yesterday. Sadly, my self-sabotaging brain is at work and reminds me I shouldn't act too bold or... I really want him to believe I am not a whore and... *NO, GIANNA! Don't you dare ruin this!* I yell at myself. It's best if I just let him take the lead on this.

I have never allowed it before with my one-night-stand lovers, but I think I might naturally be inclined that way. Letting him be in charge is not a chore but something I apparently crave. Never too late to learn things about yourself, it may seem. I believe this makes me the ideal woman to a Tarrassian man. It doesn't take a genius to know what these guys like in the bedroom. Or anywhere else for that matter.

He puts one large hand under my head, like a cradle, and another one to my cheek, keeping my face still for a kiss. I expected a slow start, but he goes straight for sucking the brains out of me. *His taste! My god, his taste!* It's like a drug to me. I don't even have anything to compare it with, but it's the best thing I ever had. A bit sweet, and maybe their food is to blame for that, and a whole lot of male, if there is such a thing. *You taste like mine!* As he sucks my tongue deep into his hungry mouth, I involuntarily bring my knees up and push my pelvis into him. Without breaking the kiss, he uses one hand and body weight to push my legs back down. Okay, so no initiative. He wants to control this and that's fine by me. I allow myself to relax all the way and go completely limp under his touch. He can do whatever and whenever. Ideally sooner, but I can wait. I can be good, just the way he likes me.

He pushes with his legs at the furs until there is nothing covering our naked bodies. At the same time, he lifts both my arms up by my head and presses my hands into the cold metal bars of the headrest.

"Keep them there, please," he says, breaking the kiss to look me in the eyes. There is a question, I think? Does he want my permission? Is that it? Doesn't he know I trust him? I reach for his face with one of my hands to give him the reassurance I think he needs. The sudden pain in my wrist startles me as he grabs it and brings it back above my head.

"I asked you to keep them there, beautiful. Unless you missed the organic restraints, of course," he says and watches me with no trace of a smile or amusement in his eyes. "Now, let's do this again," he says with a sigh. "I say, *keep your hands there, please,* and you say…?"

Good Lord! Why does he have to be such an asshole? And why do I have to find it so hot? He wasn't asking for freaking permission. He wanted me to answer just so I can't say I didn't hear. I should know by now. Answering when spoken to is my rule number... whatever. I really need to write them down.

"Yes, Zaan. I will keep my hands here," I say without managing to remove all the sass out of it. He raises one brow, but the amusement is back in his eyes. So is his kiss. Just when I am about to do some tongue-sucking of my own, he moves his lips down my neck, pressing his lips against the scar left by his fangs. Right now, even the memory of that feels hot. He practically licks and sucks every inch of my skin as he goes down my shoulders and chest. The next thing I know, my nipples are on fire as he attacks them with a passion that leaves me panting. There is biting and sucking, and none of it exactly gentle. But then there is a whole lot of licking, which soothes the pain. When he moves down my body, I let out the breath I've been holding in. I am not sure if it is the relief I survived the assault or the loss because he stopped. The sensitive skin on my belly gets the same wet-tongue treatment. That, combined with the feel of his beard moving all over me, has turned me into an even wetter mess in between my legs.

Do not come all over my bedding furs. I want it in my mouth, beautiful," he says in my mind without taking his mouth off me.

Then hurry the hell up, I only tell myself because I don't dare say it to him. I am not the one giving instructions or setting the pace here.

His hands move under my knees, and he pushes them up, moving his head in between my wide-spread thighs. About time! It is rather strange how I went from never allowing anyone to touch me like that to begging this man to do it. But he is not just any man, is he? He is my man, and that changes everything.

Keep them there, please, he says inside my scrambled brain, pushing my knees higher and even further apart.

"Yes, Zaan. I will keep my knees there," I am quick to say before he turns the crazy back on. Or even worse, he stops. And oh, my God! I really don't want him to. He is so good at this! Not that I have anything to compare him to, but this cannot get any better. His eager tongue licks me like I am the last food left on Earth, on Tarrassia, in this case. There is sucking and occasionally biting in between licks, but it is not exactly painful. He is more careful than he was with my poor nipples, that's for sure. He is now pushing his tongue deeper and deeper inside my needy channel and staying still has become a huge struggle. I want to touch him; I am desperate to move my hands into his hair as I can feel the now familiar build-up of an orgasm. He gave me my first one and the memory of it still burns my skin. I am shaking with the need to go back to that place where there is only pleasure and absolute surrender. I can't help but push my hips up because I am so close. My ears have started to ring, my skin is tingling and the muscles in my lower belly contract.

I push up again into his tongue, and just then, he pulls it out. Before I understand what's happening, his lips are over mine, kissing me like a starved man. I respond to his kiss, tasting myself on his tongue. I love his hot mouth on mine, but I can't help the feeling of loss. I was so close, and my vagina is uncomfortably squeezing on itself. Maybe he wants me to come while he is inside me. Oh, dammit, I need both! He breaks the kiss and pulls me out of bed.

Wait! What?

I stand on shaky legs by the bedside, and I would probably collapse without his arm around my waist. What's happening? He pushes my hair behind my shoulders and places hot small kisses on my neck.

"You taste like the sweetest sin, beautiful. And I intend to drink it every single span for as long as I live," he says, nipping at my skin. "For now, I'd better feed you first. You didn't have much food last span, and you know I do not like it when that happens."

What? That seems to be the only word my brain can form. I push slightly back so I can look at him. Because of our height difference, I have to tilt my head backward quite a bit. Okay, so he doesn't seem upset or anything. His golden eyes watch me like I am edible, as usual, and his huge hard cock pokes at my belly, trying to reach for me, also as usual. So, what is wrong? Is he actually that worried about my diet? This is super strange, and I am trying to find the best words to tell him I need him inside me more than I need breakfast. Once again, my stupid insecurities about my past show their ugly head. *I am not a whore! I am not!* Maybe I can point out bigger things, like literally.

"Breakfast can wait, Zaan," I say and lift a hand to his face, caressing his beard. "I am not sure this can," I say with a smile, looking down at his angry, scary cock, which is now crawling up my waist as if trying to reach for my boobs. I keep my voice and smile light and playful, trying not to make a big deal out of this. Mainly because I am not exactly sure what *this* is.

"It will have to wait," he says and at the same time reaches for a fur and wraps it around my body. I watch in dismay as he grabs another one and wraps it around his waist. "I think it's best we get to know each other a bit more. The timing is perfect, and we have all this span to ourselves. I will use the cleaning enclosure; you have the bathing pool. While in there, I would like you to order our morning meal with the kitchen," he says, grabbing something from the side. He lifts my hand from under the fur and places the com in my palm. "From now on, I want you to remember this is your home, and these are your people. You are now the High Lady of this house, and you will act as such."

He stops talking and watches me, waiting. I know what he wants, but I have to force myself out of my stupor to give it to him.

"Yes, Zaan, I will make the call. What would you like to eat?"

"For now, you can inquire with the Kitchen Master. I expect you to start learning soon things like my favorite foods or the names of the Marni people. Ideally before our Mating Ceremony. We will talk more about that during our meal.

I am looking forward to spending my span with you, beautiful, and showing you all my favorite places in our home and forest," he says, placing a soft kiss on my forehead. Then, he turns around and disappears in the direction of the other cleaning room. The deadly shower is in there, so I never go there.

I catch my reflection in the huge French windows, and it startles me. Yes, my hair is a mess, and yes, seeing myself with glowing red tattoos is still something I can't get used to. But what startles me is how lost I look. Like a puppy kicked out into the rain. What just happened? He didn't seem upset or put off. Okay, maybe he thinks I might appreciate getting to know each other before jumping to sex. And I would normally find it sweet and considerate. But our circumstances are a bit different. We have been through so much and at such a fast pace. Can't we move just as fast to sex? My stupid low self-esteem tells me that's what decent men do with respectable women. They take their time and get to know each other first.

I only find it strange because… well, because I was never that decent.

You know what? That's okay. I won't moan about it. If he wants a chit-chat day, he can fucking have it! I am still a bit upset with what just happened. If he didn't plan on having sex, then why did he start it? And why didn't he let me finish? I try to remember he is an alien, and maybe things are slightly different for them. Or perhaps it is because he has never been with a woman before and doesn't get we have needs, too. The memory of the first and only mind-blowing orgasm he gave me kills both those theories. *I know what you need, and I will always give it to you.* That is what he said to me when I didn't even know I was craving an orgasm. So, he knows. But he chose not to let me have it. Again!

38

GIANNA

After a quick dip in the scented pool, I instruct the kitchen staff to prepare our morning meal in the Sacred Garden. The Kitchen Master sounded like a pompous alien. Based on the voice, I think it might be one of the skinny little ones. By little, I mean they are standard Human size. Nothing else about them is familiar as they are almost transparent. I can see freaking internal organs behind their yellow-tinged skin, and it makes me kind of nauseous. How fragile must they be when any potential enemy can see all their organs on display. They do tend to wear more clothes than most, but still.

I choose a bright white Tarrassian dress for what I realise is my first date ever. I rush through my morning routine and I brush my hair nine times instead of seven, just to spite Zaan.

Despite my less inspiring start to the day, I smile at my reflection in the mirror. I look beautiful and definitely in love. I remember seeing it on other women before. My eyes glow, there is a flush to my skin, and I have a constant smile I can't wipe off. I've decided not to make a big deal of what happened this morning. He doesn't seem upset, and he definitely wants me. Honestly, he appears in more pain than I am. So, this is really about getting to know each other and spending the day together. If we start having sex, probably that is all we'll be doing. So, it makes sense to do other things instead. *I think...*

He puts my mind even more at rest, as the first thing he does after his shower is to give me a kiss that leaves me breathless. *Definitely not upset.* He wears the usual Tarrassian white shirt and pants. Oh, Lord, how am I going to survive today? Although the white leather kilt shows a lot of skin this other garment is far sexier. For once, the fabric is so light and soft it is almost transparent and it molds to... everything. Hot muscles, delicious ridges, shimmery copper skin, covered by a delightful sprinkle of dark hair. As for those pants, Lord have mercy on me. Tarrassian men should really consider underwear. The fact that he is rock hard against the soft fabric only makes it worse. He keeps trying to adjust himself when he thinks I am not looking. Whatever silly game this is, he might be suffering more than I am. In a way, it takes all my worries away, and I decide to enjoy my day. My first date. Ever.

We sit next to each other during breakfast, and we are even holding hands. Of course, I ignore the fact he counts every bite I take and takes notice of every sip of my smoothie. That's just him, and I can't really complain. My body feels strong and healthy, and I haven't had a stomach-ache in a long time.

And then he spoils my morning by talking about my father.

"What about him?" I ask with an overly polite yet defensive voice.

"I wanted to ask your opinion on this matter," he says, watching me in the severe manner of the High Master. So, this is a work-related question. Great!

"The Humans are a lot of trouble for an already invaded and surrendered species," he says with a sigh. I can't help but grin.

Yes, I can see that is a problem, but I am so proud of my people. We may go down, as expected from weaklings, but we sure don't stay down for too long. In the end, that's all that matters. And if it makes the mighty Tarrassians pull at their hair, even better.

"I am thinking of asking your sire's assistance with this. I want to offer him the position of High General of the entire Human army. I want them to be our allies instead of our protégés," he says, and I am too shocked to even process what he is saying. He carries on explaining, giving me time to snap out of it. Not that I do. "The Council has already accepted my proposal. I will officially invite your sire to Tarrassia, and the King will make him the offer. If he accepts, he will attend our Council as a guest of honor and ally. I wanted to make sure you don't mind. I don't expect he will want to come here and not see you. If you say no, the deal is off. You come first, as always."

I am still trying to process what he is saying. I don't know what's best to say, so I just tell him what I really think.

"Despite my strange and strained relationship with my father, I care for him. Probably more than I should," I say as if talking to myself.

My father is a harsh man, but he gave me all the love he could give. Some people just don't know how to love. I still remember the happiness of my early childhood and that one memory of me running through rows upon rows of orange trees under the hot Sicilian sun. I remember being spoiled rotten and having more toys and holidays than most kids. Was my father different then? When did he turn into the harsh man he is today?

My mom's memory is hardly ever part of the picture, and all I get is this image of a shallow socialite. My *African Barbie* mother, as she loves to call herself, is more interested in shoes and make-up than her daughter. I've never even argued with her. She is as easy-going as it gets, but now, I understand that is because she didn't care. She wanted to play the cool best friend instead of being a parent. Oh, and there is definitely a gold-digger vibe to her. Hence the new millionaire Brazilian husband.

My father's family is just as wealthy and I wonder if that's why she went for him to start with. They own most of the orange mass production orchards in Italy. Not sure why my father chose a career in the army and settled in the States instead of taking his role in his family. He also refused his inheritance, and everything went to his older brother. When my uncle took over, we stopped visiting altogether. My father's choice never bothered me. He advanced to the top of his chosen career, made wise investments, and was always well connected. If anything, we were upper-middle class, but if my mom is into millionaires, I can see how that was not enough for her.

How silly, none of this ever occurred to me before. Somehow, my mind always chose to see my mom as a victim of an overly controlling, harsh, and probably racist husband. But she doesn't fit that victim profile very well. Now that I can process all this with less heat, I can tell things don't really add up. Maybe I should talk to my father. I pull myself out of my past to give Zaan what I hope is a reasonable answer.

"I would love to see him, even though I doubt he will ever come here or take you up on your offer. He is a proud, stubborn old fool," I say, and I hope he believes me. "My father is not to be trusted. Above everything else, he is loyal to his men and his military oath. You know that better than most, Zaan," I say and avoid his eyes. I don't think any of us are ready to talk about *that* subject. Maybe we don't even have to. We could just leave it where it belongs: in the past. He pulls me on his lap and caresses my hair, tilting my chin up to look at him.

"I may not be as good as the Humans at understanding body language, but I understand pain when I see it," he says, his voice gentler than ever. "Your sire helped me find those responsible for your sorrow. He was so relieved knowing I would do what he couldn't. I have visited him twice since then."

"You did what?" I ask. This man of mine hides a lot of stuff, doesn't he? And for someone who accused me of being deceiving, that sucks.

"He is lonely and lost. And he has your eyes. Somehow that combination made my choice for me," he says, and I just melt; all my anger is gone. I place a soft kiss inside the palm caressing my cheek. He visits my dad because he has my eyes? How can I possibly argue with that?

"But can you trust him?" I ask.

"Of course not; he is Human," he says, and I just roll my eyes. He does have a point. "I do trust he is a true Warrior at heart. He is desperate for a real fight, to command his army, and make decisions people follow without a question or a doubt. He is wasting away under home restraint, and he knows it. He is also a smart male. We are the new order, and his Warriors trying to fight us would only find their end. He will make compromises and adapt as any true Commander would."

"You might know my father better than I do," I say. "I think this is something he would indeed consider. As long as you keep an eye on him and don't give him free rein. You mustn't trust him with the safety of our people." *Did I just refer to Tarrassians as my people?*

He grabs my hand and kisses it, resting his forehead in my palm. His Sign vibrates softly against my skin.

"Your loyalty to Tarrassia means a lot to me," he says, then he just holds me to his chest. We are quiet for a long time, and he was right. This is not sex, but right now, it feels just as good.

"I only have one more request for you, my beautiful, regarding other people, then the rest of this span will be just about us."

"I think I already know," I say with a smile. "Ollianna and Barin, right? That is a work in progress. As you know, Natalia is pregnant and super busy with her coming Sacred Ceremony. I really don't want to push, but I have no doubt she is scheming as we speak," I say and laugh. I stop as I see the shadow in his eyes. I can feel it in my marks. I know what this is about, and I am a bit upset he wants a chit-chat day but without really asking the important questions.

"Would you like to know what Natalia did to make me stop rejecting the Sign?" I ask, and I can feel the muscles I am leaning against starting to grow. So, there are some severe anger and mistrust issues here, yet he wants to talk about Barin and my father. I grab his face with both hands to make sure he can see the truth in my eyes. Maybe the tears too; I can't help it. I blame the raging hormones.

"All Natalia had to do was mention you were about to be exiled, most likely to die a painful death and that I was free to return to Earth since I could easily reverse my Sign. The second she said that, my Sign came back to life. I chose you, Zaan. Natalia's reverse psychology only worked because I wanted to choose you."

"Do I want to know what reverse psychology is?" he asks with a small smile.

"Probably not," I reply.

"Is it a weapon?" he says, and I stop myself from laughing, because he's not wrong.

"In Natalia's little hands, it is," I say.

He wipes my tears with his lips then kisses me until crying is the last thing on my mind. I turn around on his lap and straddle him the best I can. His size makes simple tasks rather tricky. I might not have used the L-word, but that was pretty close. I think he got the message because he kisses me like he doesn't want to stop. Only, he does. *Again.* His hand removes mine from the strap of my dress as I was trying to let it slide. By mistake, of course. He gets us both up while I cling to him like ivy. Also, by mistake.

"Come, beautiful, I want to show you my favorite place in the Marni forest." Right. He's not falling for any of my *mistakes.* No sex day, I keep forgetting that.

I follow behind as he pulls me out of the Sacred Garden into the glowing Tarrassian morning. A Kartassi guard is already there waiting to hand Zaan his weapons. He only takes the sword and holds it in his hand as we make it towards the treeline. Are we expecting trouble? Do I really want to ask about the beasts hiding in the forests? Of course not. I don't need to know about that or about the reasons behind his rejection. *It's date day*, I try to remind myself and keep my spirit up.

Zaan is very cautious as we make our way through the dark Marni forest. The bright Tarrassian sun can hardly penetrate through the thick canopy of large red leaves. Because it is dark, the trunks give their soft violet glow, and as the breeze moves the branches, sun rays filter through the eerie glow. It looks magical and very alien. Despite the peaceful beauty around us, there is a dangerous feel to the forest. I know the beasts are real. I can hear their scary grunts and growls at night. They sound far away now, but I can see the footprints in the soft reddish moss covering the forest's floor. Wow, I really don't want to know what creature left those. They are huge. Zaan pulls me closer to him, as he can feel my fear.

"I would never risk you, my beautiful Lorra. This path is safe, and the beasts only venture here after the dark span, unless they smell prey," he says, and I just nod, following him through the glowing misty forest. Was that supposed to be reassuring? I am pretty sure I look and taste like prey to everything alien. It is a bit chilly out here, so that's a perfect excuse to keep myself glued to him. Maybe I should have brought my sword, too.

The red moss is moist, and after a while, my feet get soaked inside my Tarrassian sandals. They are made of the strangest foamy gel, but they feel like walking on a cloud. Probably not ideal for outdoor tracking, though. From what I've heard so far, outdoor exercise is not really expected from the delicate Tarrassian women.

We finally stop at his favorite spot, and... well, I don't know what I was expecting. Maybe some stunning waterfall or some exotic mountain view. Instead, this spot looks just like all the other spots we passed on the way. Zaan is a strange man. I know that; the aliens know that; his own parents know that; I just need to go with the flow. The moss covering the forest's floor is much thicker here, and we sink into it as we sit by the large trunk of a Marni Tree. Zaan pulls me in between his open legs, and I lean my back against his chest.

His favorite spot is just as beautiful as every other beautiful place around, nothing special. But after a few minutes, I can begin to appreciate its charm. There is a quietness here I couldn't feel anywhere else. His finger taps gently on my cheek and then points ahead. I tense as I see the movement, but then I relax. It doesn't take an expert to know this animal I am looking at is not a predator. Probably the opposite. Prey looks the same on every planet. Is it a type of deer? It has the unmistakable huge doe eyes. Its pelt is slightly curly, and it seems to be very soft, inviting you to pet it. It is also as bright as a beacon. In this dark red forest, this creature is as white as snow. Someone missed nature's lesson in camouflage. It is the size of a small Earth deer, and its four long legs are as slim as twigs. A push could break them. It has no horns, its hooves are tiny, and as it munches on the thick moss, I can see its teeth are blunter and smaller than mine. Okay, someone also missed nature's lesson about survival. How is this creature not extinct already? Especially here, in Tarrassia's most dangerous forest.

What is it? I ask Zaan in his mind. So grateful for this form of communication. I barely dare breathe.

It is an Arni, he says, and I suddenly remember he compared me to one before. Looking at it now, I am not sure that was a compliment. Yes, it is a beautiful creature. There is a certain grace to its fragility. And strangely enough, its complete lack of survival skills makes it somehow appealing. But perhaps he can compare me to something else in the future. Something that doesn't scream *I am prey and owning it*! The really annoying thing is the more I look at it, the more it reminds me of myself. That sucks. I mean, c'mon, it can't even smell us, and we are not that far. It is a useless, pretty little thing. Is that how Zaan sees me?

Don't make any movement. Watch! he says in my mind, but even that felt like a whisper.

There is a sudden crunch of a fallen branch or something, shortly followed by a growl. From the opposite side of the small clearing, a beast comes prowling, drooling foamy saliva as it approaches the Arni. The new animal is not the one responsible for the prints I saw earlier, thank God. It is only the size of a grizzly bear, as crazy as that may sound. Looks-wise, it's more like a hyena, just way uglier. The foaming mouth doesn't help with first impressions. Ugh! It looks briefly at us, then ignores our presence and decides the Arni is an easier treat. Figure that. It doesn't pounce on its prey, just approaches slowly, like it has no worries in the world. The target is willing, so why not. Finally, the Arni spots it and lifts those beautiful brown eyes to look at its killer. Why the fuck would Zaan think I want to watch this? Is this some sort of alien entertainment for first dates?

So that you know, I am about to grab your sword and chase the beast away; I give him my mental warning before I go for it.

Behave! Just watch. Trust me, he says, giving me short, clipped orders, as if he is too mesmerized by the scene to talk. It's only then I notice, the large predator is also in some sort of awe. It's still advancing on the Arni, but somehow, there is less intent. As for the prey itself, it just stands there on its skinny legs, watching death in the eyes. All it does is stare at the predator with big doe eyes.

Does it hypnotize the beast? I ask without taking my eyes off the scene in front of me.

Not according to my sire, he replies. *The Arni doesn't change the inside of its eyes as it looks at the predator, like some species do. That is not what this is about.*

As we keep on watching, the beast gets even closer to the Arni, sniffing its way, almost as if trying to decide what sort of creature it is. The little deer-like animal doesn't make a single move. It just keeps staring at the large beast into its glowing yellow eyes. Then, its wet little nose starts twitching, and it lifts its head towards the beast. The fragile neck is a couple of inches away from the predator's huge fangs. The larger animal lowers its head, and its snout touches the Arni's twitching nose. It sniffs some more, looks around a bit, more sniffing, then loses interest and disappears back into the forest.

The Arni goes back to munching on the red moss as if nothing happened. What the hell?

The Arni is the most fragile of creatures. They have no strength, no skills, no power. That is why they choose not to run when in danger. It would be useless. They face their fate and accept their fragility without fear. Fear is the luxury of the strong. The weak cannot afford to be afraid. Because the predators cannot feel it on the Arni, they assume they must be bigger predators and let them be. It took me a while to understand that is precisely what happened in the Untried Pit. You owned your fragility and showed no fear. You were just being you.

He hugs me closer to his chest, and I turn sideways over his lap, so I can hug him back. I am an emotional wreck right now. I can feel the Arni's eyes on us, watching silently, waiting for the moment we make a move on it. I press a kiss over Zaan's heart, and he peppers my hair with his. I am speechless. What can I reply to such words?

I have never felt like this. Special. Free. Finally, able to see what I couldn't before. No, I didn't grow any powers overnight. I was always special because I am me. I don't need to turn myself into a super-soldier or act manly to fit in. I don't need to skip the make-up and go for a beer with the guys, unless that's what I want to do. I can be a soldier, and I can kick ass no matter what I look like and no matter how long my hair is. I don't have to fit in. I just have to be me.

Zaan pulls me up quietly, and we leave the clearing hand in hand, the Arni's doe eyes watching us as we disappear from its sight.

39

—

GIANNA

As our *date day* moves into a sunny afternoon, it's getting harder to keep a straight head. I am drunk on love and happiness. There are no other words for what I am feeling. I am giddy, clingy, smiley, chatty... Who is this woman? Suddenly all the clichés and stupid things people say apply to me.

Walking on sunshine? Check. Butterflies in my stomach? Double-check that! Do I want to bottle this day and keep it forever? Check. Actually, do people even say that? As for being a horny mess, I'd better quadruple-check that. Even though we agreed on no sex, I mean he did, there is a whole lot of touching and kissing. He hardly ever lets go of my hand, uses any excuse to carry me around, cradles me to him like I am precious, and pulls me in for one of those consuming kisses every so often. My lips are sore, and there are hickeys all over my neck and shoulders. His intensity is overwhelming and exciting at the same time. I try not to focus too much on the fact he doesn't let me touch him much. He is always quick to grab my hand each time I let it slide down his chest. Maybe I should be reasonable. I am surprised he can even walk around with that stone-like erection his pants do nothing to hide. Probably he is saving it for tonight, and me touching him doesn't make it any easier. And yes, I have to admit all this torturous yet delicious build-up to the main event is kind of hot. *Yes, behave, Gianna!*

He shows me all the secret places where he used to train by himself as a cub. The Marni forest is dark and scary, nothing like Natalia's pretty forest. One can feel the power coming from these trees. And Tarrassians thought the Marni wood was best used for making furniture...

When we stopped at home for lunch, I asked him to show me how to use some of the super-tech equipment in the Training Quarters. To my surprise, he agreed, and then he really surprised me this afternoon with the best thing ever – a flying lesson. The low-flying ship is easier to master than I thought, and he let me have a go for a whole eight minutes. Not only did I manage not to kill anything, but he praised me for it, saying I was a natural space pilot. I know him well enough by now. He doesn't do flattery and doesn't lie. I am so happy; I feel like I could crawl out of my skin. I think I really like dating.

We have a late dinner in the stretch of the garden outside our bedroom. He must have sent away the Kartassi usually guarding the treeline, as we are all alone. Even though we are not in the forest any more, he keeps his sword at hand as the sun starts to set. Just how dangerous are the beasts living there?

He pulls me into his lap and feeds me my dinner while nuzzling at my neck. I don't even think of complaining. Being looked after is dangerously addictive. Zaan is so relaxed; for the first time, he looks his age. He is the youngest of the girls' mates and only sixteen years older than I am. That may seem a big age gap by human standards, but Tarrassians live for a few hundred years. Apparently, the Sign and living on Tarrassia will make my life equally long. Is it scary? Yes. But then again, two hundred years of Zaan? I think I can totally live with that. He tells me stories of his childhood and some crazy adventures of the Blood Fleet. He encourages me to do the same, but there isn't much to the story. Especially when it comes to my dysfunctional family. Despite the pain it comes with, I do tell him about Yara. When I mention Sia's idea to have a Resting Ceremony, he offers his family Resting Cave as they call it here.

Yara's story reminds me of something else I have to do. I lift my head off his chest and look into those beautiful golden eyes to make sure I don't miss any signals.

"The Queen asked me to be present when Brian wakes up," I start, and straight away, I can feel him tense.

"Are all the Human females going to be present?" he asks.

"No, just me. The Healers are worried about Brian's state of mind when he wakes. He might not even remember what happened to him, and I can't imagine the shock he will have walking up on an alien planet," I say, trying to sound reasonable.

"Wouldn't it make more sense for Jade to be there when he wakes? She is the only Human without mating marks. Those could be hard to explain to the Human male," he says. Why does he always have to have a point? Maybe this is wiser, and I am considering it for a while. But, no, I want to be there for Brian when the Healers wake him. For the two years he worked for Yara, he looked after me even though I hardly even spoke to him. It is my turn to look after him. I owe it to Yara. She adored Brian. It was never a crush or anything like that. He was like a protective big brother and not just to her.

"You are probably right, but Brian and I know each other from Earth," I say and wait cautiously. There are tiny specs of white and red in his eyes. I wonder if he can tell. I pretend not to notice, and I explain as casually as possible about how I met Brian and his relationship with Yara. I make sure to mention our very brief interactions, but also Brian's care for me. He protected me when I had no one else there to do it. As expected, Zaan's tense body starts to relax around me.

"According to the freed slaves from Sketos, the Human male protected them as well," he says, and I can hear the curiosity in his voice.

"That sounds just like him. Brian is very protective of those in need," I say with a warm smile. Luckily, Zaan understands it is a sibling-like affection and nothing more.

"The Human male would make a great Blood Fleet Warrior," he says, and I can only agree.

"So, is it okay if I am there when he wakes?" I ask for permission, like a *good female*.

"Yes, beautiful. Just no touching and no hugging," he says, and I just say thank you without agreeing or disagreeing.

Hello?!!! I am Human. Of course there will be hugging. Or maybe not. Brian is a lovely guy, but he can be prickly, and he is not big on cuddles either.

I don't tell Zaan, but there is another reason why I don't want Jade there when Brian wakes. Yara and I were giggling around corners and exchanging knowing looks each time Jade was present. It wasn't hard to see Brian's interest. Yeah, Jade was flirting and doing her thing, but she was like that around all the guys. Brian, though, only had eyes for Jade. I don't want him to wake up from hell to heartache. Jade didn't say it in words, but her feelings for the High General are pretty obvious. Despite saving Zaan's life and mine by proxy, the guy sounds like a proper asshole. He is mated to some Tarrassian Princess, has sex with females working in his household, including underage ones like Mirri, and he is somehow stringing poor Jade along. No matter what this is, I don't want Brian in the middle of it.

"I know we said no more talking about others on this span, beautiful, but there is something I want to talk to you about. It is related to the female called Jade," he says almost as if listening to my thoughts. He wouldn't do that, right?

"As long as it is not about her boobs," I say with a dramatic eye roll. He watches me warily for a few seconds, then finally laughs. My man and jokes do not mix; bless him.

"No, I promise not to go there," he says with a smile. "I just want you to convince her to keep her distance from the High General."

He watches me warily, almost knowing I want details. His direct superior, and mine, for that matter, saved his life. Yet I cannot help feeling he doesn't like the guy.

"She should anyway because I think the High General has a mate," I say, trying to play it cautiously.

"Yes, indeed. Princess Umbelina was mated at birth to the High General," he says, making me cringe. A lovely birthday present she got. "She is very young, and only this orbit rotation she became of age."

Wow, that should make her ideal for the guy; he seems to like them young.

"Is the Princess the King's sister?" I ask. I know Sia spends a lot of time with her, and they are close. Of course, Jade hates it, but if Umbelina is Sia's sister-in-law, that explains their closeness.

"No, Princess Umbelina is the daughter of the Elder of the Fields. She is Tarrassia's only Princess as it is. All the other Elders have sired sons. A daughter of a King would be a High Princess."

"Your people like complicated stuff," I tell him, playing with his hair as he plays with mine.

"The High General is a very complicated man," he says, not really getting my joke. "Jade must keep her distance. She is your friend and the only one who could make you laugh," he says, surprising me. "Until now, that is. You laughed plenty for me on this span, too," he adds, melting me a bit more.

"Why do I have the feeling there is something you are not telling me?" I ask, and his reply confirms my gut instinct.

"That is because it is not my secret to share; please don't ask, beautiful. I just want you to trust me on this. Jade is not safe around him. No female is, and it pains me I can't do anything about keeping Umbelina from him. Our sires are good friends, and she is like a little sister to me," he says, and I can't help feeling jealous. I suddenly remember Sia mentioning the Princess's beauty and perfect manners. As Jade would say, I have it bad for this guy. "Out of all the High Ladies of Tarrassia, Elina is probably the sweetest. She deserves better."

Jealousy aside, I can see he is distraught.

"I may find Tarrassian males a bit… intense," I say, trying not to use any stronger words, "but I do know for sure they would never hurt a female. Maybe you shouldn't worry too much."

"That doesn't apply to the High General. That is all I can say, but I hope you understand how important it is to keep Jade away from him. Without risking yourself, of course. You know your rules," he says, and I can't help rolling my eyes.

Since I am sitting on his lap, and there is no denying what it does to him, maybe it's time I make a rule.

"Speaking of rules, can I have one of my own?" I ask, and I force myself not to laugh. Dear Lord! His face is priceless as if someone just poured iced water all over him. I cuddle up closer to him and rub my bottom over his erection, all by mistake, of course. He groans, and his large hands grab my hips to keep me still.

"As long as it is a reasonable rule," he says warily.

"Oh yes, it is," I say with a smile. "I want to touch you, any way I please, when we are alone," I say. My words sound damn right shameless to me. What have I done to old Gianna?

"This is a hazardous rule, something only a Human could come up with," he says with a sigh. "I am, however, a very accommodating male, and my mate's wishes are my own."

I lift my head off his shoulder to look at him.

"Zaan of House Marni, did you just make a joke?" I ask, but then I laugh at his puzzled expression. That was not a sexual joke. He was just being serious. God, I love him so much! Even his quirks are enough to melt me.

"So, is that a yes?" I ask.

"It is a yes, my Lorra," he says, placing a soft kiss over my Sign. I take advantage of his distraction and pull his shirt up. I almost, almost have it off when he grabs my hand.

"What are you doing, Lorra?"

"Using my rule."

"What, now?"

"Of course, now. According to the High Master of the Training Pits, rules start with immediate effect," I say, and I am rewarded with his beautiful laughter. I am also out of air straight away as he takes my mouth into an intimate kiss that leaves me panting. His tongue touches every little spot inside my mouth, like a sweeping tornado taking everything with it.

Please, I want to feel your skin, not your garment, I say inside his mind as his mouth keeps mine prisoner.

Without breaking the kiss, he removes his shirt and throws it away. My hands go straight to his shoulders and make their way down his arms, trying to touch as much as I can. And there is a lot to touch. This feels like some sort of epiphany. My go-to type was the super skinny, ultra-shaved metrosexual kind of guy, mainly for safety reasons. Touching Zaan's bulging muscles, hairy body and oversized... everything is rewiring my brain to what must have been factory setting. Before the abuse and all my sex-gone-wrong experiences, that is. This is my type of man. Maybe his Astrals are not that stupid after all.

My fingers trace the glowing red swirls wrapping around his huge biceps, all the way down to the wrists resting on my hips. He watches me with intense eyes, and this close, I have to look away before it makes my eyes tear up. It doesn't scare me like before; now, I want to roll in that intensity and purr like a cat. Before I think any crazier thoughts, my lips go straight for the copper skin stretched over his oversized pecs. I nuzzle at the black hair that is denser on his chest then I allow myself a proper taste of that delicious skin. He tenses but doesn't stop me. To my surprise, he doesn't prevent my hand from going down his pants. *God, please don't let him stop me!*

I move my body to his left thigh to give myself better access to his right leg and the monster resting behind the soft fabric of his pants. Of course, resting is the wrong word for something that lively and excited. I touch his pulsing length up and down, and I squeeze slightly when I reach the large tip. The chest I am still licking and kissing heaves, and his left heart sounds like it is about to make a breakthrough, tearing his skin. This is my moment to move things along, but I struggle with a fear I don't even understand. It's not exactly shyness, and I am definitely not afraid of him. I think it might be fear of rejection. But that is just stupid. This is a man who wants me enough to give up on all his dreams for me. Scrap that, I am his dream. The woman whose eyes he has a very unhealthy obsession with – his *Lorra*.

Why would he reject me? It is a silly fear, and I push it away to the back of my mind. Why would I even think that way?

Right, moving along. His super-hot, sexy Tarrassian pants are made for sex, I swear! No zip, no buttons, just a string-like fastening and two layers of soft fabric overlapping over his crotch. No wonder he kept adjusting himself all day. How easy would it be for an erection as big and hard as his to just pop through the front opening? Just as easy as it is for my hand to squeeze itself inside. My fingers touch the smoothest and hottest skin, wrapped around his hard-as-stone length.

"Lorra?" he says, a vague warning in his pained voice. However, his hands on my waist don't try to stop me or push me away. I can't make much progress in this position, and I slither off his lap down to the soft moss covering the garden's reddish soil. My knees sink comfortably, and I position myself in between his open legs.

"Lorra?" he says again; the warning is now mixed with a question, and there is a frown in between his bushy eyebrows.

I hold his stare, despite the intensity making my eyes hurt. I am secretly hoping he can tell how desperate I am for this. *Please, don't stop me!* My fingers work at the opening of his pants, looking rather clumsy, I must say. Pulling out a cock that size is no easy task.

"Beautiful? What are you doing?" he asks, but instinctively his body moves slightly off his seat to allow me to pull the stubborn pants down. It's not much progress, but I now have enough room to pull his cock out. I have a slight moment of panic. I probably don't have to wonder about fitting; Natalia and Sia are both pregnant, so it's fair to say it fits. I do have to consider the pain it might cause. To me sex equals pain, but I decide on the spot I don't care. I would do anything for him. The skin covering his impressive length and girth is darker than his copper body, and angry-looking veins make me think he must be in serious pain. Or are those ridges? Probably safer not to ask. I don't want to lose my courage now.

Despite how much I hate sex or used to anyway, I have quite the technique when it comes to blow-jobs. It started as a way to avoid actual sex, but then I found myself in complete control while on my knees in front of a guy. Of course, that was a winner. Now it's a bit different, and not just because of Zaan's size. This is the man I love, and that makes the power shift a bit. But I know he loves me back, even though he didn't say it, so perhaps this can only be about love, not about power. There is an increasing shake in his body, almost like a vibration I can feel in my bones. I keep looking at him as I place the first kiss over one of those angry veins going up his length. All at once, his body jolts, his cock seems to grow under my lips, and his fingers grab my chin, keeping me still. His touch is very firm, almost painful. *No more growing, please!*

"My self-control might be better trained than most, but I don't think I can survive this, beautiful," he says, watching my lips intensely.

Well, that's the idea, silly! Of course, I don't dare say it out loud.

"Please, I just want to taste you, like you tasted me," I say, and I don't care if I sound desperate.

"That would make me spill my seed, and I vowed to do it inside you. I haven't even allowed myself relief since I laid eyes on you."

That is crazy! Why does he set himself impossible targets like these? Somehow, that is also very hot. To me, a man with such self-control and discipline is a bit like a unicorn.

"Well, technically, you would be spilling inside me, just in a different place, you know?" I say, trying to lay another kiss over the hot, throbbing length, now poking at my chest. And leaking... I can feel the fabric of my Tarrassian dress getting wet, where the tip of his cock touches it.

"Yes, another Human thing my species has gone mad for. If I hear snickering and gossiping around the Camp, it has to be about that," he says, his eyes glued to my lips. The intensity in his stare goes from crazy to... I don't know; whatever comes after crazy. My horny, scrambled brain takes a few seconds to register what he is really saying.

"Your people don't have oral sex?" I ask curiously. I mean, he gave me that, right?

"Our females will receive it, just not return it."

That's a bit selfish, isn't it? Just as I am about to tell him that, he says something that brings all my insecurities back.

"This is only something the pleasurers offer on the Yellow Planets and only a few species. And there is never any swallowing. That is entirely a Human thing."

There is no judgment in his voice. There isn't much else, to be fair. His words are pretty flat and quiet, as if he is not paying attention to them. His focus is on my lips, and I lick them involuntarily. It makes his cock jump and almost pokes me in the jaw. He grabs it with one hand in a rather unforgiving way and keeps it from moving.

I don't exactly know what to do here. I still want to touch him and taste him, but he just said that's something only paid whores do. What the hell? What do I do?

"Is that something you would like from me?" I ask, and I want to slap myself. What kind of question is that?

"I want everything from you," he says, moving one hand into my hair and tilting my head up. "When I tell you to stop, you stop. Yes?" he asks, and I say yes out of reflex. He likes his questions answered, ideally with a yes. I don't understand what he means, but then the fingers around my jaw squeeze to make me open for him. He directs the large tip of his cock straight into my mouth, and I almost choke. He sure doesn't do things by half. And trust him to take control of something he doesn't even know what it is.

God, he is so big! My jaw is on fire trying to protest against the invasion. I try to adjust slowly and take him one inch at a time, but he has other plans. The hand fisted in my hair pushes my head down, and there is some degree of pain as he touches the back of my throat. I wait for the sting of panic, but there is none. I surprise myself by relaxing my muscles around his girth. My feelings for him overwhelm anything else. It doesn't matter if it hurts a bit or if I could do with some air right now. Yes, I do need to explain to him later: Humans do enjoy all sorts of oral activities but there are some freaking rules. Breathing might be a good practice.

Once I focus on the feel of him, on his taste, on the panting, horny mess it turns me into, it all gets a lot easier. Suddenly there is air in my lungs, and the pain has been replaced by pleasure, even though he's not exactly gentle. Okay, maybe we can scrap the rules. Breathing is so overrated. I can hear myself moaning around him. Oh, God, this was meant to make him come, but I think I might go first. His pleasure is the biggest trigger, and my inner muscles start to spasm, and I might just...

"Stop!" his voice says from somewhere behind the ringing in my ears. At the same time, he pulls me up and adjusts his pants back in position. My legs are shaky, and I watch him with unsure eyes. He takes me in his arms just as my legs are about to cave in.

"I want you naked, in my furs. Now!" he whispers in my hair as he carries me up the stairs leading to our bedroom. The relief knocks all the air out of me, and I place my head on his shoulder. Me and my silly insecurities. Why do I keep thinking he will reject me? Of course he wants me.

Some part of my brain that still works registers the surreal beauty of the falling night around us. The twin moons are so bright, almost as if they are anxiously waiting for the third one to make its appearance. Even the scary noises of the beasts awakening in the forest seem to fit perfectly in the picture of the beautiful Tarrassian night. As we enter our bedroom, the lights come on, and he more or less growls at the MI to turn them off. When that happens, the furniture gives its violet glow and an eerie golden hue coming from the twin moons basks our huge bed in its glory.

As he kisses the life out of me, I feel and hear the impatient tear in both our outfits. There goes my favorite dress... The intensity of his kiss, touch, and everything else, leaves me a bit brainless. I am trying to keep up as if I should do something. You know... participate, maybe?

I probably could be a lot more present without him kissing me like that. The intensity, the power, and the control he puts behind it make my world turn into a very narrow tunnel. I can only focus on his taste. I feel the furs behind my back as he lays me down on our bed. His naked body touches mine everywhere, and I am trying to stay in the moment instead of black out like an idiot. I am almost tempted to tell him to calm the crazy, slow things down, but that is not who he is. He wants all or nothing, and what I once found scary, now I find exhilarating. I almost went through life without knowing this feeling. He has taken over every ounce of my body, mind and soul, and there is only one option: total surrender. Not only do I let him have it, but I drown in the pleasure it gives me. And the strangest thing? The more I surrender the more I feel in control.

His hands are everywhere; his lips haven't left a single inch of me untouched. I arch my back into his tongue when I feel it deep inside me. I don't even remember when he got there.

I am raw with emotion, but also need to release the pressure in my body. My vagina is leaking, and my inner muscles have started to contract around his tongue. He's turned me into a beautiful mess. I whimper loudly and pull at his hair when he takes his mouth off me. I feel him moving above me, and I eagerly open my thighs to welcome him. Somewhere it registers that I can't spread my legs as he is blocking them from doing so. His hot mouth is above mine, licking my lips, and I can taste myself on him. God, he needs to hurry. I have had enough foreplay, I need him, and ideally, I need to come right now! Why did I think I wanted him to slow down?

"Please, Zaan," I say like a prayer. Because it really is. I am ready to beg if that's what it takes.

"What do you need, my beautiful?" he says, grabbing my face between his large hands to keep my eyes on him. I don't care if he sees the needy tears in there or the crazy fire he lit inside me.

"You know…" I whimper again.

"Tell me!" he says, and his eyes seem to burn my face.

"I want you to let me come, and I want you inside me when I do," I finally manage to form the words. I wouldn't even dream of mind-talking with a fried-up brain.

I can feel his hot lips pressing a soft kiss over my pulsing Sign.

"And you will have that, Gianna. They are both yours to ask for. Just not now. First, you have to understand breaking my rules has consequences. You will now accept your punishment like a good female, reflect on your rules and how to obey them in the future."

He turns me on my side and moves his body behind me, spooning me into a tight embrace. I feel a large fur being pulled over us and his hot breath in my hair.

"You will travel with me to the Pits on the early span. If I know Kayon well enough, he will give you hell tomorrow and push your body to its limits. Sleep now, my beautiful," he says, and then there is just silence. After a while, the silence is broken by my quiet sobs. My face is soaked in tears, but there is just that. Sobs and tears. I am too numb to think or feel. He pulls me even closer and places soft kisses over my shoulder   . Large fingers wipe my tears.

"Please don't cry, my Lorra. This is not revenge, not even punishment. This is making sure you understand my rules are there to keep you safe. I have to trust you will obey them. If there is no pain when you don't, what is there to stop you from acting recklessly again? Please, be brave for me tonight and accept your consequences. We can start again tomorrow without any trust issues. Yes?"

"Yes, Zaan," I say softly.

"Well done, my perfect mate."

40

—

GIANNA

It turns out Zaan knows Kayon very well. By the time the afternoon session rolls in, I want to cut his tusks off. He pushes me harder than most during endurance training.

I have always been a runner. My dad used to take me for a run for as long as I can remember. Then, a few years into our routine, he stopped being slow on purpose, so I could keep up. He never said it in words because that's just him, but I knew he was pleasantly surprised by my stamina. Sadly, he got busier and busier as I became a teen, and then it stopped altogether. After that, he was hardly ever at home. However, I still used our home treadmill since I wasn't allowed to go out for a run by myself. I kept hitting the gym like a madwoman during my modelling years. Intense exercise was my thing, and I was damn good at it!

At least that's what I used to think before Kayon told me, *the weaker Untried have to do the training routine twice*. Really? Does that even make sense? I am not the only one who can't keep up with the set targets because… there are cubs in my Unit, so yeah, there is that. I finally hit the expected mileage without falling flat on my face on the death trap they call a running strip. Unfortunately, my relief is short-lived because Kayon tells me all my breaks have been cancelled. Apparently, *the weak need extra sparring*.

Zaan is not watching me like a hawk today, and in a way, it gives me confidence. He knows I can hold my own. But, once again, my enthusiasm is short-lived. Kayon shows me exactly why even the mighty Tarrassians are afraid of him. He is a deadly mixture of pure strength and skill. He is also fucking controlling, stubborn and... well, controlling. It's his way or his way. The highway is not even an option. He makes the Tarrassian men look harmless. As for words? He only has a favorite one: AGAIN! My wrists hurt, my muscles shake, and I still have to make it to my flight module. And ideally, pay attention.

"I am not in on the next span, so we do double sparring today," he tells me, but then I notice he sends everyone else to class.

"Why am I the only one doing it?" I ask. I wish I didn't.

"Because the weak need more training. Besides, when I return, you will fight me with a Tarrassian sword. No more wooden sticks."

I want to snap at him and point out in the rudest way the Marni shinai is Tarrassian. And it is not a freaking stick! I want to tell him to go fuck himself because I really thought of him as a friend. Almost a father figure, but I guess that's where things go wrong for me. Sadly, I have to hold my tongue. He is my superior, and after last night I am not getting into any more trouble. I am on my way to becoming Tarrassia's most well-behaved female. Me and their spineless Princess.

"Shall I tell you what happens when you push weaklings beyond their limits, Master of the Untried?" I sass not really able to hold my tongue. Maybe I can stick around *sweet Umbelina*, learn some pony tricks. The thing is, I hope Kayon doesn't ask what happens because I don't fucking know!

He smacks my shinai off into the sand as easy as wiping off a bug. Yet miraculously, he didn't break my wrist.

"No need to tell me, Untried. I already know. I have had weaklings before. Doesn't happen too often, sadly," he says.

What? "Sadly?" I say. I know Kayon is an alien, and he is not meant to make sense, but still.

"Under the right care, the weak can go further than the strong. They build a will and a determination that keeps on giving when muscles fail," he explains, and despite being pissed with him, I have to agree he does have a point.

"The two smallest and weakest cubs I had in this Pit are my greatest achievements. One left here to become the Blood Fleet's youngest High Commander and the other to become the High Commander of the Royal Guard," he says, pointing at my shinai, and I quickly pick it up.

Oh, my God! Is he talking about Zaan and Sarrian? How the hell were those two ever weak or small? Sia's High Commander might be all smiles, sunny disposition, and a face to die for, but that doesn't fool me. There is a reason why the King trusted him to protect what he loves the most in the world. That and the fact he might be otherwise inclined. The King's ridiculous jealousy is not exactly a secret. As for Zaan, he can fight anyone and anything. So, how were those two ever the weakest? However, what Kayon says next is the real shock.

"You, Untried Gianna of House Marni, will be my greatest achievement yet. The High Elder and the Oria birds need my care more than the Training Pits. So does my family. I am not a young male any more. It is time I spend more time with the ones I love and leave some of my responsibilities to the younglings. I will inform the Royal Council on the next span of my appointed new Master of the Untried. That would be you! Now, use that ridiculous wooden stick. I don't have all span."

Maybe Kayon should retire. He has lost his fucking mind!!!!

Is this a joke? I am trying to stay calm and not overreact or offend him by assuming things.

"Why, Kayon, because the Marni wood glows for me or because of who I am mated to?" I ask quietly. We are alone in the Pit, but many Warriors are passing by.

"I never made a secret of my dislike of glowing sticks. I've seen better tricks," he says giving my sword a dismissive look. Kayon is not easy to impress. "Your mate's deranged behavior doesn't do a thing for me. That tends to happen when you know people since they were cubs," he says with a bored expression. "You will be my successor because of what you taught little Ronnin that span," he says, looking down at me from his towering height. "I knew you were the one I had been waiting for. Now, I can finally retire without worry or guilt. But don't worry, your magic glowing stick and crazy mate work just fine for the rest of them," he says, pointing around. "They are stupid," he adds with a smirk, and I can't help smiling. To my surprise, he smiles back. Kayon is a different man when that unusual event happens. Kind of handsome. If you don't mind huge scary orcs, that is.

I go through the rest of my day in a constant state of shock. Something I don't exactly hate. It takes my mind off *my other problem;* although I am pretty proud of myself for taking it all in like a responsible grown-up, to be fair. Maybe all that has happened has finally changed me into a stronger, more reasonable person. One who can find solutions instead of self-harming, anorexia, and mindless sex.

I was absolutely heartbroken last night. There is no point calling it anything else. Yeah! Heartbroken! I was still numb when Zaan woke me up this morning with a kiss. A long, passionate kiss. There was a lot of care and attention from him as we got ready for our day. Probably more than usual. That, combined with my newly discovered wisdom, made me understand a few things. The promised punishment I had been dreading for weeks has finally happened. It was nothing like I thought it would be. It was far worse than what I imagined. But, of course, Zaan's ideas of punishment had to be different from anyone else's. It happened; I survived it; time to move on. Isn't that what he said? We start again, without any hard feelings. The more I think about it, the better I feel – no more guilt over what I did to him, no more worries about the looming punishment.

I find myself counting every minute left of my day at the Pits. And not just because Kayon is trying to turn me into Genghis Khan, but because I am desperate to be where I belong. In Zaan's arms.

"That bad, beautiful?" is the first thing Zaan says to me at the end of the day. I more or less collapse into his embrace once we are alone on his ship.

"Kayon is an asshole. The Noorranni should hire him as Slave Master extraordinaire," I say and melt my tired mind into Zaan's warm laughter.

"Yes, I remember the feeling," he says, removing dust and sand from my hair. I must look a mess!

"How did you survive?" I ask, remembering he was only a child at the time.

"Sarrian always got it worse. He really used to trigger Kayon's wrath," he says, smiling at a distant memory.

"Maybe that's the spirit. I need to push Ronnin or Mirri to the front. Have Kayon turn on them," I say, trying to joke as I collapse in my seat.

"We both know you would rather be you than them. Your care for your Unit was what made Kayon's mind up," he says, and it takes a while before my tired brain registers his words.

"So, you know?"

"Yes, he told me this span, but I knew it was coming. I saw his interest in you. It is a great honor, my Lorra. Kayon is both feared and respected amongst the galaxies. You make me proud," he says, watching me with golden fires in his eyes.

"What if he is wrong?"

"Kayon is never wrong," he says, and I am too tired to insist. Too scared to even think about the magnitude of this nonsense. Freaking aliens can give you whiplash. How can they go from no female Warriors to having one as Master of the Untried?

I will have to revisit this subject and how I feel about it when I am less tired. And hopefully less horny.

A day of intense physical activities with a stupid leather strip fastened between my legs was worse than Kayon mopping the Pit with me. Having my clit rub against the leather all day was like an extension to the stupid punishment. Zaan better do something about it. Although, it seems we are heading that way and not just because of the evidence. The heavy leather kilt can't hold that monstrous erection down. True, he was just as aroused last night, and he still turned me down.

It is the way he looks at me that makes me think my punishment is over. His golden stare has changed from intense to damn right predatory. There is intent in his touch as he helps me through my evening routine. I let him not just because I am tired and sore, but because... well, any reason to let him touch me is good enough. He spoon-fed me my dinner and removed my leather outfit. I stop him as he carries me to the bathing pool.

"Shower, please," I whisper in his ear. "I mean the pressure cleanser."

He watches me with a question in his eyes, but then I see the smile as he understands. It looks like we both have a little unsatisfied sexual fantasy involving that deadly enclosure. Unfinished business and all that. As we step under the bullet-like water drops, I cringe and make myself as small as possible in his arms. Good Lord, this one is even more powerful than the one on his ship. What is wrong with these people? I get one or two painful drops on my skin before he pushes me against the safe back wall. We are in the same position as before on his ship. And in my wet dreams... My body is squeezed between him and the wall, pressing unforgivingly into my backside. Zaan ducks my head under his chin, covering all of me from the deadly spray. Hot punishing fingers go for my folds, pinching my clit in the process. Straight to the point. Very much like him. No more freaking foreplay and my mind says a silent *amen* to that.

I am so happy and relieved I could cry. I already know we are done playing. He will finally let me have what I need. Because my body has had enough of fooling around and mainly because I am starved for his touch, it takes him about half a minute to pull an explosive orgasm out of me. Without being squeezed between him and the wall, I would probably slither to the floor.

I don't even get to be embarrassed by my eagerness before his fingers steal another orgasm out of me, then another. Wow! Is he that skilled or am I that horny? Probably a mixture of both. Then, reality becomes all blurry and distant as two of his large fingers go so deep inside it almost hurts. He curls them and touches something I can only imagine must be my G spot. So, that's not an urban myth. For whatever stupid reason it makes me cry. Luckily his brain functions better than mine and he understands my tears are caused by pleasure, not pain. Not only does he not stop, but he does it again and again. I feel like I am about to lose consciousness, and there is some panic mixed in all that pleasure. The world is too sharp and bright and my skin feels too tight to accommodate all the expanding emotions inside me. Careful what you wish for...

Zaan, please, I can't take another one, I say in my mind, and surprisingly he can hear. I was far from trying to use my newly found telepathic powers. Not with a melted brain, that is.

You can, and you will, he says and turns me around in his arms pushing me into the wall once again. His left hand goes back to my swollen clit, while his other hand finds my hard-as-pebbles nipples.

Time has lost its meaning. The world has, too. I am somewhere between bliss and damn right brain dead. I don't know if this is his way of apologising for refusing me before, but maybe a sorry would do next time. I mean, I still want the orgasms, but keep them in single digits, if possible.

It vaguely registers he takes me out and dries me off. His touches are caring, but now there is a rush. I can't blame him. I got my relief multiplied by sixty or something. I notice he doesn't even touch his engorged cock as he roughly dries himself off. It looks painful. I don't know if Tarrassians get blue balls. It is fair to assume so, as their anatomy is not that different from ours. Maybe they just call it brown balls, as his pack has now turned a much deeper copper color than the rest of his skin. I watch fascinated as his cock swells even more under my stare, and those blood veins or ridges going up the sides are pulsing and... It's either my hormones have fried my circuits, or I can clearly see tiny shiny particles going up and down inside those veins.

His gruff voice orders the lights off. Oh well, maybe it's for the best. I shouldn't look too closely. If the stuff in those veins is an industrial quantity of shiny cum, I will have a hairy copper baby by morning. As he picks me up into his arms and carries me to our bed, I am already picking baby names in my head. I hide a silly smile on his shoulder.

Because I am so drunk on love and endorphins I don't notice straight away, he tucked me in on my side, spooned me from behind, covered us with a large fur, then... nothing. I am quickly coming out of my state of bliss, and I suddenly feel cold. The kind that comes from inside you, and there is no hiding from. However, my newly found maturity keeps me grounded. I need to understand before I rush to conclusions. I am trying to turn into his arms, so I can face him.

Not easy to read much in those solid golden eyes, unlike the expressive eyes of my people, but I still have to look at him. His arms increase their hold around me, and he doesn't allow me to turn.

"You are exhausted, my Lorra. It was a hard span for you, and you need to sleep," he says, placing a hot kiss at my nape.

I had indeed a hell of a day, and the many orgasms he gave me didn't help with my levels of exhaustion either. But I can still call bullshit when I see it! I surprise myself by trying to reason with him.

"Zaan, we both need this more than sleep," I say over my shoulder since he doesn't allow me to turn. I am scared. No, I am terrified right now, but I keep my voice calm and playful. "We won't be able to rest when we are this worked up. My sweet man, you are literally dripping over my ass right now. How can you possibly think of going to sleep like that?" *Please don't reject me!*

"Self-restraint and discipline have never failed me, my Lorra. You don't need to worry about me. Please, you must rest now," he says, nuzzling at my hair.

I see. I wish I didn't. But I. Really. Fucking. Do.

"MI, lights on!" I order with a shaky voice. He is a bit distracted by all the blinding lights coming on at once, and I use that moment to get out of his embrace. I go down the steps of our sleeping platform on shaky legs. I need clothes for this; I don't want to feel any more vulnerable or exposed.

"Lorra, what are you doing?" I hear his voice from the bed. I don't look at him; I need to cover up first.

I grab randomly one of his oversized shirts. The smell of orange flowers envelops me like a dream – a nightmare in this case. My shaky fingers won't manage one of the fiddly Tarrassian dresses, and what these people call nightwear is worse than being naked. I can feel his body heat behind me, and I turn to face him. As I do, I hand him his kilt. He looks at it as if it may bite but takes it out of reflex.

"Can you please put it on?" I ask. My voice sounds weak and shaky, but there is no point hiding the hurt he caused.

He fits the kilt to his waist, and under normal circumstances, this would be funny as hell. Trying to cover that erection is not an easy task and he struggles to get it done. However, there is nothing normal or funny about the night my heart is being ripped out of me. *I allowed this to happen. I made myself a victim. Again!*

"I don't know what this is, Gianna, but you need to stop. Now!" he says. His voice is stern, his eyes are burning mine and I don't give a shit. I am also too pissed to care about the tell-tale sign of his War Beast coming to life. He has the nerve to be angry! White specs take over the gold in his eyes, and the muscles under his pecs start moving restlessly.

"Yes, I agree. This has to stop. I am not playing your twisted games any more, Zaan!" I shout, and I wish I could sound imposing and cold like Sia. But, instead, I sound damn right hysterical.

"First, please do not raise your voice," he says, staring me down with angry eyes. "Second, I do not play games, I am not Human."

"Oh, yes, there we go," I say mockingly, but all I can hear is my voice trembling with rage. "Thank you for the reminder of my people's worth. How could we ever be good enough for the perfect Tarrassians?"

"I have no idea what you are saying or doing," he starts, and I can see he is trying to rein in his anger. "It is best if we revisit this, whatever this is, on the next span. You are tired and emotional, and you need to sleep."

I am so angry, I don't even try to keep the lid on any more. My blood is boiling, and I could easily kill something right now. Or someone. My words come out as yelling, and hot tears go down my cheeks, making Natalia look like a novice. It probably shows how hurt I am, but I am past pretending to be cool with this.

"Stop fucking patronizing me and telling me what I need!"

"What you need is to mind your words. You do not address me in such a manner. Remember your rules, Gianna," he says and grabs my wrist in a painful grip pulling me closer to him.

There is a sliver of fear, and a flashback of the past ignites behind my red-hot anger. I don't know if he can see it in my eyes, but he quickly lets go of my wrist. Even though I am now free to move away, I don't. Instead, I stay right there and tilt my head to look him in the eyes. It doesn't matter if everything inside me hurts, or how much I want him right now. The reality is all that matters. He doesn't want me back. He is too fucking perfect, and he deserves better. He knows it, I know it; it is time we deal with it!

"Fuck the rules! I have something better than that. How about the good old Tarrassian law?" I say, letting my anger rule supreme. "I want you to leave. Not only for the night and not to the guest quarters. I want you out of the Marni house! According to your mother, that is the law of your people. So, if your female tells you you're out, then you are out!"

He watches me as if his translating device has suddenly stopped working. I can see when he finally gets it. There is pain in his eyes when it happens.

"Lorra, you don't mean that. Please believe me, this was not about punishing you," he says, pointing to the bed.

"What was it about, Zaan?" I ask. I probably already know, but I want him to say it to my face. "And your Astrals help you if you dare use my tiredness as an excuse."

He takes a deep breath and lowers his eyes to the floor. His fingers find his soft, long hair and start pulling at it in his usual gesture of frustration.

"I... I just can't," he says, the words that shatter the world around me in tiny needles. I can feel them all go for me at once, piercing my skin making me feel like a Voodoo doll.

"The servants will deliver your stuff to wherever it is you will be staying. Leave! And don't you dare stalk me or use the cameras to watch me. I will ask the guards to remove them anyway." As I finish talking, I hand him his sword. It mocks my stupid fragility as I need both hands and all my strength to even lift it.

He takes it and makes his way to the door. I should feel relieved, but his lack of fight only adds to my insult. Suddenly he stops, without turning to look my way.

"Your marks and Sign will hurt," he says with a calm, impersonal voice. The complete opposite of my emotional mess.

"Not as much as your presence," I reply, and then he is gone.

41

—

GIANNA

The day after sucks! I had one or two of those before, but nothing
ever felt like this. Not the day after the rape and not the one after
being kidnapped by alien slavers. This time my body is not the
one that took the impact. It's my soul, and it hurts a lot more
than broken bones.

The late morning sun scrapes my eyes, so I hide from it under
the thick red canopy of the Sacred Marni Tree. I'm tucked in a
foetus-like position at its base, trying to block the world out. As
before, its branches lowered themselves all around me, and now
it feels as if I am in a cocoon of safety.

As if I wasn't hurt enough by *him*, now I feel hurt by my own
actions. I would have liked to wake up to the grown-up version
of Gianna. Put on my slutty outfit and go to the Pits, like nothing
happened. To spite Zaan and everyone else. But, sadly, I woke up
to the run and hide version. I couldn't eat and I had to fight the
urge to scrape at my arms. And not just because my marks hurt.
Old habits die hard.

Instead of acting like a grown-up, I left a brief com text for

Kayon and all my other Pit Masters, saying I won't be coming in. Today Kayon will announce me as his successor to the King and to the Royal Council. He will put his reputation and his head on the line for me. And what do I do? I take the day off. I left my com in the bedroom as I don't want to see his angry replies. I let him down, and there is no sugar-coating it. However, the more I lie next to the Marni Tree, the clearer my mind becomes. The fiery red sap inside the now transparent trunk can heal, and maybe that is what it's doing now. But, sadly, a clear mind comes with more pain, and the ugly reality shows its claws.

I thought I was so unique and kick-ass that I was offered the top position only days after joining the Untried. My naivety laughs in my face. Having such a high position flashed at my ego didn't let me see the big picture. This is all Zaan's doing, no doubt. I joined the Tarrassian army to become a Warrior and go to actual War. They wanted me to forget all about that just because I was offered a cushy top position that keeps me safe inside the Camp. Probably the entire Council had a hand in this. Those fuckers wouldn't risk a fertile womb. Too bad their golden boy doesn't want to put his dick inside previously used vaginas. My heart doesn't find my joke funny, and more tears soak my face. It takes a while until I become aware of the giant winged guy looking like he wants to become invisible. He can't even make eye contact. Not that I blame him. I doubt his species drowns in self-pity.

"High Lady, the Queen is here to see you," says Hellaf, and I sit up looking behind him.

"What? No! Tell her I am not here, will you?" A dose of perfection is the last thing I need right now.

"Very well, High Lady, I will escort the Queen to the Sacred Garden," he says and disappears just as quick.

What the hell? Did he just ignore me? He will pay for this! What's wrong with these people? As I stand, the Marni removes its branches to allow it. I step away, and the trunk turns violet and solid again, hiding the magic inside. I quickly straighten my white Tarrassian dress and try to compose myself while waiting for Sia. Maybe I can look casual as if I am having a lovely day off work to do some... gardening. Stupid, of course. Whatever reason she is here can't be good.

A very pregnant Sia comes through the large glass doors, and I lose my anger. I keep forgetting she is almost five months pregnant and looks like she is carrying a small T-Rex in there. As far as we know, she might be the first Human ever to give birth to an alien baby. Despite all their advanced technology, a million things could go wrong. Same goes for Natalia. This is the elephant in the room we never talk about. Sia doesn't show it, but she must be scared.

The King, on the other hand, shows it a bit too much. The Healers curse the day they were born if the rumors are true. He makes them sleep outside her room and follow her around everywhere. Which is strange, considering her only companion today is the gorgeous High Commander of the Royal Guard. He stops a few steps behind her and gives me a stunning smile, fangs and all. Despite the perfectly trimmed beard covering his lower face, there is no hiding those dimples. Honestly, he is so beautiful he doesn't look real. But then again, neither does Sia. Even her huge belly is perfectly rounded, looking kind of cute behind the layers of her floaty lavender Tarrassian dress. Her eyes are grayer than I remember them, almost silver. Her long white hair has beautiful tiny braids in it, making her seem younger, somehow. And as always, she looks serene and regal, as if she floats above the ground rather than walks.

Their Astrals are so messed up and full of shit! The King is ... well, different. It would make so much more sense for perfect Sia to have perfect Sarrian as a mate. Those two would make the most beautiful babies in the universe, no doubt. Seeing them together in all their polished glory makes me wonder again how come the crazy King allows it.

"I am afraid I am too big for hugs," she says with a smile that softens her icy features. Instead, she should ask herself why she wants a hug in the first place. What happened to *The Ice Queen?*

I offer her a seat, and this time I actually remember to ask the kitchen for refreshments. Sarrian hovers around, obviously trying to give us privacy. Despite that, his eyes are always on Sia, as if he is analyzing even the air around her for dangers.

"Are you allowed to travel?" I ask, watching her trying to find a comfortable position.

"I didn't ask," she says, and I can hear a snort from Sarrian. She grins at him then they exchange a smile.

"My head might be rolling by the end of this span," says Sarrian, who doesn't look like he is that sorry for going behind the King's back. The mischief playing in his copper smiley eyes reminds me of Yara and her antics.

"I will be quick; the King doesn't have to know," she smiles at me. "I mean, I will tell him after because I don't like hiding things from him. I always tell him everything. Just later... much later," she says in her perfect British accent.

Despite what I was feeling only a few minutes ago, we both laugh. Maybe I needed a friend after all. Of course, my tree is a great company, but still.

"Do you want to talk about it, Gianna?" she asks, going straight to the point in typical Sia fashion. I choose to play dumb. I know she can see my swollen red eyes, and I-cried-myself-to-sleep face, but hopefully, she is only here because Kayon snitched on me.

"Which part, Sia?" I ask.

"Whatever you feel comfortable with telling me," she replies, observing me as if dissecting my brain. I hate it when she does that. "You can talk about Zaan and why you kicked him out in the middle of the night or the reasons for not attending the Pits today." I watch her in dismay. What the hell?

"Yes," she says with an apologetic smile, "Tarrassians love to gossip more than they love violence. And not just them. I think it is an alien thing. But, of course, Zaan's mother complaining to Jade about it probably didn't help the matter. And did I mention the two of them came to see me just before the sunrise?"

"God, Sia, I am so sorry!" I say. Crazy Jade!

"Not your fault, Gianna. The King had a word or two with them," she says with a bright smile exchanging an amused look with Sarrian.

"Anyway, I wanted you to know, the offer is there if you need to talk. Tarrassian men can be... challenging, infuriating, and..."

"Assholes?" I offer, and I don't care if Sarrian gets offended. He just shrugs and laughs it off.

"Yes, that too. Some more than others. I should know," she adds with a small sigh. "However, that is not the reason for my visit. I am here to tell you how proud I am of you. Not as your Queen, Human fellow, and not even as a friend. I am saying it as a woman on behalf of all the women out there, no matter what their species is called."

What on Earth is she saying? Sia is a genius-level kind of smart. Can't she see this so-called achievement for what it is?

"The day I visited you at the Pits, I noticed how the Warrior cubs and the Untried were looking up to you. The young and innocent are the same everywhere, no matter what planet they are from. They can see and feel what the adults have long forgotten. Where we take count of looks, garments, age, status, they only see the truth. It is not Kayon who chose you. It was the Untried, the cubs, the Marni Tree, the ones who can see inside a heart. Kayon told the Council, the Untried follow your lead the same way another generation of Warriors followed the High Elder many years ago. Tannon was nothing more than a cub himself when he trained Warriors like the King, the High General, the former and current Commanders of the Blood Fleet."

"My Queen, you can add one more Commander to that list," says Sarrian with a wide smile. Sia returns his smile then reaches for my hand resting on my lap.

"Tarrassia needs a new generation of Warriors able to stop what's coming," she says, and I wonder if she knows. Just like the High Elder.

The Tarrassians and all the other aliens seem to believe Sia has some great power. Hence, they are terrified of her. But, luckily, they love her just as much. Could Sia be the one special Human the High Elder can see in his *knowing*, as he calls it?

"Brilliant pupils can only shape the future because of the brilliant teachers who shaped their past," she says, ending her speech with a delicate sip of her flower tea, smiling at me over the golden rim of the cup.

And just like that, the fog is gone and I have purpose again. Maybe love and relationships are not for me. But Sia is right. I do belong at the Pits. Just not the way I imagined it. My father's greatest strength as a General was teaching his men. He used to say he welcomed lambs but delivered lions on the last day of training. I know I blamed him for so long, for creating those monsters. But that's just who they were to start with. That environment of power and testosterone only made their evil flourish, and no one noticed, or cared. If they did that to the General's daughter, I wonder what they did to hostages or to innocent civilians. I do know with all my heart, men like that are only a minority and I was just unfortunate to catch their interest. Most of the soldiers under my father's care turned out to be worthy of respect. They are the ones giving hell to the mighty Tarrassians from the shadows of the Resistance. Maybe I am more like my father than I thought.

I can't deny how much I love looking after the Untried, even though most of them are stronger than I am. Well, that is not exactly true. Their bodies may be strong, but their minds and spirits are not. The High Elder came to me for a reason. As he said, we mustn't ignore coincidences anymore. Not only is the New War here, but something even bigger is coming. So, I will not send my Unit to certain death. Not before they get their shit together!

"My Queen," says a less smiley Sarrian looking at his wrist com.

"Yes, High Commander, I know. The King is very vocal in my head at the moment. Let's be on our way before he comes here," replies Sia, as she uses all her strength to get up from her seat. She still manages to look graceful, as if that belly is just a fashion accessory.

"Good Lord, yes, please go," I say, already eyeing the doors. "No offense, your guy is a bit…" I start, but I don't finish. Probably I don't have to. She knows all too well.

"I will most likely see you at Natalia's Hen Party; please don't ask," she says with a sigh. "It's the British variant *of girls gone rogue*. And Jade is organizing it," she sighs again, and Sarrian groans to himself.

"How bad are we talking?" I dare ask.

"Jade ordered vodka and tequila from Earth…"

"Oh, that bad!"

"There is a silver lining," says Sarrian proving he spends way too much time around Humans. Also, he might be the only alien who gets our sayings. "If she misbehaves badly enough, the High General might lock her up again and this time hopefully for longer. An entire span rotation without Jade… bliss!"

We all laugh, and as they go on their way, Hellaf comes in. He is sheepish, which looks comical on someone that size. However, his earlier action only shows he cares for me, so I won't hold it against him.

"Please, prepare the ship, Hellaf. We're going to the Pits," I tell him, and my words are welcomed with a rare Kartassi smile.

42

—

GIANNA

As I soak my tired muscles under the velvety healing water of my bathing pool, I thank the genius alien mind who built such a wonder. I don't even know how late it is or how much sleep I'll get until I have to return to the Pits in the morning.

Time becomes irrelevant when someone is as busy or as tired as I am. It's good for the heartache, so I am very grateful for the unforgiving pace Kayon has set. The so-called hand-over took less than a day, and by the time I left that evening, people were addressing me as Master of the Untried. My mind still tells me this is weird, stupid, and very... weird and stupid. Like I said before, freaking aliens give you whiplash. Everything happens fast.

However, I owned it! *Fake it till you make it* has become my favorite motto. I only get away with it because the aliens are not aware of such a *refined strategy*. I couldn't fool a Human if I tried; luckily, there are none at the Pits. Soon, that may change, though. Every new Master of the Untried, just like all the newly appointed Masters, is allowed to install a new rule.

Mine was to open the training Pits to all the species that are part of the Coalition of the Seven Stars. An army has to fight as one. We need to collectively know our strengths and support our weaknesses. When the Warriors need to act fast or change strategies last minute, they have to do it as one. They must train together if they want to achieve any of that. Of course, the Pits will be open to only a few selected Warriors from the Coalition to start with due to space. Hopefully, Humans, too. Once they see the benefits, they will expand the grounds, and in time more will join.

I submitted my new rule to the Royal Council with all the details and backup plans. And best of all, I had it typed in Tarrassian, thanks to Sia's super brain. I waited anxiously outside the Council Cave as a decision was made inside. Jade may listen to everything from the secret passage, and Sia may barge in whenever she pleases because she is the Queen. I, however, am a soldier, Warrior these days, and I follow the hierarchy of power.

To my surprise and horror, the High General came out to give me the verdict. It shouldn't have been strange; he is the Commander of the army. I respond to him like every other Warrior. But my god, he is scary! Not giant Viking, wild-alien type of scary, like the other Tarrassians. Yes, he does have all that, but that's not it. It's the type of scary that comes from inside. He could be as tiny as Natalia and still put the fear of God into people. No wonder Jade has the hots for the guy. She is all about bad boys; nothing has changed there since Earth. But why can't she tell this one is an upgrade to a regular bad boy? And he is a fucking pedophile; I keep remembering that. The only thing I like about the guy is that Zaan hates him. The enemy of my enemy and all that. The High General handed me a massive document with the Royal Army insignia on it and stared me down with the emptiest, coldest eyes I have ever seen. *Do not mess up!* That is all he said before returning to the Cave. I had worse problems since then, so that's that.

Shockingly my new rule started immediately, as they like it around here, and loads of new aliens joined both the Untried and the cubs. There is new tension and ego battles, mainly from the overbearing Tarrassians and their alpha bullshit. Still, I am surprised to say I dealt with it better than expected. I am not stupid; I know it's mainly because I am a woman; I am mated to their High Master and because of the Marni shinai. Still, it works, and I would like to believe some respect in there has been earned.

I've been training like a possessed woman and not just at the Pits. At home, too. Now that I am comfortable with the equipment, I use it every evening. I also spar with the Kartassi guards using the Marni shinai swords. I am only allowed to use the deadly Tarrassian one when training with Kayon. No one really told me who made that stupid rule, and I am not going to ask.

Kayon joins me twice a week for sparring during my evening session at home. He is a perfect mixture of fatherly patience and kick-ass sensei, so my progress is fast and steady. Despite being stuck with a future inside the Camp, I am still attending the Flight Module. And smashing it, may I add. I am the Master of the Untried, so I have to rule by example. Respect must be earned, and so far, I haven't done a bad job at all. I can see it in Kayon's eyes, but my greatest achievement must be Ronnin. The Ninja kid stopped sassing me. Considering he talks back at all the other Pit Masters, that is quite the achievement. His respect is a rare bird.

All in all, things are better than expected, and I find myself eager to return to the Pits early every morning. And not just because while I am there, my stupid marks and Sign don't hurt. At times the pain leaves me breathless, and I have to apply healing gel to the burns. It soothes the sting but not the deep-bone pain. And it's only getting worse, I can tell. At least it's proof he is not stalking me as before, and he is finally gone. Probably he lives with his parents now, considering Talla has stopped all contact. I miss her more than words and it hurts to think she might hate me. I am just happy he's out of the Marni house. *Yes, I really am.*

None of that luxury at the Pits. Honestly, doesn't he have work to do? I know I do. He is always in my face, always fucking watching. I ignore him and pretend not to notice. Occasionally he approaches me with matters of the Pits, and I am always polite when answering since he is my superior and all that. I avoid being alone with him like the plague. To be fair, everybody does at the moment. His temper makes the King look like a saint. I guess that's what happens when you go around with blue balls, brown balls, or whatever, just because you are too good for anyone. Fuck him! I have better things to worry about.

There are only two days left until Natalia and Tannon's wedding, and it seems as if the entire planet has gone mad. Not sure if it's the thrill of an Astral's Mating Ceremony or the arrival of the third moon. The cosmic event only happens once a year, and now they have an actual Astral to bless the Moon Ceremonies. That's all the Tarrassians talk about at the moment. Apparently, the event triggers other space phenomena all around the galaxies. The night sky is brighter than ever, but the best thing must be the Astral Lights. That is what they call it, but we also have a name for it on Earth. Aurora Borealis. Trust Tarrassians to think this is only something that happens on their planet. I do have to admit, it is better than the Earth variant. It lasts all night, and the colors are so bright, you don't even have to look up at the sky. The entire planet is enveloped in a sensory show of colors. And since all their buildings are made of mirrored metal, it feels as if someone lit the Planet up in flames. Unless I pull the curtains, my bedroom is like a disco at night. Just what a *cheerful* High Lady needs.

I miss Ollianna more than expected, but she's turned out to be a real gem to Natalia. I don't think any scheming has happened yet, as Ollianna still looks sad, despite being excited by the coming celebrations. It turns out Princess Umbelina and Ollianna are the best event organizers ever, and I am happy Natalia has less to worry about. There is some tension, and I know both Sia and Natalia feel guilty. Because the Princess is always around, Jade keeps her distance, and I think she feels betrayed. She hides it well behind jokes and her usual crazy, but we know her well enough by now. And then, there was the Hen Party. It was a disaster, all right, just not the way Sia expected it.

Of course, the Princess had to attend, which triggered Jade's insecurities and mine, to be fair. To call Umbelina beautiful would be a crime. There should be a different term for all that ethereal, alien perfection. She would kill it as a high-fashion model on Earth. Who needs hair or boobs when you look like an experiment of anime meets alien fairy? And, of course, there is her perfect southern debutante behavior to top it all. Unlike Talla, this one doesn't fake it or mock it. She acts as if she is sweet perfection. *Well, fucking Zaan thinks she is, anyway.* Jade attended the Hen Party for less than twenty minutes then rushed out all teared up. Yes, there was some vodka involved, but still. Okay, maybe there was a lot of vodka.

I think Jade and I need to work on that liquor delivery from Earth and have a night out or in of our own. Just us, the damaged Humans, no perfect Tarrassian wants.

I finally allow my sore, tired body to leave the bathing pool. Without Ollianna here, the rest of the Marni people try to stay out of my way. They don't offer to help unless I ask for it. No one says anything, but I know they are not happy. I kicked their golden boy out. It's my right, so they can stuff it!

I could have done more with soaking my aching muscles in the healing water, but the bathing pool is a danger zone. It is the one place where I cannot fight the memory of him or my feelings. I didn't think missing someone could hurt more than broken bones. It is as if there is not enough air in the world without him. The world is tight around me and my insides are hollow. How long can I last like this? I would beg him if that changed anything. Begging won't wipe my past off or make me worthy, so there is no point. Fuck him! I still put on his shirt as I get ready for bed, only because it somehow calms my Sign. For no other reason.

My hollocom starts beeping like a bad omen. An unreasonable fear makes my stomach twist. Natalia calls this late sometimes, so I try to calm down as I approach the Com Unit on the wall. An unknown line shows on the glass panel, and what is more, the signal comes from outside Tarrassia. Could it be my father? I accept the call and take a few good steps back. I already know calls from the central wall unit bring out a real-life hologram of the other person. It is weird as hell; as if they are in the room with you.

This time, it is damn right scary, and I almost fall down on my backside. *I am a Warrior, a Master of the Tarrassian army, and I will hold it together,* I keep telling myself as one of my nightmares comes to life under my eyes: an enormous red and menacing horror. The Moorri King smiles at me, revealing sharp white fangs.

"High Lady of House Marni, or Master of the Untried, which one do you prefer?" he asks with that deep voice so suitable for a demon. "Or shall I just call you my *Special One*, like before?"

I brave my irrational fear to find my voice. It is only a hologram. He can't touch me.

"What do you require, Moorri King? This is highly inappropriate. I am a mated female, and it is very late."

"It is bright and early where I am, my *Special One*. As for the mated part, rumors travel fast around the galaxies," he says with an unpleasant smirk. *Great! Fucking aliens love to gossip!* He crosses his huge arms to watch me with his pleased red stare.

Bulging muscles covered in bright red skin remind me how close I was to death or worse, at his hands.

"What do you want, Moorri King?" I ask again, trying to stay strong. I am tempted to interrupt the call, but something tells me I want to hear him.

"I want a Human female," he says as if that's the most common request. I remember this is a slave owner, so to him, that is a common request. Anger replaces all my fear, and I suddenly wish he wasn't just a hologram. My Marni shinai would look beautifully matched with his red skin as I break his fucking bones!

"I am not in the slave trade; you reached out to the wrong species."

"I believe I reached the right source. The Noorranni slavers are useless. Since your crazy King took Earth, they don't have any Humans for sale," he says, and I can't help laughing. For a second, he looks like an oversized toddler having a meltdown. His favorite toy is out of stock!

"Do I look like I have Humans to sell, King Moorri? Did all that bling in your Palace finally burn your brain?" I say, and to my surprise, he laughs.

"Yes, my people like ridiculous displays of wealth. I only enjoy my slaves if it helps," he shrugs.

"It fucking doesn't!" I shout. This is ridiculous; I am ending this call and block his red ass. I haven't done that before, but I am sure it works the same as on Earth.

"You are a Human, so you must have access to a female of your species," he continues talking as if I work for him or something. "I don't care if you have to trick a female or pay a willing one. I would prefer the latter and avoid any problems with the Coalition of the Seven Stars. I will transfer to you whatever funds you require. There is no limit on the price."

I can see he is serious. There is no grin left, and he is all business now. The Moorri are famous for their trading skills, and despite his red leather attire, horns, fangs, and forked tail, something about him makes him look like a CEO from Earth. Some of my people who happen to hate the billionaires might find his demon look entirely appropriate.

"Why would I want to do that, Moorri King?" I tell him, honestly amused. Aliens are strange, and you never know. Maybe this one thinks we are friends or something.

"Because you might want Mirri back in one piece," he says, making my blood freeze. I watch quietly as he lifts his hand up as if trying to reach for something. In the background, one of his demon guards shoves a heavily chained Mirri at him. She bumps into his hard body and winces in pain.

"Gianna, please don't! Whatever he asks for, don't do it!" she screams at the camera but then cries out in pain as he grabs her neck from behind and pushes her down on her knees by his feet.

"A willing Human for the life of this useless Moorri female you seem to like so much. Not exactly a bad deal, my Special One, is it?" he asks with an evil grin.

As he waits for my answer, his hand squeezes more and more at Mirri's neck, and I can see her trying to contain her pain. My brain works a million miles per minute. He will kill her. Life means nothing to them, and Mirri is already a pariah on Moorra. They sold her as a whore, and he will give her a slow, painful death. I have heard of the terrible torture rituals they practise. The Moorri love inflicting pain, and I won't allow it for Mirri. She is not only my friend and a minor; she is one of my Untried. And nobody fucks with the Warriors in my care.

"As it happens, you are in luck, Moorri King," I start talking calmly. "I already have a Human female available and willing."

He watches me with suspicion but invites me to carry on with a very regal hand gesture.

"There is an unmated Human female on Tarrassia," I say, and I see the horror in Mirri's eyes. She hates Jade's guts, but despite her Moorri legacy, she is too decent to wish her harm. To my surprise, she reveals a different reason for her worry.

"No, Gianna, please. He won't survive the pain of losing Jade. And I won't survive his," she says quietly. Her voice turns to screams as the red asshole grabs her ponytail and twists hard.

"What is happening here? If you two even think of communicating behind my back, the Moorri whore dies right now!" he shouts at me with that booming voice. I hope the Kartassi guards don't come barging in.

I obviously can't tell Mirri this is only a trick. Why would I send any woman to this asshole, never mind one of my friends? My mind surprised me with a quick plan, and now I have to make sure it happens. The closer I keep it to reality, the better.

"There is no deceiving, Moorri King, and there will be no payment required for this particular female. However, she is my friend, and I don't want her harmed. This is not negotiable. You cannot hurt her."

"What if she likes it?" he asks, and I roll my eyes.

"Then she will tell me so herself," I say. "There are conditions you must accept. I don't want to go against the Royal Council, and neither do you. The female hasn't been mated yet, but that doesn't stop the Tarrassians from hoping she might ignite the Sign and birth cubs one day. They will take you to war if you take her by force or harm her. Jade is not a slave. If she chooses you willingly, there is nothing they can do about it." I finish talking and give him time to digest the information. He looks suspicious, troubled, and damn right puzzled.

"Why would she choose me willingly?" he asks, and I struggle not to laugh. Why indeed?

"Jade is not happy on Tarrassia, nobody likes her here, and she loves bling," I say, and a trace of a smile makes his devilish features look very Human.

"Is this one of the Humans you were taken with?"

"Yes, the one with the big boobs," I say because I am sure he remembers that. Don't they all?

"Is she still pale? I don't like pale," he says, and I really want to pinch myself. I can't believe I am even having this conversation. "And does that mean I have to mate her legally?" he adds, and I insist because he has to believe this is an actual transaction.

"Yes, if you make her your Queen, the Council can't do anything about it, real love and all that." He snorts, and I can't blame him. Love sucks!

"Why is she not happy on Tarrassia, and why do they dislike her?" he asks, observing me for signs of lying. So, I tell him the truth.

"She is unhappy because nobody wants to fuck her, and they dislike her because she bites people," I say, and boy is that a winner!

"She sounds perfect. I will take her," he says and lets go of Mirri's hair.

"Please, Gianna, don't! She means everything to him," she says, and the King pushes her out of my sight back to the guards.

"What is she talking about? You said the Human is not mated," he says, and the suspicion is back. Once again, I go with the truth.

"The High General of Tarrassia wants this female for himself. He can't have her because he already has a promised mate."

His evil smile takes over his features, and his eyes glow as brightly as my marks. Forget a winner. This is pure gold. The Moorri's eyes are just as expressive as ours. It is easy to see the sense of victory in there.

"If you give me the female *he* wants, my *Special One*, not only can you have Mirri back, but you can ask for any other favors. My Palace and the Moorri people will always be at your service," he says, proving me right. I am trying not to show how pleased I am with this new development. His hate and whatever personal history he might share with the Tarrassian General will make him ignore the alarm bells. He will fall straight into my trap because his emotions will get the best of him. Good thing everybody hates the High General.

"We have to keep this as secret as possible, King Moorri; I hope you understand," I tell him. "Once Jade is with you on Moorra, she can call the Council and explain to them, herself. Maybe you should send Mating Ceremony invites to make it look genuine. There will be no mention of Mirri's involvement or mine," I say, and he nods quietly in agreement.

If he had any doubts, they have all been quieted by the prospect of taking the High General's woman. Men and their egos!

"Let's make the exchange in two days when the Moon Ceremonies are in place. Everybody will be distracted, not to mention attending the High Elder's Mating Ceremony. We will meet in space at a location of my choosing. You can board my ship," I say, unwilling to admit I don't know how to board his. I didn't get that far in my Flight Module.

"I will come alone, and you will do the same. The deal is off otherwise. I cannot risk any witnesses," I say, and he actually believes me. I thank God for his arrogance. He thinks I am no threat.

"I will give you Jade in exchange for Mirri. It is needless to say, you must keep her unharmed until then. I will cut your red balls off, otherwise," I say, and he bursts into laughter.

"You will always be my *Special One*," he says with a sly grin, and I refrain from another eye roll.

43

GIANNA

I am very grateful to the alien woman, whatever her species is, helping with my dress. There is no way my shaky fingers could do anything right now. I need to calm the hell down! Not an easy task, considering I am in my idea of hell. We are all in Sia's Royal Quarters, getting ready for the craziest ass wedding I have ever heard of. It is probably comical to see women from so many species acting equally crazy over color-matching underwear and make-up. There is a lot of skin in several shades and textures on display as we all try to get into our dresses.

Jade and I were supposed to be the only bridesmaids as that is not even a Tarrassian thing. But trust Natalia, Miss Popularity, to have no more no less than fifteen. Ollianna is the latest addition, and she looks just as overwhelmed with the honor as the others. Oh, and we are all wearing pink dresses. It is painful to watch. Like, literally. It gives one a headache. I don't know if they provide favor bags here for the guests, but there should be aspirin in all of them.

The only male allowed in the middle of the pink hell is Sarrian. He watches everything with a charming but otherwise unphased smile. If I ever had any doubts about his sexual preferences, I can kiss them goodbye now. Tarrassians are born horny; there is no way any of them would survive so much skin on display. His bored expression makes it very clear he is only here because of Sia.

I was surprised when Hellaf took me to the Royal Palace instead of Natalia's home. I am sure someone said the wedding would be held in the High City, but I forgot with so many things on my mind.

It doesn't change my plans. It makes no difference if Jade and I leave from here or from the White Palace. There are even more ships to help myself to here. And since now I am a Warrior, I can do just that with my own identity chip. Also, I was right; this chaos is the perfect distraction. No one would notice if Jade and I went for a stroll or fell off the roof, for that matter. *Jade...* I remember with a sigh and an internal groan.

I watch her slapping at an alien woman's hand, pretending to snap her teeth at her fingers. The poor woman runs away screaming, even though she is twice as big and strong as Jade. And Natalia's moms shouldn't encourage her. One of them, I think Laura, high-fives her every time she's out of line. My crazy Human is one of the many reasons my stomach has been in knots for the last two days. I went from worrying Jade won't be willing to help with my little plan to worrying she is suspiciously keen. I knew things were not going well as soon as I finished telling her about Mirri and my deal with the Moorri King.

Her first and only words were: *Is he hot?* I wanted to face-slap myself and throttle her at the same time.

I tried to convince her this was not a joke. A million things could go wrong. Even if he comes alone as promised, he is still an alien at least twice my size. According to my latest research, the Moorri are outstanding fighters and naturally strong. Jade is way too excited about a break in her boring routine and something else I can't put my finger on. There is a desperation to her as if she is about to do something ridiculous. She reminds me of me, and that is never a good thing. It makes everything worse, and my determination feels deflated somehow. So does my confidence.

What am I doing? Other than breaking all Zaan's rules and risking Jade's and Mirri's lives, of course. I blame my confusion on being tired and the unbearable pain in my marks; since it's a holiday and everybody has time off, I haven't been around him since yesterday. How am I going to manage the following days without him? Do these people need to celebrate for an entire week? Would he come to the Ceremony tonight? Even if he does, I won't be there for long. Would he notice my absence? Would he care? It is so strange to go from sleeping in someone's arms to not knowing where they are.

"Hey, *Warrior Queen*, are we still on for tonight? I love this shit! I always wanted to play Bond girl," Jade's voice whispers in my ear.

Oh, dear Lord!

"Is that Tarrassian wine I can smell on your breath, Jade? Really?" I say, trying to keep my voice down. We are surrounded by people.

"Of course not, love, who do you take me for? It's V.A.T.," she says with a wink and a giggle.

"What the hell is V.A.T.?" I ask, even though I am sure I don't want to know.

"Vodka and tonic. Well, technically it's vodka and the piss they call wine around here. I forgot to order tonics from Earth. But these little shits say Tarrassian wine has tonic powers, so…"

She gives me one of her bubbly waves of laughter that make her boobs and hips jiggle and brainwash men. As for me, I am kind of speechless. What was I even thinking? Jade is a loose cannon. And to be fair, so am I.

"Hey," she says, looking around to make sure no one is listening. "I know people don't make much of me, but I can assure you I can be responsible. Well, sometimes. I know this is important to you. No idea why you like *Ketchup Girl*, but hey, that's your problem. I am as ready as it gets for tonight, and I won't let you down. You will have your favorite brand of ketchup back, one way or another," she says, adding more layers to my anxiety.

Why do I have the feeling this crazy woman is considering handing herself to the Moorri guy for real.

"Listen, Jade, I know you are unhappy and probably heartbroken." *It takes one to know.* "But the Moorri King is not the answer. He is a very dangerous man. There is no coming back once you belong to him. Punishing yourself for your circumstances doesn't help." *Again, it takes one to know.* "If you want to come along tonight, you will do what you're told and keep yourself safe," I tell her in my Master of the Untried voice. It is not lost on me; I sound just like Zaan.

"Yeah, yeah, no worries, love. I have one thing to do, and then I am all yours, one way or the other," she says, continuing with the cryptic shit that scares the hell out of me.

Cold, smooth fingers grab my hand, and I register Sia is pulling me somewhere. The sea of alien women draped in pink, parts and I gasp in wonder. I know Natalia is beautiful, but tonight she is more than that. She looks like a Russian doll meets fantasy fairy. Her dress is not pink, imagine that, but pure white and I try to remember if it's because she followed the Human tradition. Or maybe Tarrassians also prefer white for the bride. Her dress follows the usual style, low cut and off the shoulders, corset-wrapped waist, and tons of floaty fabric reaching the floor. The more material, the more vertical slits from hips to the ankles, and her dress is no exception. The fabric is different, though, reminding me of the Garrii's skin. It's so shimmery; under the light, it looks as if it's changing colors.

Her massive mane of red curls has been tamed in a half-updo, most likely Jade's work, and intricate braids adorn her temples and crown. Hundreds of white feathers have been stylishly added to her braids. I spent enough time in her home to know those come from the Oria birds.

Her pregnancy doesn't show yet, and her petite frame makes her look more like a flower girl than an actual bride. Well, this flower girl can tame Sphinxes, melt Astrals, and change ancient laws with a giggle and a flutter of her long lashes. This evening she is emotional, more than usual, that is, and her small face looks all flustered. It makes her freckles stand out, and her doll-like blue eyes look brighter than the triple moons.

"Oh, Bozhe Moi! Gianna, you look beautiful!" she says because it's very much like her not to notice her own looks. "Maybe you should consider pink from now on. It really suits you," she says and gives me one of her legendary hugs. More germs have been exchanged in this room tonight than in the entire universe.

"Or maybe I'll pass," I reply, and we all laugh. She does have a point. The mirror reflects back at me a stunning young woman looking like a dream in pink. But c'mon! Golden hair, lime green eyes, brown skin, glowing red tattoos, and a pink dress? No, thank you!

"Ladies, shall we gather for a picture? Maybe just the four of us to start with," says Sia, and all the alien women step aside at once.

I try not to look at Talla just like I did all day. She's been avoiding me in the most obvious way possible, making everyone feel uncomfortable. Tact is not her thing. I sense no malice in her behavior; she is genuinely sad and probably can't understand what's happening. That makes two of us.

One of the Royal attendants takes pictures of the four of us, using some alien device that doesn't look like it's doing anything. Then one of Natalia's moms takes more using a good old-fashioned polaroid. Of course, Natalia welcomes it with giggles and claps.

"Look at us," says Sia. "We've come so far from that cold metal table we woke up strapped to."

"Count me out, *Elsa*. I slept through all that rubbish. I think my brain could tell the Noorranni were not hot," says Jade, but only Natalia's moms and Talla find it funny. Typical.

I personally find it rather sad. I think the other girls do, too. They must be able to tell the pain behind Jade's crazy jokes. And I can imagine how she must feel. She is the only Human without mating marks or a mate, for that matter. Well, there is also Brian, but he's been trapped in the healing pod for months. Not to mention he's a guy. We don't know if this thing can happen to men. Jade must feel like the odd one out. This only adds to the knots in my stomach. *What am I doing?* I ask myself again.

For a while, all I do is follow the Ceremony routine. There is so much shit involved, I am grateful Jade and I are not the only bridesmaids. When there are another fourteen of you, one can afford to make mistakes. The last years of my life were manic. Always surrounded by people, fans, paparazzi, noise, you name it. I shouldn't find all this so overwhelming. Maybe because deep down at heart, I will always be the home-schooled girl with no friends. I try to be a good sport and go with the flow. This is about Natalia, not me.

It is hard to ignore myself, though. My painful marks and Sign tell me Zaan is not here. If anything, he is further away than usual, as the pain has turned into a burning sensation. Fuck him! I could do with all of my strength tonight if I am to fight the Moorri King.

I need to rush this, but how does anyone rush the Elder of the Spark Mountain? He is the one running the Ceremony, and he looks to be about four hundred years old. Just great! After a while, it gets too emotional to remember my own predicament, and I am trying to fight tears. Natalia's two moms certainly don't mind crying. They are a mess as they escort her down an aisle longer than Denver International before giving her over to Tannon. They spent the afternoon with Jade, so there might be some V.A.T. in the mix. To my surprise, Natalia doesn't cry at all. No giggles, either. She is serene, a soft smile on her lips and her eyes shine like stars as she looks at Tannon. They only have eyes for each other. I bet they can't even tell they are surrounded by hundreds of people.

It messes with me... It's not some stupid jealousy, of course. Just because I am miserable and unloved, it doesn't mean I wish it on others. I look briefly at Jade. This must be hard for her, too. Okay, maybe it's worse for her. She is acting... strange. She is fidgety, anxious, and very unlike herself. Her behavior reminds me of my own when I stupidly decided to escape from the Blood Fleet.

Suddenly I feel like everything is too much, and I close my eyes to block it all, hoping nobody notices. A thought comes to mind, and I am tempted to reach out to Zaan. Just to ask if he is okay. His marks must hurt, too, and maybe I can... God, I miss him so much! *Where are you? Don't you care at all?* There is no point pretending I can carry on with this silly plan of mine. I can't break his rules. I really can't. I must tell him about Mirri and trust him to keep her safe. A million things could go wrong with my initial plan, but most of all, it means I'll be doing things behind his back. Lying, hiding the truth, getting away from Tarrassia, putting myself in danger... basically all the things he hates. I can't, I won't!

Zaan? I must talk to you, please. It's urgent.

My brain tries to connect with him, making my decision for me. I don't regret it. It is the right one. Maybe this is what he needs. Proof of my loyalty. He must know I can respect and follow the rules. No more punishing me or whatever it is he is doing. A pang of pain twists my stomach. He said he would always answer when I call. Yet, he doesn't. All this hot and cold is messing me up. Can't he tell how much he hurts me?

A loud noise makes me open my eyes to an explosion of light. The entire ballroom, or whatever they call it, is inundated with light coming from... everywhere, it seems. It takes me a while to understand what it is. It's coming from outside, through the giant glass windows and doors leading to the terraces surrounding the hall. At first, I wonder if it's the Tarrassian version of fireworks, but no. Trust them to have an actual cosmic phenomenon as the centerpiece. The third moon joins the other two. The mirror-like Palace reflects all the colors of the Tarrassian version of Aurora Borealis, amplifying the explosion of light. It's beautiful, and there is no denying the magic of the world at this very moment. It only makes me even more aware of being lonely and... unwanted.

The ritual part of the Mating Ceremony is over, so now it's time for the celebrations to begin. A whole week of them. Before I got my wits back, this would have been my cue to grab Jade, the weapons I hid in my guest room, and make my way around the galaxy to save Mirri. Just saying it makes me cringe at my stupidity. The old me could totally justify such actions. The new me follows the rules and embraces a more reasonable behavior.

Speaking of which, I am sticking as close as possible to Jade. She is up to something, and since I watch her like a hawk, I can see the disaster about to happen. She downs another glass of whatever pink concoction and starts walking with intent towards the middle of the large ballroom. There are hundreds of beings in her way, but they part like the sea for Moses. Her short, curvy body seems larger than life, and the determination on her heart-shaped face makes everyone step aside, despite the fact they all tower over her. She looks like a hellcat on a mission, and I follow her closely, trying not to lose sight of her. I think the other people notice something is about to unfold, and there is a wave of awareness going through the room. I catch Sia's silver eyes over the alien crowd, then Natalia's. There is a pleading in both pairs saying only one thing: *Get her out of here!* Roger that.

As I get closer to her, I can see exactly where she is going. Or rather who she is heading for. Shit! The High General is talking to his mate, Princess Umbelina, blissfully unaware of the storm coming for him. He notices soon enough though and turns to face her, looking perfectly still in his pristine uniform. He watches Jade approach him with cold yet very golden eyes. The Princess finally notices Jade and takes a few steps back, lowering her eyes.

I think the whole room becomes aware of Jade as the noise has suddenly died down. She never takes her eyes off his as she comes within touching distance. There is a very crazy grin on her beautiful red lips. Almost a dare. She is trying to prove a point to him, and I suddenly understand. They never touched! I hold my breath as she takes his left hand into hers. I think the entire room holds its breath. In the sudden silence and because I am right next to them, I can hear the sizzle of skin being burned alive. Green and silver lights ignite their two hands where they touch. A swirl of glowing green fire starts wrapping around their upper palms, wrists and then… it stops. Jade finally takes her eyes off his to look at their connected hands. I wish she didn't. I also wish I could grab her away now and take her somewhere safe away from prying eyes and from the worst kind of pain someone in love can feel. Rejection.

As she looks at their hands, his marks fade as if his skin absorbs them back. Within seconds there is only a faint redness left on his upper palm and wrist, no more than a skin rash. Her swirls are just as bright as when they sparked, but they are not moving up her arm, following the usual pattern of the Sign. There is no Sign. He rejected *It* and *her* in front of everyone. Finally, her big green eyes look up from their hands to search his. Even I can see there is nothing there, and the gold is gone. She keeps looking at him with an imploring stare, waiting for mercy that will never come. It is painful to watch someone as confident and vibrant as Jade, being reduced to the plea in her beautiful eyes.

"Come, Jade, let's go," I say, and I grab her arm gently. Her skin is so hot it feels as if it's burning my fingers, but I don't let go. As she finally allows me to pull her away from him, I see the other unwilling victim of this fucking man. Behind him, the beautiful Tarrassian Princess looks just as broken as Jade. She leaves the room quietly at the same time as us, but in a different direction. The silence is crushing, and thanks to God, I can hear Sia's calm voice inviting everyone to continue the celebrations. Nothing happens for a second, then the King adds a booming, NOW. Instantly all the noise is back, and the party resumes as if it never stopped. It makes it easier to drag out a very unresponsive Jade. We finally reach her room, through the Palace's labyrinth, but she prevents me from entering.

"Are we leaving now?" she asks.

"What? Of course not, Jade. And not because of what happened. I decided it was too dangerous, and I have already asked Zaan to deal with it." I add a little half-lie. He never allowed the mind connection because, you know... rejection and all that. Jade doesn't need the details.

"Okay, love, you know where I am if you change your mind," she says, sounding suspiciously like herself.

"Are you okay? I can stay with you tonight, and you need to apply healing gel to those," I say, looking at her marks. They are beautiful. The green swirls have a silver lining like a cloud, and they look like waves, I think. I suddenly remember his grandfather is the Elder of the Waters, and it all makes sense. What a loser; how can he reject this? Her? I hope the Council kicks his ass. Their Sign is sacred, and he just killed it.

"Sure thing, love. Why the fuck wouldn't I be? Because of this?" she asks, looking down at her hand. "Oh please, I have had far worse shit than this. Trailer-park girl, here, or whatever you call it in America. My lot? We're always fucking okay. Now go kick some alien arse, *Warrior Queen*, or whatever it is you do for fun. I need my fucking beauty sleep."

With that, she closes her door in my face. I somehow believe her. She will be okay because Jade doesn't take shit from anyone. I will let her lick her wounds tonight, and tomorrow we can hit the V.A.T. together.

This still leaves my other issue: Mirri. Fucking Zaan is giving me the silent treatment, and I am running out of time. Who can I ask to deal with the Moorri King? My own answer makes me groan. He is the last person I want to talk to right now, but Mirri's life matters more than my hatred for the man.

44

—

GIANNA

I easily spot the High General back in the banquet hall. Not a difficult job, as there is always some gap around him as if people don't want to come too close. I wish I could do the same. He scans the crowd as if trying to find someone. Is he looking for Jade? He sees me coming and stops, waiting for me to reach him. I brace myself as I give him the Tarrassian salute. I might be wearing a pink dress, but this is an army-related issue. He ignores it and doesn't greet me back. And I thought Zaan was rude.

"Jade is in her quarters," I say foolishly, thinking he cares.

"Good, let's hope the Human stays there and doesn't disturb the Ceremony any more. Thank you for removing her. I am looking for Princess Umbelina. Have you seen her anywhere?"

I am trying my best not to snap. I am telling myself all the reasons I shouldn't, from him being my General to Mirri's life being on the line.

"No, High General, I haven't seen the Princess," I say with a calm voice. The soldier in me has taken over my emotions; thank God, for that. "I understand this is not a good time, but I have an urgent issue to discuss with you. It is a matter of security, High General."

"Follow me," he orders and already turns his back. Wow! This guy could teach my dad a trick or two. I follow his wide shoulders through the crowd until we reach a strange round room. There is no furniture in here, and there are no windows. Just bare copper walls.

"Speak," he barks another order.

"The Moorri King has taken Mirri prisoner," I start and pause to wait for a reaction. Only there isn't one. Cold. Dead. Eyes. That's all I get, so I continue explaining. "He wants a Human female as payment for Mirri's life." Once again, I wait, getting increasingly nervous. The guy's lack of reaction is unnerving. Is he even alive in there? "I have the coordinates where the so-called exchange was supposed to take place," I explain, bracing myself for what comes next. *How does one tell a General I was going to go rogue and stupid?* "The plan was to trick the Moorri King into thinking he was getting a Human, then take Mirri off him by force. Yes, I know what it sounds like, High General," I add with a sigh.

"Human foolishness?" He offers an answer to my dilemma. I can't exactly argue, as he is right. "Why would the Moorri King want an already mated female, Master of the Untried?"

Shit! Here comes the fun part.

"Well, I didn't offer myself, High General. Jade wanted to help, so…"

"Did she now?" he asks, but I don't think he wants an answer. "I am pleasantly surprised to see you fought your silly Human instincts and chose to behave responsibly," he says. Is this his idea of a compliment? "You would have walked into a trap. The Moorri King was never going to let Mirri go. She shamed him publicly so he will have to punish her. Also, publicly. Her family didn't sell her to the Yellow Planets. That is just part of the cover to keep her safe. Mirri is a Moorri Princess, and she was to become the King's mate, unwillingly, of course. She ran away and was caught by the Bartassi pirates. They sold her to the Yellow Planets, and luckily, I was there when it happened. I paid their fees and brought her to Tarrassia. Thank you for bringing this matter to me, Master of the Untried. I will deal with it and make sure the Moorri King learns a lesson. A painful one."

I just nod and wait. For the first time, he looks less... dead, as if he wants to say something that actually matters to him.

"I would like to ask a favor from the High Lady of House Marni," he says, and again, I nod. Too scared to breathe. What if he kills me after if I see a breach in his impenetrable mask?

"I would like you to offer shelter and a home to Mirri. I care deeply for her but living under my roof has only increased her cub-like infatuation with me. She started to spread rumors about us having a relationship in an attempt to force my hand. And while, I do not care about my reputation; I care about hers. She is a bright young cub with her whole life ahead of her. I believe she will flourish under your care."

I can't say I saw that coming. So much easier to hate this guy when I thought he was a pedophile. He is still an asshole, though, as he has not even bothered to ask about Jade. I quickly give him my answer; of course, I would love to have Mirri. Without Ollianna there, I don't have too many friends in the Marni house. And I have a feeling Ollianna won't be coming back.

I feel so relieved as I leave the High General. I know now this would have been a huge mistake. I suddenly remember Ollianna's words. *We don't follow his rules out of fear but because they keep us safe.* Right so. Now, if he could only see I have indeed changed. I am not the same silly girl running from herself. I spot just the person I need. She makes a comical attempt to avoid me, but it's not happening.

"Hanni, Mother." I go straight for the big guns. I know it is the Tarrassian custom to address your in-laws as you would your own parents. She just melts under my eyes.

"Oh, my beautiful daughter, are you well? I don't understand what is happening. Zaan is unhappy and won't talk to me, and I cannot help thinking this must somehow be Diran's fault. The Elder is not to be trusted; he is not helping with this matter, saying you two must find your own answers. How silly. Isn't that what parents do? The Elder looks all trusty and wise, but I tell you he is a pain to live with."

I try not to laugh as I take her hands into mine in a pleading gesture.

"Talla, do you know where Zaan is?"

"Yes, my daughter, I do," she says with a relieved smile. "He is on planet Wallani watching the Lorra Moon. It is at its brightest when the Astral Moons get together. Sadly, it can only be enjoyed this dark span. Planet Wallani will release its toxic gases on the next span, at sunrise. That could also be Diran's fault. The Elder is determined there is no magic involved in the phenomena. He calls everything science, and maybe he made the Astrals angry. I think..."

"Thank you, Mother," I say, giving her a quick hug and turning away as fast and as far as possible. It is the only way one can end a conversation with Talla. Out of all the many things she said, only one registered. Toxic gases. That mixed with his refusal to let me inside his mind... well, I have to wonder. And worry. And lose my shit! He wouldn't dare do that to me, would he? My reasonable mind tells me that not only is Zaan not the type to do that, but he also would never cause me any harm. He knows very well the Sign could kill me in his absence. What he doesn't know is I would die long before that if anything happened to him. God, I hate him so much! What if he gets distracted or falls asleep and doesn't leave before the gases release?

I am already on my way to the Palace's docking bays because

how hard can it be? I am still not able to fly a spaceship manually, but I am sure the MI can solve that problem. It's not like I haven't done it before. And that's when I stop walking and turn around. The last time I pulled that trick didn't exactly go down well with Zaan. Do I need more punishment? Nope, not at all. Kayon. That's who I need. Hellaf is a chicken. Without Zaan's permission, he will not take me off the planet. Assuming he can even perform deep space flight.

I find Kayon surrounded by his family. His daughter and son welcome me as if I am one of their own while he watches our interaction with a big proud smile. He is not going to like this. I pull him to one of the outdoor platforms and tell him about my predicament. I am sure he can appreciate I am behaving like a good female; I ask for permission, keep myself safe, and other patriarchal nonsense like that. I tell him if it's too far, we can perform the *Jump*. He will be back here in no time, as I will return with Zaan. Easy, right? He won't deny me this because I am his favorite; his kids adore me and all that. I explain it all to him in one breathless conversation.

"No!" is the one-word answer I get.

"What? Why?" I ask, raising my voice and a few snooty Tarrassian women turn to stare.

"He is there for a reason. A male needs his space," he says, and I want to shove his shoulder spikes down his throat.

"Please, Kayon!"

"No. He will return in a few nano rotations because of the gases. You can talk to him then. Leave me be," he says and goes back inside.

What a grumpy asshole! Not only did he say no, but he had to mention the gases. You know what, I tried to be good. I hope Zaan can appreciate my effort. I make a quick stop by my room to grab my sword. Just to be safe. I know there is no life on Wallani, and probably there won't be any visitors either. All the normal aliens are here, enjoying wining and dancing. It had to be my alien who would rather stare at a green moon.

I am a bit taken aback by the number of ships sticking out of the docking bays. What the hell? There is a sea of them. Of course, it must be because of the guests. I am trying to pay attention and make sure I get an actual Tarrassian ship. Copper and shiny, how hard can it be? I think I found one. And it's so beautiful, it's practically calling my name. It's way bigger than what I had in mind, but who can say no to that beauty?

"I believe that ship belongs to the High Elder. Rumour goes he is fiercely protective of it," says a gruff yet amused voice behind me.

"Sarrian? I mean, High Commander," I say. He laughs and gives me a front seat to those magnificent dimples, not even the beard can hide. And face. And... other things.

"Sarrian would do just fine for when we are alone, Gianna. Come, I will take you. I don't think Zaan will appreciate it if you show up alone."

"Thank you," I say, trying to accept his kindness with grace. *Wait! How come he knows about my plans?*

"Is this your personal ship?" I ask as we board a spacecraft similar to Zaan's. I am trying not to act on my anger. These freaking aliens and their love for gossip! Does everyone know my business?

"It is part of the Queen's fleet, so it might just as well be," he says while getting the systems ready for manual flight. So, he is the hands-on-deck type, the same as Zaan.

"Does she travel often?" I ask after settling in my seat.

"Not with that belly, she doesn't," he says with a blinding smile. "The Queen used to go to Sketos very often to see the Ketosi."

Yes, her angels, as she calls them. I mean, they are actual angels, but I still struggle with that information.

"So, you prefer manual flight, just like Zaan," I say, and I am greeted with another melting smile.

"I most definitely don't," he replies. "Because of the energy released by the Astral Moons, the MI is unreliable. Too much interference. We can't perform the *Jump* either. Luckily, Wallani is not far to reach. Half a nano rotation at full speed."

Dear Lord! For the second time this evening, I am being humbled by my new circumstances. Space is not safe, aliens are not safe, nothing is safe for puny Humans. I would have probably died out there and destroyed the High Elder's ship while at it. I am so reckless. Zaan is right. I do need those freaking rules! And now I really understand how much I owe Sarrian. Did he follow me around all evening? I wouldn't put it past Sia. She is very protective of us, the few Humans living on Tarrassia.

"Thank you, Sarrian. I would have probably killed myself tonight," I say, feeling a bit deflated. "I know you did this as a favor to the Queen, but I still owe you my life."

"Yes," he admits. "The Queen is very important to me as she is to all of us. This, however, was a favor to my mate," he says, watching me warily from the seat next to mine. His cautious stare and body language tell me this is not something Sarrian feels comfortable talking about. "A mate who is not even aware I am doing him a favor," he says, still watching me. I made sure not to react to the word *him*, not that it was a surprise.

"Then why is this a favor to your mate?" I ask, encouraging him to open up.

"Because he is too stubborn to accept Humans don't do things just because they are told to," he says, confusing me even more. At least he is now laughing, much more relaxed; once we agreed I am totally okay with his sexuality.

"My foolish mate doesn't understand; Humans react badly to the word NO. If anything, it only encourages them to do the opposite. And since he cares for you as he does for his own children, I had to intervene. He can thank me later," he says, giving me a cheeky smile.

It takes a while for it to click.

"Kayon? Your mate is Kayon?" I ask in disbelief, and he just agrees with a smile. I am happy to be sitting. How crazy is that?

"Does anyone know?" I ask before I can stop. Maybe he doesn't want to talk about it, but I would rather be aware if it's a secret. As if the aliens can keep one.

"Only the Queen, and maybe the King. And most definitely Zaan," he says, and I can see this bothers him. "Kayon would be furious to hear that. In my defense, Sia worked it out herself. She is just too smart."

No arguments there. I still don't get it, and I only ask because he seems to need someone to share his burden with.

"I thought Tarrassians were not bothered by people's sexual preferences. And the High Elder has abolished the law of no mating with other species."

"Those statements are both true, Gianna. But, Kayon is a Neflay, and his species doesn't approve of such mated pairs. He worries about his children's reactions. The fact I am younger than they are doesn't help. Like I said, Kayon is a stubborn old male, always complaining about something," he says, and we both laugh. He is not wrong there. "He lost his mate in cubbirth, and for some reason, he still feels responsible after all this time. Kayon loved the mother of his cubs very much, and now he loves me. It is that simple, but the Neflay like to complicate things," he says with a frustrated sigh.

"So, he cares about me," I say, trying to change the subject and lighten up the mood. I don't like seeing Sarrian sad. His face was made for smiling.

"Very much so," he admits. "Kayon talks about you just as much as he talks about his own children. I have to admit something silly. I was a bit jealous to start with," he says, and we both laugh. "He made it very clear a long time ago, I wasn't allowed to tell his children, but he didn't mention you."

"Well, that's because I wasn't in the picture at the time," I remind him.

"Facts are facts," he says with a grin.

"You are spending way too much time around scheming Humans," I say, laughing.

"Don't remind me," he says with a groan. "Besides, this is my chance to have someone I can call family. My parents were killed by the Noorranni shortly after I was born. Never had anyone else other than Kayon to call my own. He keeps me away from his children, but the silly old male forgot to mention you. Also, this is something you don't need to hide from Zaan. I have a feeling he always knew."

"Kayon will be furious over this; I hope you know that," I say, pointing out something he must already know.

"Do you think anyone will tell the difference from his usual sunny personality?" he asks, and I tear up with laughter. God, I wish Zaan could get jokes and innuendoes this way.

"Kayon is a grumpy soul; bless him," I say.

"Yes, and now prepare to face your own grump," he says as we go through the atmosphere of the planet. And then, I see it! The night sky, the sea, the rocky terrain, the long stretch of sandy beach, everything has the exact shade of green as my eyes. Oh. My. God.

45

ZAAN

My obsession with the Lorra Moon is known to all. What they don't know is my other reason to enjoy the planet. It is blissfully quiet. Yes, the waves of the Wallani Sea are always roaring, but there is nothing else disturbing the quietness. Nothing alive, anyway. I know the best times to avoid visitors, and this dark span's timing couldn't be any better. The Celebrations of the Astrals' Moons and the High Elder's Ceremony mean everybody else is busy, and I have the planet to myself when the Lorra Moon is at its brightest. Sadly, I only have this span to enjoy it, as this orbit rotation, the phenomena coincide with the release of the toxic gases.

I probably shouldn't be here, so far away from Tarrassia and my beautiful mate. Her marks must hurt. Mine do, but everything else hurts without her anyway. Even my mind is playing tricks on me. I swear I could hear her voice in my mind. Watching the Lorra Moon is the closest I can be to her. I needed this. Soon I will have to do something about the distance between us. I can't have her in pain. She will not like it, but the Sign's rage at our separation must be too much for her fragile skin.

My whole body prickles with awareness and annoyance. I reach for my sword, even though planet Wallani is under the protection of the Coalition. No enemy forces would dare come here. The ship I can feel approaching is not a threat, just a pesky annoyance. The planet is not that big, and it feels like an island suspended in space from where I stand. The long stretch of beach is the best spot to enjoy the view and to sit comfortably. Except for the soft silver sand of the shores, everything else is covered in rocky terrain. The visitors will no doubt come this way. The info on my com makes me groan. It is best if I leave now; my peaceful moment will shortly be spoiled. My com recognized a Tarrassian ship. Not any ship, but one in the Queen's fleet. She is too heavy with her cub to travel anywhere; I know the King won't allow it. This means whoever is coming must be some rowdy guests trying to extend the fun of the Ceremonies where nobody can keep an eye. I swear to the Astrals, if I find any of my Untried sneaking away on that ship, there will be blood to spill.

I get on my way to meet the unwelcome party, but then my marks start glowing and my Sign pulsing. And now I am really angry. Can this female of mine ever learn anything useful? How dare she risk her life? Maybe a different sort of punishment is in order. My new heart doesn't care about my anger. Breathing becomes painful as I lay eyes on her. She trails behind Sarrian, observing where she steps on the sharp-edged rocks. Her pink dress is a hazard in itself, and Sarrian keeps a close eye on her movements. I know his instincts tell him to help her, but he knows better than to touch what's mine. I stop walking and wait for them to reach the sandy beach. I don't know if I can move. To see her flooded in the green light of the Lorra Moon feels like a span life dream came to life.

This is what I felt that dark span when I was sixteen orbit rotations old. Before that moment, the Lorra Moon only meant beauty. After, it became an obsession. And seeing her now, it feels like everything has come in a circle of closure. Perhaps I will never understand why.

Only it can't... I can't...

As always, her beauty and her proximity weaken my knees. The puffy mane of golden curls absorbs the light of the moon like a halo. She looks like some enchanted alien creature. Which makes sense, considering she is. As they step from the rocks onto the soft sand, she lifts her eyes and looks at me. The Lorra Moon reflects in them or maybe the other way around. My sire says this is a scientific phenomenon, easily explained. Only magic can explain why a sentient being would have moons inside her eyes.

Sarrian pulls me out of my trance, waving a hand in front of my face, and my anger reignites. He quickly puts his hands up in a defensive gesture.

"High Master, here is your High Lady delivered safe and unharmed," he says with the charming smile he's well known for. The fool is so cocky! And vexing reckless; no wonder he gets on well with my female. They have a lot in common. I don't know how Kayon can cope with this kind of behavior, but I won't.

"Why are you here, Master of the Untried?" I ask her, ignoring him. My anger reaches unbearable limits as my harsh words make her seek shelter behind his large body. I can't even see her any more. Doesn't she know what happens if she hides from me? Sarrian does know our customs and quickly steps to the side.

"As the Humans would say, don't act like an asshole, Zaan," he says with his carefree grin. However, his eyes closely watch my hand, resting on the pommel of my sword. "Your mate requested my help and protection to reach you safely. At no point was she at risk or in any danger. Maybe next time answer when she calls you, vexing idiot," he says, knowing he is one of the very few who can get away with calling me that.

"My High Lady, I hope you enjoy the rest of the dark span, even though the company is lacking," he says, pulling a little smile from her.

"Maybe I should mention your little adventure to Kayon; what do you say, High Commander?" I know I am acting like a cub having an upset, but how dare he bring her here without my permission. "I bet he has no idea of your whereabouts."

"Oh, I am so scared now, look, my hands are shaking; how am I ever going to fly back?" says the fool laughing all the way back to his ship.

My beautiful, perfect mate is only a few steps away from me, watching me warily. I am going to kill Sarrian. He just left her here alone with me. I feel my muscles starting to grow, responding to my anger. Good thing I wear my Warrior Kannicloth. As for her, I don't care if it frightens her. She is about to meet my War Beast in person. And while before it was out to keep her safe, now it wants out to make her pay.

"Explain yourself, Gianna," I say, trying and quickly failing to keep control.

Then, it's all gone. Anger, worries, fear, and especially control leave me all at once as her arms wrap around my waist. Her body squeezes mine with all her might, not stopped by the fact her arms can't even reach all around me. Her precious face rests on my chest, and the heart underneath goes mad. The heart that lives for her.

"I missed you so much," she says with her lips pressed to my chest. Her touch is burning my skin; her words are blistering both my hearts. Needless to say, all my anger is gone, and without that to cling to, I have no defense against this female.

"I thought I could do this, Zaan, live without you, but I can't."

She talks with her face buried in my chest, but I can easily hear her over the roaring of the waves and the noise of my hearts.

She isn't talking inside my mind, yet it feels as if she is talking inside all of me.

"And it is not because of the Sign," she says, and I can tell the anguish in her voice. "The pain in my marks can't compare to the pain in my soul. It's crushing me, and I tried to be strong. I tried to keep some dignity. I really did. Right now, it feels like I have never been more vulnerable, easier to hurt or reject. This is my most fragile moment ever, but also my strongest. I think love is meant to be like that. I know you find it difficult to trust me, forget my past, and put away the memory of the men who came before you. I also know we are connected by the Sign, and your body craves mine, despite whatever feelings you might struggle with. Those two things are something we can build on. Let's take it easy, let time heal and find each other when we are ready. But we can only do that if we stick together. I will be patient, no matter how long I will have to wait. And if you try to get away from me, I won't let you. Remember? *Where you go, I follow.*"

I grab her upper arms gently and push her away from me, so I can see her face. I need to look her in the eyes while trying to make sense of her strange words. She is the quiet sort, and this is more than she ever said in one go. At first, I understand she just confessed her love for me. As I process more of her words, my joy is quickly replaced by horror.

"You think I don't want you because of the life you had before me? Or because of what was done to you against your will?" I am trying not to sound angry, but that's not happening.

My rage is only aimed at myself, though. What a vexing idiot! I didn't give her any explanation for rejecting her, so of course, her mind came up with a resolution of its own. One that is worse than the truth. When people don't tell us things, we assume our own, and most times, those are more damaging. Haven't I learned anything from my sire? He says love can start a bond, but only respect and communication can keep it alive.

She doesn't answer my question, and I don't expect her to. Instead, I grab her in my arms and take her along the beach, to my favorite sandy dune, close to the crashing waves. I remove my sword and lower myself into the soft sand, taking her with me. She allows me to place her across my lap, looking unsure and a bit lost. I don't press her close to me because I need to be able to see her face. I want her to see mine when I tell her the truth. I lift her chin up, and the green in her eyes hits me like a stone wall. There is also moisture in there, and I know she is holding her cub-like tears from spilling.

"I ran away from you because I am a coward," I tell her.

No matter how bad my truth may be, it is less upsetting than the explanation she came up with.

"I don't know how to help you get over the trauma of your past. But most of all, I don't know if I can survive seeing you go through another memory episode. One triggered by my touch, nevertheless. What happened the last time I made you relive your past took all my strength away. It took away my sleep, my hopes, and all my dreams of a future with you. I don't know if I can manage to witness it again, knowing I caused it. I left because I was scared. I still am."

I tell her words I have never said to anyone before. A Tarrassian Warrior doesn't feel fear. That is what we are taught from as soon as we can understand words. What they don't tell us is that fear may happen, no matter how strong one is. What do you do then? How can you fight or understand something they say just doesn't exist? Perhaps, this is the most important lesson my species can learn from hers. Humans take things like fear and fragility and turn them into weapons, like the Arni. The power of the weak can be humbling to the strong.

My words have stunned her somehow. They probably hurt her, too, as now she understands our relationship is doomed by no fault of our own.

"Oh, Zaan, my love," she says with a sigh, and a lone tear goes down her face. "I never thought what that episode must have done to you. I don't even remember how bad it was, just that I came out of it numb and with a sore throat. Probably from screaming. I won't lie, I had nightmares before, but never like that, or while awake. All the stress of being taken from Earth, Yara's death, the Moorri King, the bite, the marks, feeling like I failed at everything, it was all too much. I was already in a dark place, and you just happened to be the trigger that made it all explode. It freed me more than you could ever understand. It let it all out. It must have been intense and scary, and you got to see it all. I thought you stopped chasing me after that because you were disgusted."

"Lorra," I start with a pained moan, but her soft palm presses over my lips.

"Please, let me finish," she says. "I might have tried to punish myself for years after the abuse; I might have gone the wrong way about it with the healing process, but I would never allow those memories to come in between the man I love and me. That would mean letting those men win, and that simply doesn't happen. Loving you gave me the clarity I needed to finally see myself; the real me. Some people are something on their own but most are something because of others. I am Gianna, High Lady of House Marni, Master of the Untried, mate of the High Master, daughter of the High General of the Human army, kind of adoptive daughter to an orc, best friend to some crazy-ass Humans, and a glowing tree, but above all, I am a woman in love. I don't lose any battles!"

She stops talking, a gentle smile on her full lips and a fierce look in her green eyes. I don't understand half the things she said, but I get the idea. I was an idiot! I know she wants a reply, but I am too humbled by her fragility, strength, resilience, and most of all, her love. How can someone who was hurt by people have so much love to give to so many people?

Suddenly, she hides a burst of laughter in my shoulder, and it takes a nano to understand why. My tongue may not be working, unable to put words together, but my cock does, and since she's sitting on my lap, she gets to feel exactly how much I missed her, need her, obsess over her.

"Shall I take that as your answer or will there be actual words at some point?" she asks with a light, teasing voice. It is precisely what I needed to take some of the pressure away. We have a life span for communicating, as my sire says. Now, it's only about claiming what is mine.

"There will be plenty of words, my Lorra. Especially about your little adventure with Sarrian."

"I didn't... I mean, as Sarrian explained..."

"Did I say you could talk?"

"No."

"No, what?"

"No, Zaan," she sighs.

"Did I say you could roll your eyes at me?" I ask, and even though I am serious, she laughs. That does it. I pick her off my lap and lay her on her back in the sand. I keep my eyes glued to hers as I remove both our garments. She helps me with hers because... who makes these things? My mouth goes for her lips with all the frustration and the desire of the last months. My kiss leaves her breathless, but she is eager to meet me halfway. As I lower my body over hers, I can instantly feel a wary question in her mind. I pause the kiss and lift my head to look at her.

The Lorra Moon reflects in her eyes, and the effect makes me feel dizzy.

Her eyes, one moon, my hearts, one love.

"No punishments tonight, Zaan. No more waiting, not even foreplay. I want none of that. I just want to be one with you," she says, and I understand exactly what she means.

Everything in our relationship was a fight and a struggle from the very beginning. This span, we keep it simple, and we leave all the worlds and their problems out. No better place than a deserted planet for it.

I lower myself over her, sheltering her body from the occasional spray of the waves. As the moon reaches its peak, the sea becomes more agitated. I feel the squeeze of her legs around my waist, and she arches her body towards me.

"Please, Zaan, I need…"

"I know what you need, my Lorra, and I will always give it to you," I whisper in her ear to make sure she can hear me over the noise of the crashing waves.

Mind-talking doesn't seem right in this nanoclip. I want to hear her voice. I need to! I also want to look her in the eyes when I enter her to ensure she is okay. She is small and fragile and the naked body underneath mine seems as breakable as mallenni glass. Our difference in height makes things more of a challenging task. I uncoil her legs from around my waist and push them up, bending her knees and keeping them spread. In this position, it is easier to have my face above hers and drown in the beauty of her eyes. It is also easier to see any sign of distress. I press my lips over hers because I want to swallow the scream; I know it's coming.

I enter her in one go; there can't be any other way. I expected the wetness because the air around us is scented with her arousal. I didn't expect the tightness. If I feel pain, so must she. I take notice of the slight wince she is quick to cover with a moan. This was never going to be painless but I think she already accepted that; especially if she wanted me to skip on the foreplay There is tension in her body, and I take her mouth in an equally intense kiss to distract her from the pain. I let my forehead touch hers and our Signs soothe each other. Soon enough, her inner muscles start squeezing around my cock. My first instinct is to keep my need to come under control. Only this time, I don't have to. No more waiting, no more self-discipline. All I have to do is bring her there with me. It doesn't take long before she starts panting and her body contracts underneath mine.

"Gianna, open your eyes, beautiful," I say using her given name. It hurt when she accused me of not knowing it. Her name is forged inside my hearts. How could I not know it? She is so lost in her release, she can't even hear me. I stop moving inside her, and she soon opens her eyes, a trace of panic in them.

"Keep them open, beautiful. New rule. When I am inside you, you keep your eyes on me, yes?"

"Yes," she says with a weak voice.

"Yes, what?"

"Yes, Zaan."

"Good," I say, and I finally allow all my control and self-restraint to slip away. I should hold on to some for when I give her my mating bite. I can't allow myself to harm her like I did last time. She probably doesn't expect another bite, but I want to do it right. I need to! Just as I start moving inside her again, she explodes around me, and I find I can't hold onto any self-restraint any more. She is so tight it hurts. So wet and hot, and her inner muscles keep rippling around me. Time and space lose their meanings, the longer and harder I push inside her, the more we become as one. She is mine, and I am hers, and I want her to tell me she understands what it means.

"Tell me you want me to always watch you," I say. In her haze of arousal, she doesn't hear or understand a word I say. So, I stop moving until I have her full attention again. I can see she finds my words strange, but she agrees, nevertheless.

"Yes, Zaan, I want you to always watch me," she says and moves her hands tenderly through my head fur, she calls hair.

"I promise I will always watch you, my beautiful Lorra," I tell her and allow myself to claim my mate. The one I spent a life span waiting for. My only one. As my body explodes inside hers and another orgasm makes her tremble in my arms, I let my fangs pierce the skin of her long neck, over the old scar. Her sweet blood tastes just like the first time. It tastes like it belongs to me.

46

—

GIANNA

It could be that our bodies need things like orgasms. Maybe it's a healthy natural release. It explains why my long-denied body can't stop orgasming now. I think he had been holding me tightly for over half an hour when I finally stopped shaking. Things like senses and awareness slowly return to me. His orange flowers' scent mixes with the intense salty smell of the sea and the smell of my blood. Because... yeah, he's done it again. There is slight pain where he bit me, but it somehow feels superficial. It's either that, or I am getting the drift of Sia's crazy kink for biting. To be honest, I enjoyed the hell out of it this time around. It felt crazy hot as if he was claiming my body, soul, and blood simultaneously. No wonder my inner muscles are still clenching, trying to get the fullness and the pressure back. And there was a lot of that.

I expected some pain because his size was always going to take some effort to accommodate. He probably could have been a bit less intense, but that is not how he does things. It feels like every cell of my body has been claimed. As for my soul, he got that long ago.

Tell me you want me to always watch you. That has got to be the strangest thing any man has ever said to a woman. I am not entirely sure what I agreed to here. It feels like some strange pact with the Devil. Yes, he definitely claimed my soul.

"How is the pain?" he asks with his lips in my hair. Walking might look funny for a day or two, but I cannot tell him that.

"It was less than I expected, and it's wearing off," I say, nuzzling at his warm chest. Not exactly a lie. But that is only because I expected a lot of pain.

"Good, because I need to do it again," he says, and, good Lord, I think he means right now. Under my hip, his hard cock becomes harder, and there is a growing pulse as if it's got a heart of its own. Yeah, he definitely means now. So, I am looking at a week of funny walking. Good thing it's a holiday. In a way, maybe intense bruising sex, Zaan's style, is better than thinking. That part is far scarier. His fingers go under my chin and make me look up at him.

"Tell me."

It is all he says, but I know he can feel my anxiety. I was connected to him in so many ways from the very beginning. Having him inside me has brought it to a whole new level.

"It's nothing, Zaan," I start, but I instantly understand that is wrong. We have suffered enough for not being able to communicate and say how we really feel. He needs to know how I feel.

"I am just scared this is too good to be true. Which is stupid, of course. When terrible things happen, we don't ask ourselves if they are too horrible to be real. We shouldn't question happiness."

"Then don't ask yourself anymore, my Lorra. Accept the good with the same bravery you accepted the bad," he tells me while running hot fingers up and down my back. Hard to remember the bad when he does that.

"Trust me, I am trying to," I say. "Humans are complicated like that. It's just that so much has happened in a short period. It might seem strange to you, but Human relationships take longer. Sometimes couples date for years before committing to each other."

"No offense to your people, beautiful, but that seems very silly to me. If you are not sure from the beginning, how is time going to change your mind? One will just try to look for excuses to either continue that relationship or leave it behind. If you need to think about it, then it's not right for you," he says.

Perhaps there is some sense in what he says, but I am too Human to accept that. My people are all about compatibility; take your time, watch out for red flags.

"Until now, I haven't fully appreciated Sia's courage," I say. "She and Tars went from strangers to future parents in only a few days," I remember with an inner groan. *God, I am so not ready for a baby!* And although a crazy passionate relationship might have been expected from someone like Jade, it was very unlike Sia. I remember thinking she was undoubtedly the last one the aliens would go for. The Sign works in strange ways, but so does love. And according to Sia, the Sign is just an excuse to be who we really want to be and forget our inhibitions. Well, she definitely forgot hers.

"Do you think this is happening too fast, my Lorra?" he says, pulling me up until our eyes are at the same level. "It hasn't been fast for me. I spent too many dark spans on this very planet to remember. Watching the Lorra Moon, obsessively trying to find its particular shade of green in everything. It was like a game when I was a cub. See how many objects I could find to match it. But then, it became more than that. I remember the dark span when it changed from random obsession to knowing obsession. It was the span I turned sixteen orbit rotations. It was then when I knew without any doubt, there was a connection between the Lorra Moon and the one who would become my mate."

Something puzzles me in what he said, I just don't understand what. He was sixteen. That is the age gap between us. I am already learning about their different ways of telling time, seasons, or days of the week. It is really complicated, and so far, it makes no sense to me.

"Zaan, can you tell me the exact date?" I ask with a trembling voice. There is a chance the device will just damp on me some alien numbers and rotations of whatever. I mean, it refuses to translate things like beard and hair. But then he says it, and the device changes his words into perfect English in my ear.

"I can tell you everything about that span, my Lorra. It was the 18th of May," he says, smiling at the memory. His smile fades when he sees the tears in my eyes.

"Lorra? What's wrong?"

"That... that is the day I was born, my love. The 18th of May is my birthday and there are sixteen years between us. Can't you see what it means?" I ask with a trembling voice, raw emotion choking me. "You are right, Zaan. This is not happening fast. It was a long time coming." *There are no coincidences!*

47

—

GIANNA

I am unsure what wakes me first, the tongue pushing inside my mouth or the fingers pushing inside my already soaked core. This is so embarrassing; who gets this wet in their sleep? Maybe that's because Zaan doesn't stop touching me throughout the night. I know I am paranoid, but I swear to God that he watches me even in his sleep. Oh, and the cameras were back the very next day we returned from Wallani.

Hot, wet kisses go down my neck, my chest... I brace myself for the pain, and he doesn't disappoint. Despite the sting of his fangs piercing my skin, I am smiling to myself. He is so predictable. Now that we are fully mated, I heal as fast as any Tarrassian. Zaan's intensity does leave bruises, but they don't last long. It was expected of him to give me fresh ones this morning. I have a feeling he loves his marks on me.

After a week of celebrations, Tarrassia is back to work, and today we return to the Training Pits. Of course, he wants everybody to see his ownership of me. Because bright red tattoos and the pulsing Marni leaf on my forehead are not enough. And, God, I don't even want to think about the way I smell. Now that my senses are enhanced, I can tell exactly what everyone will sniff around the Pits today. When your body is filled with industrial quantities of cum, a bath does nothing.

These last few days we spent together felt like a lifetime. We didn't see or talk to anyone. Food was delivered on time, and even the bedsheets were changed daily, because... yeah, that was necessary. Unless there is a species of invisible aliens living in my house, the staff must have been instructed to stay out of my way. I am still surprised why his over-the-top possessiveness doesn't bother me anymore. Maybe because I don't have a choice. He comes with all the crazy, but... Oh, my god, he also comes with that skilled tongue.

I flinch and twist my fingers in his long hair as he nips at the sensitive skin inside my thigh. And then he bites it.

"Hey, that was totally unnecessary," I wince, only half upset. "No one is going to see your claiming mark there."

Yes, but I'll know it's there. It will ease the pain of having to share you with everybody on this span, he says inside my mind because his mouth is busy licking the life out of me.

You have no idea how much I wish I could keep you locked in here forever, my Lorra.

"Oh, I think I have an idea." Orgasming and mind-talking simultaneously don't work for me, so I don't even try it. "That is why I love you more for not doing it," I tell him. I take a huge intake of air as he enters me without any warning. I got from being tongued to balls deep in less than a second, and it's messing with whatever is left of my horny brain.

"Sorry, beautiful," he says with his lips pressed against my forehead as his body moves inside me. "We have to rush this time, not long before you have to go."

"You are so not sorry," I say, holding him close to me. My legs and arms cling to him, and he has to fight them just to keep his large body from crushing mine.

"So not sorry..." he keeps saying in my ear, in my hair, in my mouth, in my head.

After having him inside me so many times these past days, I know every single detail of him. Every tell-tale of his arousal and his needs. The pounding reaches almost unbearable heights, and his already huge cock swells even more, making me feel full to the limit of pain. I know it means he is about to come, and that is enough to make my own body shudder. We are in sync, a perfect rhythm that makes two people feel like one.

As we get ready for our first day back, I decide to wait until we are on his ship before I tell him. Despite all the smiling I get this morning, I know he is tense about sharing my attention with other people. I don't want to give him a reason to lock me up in our bedroom. I bet he would love that.

I give it a while until we are halfway there and too late to go back home. Not that he would care about being late if he's really pissed with me.

"I am listening," he says from his control seat, next to mine.

Right, of course, he can tell I am anxious.

"I did something; I mean, I didn't go through with it," I start blabbing and then stop trying to find words.

"Yes, my Lorra, I am aware," he says, watching me closely.

What the hell? He is not smiling but doesn't seem that upset either.

"The High General informed me," he says, and now I am the one who is pissed. I was going to tell him myself. That guy is something else! Did he have to go behind my back and tell on me? I can see Zaan wants me to explain myself.

"I am sorry," I say, deciding to just tell him the truth. "Old habits die hard. I only had myself to solve my problems for so long, so I went down that path. I thought I had everything in place, and I was eager to teach the Moorri King not to mess with my Untried. Then, I remembered I was not alone any more. I have family, friends, and the entire Tarrassian army behind me. I remembered I told the Untried we must fight and think as a united front when facing our enemies. But most of all, I remembered your rules. I couldn't let you down again. And I am happy I chose to trust your rules, Zaan. My little mission would have been a disaster," I tell him, and I hope he believes me. We are in such a good place. I don't think I could deal with his disappointment right now.

And then, he smiles.

"I know, my beautiful Lorra. I appreciate your decision, especially because you had to fight your old ways," he says and reaches over our seats to grab my hand. Our swirls ignite with color.

"You are not upset," I say, and it is not a question.

"No, I am not. Your other adventure, though, you know, the one Sarrian saved you from? We will have a little chat about that one later, after the Pits," he says, and there is a flash of something in his golden stare. Nothing good, I presume. Oh, well... I did mess that one up.

"The High General had no right to tell you," I say to change the subject and because it needs to be said. That asshole!

"I expected him to tell me because I am your mate, but also your superior. And you must know, he had high words of praise for your decision and how you organized the rescue mission. He actually carried on with it following your initial plan. *The sensible part of it*, as he put it. I am sure you know what he meant by that."

I am speechless. The High General followed my rescue plan? And he praised me? The man is such a confusing asshole. At times he makes it really hard for people to hate him.

"Is Mirri...?" I am scared to ask, and I feel bad for not even thinking about her all these days. Apparently love makes me selfish. Besides, I assumed if anything went wrong, they would have informed me by now. As they say, no news is good news.

"Mirri is back at the Pits, and I have also been informed by the High General she will move in with us," he says with a smile. Oh, a smile is good because I agreed to that one without even asking him. Was there a rule about house guests? I must write the freaking rules down!

"The Marni house will always be open to the ones in need of protection, beautiful," he says, putting my worries to rest. "Ollianna was never a servant, despite her willingness to help around. I think she was just trying to keep herself busy. She was always family, and so will be Mirri. However, Moorri are no Garrii, so we need to keep an eye out for trouble," he says, and we both laugh. I am curious to know what happened, but I have a feeling my man will lose it if he hears the Moorri King's name on my lips. Nope, not going there. I am sure Jade has all the juicy details. Jade... I forgot about her, too. It's either Zaan is frying my circuits or I am a shit friend.

After we docked at the Pits, I expected Zaan to go his way, but of course, that was too much to ask for. As we walk side by side, I realize this is the first time we are here as a real couple. A couple by our choice instead of just the Sign's making. I thought Zaan would switch to the High Master persona; instead, he doesn't even pretend not to dote on me. We are not holding hands or showing any PDA, but his body language says *this woman is mine and damn proud of it*. By the time we reach the Pit of the Untried, it's pretty obvious no one finds it strange either. We are a mated couple, and that is not something to be ashamed of, just because we are in an army camp. I think aliens are growing on me.

When we reach my Unit, I try my best to keep a straight face at Zaan's struggle. He wished me a good span, kissed my forehead, then... nothing. He is still staring at me, and I can see the desperation building up in his golden eyes. He can't bring himself to walk away from me. It is annoying as fuck, but also incredibly cute. Sort of. The longer he stands there looking down at my face as if it's precious, the more people notice. I love this man with all my heart, but boy, does he have issues! Now, we have separation anxiety to add to creepy stalking, obsessive behavior, and an inclination for extra rough sex.

Something catches his eye behind me, and I can see it brings him out of his dilemma. There is a funny look on his face, and he takes a deep breath. I am pretty sure it must be Kayon who caught Zaan's eye. I was hoping he wouldn't be around today, considering my little episode with Sarrian. He will give me shit over it. Technically Kayon shouldn't show up here anymore, but the guy just can't keep out of my business.

Zaan's eyes move back to me, and there is a vague smile on his beautiful lips. Is that emotion in his eyes? And why is the camp so quiet all of a sudden?

"I won't thank you, Master of the Untried," he says, watching me with his intense golden stare. "I am sure the High Elder would want to be the one thanking you on behalf of Tarrassia and the Coalition of the Seven Stars."

Say what now? What is he talking about? All of a sudden, I am scared to turn and look. Whatever this is, it must be about what or who is waiting behind me.

"As for me, I can only say, I am proud the Astrals gave you to me. My beautiful, special mate," he says, and the smile shows his blinding white fangs and teeth.

"Zaan, what is happening?"

"I'd better leave you to your duties, Master of the Untried," he says, taking a fist to his chest, the Tarrassian salute. "You have a new recruit to welcome to your Unit." He leaves without any other explanation, and now that I am alone, I run out of excuses. I have to look. So, I do.

The young girl waiting outside the Pit of the Untried watches me warily. The same way she looks at everything and everyone.

There is wariness and a bit of fear, but they pale next to her excitement to be here. Her perfectly shaped nose breathes in the air of the camp, and it makes her smile. She likes the smells. She belongs here. She keeps her big copper eyes on me as she enters the Pit. Her outfit is a perfect replica of my own. Because she is skinny, tall and her boobs don't stick out, the white leather garment doesn't look as slutty on her as it looks on me. I think she is pretty young, probably on the small side of her teen years. Her perfectly shaped bald head shines under the Tarrassian sun, accentuating her surreal alien beauty.

"Hanni, Master of the Untried," she says, taking a very bony and delicate fist to her equally skinny chest. Her voice is a bit shaky, but it doesn't stop her. I have a feeling nothing ever will.

"I am Raella of House Farris. My grandsire is the Elder of the Caves. I am here against his will and against the will of my entire House. I have permission to join from the High Elder. They cannot go against his word. Our Astral said, you are the Scholar who doesn't mind teaching anyone who wants to become a Warrior. He assured me you won't care about things like my species, my gender, the color of my skin, or my weaknesses. He said you are a Scholar for all. Will you teach me?"

"Yes, Raella of House Farris," I say. My calm voice shocks me. It is nothing like the storm inside me. "Welcome to the Unit. Please find Untried Mirri and ask her to show you around. Oh, and please tell her to drop the catsuit. I expect her to show up in full Tarrassian Female Warrior garment on the next span."

"Catsuit?" she asks, looking at me with those huge copper eyes.

"Don't worry, she will understand," I tell her with a smile.

I watch her make her way through the busy Pit of the Untried. Most of the alien species just watch her with slight curiosity but accept her presence without fuss. The Tarrassian Untried... well, that's another story. Their eyes are basically glued to her ass and long, slender thighs as she moves through the crowd. My Marni shinai will soon say hello to a bunch of dicks. Like, literally. The young girl notices but doesn't let their attention stop her. She looks fragile and out of place. She is perfect!

"Do you think she has a mate?" asks an annoying voice near me. *Sigh...*

"Yes, Untried Ronnin, she does. One who is a bit older than a newborn cub," I say, and the little shit growls at me. He soon realizes his mistake and takes a step back, almost falling over himself.

"Sorry, Master of the Untried, I didn't mean that. As for the female, it doesn't matter," he says with a sulking voice. "I like boobs, and Tarrassian females don't have any. I will mate a Human female when I grow up."

He takes another step back and watches me warily. I think his lack of filter shocks himself, sometimes.

"How many Punishing Challenges did you have this orbit rotation, Untried?" I ask, trying to keep a straight face.

"Two? Five? Okay, maybe eight," he answers with a sigh. The kid is too cute for his own good.

"Let's not make it nine, shall we?"

"Fine! I will be good. What are you teaching us this span, Master of the Untried?" he asks as he follows me inside. I watch him thinking he is trying to distract my attention from his out-of-order behavior. Instead, his big copper eyes twinkle with excitement. He looks young and full of hope. Why wouldn't he? He has his whole future ahead of him, and it is up to me to shape it right.

Warriors don't always come with sharp weapons and oversized muscles; they don't always bring destruction, have superpowers, save the day or live adventurous lives. They come in many forms and trades. And sometimes, the best Warriors are the teachers who shape our future.

EPILOGUE

—

GIANNA & BRIAN

The tiring, challenging day at the pits couldn't take my mind off this moment and everything that might go wrong. Soon after the sunset, the Elder of the Healers will wake Brian. The King wouldn't trust anyone else to do it other than Diran. No one said why it has to be after sunset, but these are aliens we're talking about. There is some sacred ritual for everything. I knew this moment was coming for the last couple of months, but I had more imminent things to worry about.

I talk to my father almost every day now, and he is due to visit soon. It's rather strange; we talk more now when we are galaxies apart than when we used to share a house. Zaan was right; the stubborn old man finally gave in and accepted the position offered by the Tarrassians. He is now the High Commander of the Human army. Personally, I think only aliens believe such a thing could work. Humans are too individual to keep them all under one umbrella. But if anyone can make it happen, it would be my dad. He knows how to inspire loyalty and gather followers. Time will tell. I didn't want to push our fragile relationship and invite him to my small and very private Sacred Ceremony. And I didn't even think about telling my mom. I am pretty sure one of the Elders might ping her gold-digger radar. No, thank you! Instead, I asked Kayon to give me away. I more or less twisted his arm and asked him in public to ensure he wouldn't give me one of his favorite words: NO! He looked pretty emotional, the old grump, something he would never admit.

Despite Talla's massive tantrum, Zaan and I had the very small and private Sacred Ceremony we both wanted. We mainly invited all the couples we love and a few selected others. After so many weeks, I still avoid being alone with Kayon. I don't think he appreciated the *mated couples' invite* I sent him and Sarrian. To be fair, he only looked angry for the whole of five minutes until he saw the happiness on Sarrian's face.

I had another unexpected couple there, one that was all Natalia's doing. I don't know the juicy details because I am still not part of the gossip squad. But then again, who needs details? Ollianna's face and shimmery golden skin as she walked in clinging to Barin, said it all. What is it with aliens and gold? Is it like their universal color of love or something? Now that she is happy, it turns out she is just as chatty as her sister. *A Garri thing*, as Natalia of all people would say. Her newfound love for non-stop word vomit is the only silver lining in letting her go. No matter how much I care for her, I understand she wants to live with her man. Okay, maybe I don't. Having friends after all this time and especially after losing Yara turned me into a possessive little horror. Or maybe Zaan's madness is contagious.

As expected, the hardest part was to have Jade there. She never said it or showed it. Her devil-may-care attitude can only fool the aliens. The mating marks that developed on her right hand and wrist never went away. They are as bright as when they sparked, mocking her silly infatuation with a man who doesn't want her. Most Tarrassians must wonder why her marks are still alive. We, the Human girls, know the answer to that question. You don't stop loving someone just because they don't love you back. Luckily, the High General sent us an expensive over-the-top present, made his excuses, and had the decency not to show up. I hate the guy, but things must be just as challenging for him. Because Jade's marks are still visible, they are a mated pair as far as stuck-up Tarrassians are concerned. Nobody gives a shit if the 'happy couple' doesn't even acknowledge one another. The Sign comes before people and their feelings.

Jade is not the only victim of the Stone-Age mentality. What they did to Princess Umbelina is damn right cruel. Couples mated at birth stay that way for life. They cannot be rejected unless the Sign chooses differently. Jade's stupid decision to touch the High General turned the Princess into a social pariah. They refer to her as a rejected mate. A forever spinster no one wants. Because her relationship with the High General was a sure thing, she lived as a guest in his home while helping Sia with her Mating Ceremony. To archaic Tarrassians, no matter how advanced they fancy themselves, it only means one thing. No one else can have her now. No mate means no chance at popping babies, so they kicked her out of her home. I know the girls are furious, and Sia feels helpless. This is not some written law Natalia's scheming could change. This is a Tarrassian mentality shaped over thousands of years. In their eyes, the Princess is useless to their society. Her father is the Elder of the Fields, the most remote Tarrassian outpost. Whoever the Oria birds choose as his successor will also inherit the Country of the Fields. She is now mateless and homeless. The King and Queen have offered her shelter at the Royal Palace, and she only sees Sia these days, preferring to keep to herself. I know Jade won't admit it, but the guilt must kill her. Despite her over-the-top persona, Jade has a big heart.

Luckily, my other single guest was as annoyingly happy as they come. Since living with us, Mirri has blossomed into a kick-ass, sassy, over-the-top teen who loves messing with my Untried and their hormones. Her infatuation with the High General was as childish as they come. Easy to understand why. He saved her from a life on the Yellow Planets and turned himself into her personal hero. Twice he saved her now, but this time around, there is just gratitude without infatuation.

My wedding day was just as perfect as every second of my new life. My new job at the Pits is one big challenge, but even that is part of this new state of happiness. Every day, I pretend I have things under control, and I enjoy the chaos. And it works because… yeah, aliens don't really see past my kick-ass persona, my Warrior Queen outfit, or my *glowing stick,* as Kayon calls it. Okay, maybe they can see a lot of skin past my clothes, but they really, really try not to look. Heads rolling and all that.

Zaan can see *me* despite all my pretenses because he always could. For someone who is so black and white, that is unexpected. I can also see *him* behind all his quarks, rules, and obsessive behaviors. I still hate myself for all the time I spent pretending I couldn't. There are downsides to knowing one another so well. There is no hiding and no privacy. Zaan doesn't understand those concepts when it comes to me. My new condition doesn't help, that's for sure. Diran confirmed I was just over a month pregnant. I don't know if it's the Sign or damn Zaan who can't keep it in his pants, Kannicloth, whatever. We don't admit it, but we are both a little bit scared. Zaan is just his overprotective self but all I can think of is the other pregnant girls. Sia looks like she is about to pop out a T-Rex, and Natalia might be pregnant with Godzilla.

I try not to fuss about the timing. I've only just started on this journey at the Pits, and having a baby will put some things on hold. I find relief in knowing there is no other choice. I can almost imagine myself mentioning birth control to Zaan and the Elders. Nope, not happening. Besides, I am strangely looking forward to my own little Viking. If this baby looks and smells like his father, I don't care how many sacrifices I have to make. As for Zaan, I know what he wants, especially now that I have pretty severe morning sickness. Lock me up and throw away the key for the next seven months or so. Also, not happening. Sadly, I can't say no to the whole new level of stalking. It is overwhelming, no matter how much I love him. He is always in my face, in my space, and in my other more intimate places. And he wants to know what the baby does every twenty minutes or so as if I would know, or something.

This is why I am going to enjoy a few minutes away from him. And maybe breathe just air instead of him. Zaan agreed to me being there for Brian, and now he can't take it back. He still escorted me to the Royal Palace, but the King quickly dragged him off somewhere. Rumors are not wrong. Brian might be the reason why Earth is now an invaded planet. He is obviously very important to the King, because the big guy looked just as nervous as I feel. I'd better not mention this to Brian when he wakes. I suspect all this has a lot to do with whatever happened to him on Sketos. Sia can't bring herself to talk about it after all this time. In a way, that's what gives me faith and hope. There is no way Brian survived all that for things to go wrong now.

Diran and an imposing number of Healers meet me halfway to the Royal Med Bay. It's a private facility, only for the use of the Royal Family. Yet, the King gave it to Brian. He was there all by himself all these months, submerged in the healing pod. Sia said it looked scary inside the slushy gel-like texture of the pod. Then she quickly and politely apologized as she realized that was the Marni sap she was referring to. I took her advice and didn't visit him, not that he would have known any different.

Diran gives me an encouraging look as we reach the large metal doors of the Royal Med Bay.

I take a quick breath and mentally prepare myself as the large metal doors open for us with a zoom. Diran and I both stop before we walk straight into the ethereal creature leaving the Royal Med Bay. Her huge copper eyes take our party in with obvious mortification.

"Princess, it is nice to see you again," I say with a nod. My newly found social skills keep surprising me. I blame our Queen for that. Everyone needs a Sia in their life.

"High Lady Marni, Elder, Healers." She greets us all with a nod and lowers her strange eyes. Her long fingers twist nervously around each other.

I don't know what to say or if I should enquire about her health or something. Is she ill and looking for a Healer? She is a head taller than I am, so I can still see her eyes as she looks down. She seems... I don't know. Tarrassian eyes are not easy to read, especially the women's. They are vast orbs of shiny copper that only reflect whatever they are looking at.

Diran and the other Healers return her greetings, then the Princess steps away, looking as if she will be on her way. Just as I am about to enter the med bay, she addresses me with a small voice. I can only hear her because of my new enhanced senses.

"Will he survive this?" she asks, and I take a moment to understand her words. *He?* Is she talking about Brian? Of course, she is; there is no other patient in there. It still doesn't explain much. Now is not the time to ask, nor is it my business.

"Yes, Princess," I tell her with a reassuring smile. "Brian is what Humans call *a force of nature*." It's probably not a good thing to say to an alien who takes everything literally. Thanks to the King, they already believe Brian has some superpowers.

"Thank you, High Lady Marni. I wish you a pleasant dark span," she says in her perfect manner before walking away. I can't help inhaling her delicate fragrance. Why do Tarrassians have to smell so freaking nice? My brain can never dissociate Princess Umbelina from the scent of honeysuckle. It follows her like her personal cloud.

Once again, I brace myself for what comes next. Diran has already told me the plan. Luckily, I won't get to see Brian in the pod. The Healers will transfer him to a smaller room that looks less alien, according to them. Brian will totally think the ceiling with the hologram of a fake purple moon, and the reflective metal walls look just like any standard room at the New York-Presbyterian. It is hilarious, and I am doing my best to stop a nervous laugh. I can't blame them for trying. Besides, I don't look that Human, myself. I have a pulsing red leaf on my forehead, so the alien room is probably not the biggest issue. This is not going to be easy.

Brian is still asleep when they bring him into the room after a rather lengthy weight. I hope Zaan doesn't lose his patience and come looking for me. Our baby is not the only one with an umbilical cord attached to me.

Diran said Brian should wake up slowly in the quiet room, and there would be just the two of us. However, they will be watching and monitoring him from very close. To my surprise, Diran gives me a tiny and very unassuming-looking tranquilizer gun. They have never had anyone in a healing pod for so long. Or that injured. There are worries about Brian's state of mind, and the Elder wants me to be safe. I don't argue because I do see the point. Who knows what that kind of trauma can do to someone?

They bring Brian in on some kind of floating stretcher. It is entirely operated by the MI. I am just about to point out a floating bed might not look very Human-like when the stretcher beats me to it and releases four metal legs when landing in the middle of the room. Now it seems like any other hospital bed. The alien variant. After the Healers leave the room, Diran checks Brian's vitals, and the systems well hidden behind what I can now see is a hologram of a metal wall. Maybe the Tarrassians did go the extra mile to make this less threatening.

When I am left alone with Brian, I finally look at him. I ran out of excuses not to. They dressed him up in a white tunic and pants that are way too big for him. And not just because they are Tarrassian-sized. Brian is a big guy; he should be able to fill those better than any other Human I know. Only… he is not that big any more. He looks less than half his former size. I can see skinny elbows and pointy kneecaps protruding. His square jaw looks sharp, and his cheeks are hollow. I know the Marni sap gave him all the necessary nutrients to survive in there, but boy, does he need a steak! I hope he doesn't mind bright blue meat.

I swallow hard as I watch him breathe regularly. I expected the worst, but the reality doesn't even come close. Brian had his fair share of scars back on Earth. They were part of the scary package that made anyone think twice before even looking at Yara. His heavyweight boxer-like body, a broken nose, and extensive ink work complemented the scars. He looked badass. Now he looks like he shouldn't even be alive. The clothes cover a lot of him and probably most of the wounds. What I can see is just as bad. I can't find it in me to be scared of him and even less of his appearance. But I do hope he doesn't go back to Earth. Humans like to stare and make the unusual people stand out, not always in a good way. Good Lord, probably even the aliens are going to find Brian scary.

Because he is Human, there wasn't much self-healing involved here. The Marni sap could only knit his bones, restore organs and close his wounds. The scars left behind are a different story. There are cuts and heavily damaged tissue even on his hands. The strange-looking marks on both his feet make me believe something sharp went through… Good Lord, why did I agree to this? My morning sickness is not helping.

His face is just as bad. There are many scars, criss-crossing randomly as if someone did that out of boredom. The right side of his face looks like burned tissue. A more visible scar starts at his temple and goes down his face over his closed left eyelid. Who does that to another being? Why not just kill them?

His long lashes start to flicker, and I force myself to put a smile on. It is so fake it hurts my jaw. Did Sia make a mistake? Maybe she should have let the King put Brian out of his misery when they found him. His eyes open without warning, and his familiar green stare stops on me. I smile like an idiot without a single suitable word to say. He looks at my forehead Sign, then carefully takes notice of the glowing swirls wrapping around my arms.

Say something, woman! I scream at myself, but it doesn't help.

Brian's eyes roam around the room in what looks like a quick scan for immediate dangers, then they stop on himself. I decide to give him time, let him see that he is okay and able to move his limbs. He gets into a seated position, then turns around on the bed, allowing his scarred feet to touch the floor. He bends his fingers, then his elbows, and wriggles his toes.

"The Healers didn't say, but I don't think you should stand just yet," I tell him, finally finding my words. He watches me quietly, and maybe he doesn't even know who I am.

"My name is Gianna; I am not sure if you…"

"I know who you are, lass. Are we on Earth?" he asks with a rough, croaky voice as if his throat hurts. He hasn't spoken in over eight months, so that's normal. His Irish accent seems heavier than I remember.

"No," I say, not knowing where to start.

"Are we prisoners? Are you safe?" he asks, watching me carefully as if looking for some secret signs of distress. Only Brian could do that. He wakes up on an alien planet covered in scars, yet he worries about my safety.

"No, we are not prisoners, and we are safe. Free to do whatever we want and even go back to Earth," I say. Technically that is true. In practice, I don't really know. What if the King has other plans for Brian? No matter what, he needs reassurance right now. "I don't even know where to start. What do you remember, Brian?"

"Everything. I still don't know how I got taken from Earth. But I remember everything after waking up on the alien ship." He watches me with eyes that can't hide the pain or the memory of it. I don't want him to put himself through that, so I go there first.

"I know about Yara, Brian. I also know from one of the girls how hard you fought for her and…"

"I don't want to talk about Yara, lass. The dead are dead. Are the other women safe?"

"Yes, they are all here," I reply quickly, hoping he won't ask for too many details. I am very grateful the King and Sia want to tell him about the Earth invasion. "We are on a planet called Tarrassia, and the people living here are not a threat to Humans." Do I sound stupid, or what?

"Why are you all still here if we're allowed to return to Earth?" he asks, and at least I have an answer to that one.

"Because of these," I say, pointing at the red swirls on my arms and my forehead Sign. "They are mating marks. Three of us are married to Tarrassians." I consider mentioning our pregnancies, but Diran advised against information overload. My belly doesn't show, especially with my Warrior kilt covering the slight swell. He will tell for himself when he sees Sia and the T-Rex. Still, I must give him some information. Glowing, pulsing tattoos must be hard to understand. "It's complicated," I start, "but the mating marks are…"

"Lass, I don't give a fuck about mating marks," he interrupts me, and I startle involuntarily. Brian doesn't sound angry tough, just genuinely not interested. I suddenly remember I am talking to a Human male. One who lives by the shitty macho code our kids learn as little boys. This is not some alien guy who thinks mating marks and a forever mate are cool. I haven't been around

Human males in so long, I forgot the basics. "Do all the girls have these... things?" he asks, and now that he knows what they are, his eyes avoid my marks on purpose.

"Not really," I say, and he arches a dark honey-colored brow. I know I don't make any sense, but what happened to Jade can't be explained in a few words. So, I leave it out. "Only the three of us who are married," I say diplomatically.

"Is Jade Mitchell the third? I know the white-haired lass has the marks and an alien lad in tow," he says, and I try to stifle a laugh. There is nothing wrong with Brian's mind. He just called our scary alien King a *lad*. The thought of anyone calling him that is hilarious. And if there are things like PTSD, Brian doesn't show it. I also know he won't accept any therapy either. Shitty macho code and all that. But I am Human too, and I know how it works. If you are strong enough to fake it, then you are strong enough to make it. What worries me more right now is that he remembers Jade and the surname I didn't even know. And I talk to the girl every day. Is this going to be a problem?

"Jade is single," I say, trying to play it safe. And basically, that is the truth. Sort of...

"Good," he says, but by the little spark in his green eyes, I know this is anything but good. She is not that single. "Then you don't mind if I'd rather talk to her, lass," he says, more or less dismissing me.

"And I am sure you will, Brian," I say, trying to play dumb. "If you remember everything, you understand you need to take it easy. The Healers, I mean the doctors, said you are looking at months of physical recovery. I know things must be hard to take in because so much has happened. Sia Bentley is indeed married to the alien *lad*. He also happens to be the King of Tarrassia. As you know, the two of them found you on Sketos." This is just ridiculous. The poor guy has no idea what Sketos is, and I really suck at this. He needs someone calm and diplomatic like

Sia, or someone sweet and emphatic like Natalia. "Sia and the King are very fond of you, even though you might find it hard to understand. They would like to talk to you and explain things better than I can, that's for sure."

The thing is, Brian is not making it easy for me. I thought he would have a hundred questions. I know the answers; damn it, I just don't know where to start. Brian was never big on talking, but he was kind of sweet the few times we chatted. Yeah, the Human macho version of sweet, but still. Why is he not asking much?

"The Healers will move you to your own quarters in the Royal Palace. Probably tonight if you feel up for it. I don't know about you, but a hospital is a hospital, no matter how fancy. You will be more comfortable there. I can come and visit you as often as you would like me to and explain things. I am sure Sia and the King will do the same. I know it's all too much right now, so let's just do this one day at a time, yes, Brian?" I ask. At this point, I am just talking myself deeper into shit and not helping.

"If you don't mind, Gia, I think I would rather just talk to Jade for now. And I don't need any alien healers' help, either," he says, and his tone tells me this is not really a suggestion. It is a fact. And yes, his interest in Jade is worrying, but I think there is more to it. Does he trust her because she has no mating marks? Well, she had better cover her hand. A sudden memory darkens my mind at the names people on Earth had for me. To them, we are probably traitors. *Aliens' whores*, right? His lack of trust hurts, but I can't blame him. I used to think the same.

"I understand, Brian," I say, giving in. "You settle in for tonight and get used to your new quarters. Jade will visit you in the morning, explaining all the important stuff. Just, you know, filter everything she says. This is Jade we're talking about," I say, and there is almost a twitch of a smile on his lips. Hard to tell under mangled skin and scars.

"Did Sia and the King lad find the Human woman who escaped the tunnels?" he asks unexpectedly, and I dig my useless brains for information. What woman? I really need to join the gossip squad. Sia doesn't want to talk about the tunnels in Sketos and what they found there.

"I think you'd better ask Sia about that," I say, and I can see the shadow in his eyes. What I do know for sure, the woman he's asking for is not here. There is no way Sia would have left her behind on an Ice Planet, with a crazy Sphinx lurking around. It only means she must be long dead.

"Is the alien girl safe?" he asks, and once again, I feel like an idiot. What alien girl? Why can't people tell me shit? "The blue-haired one, with elf ears. I can't believe I am saying this rubbish!" he adds, with a groan, moving a hand over his face. Well, I know the feeling. Having a casual conversation about elves and orcs is not something one can easily get used to. I also understand he must be talking about the Garrii young girl he was rescued with. The crazy one who turned out to be the heir to Garria's throne and underage. She was hiding both just because she was crushing hard on Brian. Apparently she lost it when Sia found out and shipped her back to her royal daddy.

"Yes, she is fine. Back on her home planet. Again, Sia is the one to ask." *Coward!* I stand, and he watches me trying to avoid my Sign and marks as if it bothers him. "It's best I let you rest," I say. "And please, Brian, I know you are probably tempted to, but let's not attack any aliens. No matter how scary or strange they might look, I promise you, every single species living on Tarrassia is safe. There are no enemies here." I wait for an acknowledgment, but he's not buying it. Great! Why do all men have to be so freaking stubborn? "This is called a wrist com," I say, placing the device next to him on the bed. I have a feeling he won't take it from me. "It's basically a smartwatch, amongst other things. It has some complicated features, but basic texts and calls are relatively easy. I stored the numbers of us four, and please use it if you need anything at all." I give him a quick demonstration on my com, and he observes everything attentively.

"Can I call Jade?" he asks, and, boy, do I feel trouble coming!

"Yes, Brian, I think she will love to hear from you," I say because he needs to know he is not a prisoner here. The restrictions are for his own good, but he won't buy that. He nods in agreement, and I take that as my cue to leave. I can feel it in my bones and my marks; Zaan's patience is over. I'd better go before he comes barging in. An idea comes to mind. A perilous, reckless one that might get me into a lot of trouble. The High Elder was the first alien to win my trust by offering me a weapon.

"Would you feel safer if I gave you a gun, Brian?" I ask quietly.

"No need, lass. I prefer smashing alien skulls with my bare hands," he says, and I can tell he means it. I also understand why the King likes Brian. They are kindred spirits. God help us all! It is my turn to nod because what else is there to say? Just as I am about to go through the vertical slit of the magnetic doors, his voice stops me.

"This is not some sort of experiment we are all part of, is it Gianna? Are we on Earth, in some secret facility or something?"

Of all the things, I didn't expect that one, and I can't help laughing. Why would he think that?

"Gosh, no! I promise you, Brian, this is a very alien medical bay in the middle of a very alien planet," I say. Is that more reassuring than being part of a NASA experiment? Probably not to him.

"If this is an alien planet, why does it smell like honeysuckle in here?" he asks, watching me closely as if waiting for some secret signal of distress.

"Well, there is a very good reason for that," I say, and I can't help the smile. "A very alien reason, to be precise. I am sure you will find out all about that soon enough. For now, just remember: one day at a time, one foot in front of the other, survive to see tomorrow. Basically, all the things Humans are the best at."